THE HARPER EFFECT

THE HARPER EFFECT

TARYN BASHFORD

Sky Pony Press
New York

Visit our website at www.skyponypress.com.
www.tarynbashford.com.

10 9 8 7 6 5 4 3 2 1

Library of Congress Cataloging-in-Publication Data available on file.

Cover photo: iStockphoto
Cover design by Kate Gartner

Hardcover ISBN: 978-1-5107-2665-9
Ebook ISBN: 978-1-5107-2670-3

Printed in the United States of America

For my brother, Warwick, who continues to hurl fireballs.

ONE

THE DINING ROOM IS WHERE *the ghosts and monsters play.* That's what Jacob said when I was five and he was six, our necks curling around the half-open door, our eyes blurting fright. On a dare, we'd tiptoe into the room, dash around the table then jump through the French windows into the garden, screaming with delighted terror. Nearly twelve years later, it's still my least favorite room in the house. Maybe that's because it's where the recent pep talks have taken place and the grandfather clock seems to count down the seconds to the end of life as I know it.

So when Dad and Coach Kominsky invite me to join them at the dining table, the cream-cushioned chairs imprinted with the bums of Jacob's make-believe ghosts, I wrap my arms around my chest and respond with a brisk, "I'll stay standing, thanks."

"There's not an easy way to say this, Harper," says "Killer" Kominsky in his clipped Czech accent. He smooths a hand over his perfectly round shaved head, no freckle or bump daring to blemish it. "So I just speak the words. It is time for me to move on. I do not believe you are good enough to make it to the top."

The ground falls upward. My chest squeezes.

So this is why we flew home between tournaments.

I contemplate leaping out the window, but after all the sacrifices I've made—summers at the beach, friendships that held me together, lost moments with my family—tennis is who I am. I have to change Kominsky's mind.

I grip a high-backed chair; add some flint to my gaze. "How can you say that?" My voice wobbles. "Maybe some kids turn pro and hit top ten in one season, but I'm only sixteen—"

"Sixteen-and-a-half, Harper," replies Kominsky, tapping his fingertips together. I glance at the *Sydney Morning Herald* sports section lying flat in front of him. He's trained me to become a world-class tennis player for five years, but I've never featured on that page. Perhaps he's right, and I'm not good enough.

"Dad?" I say.

My father startles, flicks the hair out of his eyes, and squints at me as if he's staring into the sun. His smile looks worn out. He glances toward Kominsky instead. Kominsky has *been* the sun these past few years, our lives revolving around his every word and action, so that's no good either. Dad gazes out the windows into the afternoon sky, his eyes glassy behind frameless specs.

I unravel the pair of loose braids I put my hair into this morning. My hands tremble.

Kominsky stands and rolls up his newspaper, ready to walk away from me forever.

There's a whooshing feeling, a this-is-it, life-changing moment, and I seem to hover near the ceiling with Jacob's pretend ghosts. The movie of my life so far flashes before my eyes; how, even as a three-year-old I'd trail a too-big racquet around the backyard tennis court and try to copy Dad and his buddies as they played. All of them had, in their youth, hoped to be where I am now. To me they had seemed like gods throwing fireballs at each other. I longed to have their power, their grace, and speed. They were magical. They were heroes.

And for a while my talent was a little magical. For a while, touring the junior circuit, I believed I'd be someone's hero, too. But turning professional nine months ago had changed everything; the fireballs I'd learned to hurl off my own racquet had transformed into a stupid yellow ball that had it in for me.

Dad said the only thing it changed was that I could win money, "But don't let that get to you—money's not important right now."

It isn't the money, though. Before, I was living my

3

childhood dream, touring the world, and now I'm fighting to keep my scarily grown-up job. I've staked my claim, and everyone is watching.

Kominsky cracks the knuckles on both hands, his elastic lips set in a long straight line. "Physically, you have all the potential you need to be the best. But as a singles player, you are putty, Harper. Hard and tough until the heat turns up. Then soft. Easy to control. Easy to beat." He points a long finger at his temple, prods hard enough that it must hurt. "Not tough enough up here. I cannot waste my time any longer."

"Waste?" I collapse into a chair, my arms as floppy as empty sleeves. "I almost got to the second round at Washington this week. I almost broke the first-round jinx—" I look to Dad for backup, but his gaze is trained on the view of the Sydney Harbor Bridge. "Who's taking me to Cincinnati next week—the US Open? I'm young enough to—"

Kominsky holds up a hand. He's not into discussion, only commands.

Other players say their coaches are like second fathers to them, but Kominsky's never been that. Still, how can he abandon me? He's going on to better things—without me. If mental toughness means being so unfeeling, I will *never* be strong enough.

"Almost is not enough. I go home now," Kominsky says, glaring at Dad's profile. "The body I can train. The mind is for you to train, Harper." In the sunny room, his whitewashed blue eyes drill down on me from his freakish height. He leans closer and pulls the final thread on my career. "Being at the top is about winning the mind game." He extends a stiff hand in Dad's direction.

Each word is a tennis ball being smashed into my chest. If Kominsky doesn't rate me—where does that leave me? He's never been wrong. My throat swells with forbidden tears. Kominsky doesn't tolerate crying.

Dad stands. He runs three fingers through his floppy silver-white hair, and I realize it's not just me who's getting dumped.

Kominsky pumps Dad's hand. "I recommend doubles tournaments if she want to continue."

If I want to continue?

Where would my life lead without tennis? Would I go back to high school instead of being tutored? Would I take up basketball or swimming or piano and make friends—and keep them? Would I allow myself to eat ice cream and hot dogs? Would I have time to hang out with Aria?

Without tennis, what's the point of me?

The familiar sound of Jacob playing guitar drifts into the room from his house next door, like the closing credits of a movie. Except I'm not ready for anything to end. I take the fastest exit and vault out the French windows.

TWO

THE WOODS TO THE SIDE of our house are the same now as they were when my older sister, Aria, and I played Hansel and Gretel with Jacob a decade ago. We know every rock, fork, rut, and ridge; even at night we can navigate the path to the river. It's uncultivated land that Dad's tooth-paste company owns, crowded with jacaranda trees, but the three of us have called them the Purple Woods since forever. In spring, the trees become fountains of color, the blue-purple flowers waterfalling from each branch, and when the wind gusts, purple blossoms ride on the breeze. The ground transforms into a violet carpet, and the river is peppered with petals as if a wedding had passed by and everyone had gone crazy with confetti.

It's because of the woods that childhood is, for me, the color purple.

Today, the woods are sleepy and gaunt. Wispy branches hang on to the last of their yellow foliage and spindly evergreens hunch until spring, or as we call it, Purple Time. Twigs crack and dead leaves crunch under my tennis shoes as I run. Right now, I need to let the woods swallow me.

Running headlong toward the river, I hurtle back into a world where Kominsky doesn't exist, and collapse under the Mother Tree. Once upon a time, I declared this the mother of all the trees because it took all three of us, fingertips touching, to circle the trunk. Its low, solid branches became home to a zillion childhood games. Being here is traveling back into the past, back to when life was simpler, when nothing was expected of us but to return in time for dinner.

The problem with being a professional player is that everyone judges; coaches, players, the media, even inanimate objects—the hiccuping whir of the air conditioner in my last hotel bedroom seemed to mock my inconsistent serve.

I curl up and hug my knees, afraid that pieces of me might drop away, lost forever. Kominsky has not only been my coach, he has organized my life—I just arrive on time every morning.

Finally, I let the tears come.

The sound of someone scuffing through leaves as they approach makes me scrub at wet cheeks with the inside of my wrists.

"Harps. Wassup? Saw you take off." Jacob's lean frame lopes closer, even now gripping a guitar by its neck as though he left home in a hurry and forgot he had hold of it. He's just washed his hair—long blond waves touch his collarbone, leaving damp patches on his blue T-shirt. When he grins, he morphs into the small boy who became our best friend—we were no longer Aria and Harper, the Hunter sisters, but Aria, Harper, and Jacob, the barefooted, adventure-seeking Ragamuffins, soon shortened to the Raggers.

"Were you eavesdropping again?" I ask, pulling on a smile. Jacob's music studio is to the side of his home, close enough for him to listen in if he sits on the doorstep.

"Couldn't hear much. You guys need to shout louder." He plops to the ground, shoulder-bumping me. "Your dad told me to stay away. He said he needed to talk to you about something important."

I push Kominsky's words from my mind. "Never mind that. How's school?"

"Skipped today. Surf's pumping." Beaming cheekily, he nibbles a fingernail on his fretting hand. Cinderella-blue eyes study me. My heart backflips.

I remember the precise moment I fell in love with him. He'd come to support me at a local tournament when I was thirteen. My opponent's dad was sitting behind me and every time I hit the ball into the net or out, he cheered. Kominsky said I should get used to heckling, but during the changeover Jacob approached the dad, a guy built like a skyscraper, and the mocking stopped for the rest of the game. When I asked Jacob about it he shrugged, saying, "I'll always protect you from dicks like that."

Love exploded into my heart and has never left.

But as Kominsky drummed into me year after year, I didn't have time for boyfriends—or friends, or parties, or shopping. And so that I could play more international tournaments, a tutor replaced school. Jacob became my last remaining friend—another reason to ignore my heart. But I was on the junior tour, often away from home, and the autumn I turned fourteen, I returned from Europe to find Jacob kissing Aria on the back deck. They've been joined at the pinkie finger ever since.

I hug my knees and pluck a string on Jacob's guitar. We watch it hum until it hushes, then survey the river flooding over rocks and gullies. The surge is constant, reassuring—the same as it's always been.

"Spit it out." Jacob flings an arm around my shoulders. "What's happened? How was Washington?"

I twist my hair into a chestnut-brown rope and suck the end. "I've beaten Alexia in qualifying like, five times. I was three points away from going through to the second round."

"First-round jinx strikes again." Jacob snatches the hair rope and flicks it out of harm's way. "You'll do it next time. You're an amazing player."

My chin quivers and my lips twist. "But not good enough. Kominsky ditched me."

"He what? Why?"

"Said I'm a waste of time." Unable to hold back any longer, I'm shaking and wilting into Jacob, darkening his T-shirt with tears. He's always been a good listener, and a good hugger.

"He's the frigging waste of time." Jacob's chest vibrates. I cling on, our denim-covered legs interlocked, and though I should let go, I don't. I can't. Even though it's winter, he smells of summer—salty air, surf wax, and vanilla ice cream, and when I breathe him in, I feel the tiniest bit brand new.

"Kominsky's a dick," adds Jacob. "What did your dad say?"

"He always agrees with Coach," I say, still sobbing.

Even when I'm cried out, I don't move away, and Jacob doesn't unwrap me. Only when he rests his cheek on the top of my head do I draw back and scramble for the lowest branch of the Mother Tree. Jacob vaults onto the branch beside me and we face each other, riding make-believe horses. But we don't pretend to whip the branch as we used to, or squish it with our thighs to giddyup the horse, or shout "yeehah" while swishing imaginary reins.

Jacob clears his throat. "Kominsky might change his mind."

I shake my head. "Apparently, I don't have what it takes mentally. He's moving on to someone who does." With my eyes, I trace the carved letters of our three names in the trunk above Jacob's head. They've been there since before Kominsky. I snuck the knife we used from our kitchen, egging on Jacob and silencing Aria's protests. Jacob got into trouble when he cut himself, but he never snitched on me. The pale half-moon scar still bisects the heart line on his palm.

"I don't think I can give up tennis, though. As pressured as the circuit is—as lonely and scary as it is on court—not having tennis anymore . . ."

If I stop playing, it'd be like denying who I am. It'd be like telling the Mother Tree that nature just ran out of purple and to flip to plan B and grow yellow blossoms instead. Or like demanding the river flow up the hill, or banning the birds in the woods from singing. It's why I'm on this earth; rivers flow downstream, birds sing, the Mother Tree must blossom and grow—and I must play tennis. Dad once said every racquet is the same until it's strung. Then it's unique. My dream is not to be the same as every unstrung racquet in the factory. I want to hurl fireballs. I want to be an inspiration. Someone's hero.

For a moment, everything blanches, my life wiped out by a nuclear flash.

"Tennis makes me count. I'm *someone*."

Tennis is my whole world. I have no plan B.

"You'll find a better coach," says Jacob. "Anyone with a brain knows you'll be a star."

"If Dad will keep paying." Dad had sacrificed the day-to-day running of his company to his number two in order to tour with me these last few years, and it's not like I'm as profitable as his company.

Jacob lies back on the branch, hands clasped behind his head—Mowgli in his jungle. "You're earning prize money now."

"But is it enough? It's not just the coach. It's the tutor, the travel, the hotels. And Kominsky's right—I can't seem to get past the first round. Maybe I'm not good enough."

And I'm not sure Dad believes in me anymore.

I wait for Jacob's words of reassurance, but he keeps his gaze in the sky. "Must be the week for big changes," he says, so softly I barely hear him over the rush of the river.

"What do you mean?"

He straddles the branch again, picks at the bark. "Seen Aria since you got back?"

"No. I think she's working at Mo's today." Mo's is a local music center, and the owner loves the fact that Aria can play six instruments. His sales spiked after he employed her.

Jacob swings to the ground, sits cross-legged, guitar in his lap. It's the one he got for his seventeenth birthday earlier this year, and it's worth thousands. He plays a chord. His hands are soft and smooth. "We broke up."

"What? *Why?*" Why hadn't Aria called me? But I already know the answer. Choosing tennis meant letting the bond with my sister crack.

He moves to form a new chord and strums. Strums again. "Didn't work out."

"She okay?" I ask, scratching *holy crap* on the branch with a piece of bark. *What about the Con?* I wonder. After graduating from high school last year, Aria took a gap year before applying to the Sydney Conservatorium of Music so that she and Jacob could attend together. But now I feel a sense of something shifting, like a kaleidoscope changing its pattern.

"Guess so. Haven't seen her since. Buried herself in her music," he says.

"I bet you've done the same, knowing you."

He chucks a twig at me, and smiles into his lap.

"Who broke it off?" I ask.

Jacob clicks his jaw from side to side. "Me."

Inside my belly, something sparks and my eyes stick inside his so I can't look away. *Got to get a grip.* Even though we've been best friends since kindergarten, he can never be mine. Not ever. That would break the sisters' pledge Aria and I made when I was eleven. We'd sworn an oath, pricked each other's fingers, and smeared our blood on Aria's pink guitar picks—one each as a reminder to never steal the other's boyfriends. Even though we're not as close as we used to be, oath or not, she's my sister, and I couldn't do that to her.

Jacob plucks an intro. While he sings some boy band cover, I climb higher into the tree, away from the desire to stroke his neck as it arcs over the guitar. Away from the need to touch the small cleft in his chin. Away from the temptation to watch his curvy lips as he sings.

Away.

But when he finishes, he leans the guitar on the trunk and scrambles after me, pouncing onto the first branch, then the second, and the next. He's deeply tanned from surfing, barefooted, and his blond hair, now dry, flies out behind him.

He comes level with me and sticks his tongue out. "Last one to the top's a stinking cane toad." His long limbs reach upward, past the branch still spiky with metal nails—all that's left of a tree house the Raggers built the summer before I went on the junior circuit.

All for friends and friends for all. I chase after him, our childish Musketeer chant repeating in my head. He catches my wrist to help me up the last few branches, even though I've done it myself a gazillion times, and we poke our heads through the sparse canopy. A sea of yellow leaves, polkadotted with spiky branches, sweeps toward the houses at the top of the surrounding hills—an ocean wave and we're in the trough.

We grin; bodiless, floating heads above the foliage.

Eventually, Jacob says, "You'll always have me and Aria. And we'll love you whether you're ranked ten or ten thousand." Our long hair flickers in the wind like lions' manes.

"Thanks, Jacob." I peel my gaze away and concentrate on both feet as I climb down. If Kominsky knew how hard it's been for me to watch Aria and Jacob together, how hard it is now to move away from Jacob, he wouldn't call me weak.

THREE

"THIS IS JUST PERFECT," I groan, crossing my arms. "Kominsky's goodbye gift—an injured doubles partner." Aria gives my shoulder a sympathetic squeeze. Two weeks later, still coach-less, I inspect the players on several courts as they warm up for round two of the Western and Southern Open in Cincinnati.

"It's not Kominsky's fault Saskia twisted her knee," Dad says, curt. When his gray eyes aren't sparkling, they appear small and too close together. I hate it when they don't sparkle, because it's usually my fault. He made it as far as national level tennis, but once admitted he didn't have the mental strength to make it professionally. *Guess we're both terrified I inherited that trait.* Judging by his pinched expression now, he's probably wondering whether I'll ever live up to my name: Jack Harper was an Australian tennis player from the 1940s who still holds the record for the shortest singles match ever—eighteen minutes. The only record I'll probably ever set is for highest number of first-round knockouts. "Kominsky's going to help us," Dad adds. "He'll call back after he's verified the lucky losers. He'll find someone to pair up with you soon."

"Great," I say under my breath. I know I'm being a brat, but when the earth is shifting beneath my feet with every step, it's hard not to be defensive. Before we left for the airport, Mum advised me to let Dad worry about a new coach so it doesn't affect my game. "This time next month, you'll have forgotten all about this problem," she said as she hugged me goodbye. "I bet you can't remember what you were worrying about this time last month."

Aria pokes me. "What's a lucky loser?" A droopy bow adorns her messy, half-up hairdo.

"Someone who lost in the qualifying round who gets called up to replace dropouts. Great for them, crap for me." I've got a bad feeling about all this—no coach, I lost in the first round of the singles event, again, and an injured doubles partner. Kominsky was right—physically I've turned up, but I've pressed the self-destruct button on all iron-willed cerebral activity.

Aria nudges me in the ribs as Dominic Sanchez saunters past. He's number 3 in the world. She pops on a pair of sunglasses so huge I could be staring at a panda in a tartan maxi-dress. "This is so cool. Why haven't I come with you before?"

17

Because Kominsky wouldn't allow the distraction. Because you didn't want to leave Jacob's side.

I take a sip of the green smoothie Dad made.

Aria's not exactly hacking it since the breakup with Jacob. It's the real reason she's here with me and Dad. She'd packed herself away like a broken doll, staying after hours at Mo's to practice, barely seeing the light of day. She's always been pale, but now she's translucent. She won't talk about Jacob, either, and that hurts—sisters are meant to talk about this stuff. Thinking about the bond we've lost used to make me want to hit myself over the head with a tennis racquet, but I figure it's not wrong that I chose to play the junior circuit. After all, she chose to be a musician. She also spends hours alone practicing. Except I suspect it's not as simple as that; sisterly bonds tend to need more than absence to break them.

Today, though, I need her here with me like it's my first day of school. I wonder if I can heal us. The thought of becoming close again has only just occurred to me—probably because Kominsky has turned my world upside down. Or is it because she's no longer with Jacob?

Relieved that a natural smile has replaced her clip-on one, I sling an arm around her. "Glad you're here, sis. I totally mean it." She yanks my ponytail, which is the exact same shade of chestnut as hers. Despite her smile, a shadow crosses her features. I poke her, in case her mind is wandering back to Jacob.

We're waiting in what's become a thoroughfare and when Aria tickles me back, I jerk away from her. The last of my green smoothie escapes out of the bottle and onto a man's black T-shirt as he picks his way through the crowd. My eyes go wide.

He's tall. Given my own height, I figure he's well over six foot. He also has a solid, athletic build and a chin shadowed with stubble. You wouldn't want to bump into him in a dark alley. But when he swings around, it's clear from the deep-set eyes to the arch of his cheekbones that he is someone you'd want to bump into on your first day of college. And he can't be much older than me, even if he is man-sized.

I throw on my biggest smile. "I'm really sorry—bit crowded here." My smile falters when he stares back at me, actually *into* me. His espresso-colored hair is short and spiked at the front, revealing a small widow's peak, and his skin is a deep tan, similar to mine. He must spend a lot of time outdoors.

I try another smile, stashing the bottle behind my back. "Sorry. We were goofing around."

"Harper Hunter," he says, low and smooth—a man's voice. I'm not sure if he's asking or telling. I nod. "Another one," he snaps. "I'll be sure to avoid you in the future."

My mouth pops open, but the words, *Another what?* remain hooked in my throat.

He pivots and strips off the smoothie-gunked T-shirt

as he walks away, revealing muscles that didn't just grow there on their own. And judging by the fact that his right bicep is slightly bigger than the left, he's a tennis player.

"I'm not sure if he's amazingly rude or amazingly sexy." I half laugh. "Who broke his tennis racquet?"

"Is he famous?" asks Aria.

"Obviously *he* thinks so." From his accent he's American—how does he know my name?

"Those eyes. Perfect for drowning in," Aria adds. She's saying the words, but by the far-off look in her eyes, she's actually talking about Jacob.

Dad's phone rings. He's been watching the match on Court 4 and walks away from us, one finger stuck in an ear, his round glasses slipping down his Roman nose in the heat.

Aria and I lean on the railing to inspect the play below. Dad thinks this doubles idea will give me more match play, get my name known, and maybe if I have a partner to buoy me, I won't choke when the pressure's on. Maybe I'll even get past round one. Even though the words are a repeat of something Kominsky would say, I don't argue because it pleases Dad and might get me a new coach.

"Let's go." Dad pulls us into a group huddle. "Kominsky's come through again. We're meeting a potential coach in the players' lounge. You've heard of Milo Stein from Germany?"

I hug myself and don't move. *What if this coach is worse than*

Kominsky? He might also tell Dad I don't have what it takes. "Dad, I'm on court in three hours. What about a new partner?"

"Partner's taken care of, but this is important. This is the long term." He tweaks my nose, then weaves through the crowd, Aria and I trailing behind.

The players' lounge, normally filled with cliques and gossip, is almost empty. It's easy to spot the guy I chucked green smoothie on. Still shirtless, he's talking to an older man with such long silvery-brown hair it could belong to a girl—except he has a beard.

Dad heads for Mr. Shirtless.

"Oh, poop," says Aria. She winces on my behalf.

While Dad shakes hands with long-haired guy, I hang back and count Mr. Shirtless's six-pack. I'm used to seeing Jacob without a shirt on, and he's ripped, too, but he's wiry and boyish, smooth-chested. This guy's wide shoulders narrow into his shorts, and his muscled chest is covered in a smattering of dark hair.

Dad beckons us. I slow, twirling my ponytail and sucking the end, and decide Mr. Shirtless was plain rude before. How dare he say he'll try to avoid me? It was an accident, Mr. Humorless.

The guy Dad's talking to—my possible new coach, I assume—is wearing flip-flops with jeans, rather than the usual sneakers or tennis shoes. He has the air of someone on the way to a music concert—or a bikers' reunion.

"Harper," says Dad, "this is Coach Milo Stein, and say hello to Colt Quinn."

Even though Aria's older than me, I'm an inch taller. I pull up to my full 5'8" and extend a hand to the coach, who is younger up close—maybe late thirties. The stress of tennis must've turned him prematurely gray. There's a tattoo on his neck almost covered by the collar of his shirt that reads *Train insane or remain the same* in black cursive.

Steeling myself against his judgment—*this is the girl who never gets past the first round*—I'm surprised to find Labrador puppy-dog eyes. But they don't say hello. They seem to gently look right into me as if leafing through a book. His grin expands as he says, "Well, the rabbit lies in the pepper."

What? I wrinkle my nose. Great. He *is* insane. Irritation prickles under my skin.

Switching to Colt, I say, "Sorry you couldn't manage to avoid me." I point with my chin toward the black T-shirt he's left in a heap on the table. "And what did you mean by *another one?*"

Colt's handshake is as firm as stone to match his manner, but instead of replying he turns to Aria. "I didn't know you were a twin," he says.

"Not twins, I'm nearly two years older," says Aria, squashing down the annoyance I see flickering in her eyes. "And we're nothing alike, you know." Aria's words speed up, a dead giveaway she's nervous. "Harper lives for tennis.

I live for music. She's addicted to coffee. I hate even the smell of it—"

I nudge Aria's calf to stop her prattling. She never could talk to boys—other than Jacob.

Colt keeps inspecting us. "You have green eyes and Harper's are blue."

"Impressive," I say, sarcastic. "You can tell the difference between blue and green." The words land in an awkward heap in the middle of our circle.

"*Harper*," reprimands Dad.

"A smart-ass, I like it," says Coach Stein, slapping Dad on the back. I'm surprised that his accent sounds mostly Aussie, with a tinge of something foreign in the background.

"A smart-ass with a soft heart that stops her from winning," adds Colt, pronouncing my death sentence.

"Is that right?" I snap. For the first time, I notice he has a tattoo on his arm—no doubt a naked lady or something equally offensive—but I refuse to show any interest in it.

"Good court speed. Tight footwork. Powerful ground strokes. Takes the ball early, can play defense and offense, double-handed backhand, but you have a wandering ball toss when you serve, thankfully made up for by a strong, consistent return of serve. Singles ranking top hundred-fifty in the world, a position you've not improved for several months thanks to a tendency to go soft on your opponent when you start beating them."

Flames rise through my cheeks and to the tips of my ears. "It seems you know me better than I know myself." He doesn't flinch but stares back—no humor, no embarrassment. No nothing. Is he a robot?

"I'll be watching your doubles game this afternoon, Harper Hunter," says Milo Stein. He pops on a pair of aviator sunglasses, even though we're indoors. "I'm told you're in need of a new coach."

● ● ●

I lose the doubles game in front of both Coach Stein and Colt. Though I pretend they're not there, the pressure to perform is sky-high, and as Kominsky predicted, I turn to putty. Plus my doubles partner and I don't gel; she's too greedy for the ball. My mood worsens when Dad informs me he's agreed to help Milo Stein by putting me up as a doubles partner with Colt for a practice match.

I chuck stinky socks across the hotel room. "I'm out of the tournament. What's the point?"

"Colt is, too. Milo asked for a favor, and I'm not about to say no to a coaching legend who's considering taking you under his wing. And Sebastian Norman is coming. Norman's high up in one of the sports agencies. He wants to see Colt play, as well as your opponents."

But not me.

Dad says Colt's from Florida, but if he's so good, why's

24

Milo looking for a new player—especially considering I live in Australia?

When it's time to leave for the warm-up, Aria's still got curlers in her hair. "You're not going to the royal box at a Wimbledon final," I yell as she pulls free the last curler and scoops her hair into a messy updo.

"And neither are you. I had to practice my flute."

"But did you have to play the same piece a hundred times over?"

"I have to perform each piece—"

"Twenty-five times. I know. But today?"

Her narrowed eyes inspect me. "You could do with varying your ponytail—I mean, what statement does that make? It's so clichéd."

"I'm not trying to make a statement. I'm trying to get to a tennis match on time."

I wonder what happened to the Aria who'd trail around after me and Jacob, who'd agree to all my suggestions about games and movies to watch and what to wear. Now we can't even agree on a ponytail.

But remembering that Aria hates to be rushed, Dad has fibbed about the start time so we're only delayed by five minutes. When we walk onto the practice court, Coach Stein is expertly juggling three racquets. He catches each one by their grips before waving. Colt keeps hitting the ball against the back wall like he's punching someone in the face. I grasp my racquet tighter and scowl at Dad.

"Sorry I'm late, Coach Stein," I say.

"Call me Milo—just Milo," he says, the aviators reflecting the glare. "Colt! Over here."

Colt switches to backhand and keeps hitting against the wall as though I don't exist. Just as Milo opens his mouth to say something, Colt takes off for the service line. Milo tuts to himself. I trudge to the opposite end of the court. This is a huge mistake.

Colt's serve is fast, powerful, dangerous. I stick my racquet out and block it, but the return spins out. *What's he playing at?* We're supposed to warm up, not kill each other. He goes for a second serve and this time aces me.

That's it. I storm to the net. "What's your problem?"

Colt strides toward me. "My problem is you're late." His eyes flash. "This is my career, not some playdate. You're selfish, spoiled, and you think you're too good for me." He doesn't shout, but speaks as if reading from a list he prepared earlier.

My brain empties of words like a leaking water bottle. I *was* late, but I refuse to get into a discussion about hair curlers. As Milo approaches, the best I can come up with is, "I think I'm too good for you?"

Colt spots Milo, ditches his racquet and jogs around the court. Milo and I watch Colt, his arms spinning in circles, doing crossovers, high steps—anything but engaging with us. I slouch at the net and shake my head at Dad.

"Sorry, Harper," says Milo. "Just give him a moment."

Milo joins Dad on the side of the court, leaving me thinking that Colt must pay Milo heaps. Colt eventually retrieves his racquet and proceeds to his baseline where he hits the ball. It plops over the net next to me. I glare at him. He stuffs two extra balls into his pockets. Dad motions to the baseline with his chin.

I want to hurl the umpire chair at Colt, but somehow I drag my mood under control. We rally hard for twenty minutes without exchanging a word. My body gradually uncoils while we go through our strokes, taking comfort from being in a well-worn groove.

When we depart for the match court, I whisper to Dad, "I don't think he brings out the best in me."

Colt stops. I almost walk into him. He sizes me up as he says, "In case you're interested, my strength is my serve. Solid placement, lots of power. My weakness is net shots."

He strides away, overtaking Milo, who waits for me. "Don't mind Colt. He takes things real seriously at tournaments. Great player, though."

"I've never heard of him. What's his ranking?" I ask.

"His ranking doesn't reflect his ability. What that boy's gone through to get here, my little *Dampfnudel*—let's just say rankings are not only determined by how good you are."

Unless he's killed some dragons, survived shark-infested waters, and solved world hunger, I'm not interested in what Colt's been through.

FOUR

THE COACHES HAVE PULLED SOME strings to get an umpire and linesmen, giving the match an official, competitive atmosphere. Sebastian Norman is a *really* important guy.

I have two brains. Or perhaps there are two voices in there. One is the glass half-full type, the other is not. Either way, both are whispering the same thing right now. *Holy crap.*

Our opponents give us the once over, whispering behind water bottles. Colt stands next to me fiddling with his racquet strings. A small group of spectators take their seats. I scrutinize them, but a sports agent is unlikely to be wearing a flashing name badge.

We win the toss, and Colt declares he'll serve. We take the first set without dropping a game and without looking at each other. Colt's a strong player and hits with such power he makes a grunting sound with each shot. It's low and guttural and, I can't help thinking, kind of sexy.

As we take a break between sets, sitting next to each other on blue plastic chairs, Colt swigs from a water bottle. "Nice play," he says.

"You, too." I make nice back. "Sorry about that net shot at the end."

"Don't ever apologize." He places the bottle on the ground. Nothing I say is ever right.

In the second set, our opponents step up. So I'm meant to step up, too. I make several unforced errors instead, and soon, I'm fighting the negativity in my head. *Kominsky's right.* This is me turning to putty; whenever I'm winning a game, the fight to pulverize my opponent dribbles out of me like gas escaping from a slit helium balloon, and next thing I know, the hole's too big to plug. I lack the killer instinct.

They take the next set 7–6.

As I pass Colt a ball, instead of taking it, he wraps strong fingers around mine and the ball.

"We got this," he says. One side of his mouth quirks up, instantly transforming him from hot guy in tennis whites to a total Adonis. I command myself to stop staring.

We got this. I can't let Kominsky be right. Because if he is—

I can't let Colt be right. *A smart-ass with a soft heart.*

My world narrows to the court, the net, my racquet. I win points with tactical drop shots twice in a row and Colt raises a palm for a high five. He puts a spin on the next return, giving me the chance of a smash, which I execute. He jogs past and fist bumps me. The energy rises on court, and I rise to it. I haven't felt this confident in ages—I truly want to win—not just for the coach, or Dad, or the ranking points. My competitive streak swings into action, as if it's a hibernating bear being poked awake. When did it go to sleep? When did I stop playing for myself and start playing for everyone else? But just as I'm getting cocky, I move close to center, and Colt's racquet cracks me in the face. I clutch my cheek. Tears ambush me.

"Let me see," commands Colt, peeling away my fingers. "We need ice," he yells over his shoulder.

He walks me off the court and parks me in a chair. I concentrate on controlling my erratic breathing. Shoulders hunched and the breath pinched inside my throat, there's a rush of relief as someone places ice on my cheek and cups my jaw. After a minute I open my eyes. It's Colt doing the holding, his face inches away. In other circumstances, he could almost be about to kiss me.

"Okay?" he asks. I can only nod.

"Can she play on?" I hear someone say.

"Jeez, give her more than a minute," Colt bellows.

Though my cheek pulses, I push away the ice to test whether I can see straight. "I'll be okay," I say. "In a minute."

I pull the ice back on and watch Colt watch me. He's kneeling in front of me. My nerves snap and crackle. Maybe

I need to relieve the tension because, even though it hurts, a laugh jumps out of my chest. It keeps going. Colt's expression spins from anxious to confused to amused. And then it happens. He smiles. And his whole face unfastens like a window blowing open in the breeze letting in the fresh air and sunshine. It's as if I've witnessed one of the Seven Wonders of the World; seen something not many people get to see. . . .

We continue the game, my sight somewhat affected, my cheek throbbing, but I'm on a high and playing for the next fist bump. Our winning point comes when I respond to a lob with a tight drop shot. My arms shoot into the air. I whoop and twist to Colt. He's already there. His hug is brief but strong, a wall of muscle.

"You're tougher than you look," he says, then jogs toward Milo, who's leaning over the barriers. Colt double high-fives him.

Dad races to the edge of the court, Aria following in her own good time.

"Brilliant game, honey. You beat two players ranked 79 and 92." Dad is beaming and I've made his eyes sparkle again.

"That was really exciting to watch," says Aria, her earbuds still in place.

I trek back to where Colt is packing up, zip shut my bags, and stow the water bottles.

"Sorry," Colt says. He focuses on the swollen cheek and winces. "Impressive comeback, though." For a moment, I see that inside Colt Quinn the robot there's a tiny piece of human.

But he brings out the steel in me. "I thought you said never apologize?"

Stapling a gaze to the ground he smirks. "Touché." He throws his tennis bag over a shoulder. "Game over."

FIVE

"NICE HALLOWEEN MASK," SAYS JACOB, sticking out his tongue when he falls in beside me. Despite my face being yellow and black after the cheek-smashing incident three days ago, I'm determined to continue with my training.

I rotate my arms as we run. "You heard, then?"

"Don't worry," he says, picking up the pace to show off. "We'll still love you, even if you're ugly and deformed."

We reach the base of the hill I usually challenge myself to sprint up. Jacob's tied his hair into a short ponytail, and I tug it and yell, "Last one to the top's a soggy banana." Jacob thrusts out an arm to block me, sniggering through heaving breaths. I crease up, pushing at him all the way. At the summit, we slide to our knees on the grass verge, huffing and groaning.

I suck in the salty wind, squinting at the sun setting behind light-gray clouds that are reflected in the ocean below. "You are so childish."

"Can't let a *girl* beat me."

"We'll see about that." I'm up before he can grab me.

When we reach the beach, Jacob bends himself in half. "Jeez, I'm out of shape." He's not. He has a hot body. I'm just more fit. "How'd you go, Harps? The tournament?"

I think of Colt and how we won our game, how he held the ice to my cheek, how I glimpsed a different version of Colt behind the intense mask. Was that version just his game face? My own had swelled overnight, and a doctor confirmed a small fracture in my cheekbone. Luckily, there's no bone displacement, and it'll heal without surgery.

"I've had better tournaments"—I bend to remove my sneakers, plunging sweaty toes into the sand—"given I lost in the first round, my doubles partner got injured, and some guy broke my cheekbone, and then flew home without so much as a *see ya later*."

"You're kidding. He fractures your face and leaves? Jerk!"

First Colt had refused Dad's invitation to dinner, saying he needed to rest. Even though he was probably being sensible, I felt hurt. We'd had this amazing win, but it seemed to mean nothing to him. And after the doctor confirmed the fracture, only Milo came for lunch the next day. Colt had changed flights and gone home.

"Like I said, I've had better." The stretched sensation in my chest springs up my throat, making my voice break.

We stroll along the jetty above the churning breakers. When we reach the end, Jacob throws an arm across my shoulders. "Poor Harper." My heart whimpers.

"You stink of sweat," I say, shoving him. He smells of peanut butter today; the last time I saw him, before I left for Cincinnati, he smelled lemony. I sit down and swing my legs above the slapping waves.

He sprawls next to me. "How's Aria?" he asks, mournful.

"She's okay. Not quite herself yet."

"I miss her, Harps."

My face whips up a frown. He adds, "I miss the three of us hanging out together without me feeling like the bad guy. Being able to come over whenever I please."

"Whenever you're hungry, you mean."

Jacob pokes me. "Wish we could go back in time. We used to hang out every spare second we got. Remember the rock pool search expeditions?" He points to the rocks near the café. "And the summers we hung out with that old radio, and got great tans and surfed and taught your dogs to fetch sticks."

The smell of burgers and coconut sunscreen and wet dog floods my nostrils. Mum had brought home two sheepdog puppies from her vet practice. I named mine after Venus Williams and Aria named hers Adagio—something to do with music.

Jacob's eyes still lit with memories, he adds, "Remember how we believed the Purple Woods were magical and somehow joined our souls—" His smile wobbles. "Hasn't been like that for forever."

Since you and my sister became joined at the lips.

We track the soaring seagulls testing the thermals. Waves splatter our legs.

I remember how Mum used to say Aria and I were joined at the brain. When we were younger, we'd simultaneously have the same nightmares and even once had an ache in the same tooth. One year, our report cards were so similar our parents swore the teachers had us mixed up— we did look alike. Sometimes, we'd trick people by wearing matching dresses. Now Aria prefers skirts so long she trips on them, and quirky hats, and anything with feathers, while Mum buys jean shorts and tank tops for me in bulk. We used to have the same favorite color, read the same books, share our shoes, write identical Christmas lists. Now I'm not even sure of the name of her best friend— except that it's no longer me.

"Do you think we can go back there, or is everything messed up now?" asks Jacob.

"Aria postponed her audition for the Con so you could go there together. Now there *is* no together. I don't know . . ."

Jacob scans the thickening clouds blotting out the sun. I figure this has scratched at him for a while.

"Why did you break up?" I ask.

"Aria hasn't told you?"

I shake my head. After five years, the crack in our sister bond is now a chasm, and I don't know how to bridge it. "She says she's not ready to talk about it."

"I tortured myself to death about us breaking up. There was the Con and also your parents—but Aria's more of a sister to me now." His eyes ensnare mine. "I hate not being part of your family. It's not like I have a real one. I'm like a boarder at home. Without you guys . . ."

Jacob's parents, both lawyers, leave the house by seven and don't return until late. They've employed the same efficient housekeeper for ten years as a parent substitute. It was no wonder we'd practically adopted Jacob.

A drop of rain startles me. The cloudy sky has turned pewter in the dimming light. "You'll always be part of our family. Besides, the dogs would miss you."

Jacob shoulder-bumps me, and we fall back into silence.

Everything is broken and messed up—I still don't have a coach, Dad's casting around for our next step, Aria's lovesick, Jacob thinks he's been evicted from my family, and I still don't know what to do about tennis. Most of the time I feel like turning pro has put me on a pedestal and everyone is trying to knock me off, but I'm not ready to give up even if everyone else thinks I should. The game with Colt proved I've still got some fight in me. Maybe my dream isn't over yet.

When I imagine my future, I'm certain tennis is what I was put on this earth for, because nothing else makes me feel like I'm glowing from the inside out. Nothing else gives me that sense of purpose. Tennis has always called to me and still does. If I stop playing, I may as well carve away a piece of my heart.

As if to prove it, my heart flinches.

Jacob hugs his knees.

I flick his calf. "I'll talk to Aria." Maybe this is one part of my life I can fix. "We can try to get back to being the Raggers again."

"Yeah? Thanks, Harps." He smacks a kiss on my shoulder as if merely kissing a boo-boo away. A starburst of heat floods into my chest, even though he probably sees me as a sister, too.

When I get home, Aria's in the kitchen making a snack. Mushroom-colored feather earrings swing below her suede cowboy hat as she sets down a tray of chocolate chip cookies to cool on the countertop. The radio blasts a nameless piano concerto. I can always tell if Aria's home and which room she's in, based on which room is filled with classical music.

On the run home, I rehearsed what to say. We should've had this talk a long time ago, but she had Jacob, and I always thought it was my problem, not hers. If I can get the three of us back on track, I'll feel as though life isn't splitting apart at the seams.

"We need to talk," I say, switching off the radio and perching on a stool at the island bench. She slaps butter on bread as if it won't sit still on the plate. Her nose scrunches.

My knee bounces rapidly. "What's happened to us? Why don't you talk to me like before? We used to share—"

"You're hardly ever here, Harper." Aria's mouth tightens. She unwraps a block of cheese and slices too-thick chunks.

I slap the counter to get her attention away from the cheese. "And when I am here—"

"It doesn't work like that." Ditching the knife, she yanks off her hat and tosses it across the room onto the farmhouse kitchen table, where it skids to the floor. She's so fired up, I realize she's been bracing herself for this conversation, too.

"Why not?" I say.

Aria crosses her arms and bites her bottom lip. I expect a death stare, but instead tears spill down her cheeks. "Did you ever wonder how I felt when you started on the junior circuit? You weren't the one left behind with reminders of the Raggers—every room filled with you. I realize you missed me, but you had a new life. I had to learn to rely on you less."

I swallow my own tears. "But I haven't made a life without you. You're as important as ever."

"When you go away, that's your new life for a couple of weeks, a month. Tennis is your life. Then you visit with us

39

until the next tournament and home becomes 'The Harper Show.'"

"That's not how it is."

She comes around to my side of the countertop squeezes both my hands in hers. "But it's how it feels for *me*. We were the Raggers and soul twins, and when you went—it wasn't easy. But I made my own life with my school friends, my music, of course—"

"And Jacob," I add. The words sound spiteful. Jealous.

"Yes. And Jacob. Without him, it would've been ten times harder."

If Aria had left me for the circuit when I was eleven? She's right—*not easy*. My world also changed, but I was going after a dream, not being left behind. I stare out the window at the tennis court and swimming pool below, wading through my emotions to find the right words.

"When we waved you goodbye that first time, Jacob and I marked off the calendar every morning before school. When you came home we packed in so much, but then you vanished again. The fun went out of waiting for your visits. Our lives became dull. Every day we waited for *your* news. We were living in your shadow." My fingertips turn white from Aria's grip. "It took a while, but when it hit us—that life as we knew it was over. I'm not being dramatic, but it was as if you had died. No one understood how Jacob and I felt."

I disentangle my hands from Aria's and reach for the

cheese knife, spinning it in circles on the countertop. *My leaving pushed Aria into Jacob's arms.*

"I'm sorry. I'm glad you had each other." I don't explain how hard it was for me, how I left behind all that was familiar and safe, how it felt like I was breathing through a straw the whole time I was away, how coming home felt as magical as Christmas day had when we were little. I study her short, neat nails, glossed with light green polish.

"But I'm used to you coming and going now," she adds. "I have my own life. I'd like to spend more time together—especially now that Jacob and I—"

"Promise. I promise we will."

Aria gives me a look that suggests she doesn't quite believe me, but then takes my hand again and leads us to the twin sofas in front of the fireplace. Her warm smile gives me hope.

"How do you feel about Jacob?" I ask, and crash next to her.

"I want him back." Her eyes glaze over. "I miss him. I love him. Proper love, you know?" Outside the window, the drizzly rain masks the view of the Purple Woods. "But these last few months something was wrong. . . . He became hard to reach. Like he wasn't with me—was somewhere else—with someone else."

I pick at a dry cuticle, swallow hard. "Is there someone else?"

She studies me, grave. I hug a cushion.

41

After a silence that's too long, she adds, "I think so."

My jigging foot stills. "*Who?* Someone at school?"

"He denies it. But—" Aria flops back on the sofa, arms crossed over her face. She giggles—"we slept together."

The floor rushes at me and the world tilts sideways. "*What?* You've . . . had sex?"

With Jacob?

She nods. I leap to my feet. If I'd felt like the outsider before. . .

"When? I can't believe you didn't tell me, Aria . . . something that big in your life. How *could* you?" How could Jacob?

Her face scrunches. "I clearly wasn't going to get your approval." She springs off the sofa toward the windows.

Jagged thoughts pin me to the spot. My heart thumps and churns, wanting out of my rib cage. Does every sister feel this way? Or is it because I've known Jacob forever, loved him even? He's not just some random boyfriend of Aria's.

"And it's not like you're ever here to talk about this stuff," she adds.

I chuck a cushion to the floor. "I'm sick of this. It's not my fault I have to travel. I get lonely, too, you know. At least you have family, Jacob, school friends. You get to go to the movies or eat junk or hang out on the beach. I have tennis racquets to cuddle and a moody coach who runs my life."

"You have Dad all to yourself."

"You have Jacob all to yourself."

"*Had* Jacob." Her mouth twists as she runs from the room and takes the stairs in twos, slamming her bedroom door.

A blast of opera music makes the walls vibrate. I pound my head into a cushion, but my cheek hurts. The music gets louder when a door bangs into a wall.

"What's your problem, anyway?' screams Aria, over the banister. "Just because you're lonely in those hotel rooms doesn't mean you get to be jealous of my boyfriend." She slams the door again.

Ex-boyfriend.

But I won't let her have the last word, and I pound up the stairs, thrusting at her door and smacking my head into it; she's locked it. I march into my bedroom where tennis posters cover every wall, through the bathroom, which links our rooms, and into Aria's room. It smells like her—a mash-up of flowers, violin rosin, and cake batter. Even though bras lie scattered on the floor among high-heeled shoes, lash curlers, and mismatched bikinis, dolls also balance in neat rows along both chests of drawers, the curtains are the same frilly ones she's had since we turned seven, and framed pictures of ballerinas line the walls. She refused the makeover Mum offered for our twelfth birthdays.

Aria's perched on the double bed, a pale pink blanket hanging half-on, half-off the mattress. Her violin is cocked beneath her chin, bow at the ready to accompany the opera music. But she's not playing, just frozen in that pose, her face contorting.

A spark of sympathy makes me claw back the words I was about to expel. Instead, I shout over the music: "You two had this big secret. Why didn't you tell me?"

She slinks off the bed, leans her violin against the drawers, turns the music down. "Jacob didn't tell you, either, so go be mad at him."

"But we're sisters."

Still facing the wall, she hugs herself. "I wanted to. But it was never the right time. Or there wasn't enough time."

I recall how years ago we would jump into bed and whisper until the middle of the night, or sneak downstairs for midnight snacks, climbing the Mother Tree in our pajamas. Those moments stopped because I was exhausted by hours of training and school and traveling. Everything's changed. It's my fault. I broke us.

She swivels. We look so alike that my own blotchy features stare back at me. "Besides, I'd bet my violin you don't tell me what's going on in your head these days, either."

A door slams downstairs. "Aria? Harper?'

Aria's face gusts shut. "Is that Jacob?" she shout-whispers.

"I invited him for pizza. I thought we—I don't know what I was thinking. I'll tell him to go."

"No. I've got to get over him. I've been trying. I know everyone misses him. Even Mum."

"He did eat practically every meal here." I picture Jacob

sitting shirtless at the breakfast table; how I struggle to ignore the way his shorts hang low on his hips. "We can always squish pizza in his face if you can't hack it," I say, tentative. Food fights are a common occurrence in our kitchen. Even Mum starts them. I'll never forget the green bean that hit Dad right on the nose because he kept checking his iPad during dinner.

Aria turns to switch off the music.

There's a rap on the door. But when I open it to find Jacob on the other side I'm overwhelmed by the image of him and Aria kissing—doing it. I gulp against a pinched-up feeling inside and swing away from the newly showered, lemon smell of him, from his tousled wet hair, from his Aria-kissed lips and those eyes that seem to search for something in my face.

"Ready for pizza?" Aria asks, taking her earrings out and keeping her eyes on the mirror.

Jacob leans against the doorframe, arms crossed, lazy grin settling in place. "Does Mr. Greedy need dessert?"

We traipse into the kitchen and Aria orders pizza for three—Mum and Dad are out. Venus and Adagio paw and yelp at the door. Jacob lets them in and falls to his knees to play. He mashes Venus's head, pushing his own lips into a fish mouth and making kissing noises. He's a shaggy Old English sheepdog himself—even his hands and feet are too big for his body.

I grab bottles of Gatorade and turn on the sports

channel. There's no tennis, so swimming will have to do. Aria decides now's the time to make another batch of cookies. While Jacob hovers, sticking his fingers in her mixture, I pretend I'm into the swimming results until the pizza arrives, and Jacob turns off the TV. He slips the remote into his pocket.

"You're being antisocial," he proclaims, then balances on the back legs of the kitchen chair, telling jokes and stories about school and flicking peanuts at us. He glows again, as if there's a sun inside him.

He doesn't appear to notice we're not back to normal; we're not the easy going Ragamuffins. Aria and I steal glimpses at each other, smiles fixed in place. We shower Jacob with attention, but remain reserved with each other. Everything is still unresolved and I don't know what to do about it.

When there are two pizza slices left, Jacob clutches his stomach. "The tunnel to my belly is closed."

Seeing a way to release the tension, I raise my eyebrows at Aria. We spring to our feet, stuffing pizza into Jacob's chops. Clumps slip down his T-shirt and onto the floor, while his arms flail to fight us off.

"Girls, girls, guys, what on earth?" says Dad. He and Mum have returned from somewhere swanky—Dad's in a suit and Mum's brown hair is a sleek bob except for one unruly curl that always flicks up at the side. In high heels, she's taller than Dad. Their smiles light up the room. Before

46

Dad's toothpaste manufacturing company took off, before we were born, they were the photo on the front cover of the company brochure.

"Your daughters' table manners are a credit to you," Jacob says, wiping a greasy chin with his knuckles.

"Fun's over," says Mum, her jade eyes glistening. She kicks off her heels, revealing soles still dirty from being in bare feet all day. She hates shoes and has been known to go to the shops without them. "Aria, you have a six start tomorrow. Off to bed with you." She tweaks Aria's braids when she gets up to give them a cuddle. Jacob demands his goodnight hug from Aria, like the old days, friendly and brief, as if they had never slept together. Over his shoulder, Aria scrunches her eyes shut, and her smile trembles.

Mum watches Aria head upstairs and throws a handful of peanuts into her own mouth. "Good to see you three together again."

Dad puts the dogs out for the night. "You kids can get this cleaned up." Slicked-back silvery hair flops across his brow. "Come on, Mrs. H. I'm exhausted." He takes Mum's elbow just as she's slipping into a chair beside Jacob.

"Don't be long," Mum says, pivoting to follow Dad and tossing a peanut at my forehead. "You've got training tomorrow, Harper, nine sharp."

As they leave, Jacob's gaze collides with mine.

I shrug-grin and stoop to collect pieces of pepperoni and onion while he washes himself off at the sink. Through the French doors, the sky blanches with sheet lightning, silhouetting the woods. Jacob chucks a sopping cloth at me, cursing when I catch it. I wave it triumphantly in the air. "I play ball games for a career, loser boy."

On all fours, Jacob sweeps up dregs with a dustpan and brush, and I move next to him, swabbing the floor. Under the table he cocks an eyebrow at me. Something's changed since he and Aria broke up, and it's getting dangerous.

When we finish, Jacob leans against the bench, arms folded over his navy T-shirt. With his hair falling across one side of his face he surveys the kitchen, then me. "Thanks for talking to Aria," he says, soft.

My gut clasps. I prop myself against the fridge and release my ponytail. When a growl of thunder sounds, I yank my gaze away from his biceps to the window. "She's so over you." I don't know why I say it.

He launches across the kitchen and tickles me. "It would take a lot longer than a month to get over me, let me *assure* you."

"Yeah, sure. 'Night, Jacob."

But it's my turn for a goodnight hug, as we've done many times. His arms wrap around my body—except this time he kisses me on the forehead. Goose bumps rush across my scalp. When he removes his lips, I glance at them, and my knees flinch. I could lift my chin to kiss him, and by the way his eyes crackle, I know he wants me to.

I admit to myself that his eyes have lingered on me

a little too long lately, sometimes roaring with unspoken words. I had dismissed it as wishful thinking.

But Aria still loves him. And our sister pledge.

Jacob clinches me to him, and buries my head under his chin. Our breathing remains quick, our chests pressing a rhythm into each other. His palms slide up my back to my shoulders, always stiff from tennis. He kneads them. Thunder unspools around the house.

I let myself stay there, confused, but feeling as if I'm in a safe, calm harbor, and press my arms around him. I tell myself it's normal. We're just good friends. But I know I'm kidding myself, because my heart sighs every time I see him.

Three years of keeping it dammed up. Perhaps this is the real reason Aria and I drifted apart—I couldn't bear that she had him for herself.

I cling tighter, knowing I haven't fixed anything today.

"Harps," Jacob says against my temple. A sensation of heat starts at the top of my skull and gushes into my belly like a hot waterfall. He lowers his chin. Our noses side by side, mouths a finger-width apart, he licks his lips, says, "Harper."

I'm coming apart in his arms, but if he says another word our lives might shatter and there'd be no way of putting them back together.

He hangs on to my elbows when I pull away. I tug back harder, glimpse his fractured expression, and go over to the sink. "That was huge." The words scrape my throat. "We're back to being the Raggers again."

I twist on a faucet and rinse a cup, blinking furiously. Through the window the rain transforms into a screen of spitting needles just as fork lightning stabs the canopy of the Purple Woods.

Jacob doesn't answer, and I don't know he's gone until the lock clicks behind him.

SIX

TEN DAYS LATER, I DON'T even reach round one at the US Open, bombing in the qualifying rounds. I'm as useless as an unstrung racquet, with no coach and a dad who's not sure I belong on a tennis court. The pressure to perform has skyrocketed, and I buckle under the weight of it.

Then there's Jacob, sitting in the middle of my heart. I can't cage the effect he has on me anymore; the secret grows more real every day and stands between me and Aria.

Dad and I fly home from Flushing Meadows early. The words we don't speak shout inside my head so that the moment we get indoors I switch on the TV to silence them.

Suddenly, Colt's in our living room; his face fills the sixty-five-inch flat-screen TV and he's serving against the number 15 seed in the first round of the men's singles. My stomach drops. I didn't see him at the Open—he must've avoided me. When I call to Dad, he doesn't seem surprised to see Colt. Instead, he settles into an armchair and praises Colt's serve, his power, footwork, and ground strokes, and I become increasingly defensive.

"Not *that* good," I say. "He's ranked 240. I Googled him." But I know as well as Dad, as well as anyone who witnessed our mixed doubles game, that he's a better player than me. *And* he's in round one of the US Open, not viewing it on TV.

"His ranking doesn't reflect his ability," responds Dad, echoing Milo's words. "He had to take time out at the start of the year, and he hasn't hit the circuit consistently since."

Milo said Colt has been through a lot. Dad says he's seventeen, yet he comes across as though he was born an adult. I wonder what happened at the start of the year.

Colt blasts through three sets, showing every sign he's a match for his opponent. The camera jumps to Milo in the break, aviators in place. But in the fourth set Colt flakes. Limbs heavy, reactions slower, he loses the match. The camera pans to him, perched on the chair next to the umpire, where he's drumming the circular edge of the tennis racquet into his palm.

"More stamina, a lot more match play, and he'll reach the top." Dad mutes the TV. "I want to discuss something with you."

My stomach pangs with fright. *Decision time.* I hug a cushion.

Dad drums his fingers on the armrests. "Milo and I . . . we've been corresponding."

"Yeah?" I had assumed Milo's silence meant he didn't want to coach me.

"He needed to clear up the schedule first—get Colt through the US Open. But he does want to team up with you . . ."

Relief winging through me, I swoop to hug Dad, then laugh over his shoulder. "I'll prove Kominsky wrong." I settle on the arm of Dad's chair. "Not good for Colt if Milo's back in Australia," I say, feet rapping excitedly in his lap. "Did Colt sign with Sebastian Norman?"

Dad removes his glasses and pinches the bridge of his nose before focusing on me. "Norman never turned up in Cincinnati. But Colt's going to be in Sydney. He's a Sydney boy originally. His family has lived in Florida for the last eleven years, but he came back to Sydney six months ago, and Milo picked him up."

I pull back. "What are you saying?"

Eyes down, Dad bunches his shirt to clean the smudges from his lenses. "Milo wants to coach you both—as mixed doubles partners. And, if you want, as a singles player."

"Dad!" I jump off the chair and loom over him. "Colt fractured my cheek and then went home without—"

I almost say *apologizing*, but then remember that I threw his apology back at him.

"Milo said Colt had to deal with a family problem," Dad explains. "I don't know the full story."

I recall Colt's intensity, how grown-up he appears, his game face. He scares me a little. "I don't think we're suited." But then again, he's also got the air of a born winner—as if he *knows* he's going to win—and somehow he woke the competitive streak that used to drive me.

Dad clears his throat and pops on his glasses. "Forget Colt for a minute. Milo was a great player nine years ago—top fifteen, and ranked number 1 in Germany. Since then, he's coached men and women from all over Australia, plus helped Acker turn professional. Consider how she's developed."

I think about how Aria and Jacob are going to have to attend the Con together. Just as they'd be crazy to give up on their dreams because it might be a bit awkward, I can't give up on tennis because of Colt. Without tennis, I'd be that river that fails to flow uphill. But maybe with someone like Milo . . .

"And he's interested in you," continues Dad. "He says he thinks you have what it takes to reach the top."

My body fills with hope so buoyant and glossy and big I could float over Sydney Harbor. "He said I have what it takes?"

I've heard those words from family and friends, but never from a respected international tennis coach.

Kominsky thought I was mentally soft and stopped believing in me a long time ago.

This is my last chance to hurl fireballs across the court.

It's the only reason I say yes.

SEVEN

TWO DAYS LATER, COLT CHOOSES the time and location of our training sessions: the dashboard clock reads 5:16. And even though we have a court at home, Dad drives me to the training courts nearer Colt's home. It's hard not to believe I'm the second-rate player.

I'm wearing a tennis dress—the only type of dress I wear. As Dad talks, his eyes sparking again, I fidget with the hem of the miniskirt and sip my coffee too quickly, burning my tongue.

Milo's dressed in the same white cotton shirt he wore in Cincinnati, one button too many left undone, except he's paired it with tennis shorts instead of jeans. He's already on the court, warming up with Colt. I stop to retie my laces, letting Dad go ahead. Milo slaps Colt on the back and says something I don't hear. Colt gives a close-lipped smile and tracks me over Dad's shoulder. It only takes one look from those dark eyes to unleash the butterflies in my stomach. I have to admit, I'm a little excited. I pull up tall and join them. I refuse to be scared of either of them.

Colt's navy T-shirt, almost gray from over-washing, boasts a V-shaped sweat stain down the chest area already. The skin of his hip is visible through two small holes. *Must be his lucky shirt.*

"Hi, Coach—um, Milo," I say, juggling my coffee cup to accept a firm handshake. He beams, warm and calm. I swing to Colt, awkward.

"Cheek's better," Colt says. He switches his focus from the cheek in question to my eyes. "I needed to leave Cincinnati on short notice, but Milo kept me posted."

I tug at my tennis skirt. "I heard you had a family emergency." Colt cuts his eyes to Milo, expression loaded with reproach. Milo shrugs. I almost mention the US Open, but decide Colt won't want to be reminded of a loss, even if it was a good one. Instead, I go for humor. "I see you're wearing your lucky T-shirt."

Colt's expression shutters. He pivots and speeds toward the baseline, smashing a ball into nowhere.

I study Milo from under lowered lashes. "Guess he's mad at me for poaching you."

Milo lobs a racquet into the air and catches it. "Nope. Colt has other issues." Milo turns to Dad, instructing him to return in four hours.

When Dad hugs me goodbye, I whisper, "Stay."

"You'll be fine." Dad glances at Colt. "Time to stand on your own two feet. A new era."

Colt bounces the ball, then cracks a flawless serve. He eyeballs me, clearly irritated, and serves again.

"Let's get started," says Milo. "Coffee down, Harper. Dairy's a no. You're not a cow, unless you've acquired four stomachs."

After a tough warm-up, walking on court to play Colt is even tougher—as scary as being shoved into a cage with a tiger. Except this time, Colt doesn't attempt to kill me with his serve, and we hit a few rallies.

A couple of guys arrive. Milo beckons me and Colt over while they limber up. He passes us cups of homemade electrolyte he calls Milo Potion. Colt downs his in two seconds.

Milo spins a racquet in a three-sixty. "These boys are here for doubles practice. Your goal is the Australian Open mixed doubles final in January—less than five months away."

I glance at Colt, wondering if Milo's joking, but Colt's staring into the distance; he's heard this before.

"We're attempting something that's going to stretch us all." Milo balances the tip of the racquet on the toe of his tennis shoe. "Ultimately, it'll get you both noticed, and that means wild cards, better rankings, sponsorships, and an agent. It means your careers get a kick in the butt."

"Ha. I can't even make it into a women's main event final, never mind the ultimate Grand Slam final," I say.

"Sort of the point, Harper. And achieving this goal will improve your singles games, help you earn money faster, meaning you can *keep going* on the singles circuit, and it'll confirm what a damn fine coach and tactician I am. Remember this: one hand washes the other." Milo tosses his racquet into the air, seizes it, and performs an elaborate bow.

The two guys join us, and we rally to warm up. Colt seethes. It's like playing tennis next to a pit full of vipers. I can't concentrate. When the game starts we go for the same ball—twice—our racquets clattering. I flinch to protect my cheek. Next, we both leave the ball for the other and it bounces in the space between us.

After the first set, which we lose, Milo calls us over. "Not quite Cincinnati," he says. "How are you going to learn to become winners together? Is it the power of your serves? The consistency of your ground strokes? Is it your speed . . . ?"

"Trust," says Colt from behind me. I can hear the eyeroll in his tone.

"Thank you, Peter Patient." Milo leans forward to pass out more drinks. "When you played in Cincinnati, what I saw was chemistry. Underlying whatever's eating you today—and let's hope you put a lid on that box—there's chemistry."

I splutter on a gulp of Milo Potion.

"I'm not talking the love kind of chemistry," continues Milo. "I'm talking about what makes two people connect as doubles partners, even before they get acquainted and understand each other. That's important, and you have it. And yes, trust is needed, but what comes before trust?"

Colt sighs. "Jeez, Milo. We're not children. Spit it out, would you."

"Okay now, Colt. You're a dangerously good player, physically and mentally, yet you still have many flaws." Milo's tone stays smooth, steady. "Luckily, I know that crooked logs also make straight fires, so can I suggest you let me coach? You acknowledge you have a lot to learn?"

Colt's stare challenges Milo's. His Adam's apple ripples. "Never said otherwise."

"But you *act* otherwise. It's okay to accept help from people around you. Me, Harper—let us in." Milo massages his temples. "Tennis is a serious business, but there needs to be balance or it'll eat you alive. You need to hippy up. *Upsize* the child in you, Colt. When you're on court, you must loosen up, otherwise when the pressure builds, your strokes become fixed and robotic and, mentally, like concrete in the sun, you crack."

"I get it, but can we talk about this stuff another time— when Flappy Ears over here isn't listening?"

Flappy Ears? I want to wrap a tennis racquet around *his* ears.

"Before trust comes communication," continues Milo, giving Colt a warning glare. "As doubles partners, you need to read each other's minds—or bodies. Wordless communication. That's why I'm saying all this, Colt. Not to embarrass you, but to bring Harper into the circle. This is a partnership, and she needs to be aware of this stuff."

Colt swerves stiffly side-on.

"Harper," says Milo. I flinch. "You're a talented player. Experienced, strong, committed. But you nurture a chip on your shoulder as big as Texas."

"I do not!" The words drop out like bombs. "Sorry. I mean—no one's told me that before. My flaw is that when I'm under pressure, I turn to putty."

"The two-inch version of you right there?" Milo points at my shoulder. "She's the spitting image of you, and we both know what she's saying."

I hunt at my feet for a hole to fall into.

"She's screaming it from your shoulder. *I'm not good enough.*" Milo picks up a second racquet and spins two at once. "But you *are* good enough and you *can* do this. You must commit *more*, work *harder*, get *stronger*, to compete at this level. It's inside you, and only you can access it . . . but I can open the gate. When you believe you can do it, you'll become a winner. What are you afraid of? Winning?

"And what you said before about turning into putty— you rely on others too much. There's always someone there to hold your hand or pump you up or catch you when you

61

fall or tell you what to do. So, when it's just you on that court, you crumble. We've got to independify you. Then we'll see your singles game take off."

I grind the words I want to spit out until they're small enough to swallow—because I suspect he's right. When I started playing competitively at the age of seven, that's what I demanded from my family, from Jacob, my other friends at the time. What was the phrase Aria used? *The Harper Show.*

"Okay, now check out how you just played," says Milo, spinning his two racquets. Colt and I shuffle. "You resemble ice cubes in a bowl of water, jostling and crashing into each other, going in different directions. What you need to do is melt into the water and then you'll find yourselves moving as one entity, in tune, in flow with each other. Don't question my methods, listen to what I say, and it'll happen."

Colt and I jog back on court for the second set, but within minutes we collide and I'm knocked to the ground. Colt helps me up without looking at me. At least I'm left with all bones intact. Milo stops the game and thanks our opponents.

"Let's go," he says. We follow him toward a shady spot on the bleachers. "Sit."

I plop down where I am and Colt sits two rows up.

"Let's play a game you're going to get extremely good at. It's called mirroring. Colt, get down here, next to Harper." The bleachers rattle as Colt moves beside me. His shoulders hunch, elbows on knees, attention on Milo. "It works like this: you become the other person's eyes and hands. You *see* the other person's need and your *hands* fulfill the need."

"Sorry, explain again. I don't understand," I say, sensing this is going to be embarrassing.

"No problem." Milo pulls at my shoelace. "Colt. You *see* Harper's shoelace is untied. You are Harper's hands. Do up her laces."

Laughter busts out of me. "No way. Wait. Yes way. Colt, go ahead. I can live with that." Colt scratches the back of his neck, then bends to tie the lace.

"Harper. Colt's neck is itchy. You're his hands. Scratch his neck." My laughter breaks off. Milo isn't kidding.

I lean forward to reach around Colt's square shoulders. His neck is sweaty. I scrunch my nose and rub my fingers on my skirt.

"Colt. Harper's ponytail has come loose. No way can she play tennis. Fix it for her."

Colt gets up, kicks at his bag. "Am I going to take a leak for her, too?"

"Quite possibly," says Milo, stern. "But not now. The problem right now is her hair needs fixing. Up, Harper."

I comply, amazed that Colt is taking orders from Milo.

Colt moves behind me. There's no gentleness as he abruptly scrapes my hair back into a ponytail and secures it with the elastic. I wince.

"Sorry if I pulled," he says, stepping back.

"Harper. You're Colt's eyes. What does he need? Look at him."

Colt's squinting into the sun, impatient. "The sun's blinding him."

"Get his hat." Milo points to Colt's bag. I unzip it and find the tennis cap—next to a motorcycle helmet. Mum and Dad won't like that; they've warned me to stay clear of motorcycles.

I pass the cap to Colt.

"Stop," says Milo. "You're his hands. Put it on." I step closer, perch it wonkily on Colt's head.

Colt straightens the hat. "When do we play tennis?"

"You can play tennis already." Milo slaps Colt on the shoulder. "Being a top doubles partnership entails more than being top players. You proved *that* when you lost to those two barely ranked muppets today." Colt kicks at the dust and slumps onto the bleachers.

Milo pulls the aviators off, perhaps the better to glare at us. "What don't I know? You appear to have a problem with each other. It needs to get stated right now. Ladies first." The look Milo gives me could snap racquet strings.

"What? I don't have a—"

"You're about to become the greatest mixed doubles partnership ever. Because I *know*. You will discover each other's flaws and embrace them. You'll love each other's strengths, smooth out any sharp edges, and toughen up the weak parts. Don't go shy on me now. Spit it out, my little *Dampfnudel*."

The remains of Colt's annoyance swirls around us, and I turn away.

"I'll start then," says Colt. "She's another one of them—a tennis brat."

Is that what he meant when he called me "another one" in Cincinnati?

"Why are you telling me? Tell Harper." Milo settles on the ground, cross-legged, happily staging a sit-in—or a yoga session. What's next, flashing the peace sign?

"Fine," says Colt. "Everything's given to you on a platter. You don't need to struggle for anything—"

I swing to face him square-on. "You're kidding, right? You think I got the ranking *given* to me? Or perhaps I paid for it? You don't think I trained and trained and sat on the same flights as everyone else, lived in the same hotel rooms? I sacrificed family life, friends, a social life, got a tutor instead of going to school, gave up my childhood—"

"My point exactly." Colt folds his arms. "Hotel rooms? Try youth hostels or trailer parks. A tutor? Try keeping up with schoolwork at midnight. Friends? Family?" Colt almost chokes on the last rage-soaked words. He glares at Milo. "She has no clue."

"But why be angry with Harper?" says Milo. "Should she get kicked off the circuit because she has a tutor and stays in better hotels?"

I flex my fingers. "He'd love that."

Milo bounces a tennis ball. "You're angry because you

don't have that, Colt, and that's allowed. But don't take it out on Harper."

Everyone's wrapped in a boiling silence.

I start speaking softly. "I'm a bug under Colt's shoe. He thinks he's too good to breathe the same air as me. Maybe I should kiss the ground he walks on."

Milo claps once and rises. "Harper, this is where you're not familiar with Colt, and you'll find it's simply barriers. It's just that he doesn't know you. When he does, he'll let a more human version of himself come out from behind the barrier. Right, Colt? As I've said, life is extremely serious for Colt."

"Maybe that's because life is serious," Colt says. "Tennis is not a joke for me. Not something I may or may not do. I'm going to reach number one and some spoiled brat isn't going to get in the way."

"Perhaps you should tell Harper about your life. It'll help explain—"

"No way, Milo." Colt looks as though he's seen a ghost. "I'm done." He snatches his bag and strides away.

EIGHT

"DAD, IT WAS LIKE MARRIAGE counseling. Worse—divorce court. We barely hit a ball. Milo is some sort of hippy and Colt rides a *motorcycle*." I glare at Dad as he drives me home. After Colt stormed off, Milo went to talk with him, and Colt had remained astride his bike.

"Milo's the expert, Harper." Dad's back to thinking the tennis coach is God and every word He utters should be immortalized in stone.

Even a long shower doesn't stop my insides from feeling unsettled and stretched. Something big is about to change, and I'm not ready for it—like that moment when you're learning to swim and you *want* to jump into your mum's arms in the pool, but what if you miss or she tricks you and steps aside to force you to swim?

And what if you can't do it?

I need comfort and abandon my schoolwork for the Purple Woods. Gazing across our pool and tennis court toward the woods, I remember that "brat" word. I *am* grateful for what I have, though . . . I've always known we're lucky, and that it's thanks to Mum and Dad I have the freedom to follow my dreams. But is it possible I've started to take it for granted?

"Hey, you." Jacob's head appears over the wall between our houses.

"Hey, back. You cut school *again*?"

"Keep me company?" He never asks me over. Guess he's not spending hours in the music studio with Aria anymore. The studio was built a year ago, and I haven't visited it since the grand opening. It was *their* space. Best to keep it that way.

"Nah. Going for a walk."

He cocks his head to one side and makes whining dog noises. "Pleeease. I've had a crap day. Need cheering up."

"What's up?" I ask, frowning. Jacob usually falls in with what Aria and I want to do.

"The record label my band sent a recording to? Straight rejection. Flat no. Nada. No way. Forget it." He nibbles at a nail.

"*They're* crazy." I approach the wall. "Couldn't spot talent if it prodded them with a drumstick."

"And my piano teacher says I won't get a good grade on the exam next week—can't get this set piece right. Why

can't we choose the music we like to play for these freakin'
exams? It could affect my chances of getting into the Con."

"You win. Your day's worse." I haul myself onto the
wall and straddle it. "What's your band called these days?"

"The No Names. We still can't agree. Come drown my
sorrows with me."

Jacob leans against his side of the wall. He's dressed
in a loose tank top and board shorts, his bare feet on the
firewood box. I jump down onto the box, purposefully
knocking him off. He sprawls on the grass, blond hair fan-
ning around him. I welcome the warmth of those bub-
bling eyes. Jacob makes me feel safe and as if my life isn't
whirling down the drain.

Slumping next to him in the grass, we gaze up at the
fast-moving clouds. Their rushing makes me dizzy, though.
They need to slow down and let me feel calm inside. I push
myself upright, pulling at the grass.

Jacob rolls onto his front, stands. "Coke or OJ?" He
strides away, bathing me in that billion-watt smile.

The music studio appears small from the outside, but
inside the room swells, cave-like. It's all soundproofed walls
with high-up slits for windows, and it's filled with instruments—a saxophone, a grand piano, a drum kit, guitar stands
with six different types of guitars. The ceiling is enclosed
in material-covered squares—something to do with sound
quality. At the far end is a door that opens into a recording
studio. Bowls of unfinished cereal and plates of half-eaten

toast clutter the carpet, along with glasses containing sticky orange juice pulp, beer bottles, sheets of random music, drumsticks, and vinyl records. The odor of sweet cola only just overpowers the smell of leather from the sofas.

Jacob often sleeps all night on the sofa that's shaped like a pair of oversized red lips. It's sad his parents don't notice. The other sofa looks like it's made from giant, multi-colored Lego pieces, but I remember that it's spongy and squishy. It slumps when I sink into it.

The door to the studio closes and blocks out the world beyond. The tension leaches from me. Jacob whoops and makes a flying leap, almost landing on me before I roll to the side. The sofa sags further.

"Devastated, are you, Jacob? Where's that OJ?"

Struggling out of the sofa, he pushes aside a sax to open a fridge loaded with drinks. He twists off the lid and gives me a bottle of juice. "Ran out of clean glasses."

"Tell me something," I say. "Do you think having this studio means you don't work as hard as someone who doesn't?"

"*Whoa*. Philosophical much?" He steps lightly onto my toes, wriggling his against mine. "I don't practice any less than anyone else in the No Names. And if this place burned down tomorrow, I'd find somewhere else to practice. Why so deep?"

"Tough day. First session with that Colt Quinn and the new coach."

"Didn't go well?"

"Don't know. It's twisted me up inside. But I want to forget about it for a while."

"This'll help." Jacob produces a small bottle of clear liquid from a pocket. "A little happy juice in your OJ?"

I hesitate. Although I've drunk a little alcohol before, Kominsky preached that my body is a temple. But I'm fed up with being told what to do, what to eat, what to think. And this new training world Dad's thrust me into is scary. Besides, Milo said I should be more independent.

"Just a little," I say, settling back into the Lego sofa.

While I sip my drink, Jacob plays a cheerful, jazzy number on the piano. Music isn't my thing, but I like how it makes me feel. I let the tune's merry mood relax me. Jacob plays another, then another, and fetches more OJ before settling cross-legged on the floor, cradling a guitar. He sings something quirky. It makes us crack up and the world slows down, and the events of today don't seem that bad. In fact, the memory of how Colt tied my shoelaces makes me giggle. Jacob wants to know the joke. Then he leans against the sofa, his torso touching my legs, and tells me about a song he's writing.

Later, Jacob gets more drinks, taps on an iPad until music I recognize from a past era about being "easy like Sunday morning" filters into the room. When he plonks down next to me on the sofa, the sides of our bodies press against each other. I wonder at the way the squares on the ceiling move in slow, swaying circles, and we sip our drinks, talking, warm and happy, until my eyelids droop, and I decide not to fight it. When I close my eyes, there's a sweetness to everything in the world.

When I wake, the music has stopped and a dim twilight fills the space. I've rolled over, head on Jacob's chest. We've cuddled like this before, except not for a long, long time. I should move, but I'm sleepy and fuzzy and peaceful inside, and I don't want the sensation to go. I remain motionless in the muted light, aware of his chest rising and falling as the sunset smudges red across the sky.

I don't know why the tears prick in my eyes, but what I do know is that I need more of this feeling. And when I think of tennis and Colt and Milo and Dad and the future, my body tightens and seems dark and bruised inside. I yank my mind away from them, from anything outside this room, and when Jacob strokes my cheek I don't pull away.

For once, I stop the battle that is a part of every day of my life, whether it's keeping Dad happy, sucking up Coach's criticism, training until I can't stand, coping with another first-round defeat, doing schoolwork until I fall asleep mid-assignment, or denying myself ice cream in favor of protein balls. And I stop fighting the fact that I've been in love with Jacob since I was thirteen.

His hand slides down, finding the strip of exposed skin above my shorts. Warm, soft fingers caress the flesh there.

My insides flip-flop. He presses harder, kneading the rigid muscles up my spine, and there's such a sense of relief I let out a small groan.

Jacob shifts onto an elbow. Our eyes crash into each other, and I see the instant his say, *We can't.* But that's chased out by *Just do it.* Mine must say the same thing because his mouth moves closer. All thought turns loose and wafting and won't be pinned down. His lips graze mine, light, like he's testing if they'll burn. He pauses. An invisible force holds me still. Desire floods like a hundred hot rivers along my veins. He brushes my lips again. I open mine to him and he whispers into my mouth, "I don't know how to stop."

His tongue slips between my teeth and there's a sensation of bones dissolving, of skin trembling, of a heart pounding loud enough that it might be heard outside the soundproofed studio. He knows what he's doing. My body also seems to know. I follow its lead until we flow together, our mouths craving, our hands finding the places we've needed to touch for too long.

I kissed a boy at a school dance years ago. It felt awkward and fake, like kissing a friend. Worse—he practically licked my tonsils. And I was at a player's party last year, talking with a guy I'd become friendly with. He kissed me what you'd call passionately and all I could do was make myself kiss back.

But kissing Jacob is wanting it to never end. It's needing

a signal for *Don't-stop-Don't-stop* so I can kiss him forever. I cling to him as though he's the answer to every question I ever asked.

It's dark in the studio now, the sun having winked goodnight, and it makes the floating sensation stronger. It makes the sudden knock and Aria's calling louder.

Springing apart, I pull down my T-shirt and Jacob leaps up, running fingers through mussed hair. His expression is so close to regret my heart wants to cry. He puts a finger to his lips. He's not going to answer the door. *He locked it.*

When we hear Aria move away, I'm still stinging with the memory of Jacob's stricken face. *He wishes we hadn't—*

I stand, ready to go, to never return, to never go back to where I shouldn't have gone in the first place. But as I step away, he moves nearer, sliding his arms around my waist.

Not so long ago, it was Aria he hooked up with, right here in the studio.

I break away and run from the sound of him calling me back.

NINE

EACH TIME A PEBBLE HITS my bedroom window, it's a reminder of what we've done.

Why is Jacob trying to reach me when there's nothing more to say? I'd ignored his chain of texts through the evening begging me to come over, but he hasn't taken the hint.

I should be worried about Aria finding out and concerned about Mum and Dad's reaction. They would never accept how I could do such a thing to my sister. And I should care that the Raggers could break, our childhood wiped away in one night, because all our memories would become taboo. But all I can think about is how Aria slept with Jacob, and I wish it had been me.

It's midnight and another stone hits the windowpane, louder than the others. Without turning on a light, I find the guitar pick still smeared with dried blood from our sisters' oath and clutch it through the plastic bag it's been stored in for five years.

I've betrayed Aria. The Harper who, aged seven, squished sausage through Aria's keyhole because she was sent to bed without dinner for drawing on my wall, is gone. The Harper who brought Aria gifts from her travels—a flower from Beethoven's birthplace in Germany, violin rosin from Italy, a rock from outside Strauss's home in Austria—vanished years ago.

Like Colt said, I *am* a spoiled, selfish brat.

The sound of Aria practicing her violin wakes me before my alarm. I've had three hours' sleep. I thrust arms into sleeves and feet into socks, angry that Aria had to love Jacob, angry at myself for being weak, angry at Jacob for disturbing the heart I'd sent to hibernate forever. And angry because I can't forget Jacob's mouth on mine—can't stop wanting more.

When we arrive for training, I'm in the mood to wrap the tennis net around the throat of the first person who speaks to me. I march onto the court and throw my bag at the ground. Colt stops stretching his calf and cocks an eyebrow. There's no sign of Milo. I slump into a chair.

Colt's footsteps approach. He wafts a take-out coffee

cup under my nose. "Glad I'm not the only moody bastard around here."

I inspect the dark stubble around lips that could belong to a poster boy, and almost retaliate with a smart-ass remark about getting everything I want—including coffee. Almost, because being a smart-ass could be interpreted as being a spoiled brat. And Colt's expression is warmer than I've seen it, conciliatory, even.

I take the cup. "Thanks."

"Sorry I took off yesterday. Milo enjoys pushing my buttons."

"Bit intense, wasn't it?" I inhale the coffee aroma.

"He's right, though. I figure he was born aged seven hundred." Colt scuffs his bag with the toe of his sneaker. "Listen, I know it's not your fault—the hotels and the tutor and stuff." He does that thing where he unzips me with his eyes and rummages around inside me; he must have learned that from Milo. But this time, instead of looking switched off, something's changed. Colt's here, in the moment. With me, not against me.

I blurt, "You're awfully judgmental." His gaze releases me, and I sense the relief of being put down.

He watches Dad hovering at the gate. "Milo tells me you're not a tennis brat. Spoiled, maybe, but not a brat."

"Thanks a lot." I kick at his shin. "How do you define a tennis brat, anyway?"

"You've met the type—parties late, drinks a lot, spends

all of Daddy's money while off the leash on the circuit. Ungrateful types who waste their talent."

I chew on my lip and scold myself—not for any partying, but I'm probably guilty of being ungrateful. I'm not sure I'll make it as a professional *without* Milo, yet here I am, complaining that he and Colt aren't right for me. I have to admit the mixed doubles plan makes sense. It'll get my name out there for an agent, improve my ranking, and pull me out of the first-round graveyard. Suddenly, my tennis goals seem easier than anything that's going on at home.

"And I don't think I'm better than you," Colt says, dropping into the chair next to me. "I envy you. You've got all the talent and everything you need to make it. Truth is, I need you—this mixed doubles gig—I need to earn some big prize money."

"So you can afford to go to more *singles* tournaments?"

He stretches a straightened arm across his chest to warm up. "Don't take it that way. I need this for my family. You need this gig to improve your own singles chances, but it doesn't mean the doubles game isn't important to you." He extends the other arm. "I guess I can be pretty stubborn, but we're partners now. I won't judge you if you won't judge me." He grins—a precious gift made just for me.

Something inside me comes unstuck and falls away.

"Okay," I concede. "Where do we go from here?"

Colt bends to remove a racquet from his bag. "Forward. As Milo always says."

I savor the coffee on my tongue before swallowing. "You remembered what Aria said—that I'm addicted to coffee."

"I'm your eyes and hands now." Colt stands and rubs a bicep, revealing the tattoo under his sleeve. *I can and I will.*

By the gate, Dad greets Milo before leaving me to it.

I jerk my chin at the tattoo. "*I can and I will* what?"

Colt raises an eyebrow, then goes to help with a bag of rope Milo's carrying.

"*Guten Morgen*," says Milo with a guttural German accent. "Hope you slept well. Now we work." I groan into my cup. Milo throws Colt's racquet to him. "I'm assuming that as it's 6:10 you're warmed up?"

There's a silence in which I hug my knees and Colt walks to the baseline.

"Up and at 'em, Harper. The devil's favorite furniture is the long bench. And I hope that's black coffee." Milo tilts the chair forward, and I spill out of it. I gulp at the cappuccino and pick up a racquet, dragging it behind me. A ball bounces on my back and I assume it's Colt hurrying me up, but he's smirking at Milo.

"*Morgenstund hat Gold im Mund,*" shouts Milo across the court. "The morning hour has gold in its mouth, Harper."

Colt sends a gentle lob across the net. I smash the ball at his feet. He tracks me, amused. I send over a couple of balls, one after another. Colt reaches the second and I return it, putting my entire body behind it. It slams across the net. Colt drops back, returns it, but it's high, and I go

79

in for the kill. I think I even aim at him. It slices the air and wallops Colt on the thigh. He laughs out loud. I check to see if it happens again. It does. Straightaway, I'm enchanted by his oversized smile. It's better than a hard-earned match point. It's not just the way his face opens up, it's the look in his eyes, like he's admiring me for making him laugh because it's something rare and hidden and infrequently awarded.

"What's with the rope?" asks Colt, breathless, when Milo calls us over.

"You already know in doubles that you need to keep a similar distance between you to avoid creating holes for the opponents to hit into. And I take things literally."

Milo loops one end of the rope around Colt's waist and secures it, then does the same with me. I shift my gaze to Colt, checking in, but he simply snaps up a racquet and gets into position, assuming his self-appointed spot on the service line. I move nearer the net and the rope pulls taut.

"That's the distance you want to maintain—you'll trip if the rope slackens," yells Milo. He sends a gentle shot across the net and I return it. Next, he makes me move left and the rope tugs, but Colt follows and the rope loosens. The next shot is high and goes overhead to Colt. I should step back farther, but I move too late. Colt yanks me with him and I skid and bump onto my butt. Milo chuckles, but Colt has the decency to keep quiet, and helps me up.

We return a few shots until Milo lobs a ball at the gutter

and I go for it. Colt is too slow. Except *he* doesn't go down—he's much heavier—and it's me who gets wrenched backward and onto my backside again. This time, I brush away Colt's offered hand, patting my grazed butt as I get back into position at the net.

"Good thing we're not playing mirroring right now." I hear Colt's words and take a moment to grasp his meaning. I can't believe Colt made a joke, never mind a flirtatious one. I glare at him, but it falls flat because Colt's smile overtakes his face. *Whoa!*

We get the hang of the exercise. It's less about knowing how to hit a ball and more about moving as one entity. The mood on court lifts, and we fist bump between wins.

"That kind of worked," says Colt, when it's over.

"Don't sound surprised," says Milo, juggling racquets. "Now we go back to mirroring. Best get your rope off."

Colt steps closer to unknot my rope. I hold my breath, vastly aware of the wall of muscle that he is. When he's done, I do the same for him, taking ages because my fingers transform into bananas.

We practice our serves. Milo concentrates on correcting my wandering ball toss. Apparently, they're a reflection of my inner confidence—shaky and inconsistent.

Then comes a new game: Milo feeds us the ball and we return it and race around half the court while the other player hits the next shot before taking their turn around the court. The snag is that if we fail to make the return, Milo doesn't slow the play by double bouncing, but straight-away feeds the next ball. The more we mess up, the harder it is for our partner and, in turn, ourselves. Neither one of us wants the blame. We knuckle down until Colt and I fall to our knees, heaving air into our lungs and begging Milo to stop.

"Colt," shouts Milo, the sun catching the mirrors of his sunglasses. "You said you're free from four on. I'll pick you up then." He turns to me. "We're going to Balmoral Beach for more torture. Plan to get wet."

"You're about as distracted as a cat in a roomful of wild dogs," says Mr. Fraser. He's been my tutor since I started junior year, and I'm pretty sure I'm his worst student. "How about we leave it for today?" He slaps his laptop shut and arranges my textbooks into a pile.

"Sorry. I didn't sleep well last night, and I have a throb-bing headache." Plus my mind can't stop replaying every-thing that happened with Jacob.

After I walk Mr. Fraser to the door, I skulk into the kitchen and lie helplessly on the sofa. The first hint of a spring breeze sneaks through the windows.

Aria wakes me when she and the dogs crash into the kitchen after work. "You sick?" She removes a floppy black felt hat and chucks it at me. It misses by a few feet. "We're making popcorn and slushies. Like the Raggers used to. Want some?"

We? I sit up straight. Jacob is bent over the snuffling dogs. My heart scurries unhappily.

I feign sleepiness and lie on the sofa, a cushion over my head. Jacob and Aria mess around, shaving ice and popping corn, the room filling with the buttery smell of childhood.

The sofa sinks and Jacob presses an icy glass against my leg. I sit up and accept the drink, leaning against the arm of the sofa and glancing behind me at Aria who is scooping up spilled ice. Jacob mirrors me, covering my bare feet with his. I inspect the slushie as though it's something from an alien planet. When Aria dumps herself between us, squishing our toes, Jacob's smile is chaotic, as if it doesn't know whether to be a grin or a grimace.

TEN

ALTHOUGH ARIA GENERALLY SHUNS THE outdoors these days, she wants us to spend more time together and walks to Balmoral Beach with me.

"I admit I have an ulterior motive for coming," she half shouts. She's slightly behind me, her flowery skirt billowing, so that I have to keep stopping for her to catch up. We're going to be late. "Colt's hot, don't you think? I could use a distraction from Jacob." She's trying to sound nonchalant, but her words don't hide the heartache in her voice.

"You've never been on the receiving end of one of Colt's glares or dressing-downs. And you don't want to be, believe me."

They're waiting for us when we arrive, a paddleboard on the sand between them. Colt is wearing nothing but navy blue swim trunks. I give him a once-over, careful not to get caught staring. *Yeah, hot.*

Milo greets us, his long gray-brown hair blowing across his face. "Before you ask, this exercise is about teamwork. You must stand up together on the paddleboard and work to get from the jetty to the restaurant, spin around, and back to the jetty. You keep at it until you don't fall to earn your supper."

"I'm stiff from this morning's session." I groan.

"He who rests grows rusty," says Milo.

"No *rabbits* in the pepper today? What did that mean anyway?"

"German proverb. Look it up. You're welcome to join me in the spectator zone, Aria." Milo points farther up the beach to a red deck chair. She seems to have lost her tongue and just nods.

I strip down to my suit, grateful I decided against the bikini. Colt's glance whips down my body so briefly I'm sure I imagined it.

"This is supposed to strengthen your core muscles," Colt says, dumping the board into the water. I wade out, whacking him with the paddle when a wave bumps me. Next, I fall off the front of the board, butt up, head first, and then cap that by slipping off on top of Colt. He seems mildly amused, but he never takes his focus off the goal.

"We need to both lie on the board, then get to our knees, don't you think?" asks Colt.

I jump on first and suddenly he's lying on top of me, lower down the board so his face is just above my butt. *This is mortifying.* He moves to his knees and I copy until we're stable in the small waves. When we finally make it upright, Colt's hands rest on my hips to keep us balanced, and my cheeks simmer. I concentrate on moving us forward until we succeed and we haul the board up the beach, our arms and legs spent.

The sunset is a violent red slash across the sky, reminding me of what I was doing this time yesterday. And that's when I spot Jacob on the sand next to Aria. A shiver of cold douses me.

"You earned your dinner." Milo strolls toward us. "And in record time. I expected you to take much longer. Next time—"

"Next time it's your turn, old man," cuts in Colt.

Colt is suddenly eclipsed by Jacob's stormy face. I hug myself, rubbing at goose bumps as Jacob approaches. He's jiggling the keys to his Jeep like they're a weapon. His glare nails me. He sizes up Colt, then swipes the towel from Aria, who's mocking our efforts, and moves behind me, wrapping the towel around my shoulders and rubs my arms to warm me. I go rigid. Aria's eyes widen, then swoop away, her brow furrowing.

What the hell is Jacob playing at?

Milo does the introductions because I forget.

"What sort of name is Colt?" asks Jacob. Colt, taller and

definitely broader, examines Jacob like he's weighing several possible responses, one of them being to pound him into the ground. He focuses on Jacob's hands, still on my arms, and appears to decide not to respond at all. Instead, he scans through Jacob to the restaurant behind him.

Milo takes the hint. "I promised you dinner. Good to see you, Aria. Jacob. See you another time, I'm sure." Relieved, I pull the towel tighter around me and Colt carries the board, leaning it against the wall of the restaurant.

At the outdoor table, Milo orders steak all round and a pitcher of water, then asks us what we said to each other on the paddleboard.

"Colt swore at me a lot. He was out of control," I tease.

Colt cracks his neck, suppressing a grin. "Suggestions mostly."

"And when one of you got it wrong and tipped you both over?"

"I cracked up," I say. "It wasn't anyone's fault. We both made mistakes. My abs will kill tomorrow."

"And how do we take this onto the doubles court?" asks Milo. "Number one: you always use the *we* or the *us* word."

I jump in with, "Never blame anyone for a lost point."

"Yes. It's never one person's fault," continues Milo. "Maybe the setup wasn't the best or someone just made a mistake. Either way, you *both* lost the point. And don't tell each other what to do. Colt?"

Colt's foot taps repeatedly. I realize he's watching Jacob and Aria exit the beach. "Keep your sense of humor," he mumbles.

"True," says Milo, then orders bread from a waitress. "And when you're physically close, it's hard to get angry with each other," he continues. "Hence the fist bumping and high fives between points. They're not just for passing on messages or encouragement, but to keep you close, almost intimate—you stay as one unit and don't break away into two when the pressure builds."

"Got it," I say, twirling a loop of hair and sucking the end.

"Too hungry to speak, Colt?" suggests Milo.

"At least I'm not eating my hair." He eyes my mouth.

"Okay, let's try a distraction technique. Truth time," says Milo with a clap. "Swap one bit of information the other person doesn't know about you."

Colt's attention is suddenly on the swinging kitchen door, then the waitress, then the table next to ours. Arms folded, his leg bounces repeatedly. The rolls arrive and he starts in on them without waiting for the butter.

I shrug. "I suck my hair when I'm nervous. But I'm sure Colt doesn't care."

"He must learn to care. This is all part of doubles strategy. Same as a good marriage—understanding each other, trust and communication."

Colt raises an eyebrow. I push down a gurgle of laughter.

"My second-favorite sport—paddleboarding," adds Milo. "It's one of the reasons I moved to Australia in my twenties." He raises his hands to the sky. "This great weather."

Colt pushes his chair back. "Need to take a—restroom."

Milo jerks a thumb at Colt's retreating figure. "I tried. But you can't milk a bull. Hopefully he'll open up as time goes by."

Colt stays away for longer than it should take to pee, returning as the waitress serves out our plates. He tucks into the potato before he's properly sat down, then orders more bread. Milo chats to me and dumps several of his own potatoes on Colt's plate.

"He has the appetite of a pack of wolves," Milo explains.

"The tattoo—*I can and I will eat everything I see?*" I tease, and am rewarded with a chuckle from Colt.

When Colt finishes his meal, after several more helpings of bread, Milo goes to pay the check. Colt's stare pries me open. "So whose boyfriend is Jacob, yours or Aria's?"

I choke on a green bean.

ELEVEN

SOMETHING STARTLES ME AWAKE. I blink, catching the 12:04 on the alarm clock. A blurry shape approaches my bed, and I make a squawking sound.

"Shhh. It's me." Jacob's fingers push against my mouth. I haven't seen him since the paddleboarding exercise with Colt earlier this evening. I told Colt that Jacob is a lifelong friend—and far more important than a boyfriend.

I scramble up. "How'd you get in?"

"Bathroom window has no screen."

"You climbed two stories and through our bathroom window?" I flick the lamp switch.

Jacob sparkles with mischief and roosts on the bed, flashing a penknife. "Done it before."

"I don't want to know." I remember Aria, and sneak to lock the door between our shared bathroom and my bedroom. Turning back to Jacob, I keep my distance. "What're you doing here?"

"Missed you. And watching that guy with his paws all over you—"

He's staring at my mouth. Pulses of heat crease through me. I drift over to the window. The blinds are open—it's easier to wake early in a sun-filled room than a dark one—and stars blink at me. The full moon is small and high. Jacob moves in behind me, holds my hips. I feel the warmth of him through my crop top and lick my lips. "What we did—"

"Don't say it. Don't," whispers Jacob. His breath on my ear makes me shudder. Warm lips press against my temple. "How can it be bad or wrong to love you?" he says. His lips flutter against my skin. He bends to kiss my neck, and I lean into him, my legs like water.

He loves me? His words hang in the air, glittering with possibility, but if I admit I love him, too, how do we come back from this? And come back we must.

But it's like trying to roll up a hill.

Hands slip under my T-shirt, splay flat across my stomach. My bones evaporate. I turn my face so Jacob's mouth finds mine. His desire is strong and alive, alight, and I catch fire and kiss him back.

But Aria—

I start to shake my head. He tugs me to face him, kisses me deeper, trying to kiss the No right out of the room. But it won't go. I draw back.

"I know. I know," he whispers. "I'm the biggest prick ever."

I'm worse. *She's my sister.*

He binds my wrists with his hands. "Don't hate me. I'd give up frickin' everything—"

I'm shocked at how cut up his face is, partly stuffed with longing and craving, part crammed with regret and guilt. We're not children anymore, playing childish games. This is real and big and hurtful and capable of blowing apart lives.

This must stop.

But the words stick in a throat that's fat and prickly with tears.

His mouth is on mine again, feverish. Desire that streaks hot and fast pulls me along as if I got a sleeve caught in the door of a runaway train. I kiss him, hard.

But Aria? My limbs stiffen.

Jacob releases me. "I know what you're thinking. But Aria was a mistake. I was with her—and thinking of you." He kisses my nose. "And now, with you, it's *intense*. Every touch turns the dial up. You make my pulse beat faster. And I can't stop thinking about you. I crave you. I write songs about you."

Something ruptures inside me and every part of me wants to reach for him. All words bury themselves, and I have to dig for them. I make my voice soft. "It doesn't matter what we feel. I know you've split up, but no one in

this way about you," he continues. "Back then I didn't want our friendship to change. Then you left on the junior circuit." He strokes my cheek. "I think it's why I eventually went out with Aria. When I looked at her, I saw you—pure torture. When I kissed Aria, I got a piece of you back. And maybe it worked for a while. But not anymore."

I listen to what he says, recognize what he's feeling, and wonder if it'll ever be okay to tell the world we're in love.

TWELVE

THE NEXT MORNING, COLT'S LATE for training. When he stalks onto the court, Milo stops our rally to study him. I wait for Milo to cut him off at the knees with some choice words, but all he says is, "Come warm up, Colt."

Milo would dish out a lot more than *Come warm up* if I arrived half an hour late. Is Colt such a Wonder Boy he can storm off, arrive late, and dictate where and what time we train?

"You're soft on him," I grumble.

"When it's appropriate. By the look of him, I'm surprised he turned up."

"What's his story?"

Milo examines me. "Best wait till he's ready to tell you."

Days pass and Colt's mood doesn't improve. As if to shut out what's bothering him, he trains harder than ever, and I follow his lead; it's the only time my head isn't full of Aria and Jacob.

Colt and Milo travel to the Chengdu Open in China at the end of the month for a men's ATP event. I'm left with instructions to hit the gym, work on conditioning, and practice with nineteen-year-old Kim Wright, a fellow Aussie ranked 113 in the world. I still haven't quite broken the 150 barrier.

Kim has muscles and a figure that belong to Superwoman. Across the net, her severely short, red hair and fixed jaw give her the air of a female warrior. But it's those green eyes, always narrowed, always strategizing, always weighing me up even when we chat, that get me shaking in my tennis shoes.

We train on the court at my house, and following our first practice match, having thoroughly beaten me, she quips, "Even without the home advantage, I can whip your ass."

The competitive streak Colt woke in me growls.

Kim's faster than me, fitter than me, stronger than me, but as the week advances I lose by smaller margins. On the day we each win a set, Kim's not impressed.

"What's with her?" asks Aria after Kim's stormed through the kitchen and out the front door. Aria twists to flick on the radio and Jacob, who's just finished jamming with his band in the studio, gives my hand a secret squeeze. A gang of butterflies attacks my stomach, and I squeeze back.

"Scared I'm going to beat her," I answer, opening my laptop to see how Colt's doing in Chengdu.

"S'pose you and Dad will be leaving for China soon," adds Aria. "Can you try not to hijack him with tennis talk at dinner tonight? I'd like a little quality time." Aria's tone is even, but her mouth looks pouty. Since she broke up with Jacob, she seems even more jealous of the time Dad spends away with me. *Is that what drove her to Jacob?* I had Dad so she took Jacob.

"It's not a territory war," I snap. Aria slams the fridge shut and storms upstairs. I flash a look at Jacob who tugs at an ear and blows out his cheeks.

"Sisters," he says.

Aria's opera music blasts from her bedroom, making the walls throb.

Part of me believes it was Aria who betrayed the sister code first. She took Jacob for herself. Sure, she didn't know I loved him, but she knew she was making something that was a threesome into a twosome. I realize now that I resented her for that, maybe enough to let our sister bond diminish.

She must've known it would change the Raggers, yet she selfishly did it anyway. Maybe my choosing to be with Jacob now isn't so bad, after all. Maybe she deserves a taste of her own medicine.

Screw her. With more force than is necessary, I scrape back the bar stool, perch, and punch in a URL on my laptop.

Jacob turns off the radio, then wraps his arms around me, watching the screen over my shoulder. His touch quells the streaking anger inside me. I click on the link for Colt's compulsory post-match interview. It's more of a sound bite, though. He'd reached the second round before being knocked out and says five words: "I executed my game plan." He looks as though he'd rather wrestle crocs in a river than endure an interview, and even before the camera switches away he swivels to leave, any hint of "human" switched off.

"What's with him?" asks Jacob. It's exactly what I want to know. "Maybe I should hook up a camera so you can watch *me* in the studio?" he adds.

"Doing what? Eating and sleeping?" I plant a kiss on his cheek.

Three days later, Dad and I travel to meet Milo and Colt at the China Open. I'm more than a little curious about being at a tournament with Colt, even though we won't actually play together; they only have mixed doubles at the Grand Slams, so we'll compete separately in men's and women's doubles matches to gain experience. But for almost the whole competition, Colt's the invisible man and doesn't even stay in the same hotel as us. I remember his words about trailers and youth hostels.

"Is he always a monk at these events?" I ask Milo.

"Colt is one-tracked at tournaments. It's complicated," says Milo, spinning a racquet. He changes the subject. "Fancy visiting the Great Wall?"

"Seen it, thanks." I recall that fight with Kominsky—he'd preferred a training session over sightseeing.

While training with Kim, I've developed a superstition of always bouncing the ball five times at the exact same height to stop my ball toss wandering. It mostly works, and I decide to try it out in my first-round match. Milo has nicknamed my opponent, Monica Moreau, Pocket Rocket. It's soon clear why. She's smaller than most players but somehow manages to reach the very inch of the court my ball bounces in every time. But my ball toss is more consistent and I feel fit and strong, and I find myself ahead after the first set.

Monica is red-faced and panting as she lunges for a net shot. Before I can stop myself, I don't smash her return but lob it back, giving her a chance. She wins the point. I check in with Milo, but unlike Kominsky who'd pace and throw up his hands and shake his head, he remains still and expressionless behind his aviators. I head to the baseline, fiddling with my strings and scolding myself. It's like I'd rather play fair than win. For the remainder of the game, I'm stiff with nerves, knowing there's something in me that would rather be liked—rather be nice—than smash my opponent.

After I lose the game, I lock myself in the restroom. *Kominsky was right.*

When I emerge, Milo says, "Fail once, try again twice. Besides, you went to a tiebreaker three times. It was close. And that's because your ball toss has improved, making your first serve more consistent. Failure makes you smart, *Dampfnudel.*"

"No matter how good my ball toss gets, I'll never win because I don't have a killer instinct. Even thinking those two words makes me cringe."

Milo cocks his head, his eyebrows raised. "Did no one explain that this is a game, not a war? It tests three things: your skills, your fitness, and your mental toughness, not your kill rating. Improve these three things and you never have to think those words again."

"There's a difference between a killer instinct and mental toughness?"

"Of course. One means smashing your opponent into the ground until you beat the game out of them, the other means staying strong and believing in yourself even when your opponent is trying to smash you into the ground. Remember that two-inch version of yourself on your shoulder?"

The one shouting *I'm not good enough.* As I follow Milo to the court where Colt's playing his second-round match, I realize Kominsky was right about winning being about the mind game. But he never explained that there are different ways of playing that mind game.

Colt's match has started. He's buried inside himself, barely changes expression, and never checks in with Milo. Powerful strokes make him a threat, but the number 9 seeded German applies enough relentless pressure that Colt cracks and loses his match.

It's October. Neither of us can reach the quarterfinals in our singles tournaments. How can we hope to win the mixed doubles Grand Slam in three months?

When my cab arrives home, the Welcoming Committee, including Jacob, waits in an excited line. I hug Mum first, the familiar smell of dog and disinfectant making my nose twitch. Aria jams me into a hug next. Her oversized hooped earrings dig into my cheek.

Jacob pulls me into his usual rough hug. I poke him in the belly so he lets go, but he wrestles me into a headlock. As he rubs his knuckles against my head, he whispers, "I missed you," his lips on my skin. My body quivers. He'd sent me a billion texts, but between matches, training, and schoolwork, there was little time to reply to all but a few.

We gather for a family meal—Jacob is family. As usual, Aria reclaims Dad by having him play a duet on the piano with her, her arm slung around his neck as she shows off. She and Jacob talk excitedly about the Con audition next month, but under the table, Jacob's bare feet cover mine.

"Who's up for a game of *Clue*?" asks Mum.

"Only if you use your French accent," I reply.

Mum twirls an imaginary moustache with her finger-tips. "*Mais oui, mon petit chou-fleur.*"

"Gotta go," says Jacob, laying down his cutlery and scraping back his chair in one movement.

"You sure?" asks Mum. "Aria made oatmeal cookies."

"Meeting up with the band at Mad Dog's house, but I've always wanted to ride a motorcycle while eating cookies." One hand collects three cookies from the wire tray on the kitchen counter. "Thanks, ladies."

"What motorcycle?" I slap my hands on the table, but Jacob races out the door. I look at Dad, inspecting his reaction.

"Parents bought it for him," Aria quickly explains. "To make up for missing his band's gigs."

"But didn't they only just buy him a Jeep? You know, the one he bought to match ours? The one he barely uses?"

Aria shrugs. "And don't forget the music studio."

"The same rules apply as before—no riding motorcycles," says Dad, through a sigh. "I wish they'd restrict bike licenses to the over twenty-fives."

"Why are you so against them again, Dad?" asks Aria.

"You kids seem to think you're invincible on them—they're not bicycles. It takes maturity to ride one safely and responsibly." I think of Colt and his motorcycle.

While the three of us play *Clue*, Aria keeps interrupting by calling for Dad's feedback as she plays her audition pieces on the violin—the same piece over and over twenty-five times before the next one, again twenty-five times.

Never any fewer, never any more. That's when she's most contented, lost in her world—creating music as if she's knitting her own happiness.

Later, the roar of a motorcycle's engine brings me back from the brink of sleep. Dad's warning fully wakes me. I sit up, suddenly anxious. I'm fooling around with my sister's ex-boyfriend, he's riding a death machine, Colt's become scarily moody, and Kominsky was right about me being too soft. *Can Milo really fix me?*

Something's shifting again, the kaleidoscope turning, but the pattern it's creating is darker, more complicated than before. I'm suddenly cold with anticipation, but not the good kind; more like being inside a thriller and suspecting the villain is around the next corner.

THIRTEEN

FOLLOWING OUR PERFORMANCES AT THE China Open, Milo puts Colt and me through rigorous strength and fitness sessions. He believes in weight training and sprint work. We race 100 yards in under fifteen seconds, with the remainder of the minute to rest, and then we do it again. Twenty times. Another day, it's a quarter mile repeated ten times.

At the end of each session, I can barely press the accelerator pedal on the Jeep I share with Aria—Dad insists I drive myself to training now. Exhausted, I drop into bed by eight each night, leaving Jacob smiling wistfully goodnight.

Whatever was happening at home must have improved for Colt, because he's much happier again. We play the mirroring game every day until Colt is retying my shoelaces and I'm massaging his aching right shoulder without thinking about it. We complete 5Ks through the park, our inside legs tied together in a three-legged race. We play tennis, one of us blindfolded to force us to use our other senses, the other giving directions. We swim in the local Olympic pool, not just forty laps, a self-imposed limit with Kominsky, but a hundred. Running 5Ks is no longer enough, and the runs evolve into half marathons.

As doubles partners we're more relaxed, not surprising when we spend half the time tied together. I'm no longer embarrassed when we trip over in a pile of limbs during a three-legged run, or lie next to each other, panting and groaning with the effort of pulling air into our lungs. Colt's also stopped scouring me as if I'm something to judge or decode. Instead, it's Colt and me against Milo, straining to survive his tests.

Two weeks after we return from China, Milo invites Colt and me for dinner at his house. We arrive at the same time, Colt on foot, and me in the Jeep. It's weird seeing Colt wearing something other than tennis clothes and he's hot, hot, hot in jeans and a black V-neck tee that stretches across his chest and accentuates his shape. I'd ignored Aria's suggestion of a dress and gone with jeans and a white T-shirt, but I straightened my hair and left it down.

Colt waits for me to park, and we climb the steps to Milo's front door together. Milo answers the doorbell, waving a blindfold.

I lean against the doorframe and groan. "Do you ever let up?"

"I'm good," Colt says, taking it. "I can eat blindfolded."

Milo chuckles. "But can you cook blindfolded?"

"Sure," Colt answers. "Just don't gag me as well."

Milo's house is an original timber cottage on the outside, but inside he's let someone who knows what they're doing renovate and decorate. The back of the house is made entirely of glass windows and it's furnished with plush rugs and wall-sized modern art. It's not as messy as I expected of a rock star tennis coach, even if it smells of old cheese and garlic. Milo pours juice at the white granite-topped island and takes a seat on a black leather bar stool.

"What am I cooking?" asks Colt as I tie the blindfold.

I assess the chopped meat, pasta, tomatoes, onions, fresh basil, garlic, and oregano. "Spaghetti, I think."

"Great. That I can do with my eyes closed."

Milo and I make a surprised face at each other. "Is this something you haven't told us about yourself, Colt? You can cook?" asks Milo.

"I'll answer after you've eaten."

"Juice." I nudge Colt with the glass. "When you're ready, take two steps forward and reach to pick up the knife on the chopping board." He sips the juice and stretches to put it down. I take it before it misses the counter. "Is this honestly helping us work as one on the court?" I ask Milo.

"Doubt it. Entertaining, though."

"Seriously?" I pass Colt the tomatoes, but he requests the onion first. He slices each end off then peels it.

"Is all the skin off?" he asks, before expertly slicing it.

"I'd have fingertips as a tasty addition to the meal by now. How'd you do that?" Jacob can barely use the toaster, never mind slice onions blindfolded.

Colt's biggest challenge is stirring—he keeps missing the pot. I hold the spoon with him to guide it into the sauce. And I help him pour water into the pot for the pasta before he dumps it over our feet. Each time I get close, there's the clean scent of laundry powder and a hint of woody aftershave rather than hot sweat and Tiger Balm.

Over dinner, which is divine, we talk about the upcoming Moscow tournament Milo and I leave for the next day, followed by another week at a Singapore event. Milo delivers a list of instructions for Colt. He's found Colt a hitting partner, merely number 60 in the world, to help prepare for a series of Futures and Challenger events in Australia—lower level tournaments compared to the World Tour. They pay less and award fewer ranking points, so it's weird he's targeting them.

"Why aren't you entering the men's event in Moscow, Colt?" I ask.

Milo lays a knife and fork on his scraped-clean plate and answers for him. "Not this time."

Colt gets up for a second helping as big as the first.

"Now, Harper." Milo sips from a glass of red wine. "I want you to think about someone or something—maybe a memory, a dream, or a place—that immediately calms you. It has to be something so potent it cuts through your nerves on the court. Take some time to get it right because this will become a powerful weapon in your mind game."

I don't hesitate. *Purple Time*. It's the Purple Woods when they blossom in springtime. It's everything the woods make me feel because of the memories they house.

"I've got it," I say, triumphant.

"Already?" says Milo. "But when you think about it, what does it *feel* like?"

"A warm blanket wrapping around me while I snuggle on the deck on a winter's morning. Or banter at the breakfast table on a lazy Sunday when I know, deep down, how fortunate I am to be totally loved and it makes my heart explode. It's being with my dogs, Venus and Adagio— always ready to play, to live in the moment and love life."

Colt stops eating. He lowers his fork and regards me in a "light bulb moment" way.

"What?" I ask.

A smile tilts his lips, but he starts twirling more spaghetti.

"Does it feel like slipping into a warm bath after a hard training session?" asks Milo.

"Yes, that, too."

"Perfect. It has the 'warm bath' effect. It's the right memory."

I insist on doing the dishes and Colt stays near, discussing the current Shanghai Masters. When I'm done, he points out the dishwasher he's leaning against. "Even blindfolded, I knew it was there."

I flick water at him, and he tickles me until I'm a ball on the floor begging for mercy. He picks me up, still balled up, and dumps me on the chocolate-brown leather sofa where Milo has switched on the coverage of the Masters.

"Now you can appreciate the reason for making you cook blindfolded," says Milo.

I frown. "We can?"

"My pig whistles, Colt. You've upsized the child in you."

Colt rolls his eyes and sprawls next to me, brushing his knee against my leg. It's the first time we've spent together *not* on a training session since the paddleboarding afternoon, and compared to then, we're more relaxed— friends even. We study the tennis, commenting on defects, strengths, and styles, and Milo passes out ice cream. Colt declines.

"A little bit of naughtiness now and again is okay," says Milo. But Colt's fixed to the screen, elbows on knees, as Ramesse serves for the match. Ramesse somersaults his racquet when he beats Dominic Sanchez. Colt relaxes back into the sofa, satisfied that the lower-ranked player won.

Milo gets up from his armchair to use the bathroom.

"Sure you don't want some?" I say, wafting my cone near Colt's mouth. I'm not sure why I do it, perhaps to get his attention; I touch the ice cream to his nose, leaving a blob behind. Colt smirks, wipes the splotch away, licks his thumb clean, but otherwise ignores me. So I dab the ice cream against his lips. Before I can pull away, he grabs my wrist and rubs an ice cream–covered mouth over my cheek and neck. I shriek, taking in the rough prickle of his five o'clock shadow and how powerful his body feels as I fail to push him away. *Holy muscles.*

He settles back on the sofa, smug, and I stop myself from doing it again.

I clean up with a napkin and lick the lopsided ice cream into shape, liking this playful Colt.

He ponders me for a moment. "I haven't seen you with your hair down," he says. There's a message in his voice, but I'm not sure what it is.

Later, Milo talks tactics and strategies—how we must know our opponents, their wins and losses, why they win and lose, how we adapt to them. "Winning is not only about how well you play, it's about how well you make your opponent play badly," he says.

I offer to drive Colt home. He refuses, but Milo pushes and Colt agrees, begrudgingly.

We drive in silence. He seems overly large for the space. I fidget. It's awkward, like strangers sharing a too-small elevator. He directs me to a dimly lit retail parking lot next to a railway station with trains screaming through it.

"You live in a parking lot?" I tease, pulling into a space.

"Yeah. See those Dumpsters over there? The blue one's my bedroom." But he isn't smiling.

Two leather-jacketed guys cross in front of us. Colt's

tense and alert, and draped in shadows as we touch on part of a hidden truth. Milo says to wait until he's ready to share. I scour the shabby neighborhood to find clues into his world and remember how Colt said he envied me.

His stare ambushes me.

I straighten. "You're a great cook, even blindfolded. I've never seen basil chopped that small." Colt's belly laugh rolls around the car.

"You admire my basil-chopping skills," he says, between chuckles. His eyes brim with laughter, and it makes my heart strut. "You're a good friend, Harper. An unexpected friend, but a good one."

The idea thrills me. To make friends with Colt—someone who doesn't appear to like many human beings—is big, important. Special.

"You're a good friend, too," I say.

"You enjoy covering me in your food, though."

"I do?"

"Green gunk in Cincinnati. Ice cream tonight." He leans in and kisses me, chastely, on the cheek. "'Night. Thanks for the lift." I clutch the steering wheel while he unfolds long legs to exit the car.

"See you in two weeks," he says, ducking back in. "Good luck. You can beat this first-round jinx. I'll be watching you online."

He slams the car door. Something inside me crumples a little. I'm going to miss him. He stays on the spot, waiting for me to leave, and I pull away, tracking his shape as it recedes in the rearview mirror.

On the drive home, I wonder what Milo means when he says Colt has a lot to deal with. I want to know more. I want to help—if I can. I want to be the best friend he's ever had.

FOURTEEN

I SLAM DOWN THE PLANE'S window shade harder than intended, blocking out the sunlight that streams in. "You and Colt were close-lipped last night. Why isn't he coming to Moscow?"

When Milo pretends not to hear, I splay my fingers over the open Jean-Paul Sartre book in his lap. He studies the movie menu screen on the back of the seat instead.

"Don't tell me to ask Colt. He never tells me anything. I don't even know if he lives with his parents, if he works, if he has any brothers or sisters. The stuff on Google is limited to his stats and it still says he lives in Florida. Why the big black hole with him?"

Milo shuts the book. "But it's not for me to tell, is it?"

"We're supposed to win the Australian Open mixed doubles together, and I don't know if he suffers from

youngest sibling syndrome or if a hereditary family disease causes his mood swings. Yet he's pretty much familiar with everything about me."

Milo presses his fingertips together, bending and stretching them so they resemble a pulsing heart. "He won't appreciate me talking out of turn. But I'll say this: his mother died when he was six. He's an only child and lives with his dad. And he's homeschooled, so like you, he'll be late at graduating high school. By the way, he's catching up on you—ranked 172 now."

"I'm guessing he's not coming to Moscow for—financial reasons?"

"Yes and no. It's a bit more complicated than that." Eyebrows wiggling, Milo reopens his book. "Give it a little longer, and I'm sure he'll let you behind his game face."

Exasperated, I lift the window shade and stare out at the blue surrounding us. Just as it's impossible to make out where the sky ends and the sea begins, it's impossible to know how much of Colt's game face is the real Colt.

I get into round one of the main draw of the Kremlin Cup. The indoor arena is full of flags from every country, making the match seem more official and important than being on some back court. I start to question if I deserve to be here.

You can beat this first-round jinx. I'll be watching you.

In the taxi to the match I take deep breaths and think of Purple Time.

"Concentrate on the facts," says Milo, "not the super-stitious first-round curse nonsense the press have decided to focus on. That's just a compelling headline. Repeat the positive self-talk we discussed." When I don't respond, he adds, "Out loud. Now."

"I *am* fitter and stronger than ever. I don't believe in curses. I believe I can get into the top one hundred. Every day, in every way, I'm better than I was the day before."

And I do want Colt to see me beat the jinx on the live-stream website.

"Good. Now visualize your serves, your drop shots, your backhand. Visualize that winning shot across the net."

In the end, Purple Time settles me down. The mem-ory of its calm purple haze, of the happy moments in the woods, resembles a warm hand holding mine. I feel less alone, less vulnerable in the middle of the court; the court becomes my turf. When I was younger, I had the heart of a lion, rampaging through life without fear. Remembering Purple Time gives that back to me.

I win in straight sets, and in that moment I under-stand why the big players chuck their racquets in the air or crumple to their knees like they're worshipping the court. But I'm not a top-ten player and I haven't just won a Grand Slam, so I keep myself together enough to shake hands across the net, thank the umpire, and drop into my chair

next to Milo. But I'm squealing inside, my heart feels like it's ten times bigger than normal, and I want to get on my hands and knees and kiss every inch of the court.

As I exit the area, Milo's huge grin and crushing hug don't match his words: "'We are responsible for what we are . . . we have the power to make ourselves.' Swami Vivekananda."

Going into the second round, Milo equips me with another weapon. "The memory you call up to settle yourself? What if your opponent is trying to destroy it?"

I'd never let anyone take Purple Time from me—from the Raggers. When we reach a tiebreaker in the next match, I'm psyched, and refuse to let my opponent take the win from me. Milo is teaching me that tennis is not just about chasing a dream. It's a one-point-at-a-time, high-stakes psychological battle.

The next morning, Dad, who Milo hadn't wanted to accompany me this time, texts a quote from the *Sydney Morning Herald*: "Stein banishes Kominsky curse."

Milo actually does curse when he reads the article. It's more about him than me, and suggests he's a Merlin-like coach and Kominsky must've cast the curse. "Don't read anything in those papers. They'll distract you. What a pile of—it suggests *you* have nothing to do with your result and that's—*Scheiße*." He storms from the room, slamming the door, and later confiscates my phone. It means I can't text Jacob. I feel unsettled, and when my partner and I lose the women's doubles game later that day, I blame Milo's no-phone rule.

In the third round of the singles tournament, the number 10 seed puts a stop to my winning streak, but it's a close match, and I know I've played the best tournament of my life.

"Defeats make you fight harder for victories," says Milo as I exit the court.

"You got a book you're writing these quotes in?" I'm coming down from an adrenaline rush and am not feeling up to philosophy. "You'll make more money from them than from me."

"Defeats are the foundation of victories," he teases. I playfully shove a bag at him and we practically float to the pressroom for the obligatory post-match conference. Maybe Colt's watching.

On the flight to the Singapore tournament, I beg for my phone. But Milo doesn't want me relying on anyone. He's still working to independify me.

"We can call your family, but all this constant texting, Instagram, Twitter, keeps your mind on things back home when it should remain a hundred-fifty percent here. What do you think players did before cell phones?"

I mope for most of the flight, not because of the phone so much as because I'm mad at myself for missing Jacob's voice more than Aria's.

While we wait for our bags in luggage claim, Milo

checks his messages, then offers me a stick of peppermint gum. I decline.

"If you stop behaving like a brat, I'll share Colt's news," he says. The sentence contains so much subtext I don't know where to start. He'd told Colt I wasn't a tennis brat when Colt had believed I was one. Maybe I am and didn't know it. I've broken my jinx, and yet I'm sulking about not having a phone so I can talk to the sister I betrayed and the boy I shouldn't have kissed. I *am* a brat. And *what* news about Colt?

I accept the gum.

Milo yanks off his sunglasses, revealing eyes fizzing with excitement. "Colt won the Futures tournament in Australia—in straight sets. Quickest final ever." And we're hugging and dancing in circles in luggage claim, whirling and twirling because it's impossible to stop, to remain static with such amazing news, and the world's spinning faster anyway, and we'd better go with it if we want to keep up.

When we're too dizzy, we clasp each other at the elbows to steady ourselves. People nearby smile and laugh.

"Oh my God, can we go home right now?" The urge to see Colt is overwhelming. I've never been this happy for someone else. Milo shifts from one foot to the other, fingers woven through his hair, smile so huge he can't speak yet.

Finally, he says, "I accepted he'd take longer to improve his ranking if he concentrated on local tournaments, but if he keeps winning—"

"Can I eat some of whatever you're feeding him?"

"You're doing fine, *Dampfnudel*. Colt's getting back to where he should be. He took time off and his ranking slipped. He was hovering around the 120s a year ago."

I'm back to wondering what happened to Colt. He'd have said if it'd been an injury or something like a death in the family. It must be something really bad—illegal even. Was he banned for taking drugs or fighting? But I had Googled him and only found some dry biography that listed his tournament results. So what's the big secret not even Milo can tell?

Excited to arrive home after a quarterfinal loss in Singapore, I smile at a sunbaked Sydney through the cab window. I broke the first-round jinx not once, but twice. Yet, while I long for Jacob's arms around me, it's Colt I want to celebrate with. The realization is disconcerting. Colt's taking up more and more of my headspace these days, but I guess it's normal because we share tennis and we spend hours training together. Still, my stomach does a loop the loop.

"It was always in you to do it, Harper," says Milo, eyes sparkling. "Just needed to make you believe it."

"That, and a million miles of running and swimming and a billion hours of training."

"You needed to step up, and you did." Milo opens his

newspaper and points to the small article we read earlier about me and Colt. "You did that. I gave you the framework, but you chose to do the rest."

"You've made such a difference to Colt, too." Colt had won another tournament while I competed in Singapore—an even bigger Challenger event.

"He was destined to win those tournaments." Milo cracks his knuckles. "Big local wins plus match experience equals increased rankings. Hell, it's a great plan, even if I do say so myself." He gives me a high five. "And he really needed that prize money. Stability in the schedule, consistency, and there's not a lot stopping him. He's got four more Futures to win before Christmas. If he does, and you keep improving your ranking, we've a great chance of landing you guys an agent, a sponsor, and a place in the main draw at the Australian Open. It'll be a cinch getting into the mixed doubles event."

Nerves sprawl through my belly. Training with Colt is one thing. Playing in a Grand Slam together for $150,000 in winnings, knowing that he really needs that money, is quite another.

When we pull into my driveway, I'm out of the cab before it stops moving. Mum's on tiptoes photographing our arrival, and Dad runs down the stairs to greet me first.

"I knew you could do it," he says, squeezing the breath out of me. I beam over his shoulder—

My brain stalls.

Colt.

He carries himself with quiet certainty, as if he knows he's on this earth to do something special, but doesn't need to shout about it. As he ambles closer, I see him clearly for the first time. He's dropped his mask, and his beaming face is jammed with praise.

My heart plunges. *Whoa.* Having Colt see me beat the curse must've meant more to me than I realized.

Dad releases me, and I rush to hug Colt, my cheek against his chest. I recognize the smell of Tiger Balm—and fresh laundry soap. "You did it," I say.

"*We* did it," he says, clinching me to him.

I pull free as Jacob approaches. Something in the way he glances between Colt and me isn't right. He punches my shoulder too hard, grinning, but doesn't hug me. All at once, Venus and Adagio bounce at us, their tails whacking my legs, and Mum and Aria tumble into me, hugging and kissing and using every word of amazement ever printed in a dictionary.

We move up the dog-clogged stairs and into the house in a big ball of inseparable human. No one finishes a sentence, but everyone talks nonstop. In the kitchen, Mum pours champagne, spilling it in her excitement. I pass around overflowing glasses. Colt declines.

Aria threads an arm through mine. "My sister is going to be a World Champion."

"A toast," says Milo, lifting a flute high in the air. "Hard-working, determined and good-looking—but enough about me. Here's to Colt and Harper."

Jacob downs the bubbles in one gulp.

After I recount every detail of the tournaments, and Milo has made Colt do the same, Colt thanks my parents for inviting him and pulls some keys from his pocket.

"Colt, you can't go now," says Mum. "Stay for dinner. This celebration is for you, too. There's apple pie—"

"Stay, Colt," I say. "We were about to leave the oldies and go down to the river. And Mum always cooks a lot. You can even take thirds."

Colt stuffs his hands into his pockets. "Thanks, Mrs. Hunter. That would be great." I catch Jacob silently mimic, *Thanks, Mrs. Hunter.* I glare at him, then mouth, *Childish.*

Aria takes forever to find her sandals—she's afraid of splinters. Jacob follows Colt and me outside onto the deck. Colt spots the tennis court. He doesn't need to say a word because his thoughts are written all over his face: *Harper has it all.* But I'm not angry. He's right. I do. And I never want to waste it.

"You can come over anytime to play," I say, making an effort to include him, wanting to be his friend. He nods and scans the pool.

Jacob inspects me, then Colt. I secretly brush Jacob's toes with my bare foot, and a grin replaces his frown.

Throwing me over his shoulder, he strides down the stairs to the garden, runs, then trips, and we tumble to the grass. Instead of making light of it, I'm irritated.

From the deck above, I hear Colt talking to Aria. My jaw clenches.

"Last one to the woods is a squished toad," Jacob yells, leaping to his feet. His challenge has been thrown out there many times but today, I'm torn between racing him and waiting for Colt.

I hesitate and confirm that Colt and Aria are following, but when I turn to chase after Jacob, my breath catches: it's Purple Time.

It appears to happen overnight each year. It's always magical, the blue-purple haze painting the woods in lilac fairy dust. I follow Jacob, my insides whirling with laughter and lightness. The tunnel of honey-smelling purple deepens. I weave down the path, our footsteps muffled by fallen blossoms, until Jacob steps from behind a tree, making me squeal with fright. He yanks me out of sight, kisses me, and, still fizzy with happiness and light-headed from the champagne, my blood spikes to a thousand degrees, and I kiss him back. But only for a moment.

When I pull away and turn to run for the river, he grabs my ponytail, making my scalp smart. We reach the Mother Tree, and Jacob brushes my jaw with his nose, nips at my neck.

"Behave yourself," I scold, my scalp still stinging.

Confusion muddles me. Kissing Jacob usually feels so right, yet I half wish Jacob and Aria would disappear so I can talk to Colt about all things tennis—and winning.

I push Jacob away when I hear Aria and Colt approaching. She barely stops to breathe between sentences; Colt seems to make her nervous. Jacob and I sit on the ground just as they come into view.

Colt is quietly taking in the surroundings. I always figured it'd be weird to bring anyone here, but it isn't. Today he fits. He's calm and at peace, as are the woods.

Aria and Colt sit cross-legged next to us. I lie back to track the shafts of sunlight forking through the canopy where the blossoms resemble sparkling lavender jewels. Aria shoves Jacob for being smart-mouthed about something, and Jacob shoves her back. Colt studies them.

I tap Colt's leg. "Time seems to stop in here. Amazing, isn't it?"

His eyes still on Jacob and Aria, he nods.

"It's this separate piece of the earth," I add. "Separate from the scary outside world. In the 1960s, the local hospital handed out jacarandas to new mums who planted the saplings and watched them grow alongside their children. That's why there are so many of them around here."

"Mum says families planted one for every local soldier who didn't return from the war, too," adds Aria.

Jacob thumps me on the stomach. "Let's hit the river."

We hop onto the rocks and leap from one to the next till

we reach the other side. I wave Colt over, but he's leaning against the Mother Tree, arms crossed, looking the other way. Jacob and Aria keep going. I follow for a while, but don't want to abandon Colt, so I turn back.

He's parked on the lowest branch of the Mother Tree, staring upward. The blossoms mimic lilac clouds stuck in the branches.

"The river transforms into this purple stream of confetti when the blossoms fall," I say. "And there's this part of the river where the trees are low and they meet in the middle, and it becomes a purple cave." I indicate downriver. "They're going there now."

Colt leans a shoulder against the trunk. "You don't need to stay. Go with them."

"'S okay. I want to—to hear more about your victories." I straddle the branch opposite him. "Guess you feel amazing. You're really chilled out."

He tells me about the break points, the tiebreakers, the final triumph when he hit that winning shot across the net. I want that to be me one day. In turn, I confess how Milo and I danced in luggage claim.

A flurry of wind makes it rain trumpet-shaped blossoms. Colt peers up at the petal shower. One lands in my open palm.

"I bet you've never climbed a tree before," I say. "Come on. Dare you."

His eyes swoop into mine. "You think if you dare me, I'll do it? Not much of a psychologist, are you?"

I shift to squat on the branch, pocket the blossom. "You never just mess around. Totally let go. Hang out. You're seventeen, not seventy-seven."

"Now I'm a boring old fart?" A petal falls onto his shoulder, and he chucks it at me.

"Yeah. You are."

His eyes cling to mine for a few beats before he stands on the branch. "You win with that crosscourt shot." He reaches for the bough above then pulls himself from branch to branch, and we race up the tree, me grabbing his ankles and him flicking me off, over and over. Where Jacob moves like Mowgli, Colt is a black jaguar.

Near the top, we blink at each other, puffing and chuckling. "This is the best part," I say, between pants. "Another few feet and you won't believe what you see."

Our heads emerge above the treetops, and I'll always remember the expression on his face: it's stamped with a childlike wonder, stripped of all attitude and fear and whatever else made him into the current Colt. I grasp what it would have been like to be his friend when he was a small boy. The swaying canopy circles around us, a vast, purple parachute of petals flickering in the wind.

"I'm speechless," whispers Colt.

"That's not saying much—coming from you."

He bounces the branch I'm perched on.

"This is my memory," I add. "The one I think about when I'm fighting the pressure in a match. This, and the woods themselves, the memories me, Aria, and Jacob made here."

"The warm bath effect?"

"Yup. It's called Purple Time and these are the Purple Woods and it's the best place on earth."

Colt smiles at me and I'm thrilled to finally feel as if I'm the best friend he's *never* had. More than that, it's the kind of smile that makes my heart fly right out of my mouth.

FIFTEEN

AFTER DINNER AROUND THE KITCHEN table, Aria plays the piano while Milo and I talk about Singapore. Colt seems to clam up in company and listens in silence, tapping his glass with his fingertips. Jacob slouches in a chair, legs sprawling, and pats Venus. His sulky glances in my direction are frequent and long. I swallow my irritation and to cheer him up I retrieve a can of whipped cream and plunk it on the table—next to an apple pie Aria's made.

He pants, tongue hanging out. "I'm going to eat as much as I can stuff into my chops." Rubbing his stomach, he sprays cream into a wide-open mouth. When he stops, I snatch the can and spray more until it's foaming around his nose and chin. He swipes at the slipping cream, licking from fingers to wrists. The table erupts with hoots and comments.

I spray a puff onto Colt's elbow. He wipes it with a napkin, smiling, and asks Milo to punish me tomorrow with a grueling drill.

"You two will never grow up," says Mum, plonking a wet cloth on Jacob's head. "Always into mischief, Milo. Two mud-covered, barefoot, wild children dragging Aria with them."

"Excuse me. They never dragged me anywhere." Aria snaps the piano lid shut, her face pouty. "They just had better ideas."

"Remember when we slept on the roof the night before Christmas to surprise Santa?" says Jacob, talking around a spoon of pie.

"The worst was when they set off to school and half an hour later they were back, uniforms dripping wet. They'd gone to the river because the jacarandas had bloomed," says Dad.

"Why were they wet?" asks Milo.

"They were competing to get somewhere and fell in the river," says Mum.

The Purple Cave.

"Actually, Harper pushed me in. She hates losing," whines Jacob.

Aria points at him. "And *you* pulled us in."

"It explains a lot," says Milo, mock-frowning. He places my phone on the table. "Don't bother bringing it next time."

I snatch it up, beaming. "He's the worst coach ever, Dad. I mean, no phone? It's child abuse."

Milo starts to leave, but gets caught in a detailed discussion with Dad. I wait with Colt as he studies Mum's sketches in the hallway. When Mum's not curing animal ailments, she's on the deck drawing while listening to Aria practice, offering suggestions to slow down, watch her staccato notes, or get louder at the crescendo. Over the years, she's framed a dozen pictures of us: Aria, dwarfed behind her double bass while wearing a towel turban; me emerging from the surf, long hair wet and tousled; Aria playing the flute; me, aged fifteen, playing the fool in a pair of bunny ears. Jacob's also there. My favorite is the one where he's balancing on one leg on the wall between our homes while eating cake.

"Great family," Colt says, bending to pat the dogs. They pester him as much as they pester Jacob, except instead of the maniacal bouncing they do with Jacob, they slide around Colt's legs, looking up expectantly. He straightens and peers down at me. "So how long has Jacob been in love with you?"

My mind splits in two, then clashes together like cymbals, leaving me dizzy.

Snorting, I jerk a thumb toward Jacob in the kitchen. "You've got it wrong. We've known each other since I was five. He's like a brother to us." Jacob flicks a blob of soap bubbles at Aria. "We're just close, that's all."

The words are dipped in poison, and I let Colt swallow each one, and hate myself, both for lying to him and because the truth is, for Aria's sake, Jacob should only be like a brother to me. I squash down the idea that I lie in case Colt is interested in me—in that way.

Later, when Jacob says goodnight, he hugs Aria first, then me. His eyes pluck at my heart when he whispers, "See you at midnight."

I shake my head no, frowning.

Aria follows me upstairs. "Thanks a lot for splitting with Colt and leaving me with Jacob in the woods."

I halt in the doorway at the sight of my bed covered in purple blossoms. Aria huffs and flops against the doorframe, knocking the side of her skull against it. "Jacob did it. He said it's to celebrate your wins."

There's a silence so thick it could be stirred.

"He never did that for me." Her chin trembles. She bites her bottom lip.

For a moment, I'm floored. How could he be so thoughtless toward Aria? So careless with our secret? For the umpteenth time today, I'm mad at Jacob. I want to hug her, but she's struggling to keep it together and the part I played in this holds me back.

I walk into the room, ignoring the blossoms. "Guess everyone's come along for the ride with me. Everyone's overexcited." When Aria doesn't respond, I assume she's gone to mope in her room, but when I look up she's still there, her face stony, her eyes questioning.

Her mouth, her brow, twists.

"So how's the audition stuff coming along?" I ask,

fiddling with the lock on my suitcase until it releases. "Going to blow them away?"

Strains of Jacob's voice reach us through the open window as he sings "You Can Count on Me." I roll my eyes at Aria, but she directs her crushed expression out the window.

"Is there something going on with you and Jacob?" she says, her voice colorless.

I hesitate, stop myself from gasping or throwing my hands in the air in pretend shock. But I can't look her in the eye when I say, "I'm not sure what you mean. He's just trying to fit in—you know, adjust to how things are now . . ."

"And how are they? Seems you two are back to being the wild ones, dragging me behind you. You two always made me feel left out, you know."

"What? You hooked up with him. I think you'll find I was the one left out."

"And now you want him?"

"Jeez, Aria. I can't deny it's good to have him back as himself and not permanently attached to you."

"But being the Raggers again. I'm not sure that's possible."

I pick at the Blu-tack on the wall where one of my tennis posters has curled at the corner. "Neither am I."

Aria stares at me, eyes searching, then disengages and approaches my bed. She scoops up a handful of blossoms. "The audition stuff is going well. Thanks for asking," she says, her tone flat. I go to hug her, partly to stop her inspecting my face, partly as an apology for the lies. "Jacob and I practice every day," she continues over my shoulder, her hands light on my hips. "It gives me hope we might be able to work things out. Does he ever talk about me?"

"Enough about Jacob. I missed you so much, and I couldn't even phone you and we promised to spend more time together and we haven't, not really."

She pulls back, grabs my shoulders. Face slightly pink, she's recovered herself and quirks an eyebrow. "Let's have a sleepover. We can talk all night. Maybe we could have a midnight snack and climb the Mother Tree in our PJs like the old days."

Nausea muddies my stomach. Jacob might climb through the window at midnight. I need Aria to be asleep while I put him straight. I unzip my suitcase, the poster eyes of almost every Grand Slam winner on me as I think up another lie. My hands tremble.

"I'd love to. But it was an exhausting trip. Tomorrow night? I promise." I'm such a loser. No, worse. There isn't a word for what I am.

"Sure thing," she says, wandering into our bathroom. "Tomorrow." She slams the door.

I don't blame her for being disappointed—angry, even. I'd promised to make more of an effort to spend time together. I drop my lying head into the muddle of clothes in my suitcase and listen to the sound of her electric toothbrush. Colt is suspicious, Jacob is being insensitive, and I can't keep my promise to Aria because I'm still betraying her.

I don't wait for Jacob to climb through the window at midnight. I'm exhausted from the tour and seething about the risks he's taken, and sneak out an hour early. When I poke my head inside the studio, a huge grin overtakes his face as he puts down his guitar and checks out my body. The grin falls away when he sees my expression.

"You have the body of Catwoman these days," he says, taking a step toward me. Suddenly, my usual crop top and shorts don't seem like a good idea. His smile uncertain, his fingertips reach for my six-pack. I sidestep and slip into the office chair at his desk. I do feel strong, my body hard with muscle, arms defined, legs firm. But my heart isn't in good shape.

Jacob doesn't get the hint and comes closer.

"Stop right there. What were you thinking, putting petals on my bed? Aria's already suspicious. And you shouldn't have kissed me earlier—"

He places a warm hand on my shoulder and strokes my arm. "You kissed me back." His fingers massage my neck. "I missed you so bad some days, I nearly ripped apart my rib cage to stop the ache."

Though I often felt the same way, the truth is that the petals on the bed hurt Aria, and knocking back an appeal to hang together tonight wounded her. If she knew . . .

"Then the texts stopped," he says. "I realize now what happened with your phone, but at the time—*freaking hell*. I couldn't concentrate or practice. If I blow the Con audition, it's your fault." He digs my side playfully.

I flinch and exhale, glance at the door.

Jacob's face cracks. "Is something going on with you and that Colt guy?"

"*What? No!*" I stand, keeping the chair between us. "Why would you think that?"

"Sorry. Just jealous. He gets to spend all this time with you. I mean, what about me? When was the last time you came to one of my gigs?"

"You know I can't do late nights. Or drink."

"And you took him up the Mother Tree—he's not part of the Raggers."

Jacob's got a point. And I'm not even sure why I did it. A heaviness sits on my chest. I decide to avoid the subject. "There's nothing going on between us. It's Aria. We can't do this to her." The words sound crueler than I intend.

Jacob stalks toward the red lips sofa, sitting heavily. "Thought we were waiting for Aria to move on. So we keep us a secret until then."

I gaze out the window at the prickly stars. It's time to be strong, to push away what I want but can't have. It's time to make grown-up choices. "It's too risky. It's just wrong."

Jacob's eyes swirl with sorrow. He pulls his knees to his chin, circling them, then shakes his head and doesn't stop.

"How can this be wrong when it feels completely right? How can loving each other be wrong?"

Chin trembling, my throat clogs. We've bottled up our feelings and refused to let them blossom for years, and now that we've allowed them to take hold of us, now that we've said them out loud, denying them is as useless as telling the jacarandas not to bloom.

But give him up I must. My mouth twists.

"Don't do this," he says, suddenly determined. "We'll do everything we can to protect Aria. I don't want to hurt her either—not ever." He stands, eyes glossy with hope. "We'll keep our secret until it's the right time. We'll love each other, but protect Aria. How can that be wrong?" Silence simmers between us.

"How does scattering petals on my bed and kissing me in the woods, with Aria right behind us, protect her?"

"I'll be more careful."

What wise saying would Milo spout now? *You can't have your cake and eat it, too.* But how do I change what I feel? I remember something Milo said when I complained about moving up the rankings too slowly: "When you stop chasing the wrong things, you give the right things a chance to catch you." Is Jacob the wrong thing?

Is Aria the right thing? We've drifted apart enough—

"I don't want to hurt you, but this can't happen right now." I tread backward and fumble for the door handle. "Please don't climb through the window again."

He pinches the end of his nose and waggles it. "Okay. I'll be more discreet."

"We can only be the Raggers, that's it."

I shut the door behind me, but not before he shouts, "For now."

Back in the kitchen, I drink milk from the carton and pace. I hit my hip bone against the table. Milk slops onto the floor. "Okay, so that conversation felt like crap, but it was the right choice," I mumble, staring at the spreading milk. I grab a cloth to clean up the mess. "That's that."

I put my bawling heart in a box and seal it with tape. *For now.*

Next, I grab butter, milk, sugar, flour—time to make it up to Aria. She has a book of her favorite recipes in the bottom drawer. Her vanilla cupcakes take ten minutes to prep, ten to cook. While they bake, I make coffee for me, hot chocolate for Aria and set it on a tray. But something's missing. I steal outside and across the lawn to the woods to gather handfuls of petals.

Aria's room is dimly lit by her butterfly night-light. She hates the dark. She's sleeping in the middle of the bed, so I sit to one side, the tray on my lap. I had spread the icing when the cupcakes were too warm. It's trickled into a puddle around each cake, but the tray still looks pretty, sprinkled with petals.

I shake her, whispering her name. As she stirs, I flick on the bedside lamp. That's when I see it: Aria's pink guitar pick resting on the same kind of plastic bag mine is stored in. Except while the pick is patchy and stained, there's no sign of our mingled blood. She's washed it.

She knows. How could she? She's probably just angry with me. Or jealous about the petals.

I wrench my eyes away. Aria squints and sits up, taking in the tray. I liberate the petals I've been squashing in one hand, like confetti. "Surprise."

But it's me who's had the surprise.

SIXTEEN

COLT AND I SPRAWL ON the grass at the top of Murder Hill after a 10K run with a sprint finish. Milo's training turns me inside out until my lungs feel as if they're hanging off the front of my body. But I'm growing stronger and fitter. My ground strokes are decisive and powerful, footwork tight.

Milo hovers over us. "I'm going to say a word and you must respond with the first word that comes to you."

"Right now it might be X-rated," rasps Colt. I splutter with laughter.

Milo searches in his sports bag for cups. "Start with the word *me*."

"Milo," we both shout from our positions in the grass.

Milo gives a thumbs-up. "Okay. Next word is *you*."

There's a beat's silence before I say "grumpy" and Colt follows with "childish." I elbow him.

"Interesting." Milo pours some Milo Potion. "I think we'll go with *child*."

"Is this some sort of intelligence test because *clearly* I'm the smart one?" I say.

"Only if intelligence is a measure of the number of times you end up on your butt," quips Colt.

"Let me finish," interrupts Milo. "What about *up*?"

"Trees," I say, and Colt says, "Purple."

Milo and I gape at him. Colt actually flushes, which has to be a first. "You should know. Purple trees?"

I roll my eyes. "Purple Woods, not trees."

"*Purple* it is," Milo says. "No one needs to understand apart from you. The last word is *alley*."

"Smelly," I say, straightaway.

"Smelly works for me," says Colt. "Are these code words for when we play mixed doubles?"

"How can we practice them when only the Grand Slams run mixed doubles competitions?" I ask.

Milo removes his sunglasses. "You'll practice with me. And you're practicing the skills with other partners, and when you add up your fitness training, the doubles exercises including mirroring, the bond rope . . ."

I don't hear the rest because I'm competing with Colt to swipe more Milo Potion before it runs out. Colt wins.

I dig his ribs. He clenches against the tickle. I'm a little thrown when I realize this feels a lot like I'm flirting.

"Attention on me, guys." Milo snaps his fingers. Colt pulls off his shirt, soaked through with sweat, revealing a new tattoo on his shoulder blade. I strain to read it without him noticing. "When Colt shouts purple, Harper, you'll know he's about to attempt a lob—up. Got it?"

"So if I'm calling for a ball, I don't say me, I say Milo?" I ask.

"Exactly. Or if you're aiming for Colt's alley, call the code for you alley—child smelly."

"And my alley is Milo smelly," Colt teases, chucking his sweaty shirt at Milo.

Milo clutches it. "I'll take the fall. You guys mustn't be two individuals playing next to each other. Come together after every point. Talk codes. Be conspiratorial, a physically close team at all times, even if you're losing. Tennis is not merely a ball game, but a mind game, and this teamship psyches out the opponents."

He tosses Colt's shirt back.

"New tattoo?" I shuffle closer to read the words. "Choose to win."

Colt uses the shirt to wipe the sweat from the back of his neck.

Something in me wants to touch the tattoo, rub it out even. "Isn't winning kind of up to your opponent as well?"

"Interesting you should think that," says Milo. "Even winning is a choice."

"You're saying I choose to lose?"

"Break it down to something smaller," says Milo. "When you call for a ball with our new code, you're saying, "I'll win that shot—I'll get there. This is my win." That's choosing to win. Winning a match is about choosing to win, one point at a time. If you lose a point, you delete it from your memory and go after the next point. And the more you practice this technique—the more you train—the better you get at it."

"But there are other factors such as weather, your opponent, the court conditions, the crowd—"

"Yes. But they affect everyone." Milo kicks the bottom of my shoe. "Think back to each match you lost. The moment you chose to lose is always clear—your body slumped, your mind told you it was too hot, or your wrist ached, or your opponent was bursting with energy, or the sun was blinding you. You forgot to choose to win."

I turn from Milo to the tattoo to Colt, who's glaring into the distance. "The other tattoo? Is it supposed to mean 'I can and I will win'?" Milo nods for Colt and I add, "You're both insane."

Milo winks at me, but Colt's strained gaze is lost somewhere in the sky and he's checked out of the conversation. I tap his arm. He jolts back to earth. "You okay? Did I say something wrong?" I ask.

Colt jumps up to go, face unbuttoned. "The tattoos are a reminder," he says, looking like he swallowed what he really wanted to say.

● ● ●

Soon after my homecoming from Singapore, Milo and Colt come for breakfast. Dad wants to confirm the new world rankings on the pro website together. After we've eaten, we file into Dad's study.

With Mum's and Jacob's arms around my shoulders, Dad punches in the website. After our talk in his studio, Jacob's doing a good job of pretending we're still the Raggers. In the nervous quiet of the study, Aria leans against the door, arms folded, a pursed smile on her face. Lately, she's locked herself away with her instruments, claiming to need more practice. Neither of us has brought up the guitar pick or the sister pledge.

Dad searches for Colt's ranking first. It's a massive jump, to 121. Colt's chest puffs out, and he beams while Milo slaps him on the back. Dad pumps his hand and Mum kisses him on the cheek. I want to go to him, but Jacob has me in a headlock, tactlessly chanting, "Harper, Harper, Harper." Annoyed, I pull myself free.

I feel rotten for Colt. His dad should be here.

When Dad types in the women's rankings search, the air in the room seems to get sucked out the door.

Dad springs out of the office chair. "You did it. Number 100." And the room is jumping up and down. There's squealing, jostling, and kisses covering my cheeks. Even Aria hugs me. But all I want to do is go to Colt who waits alone, his smile bolted on. I wrench away and bowl into him, making the air whoosh out of his chest as he stumbles backward. I hold on to the sound of his chuckle.

"Does that mean Harper can beat you, Colt—since she's ranked higher?' asks Jacob. Jacob knows perfectly well that men's rankings remain a different entity and are far more competitive, so I kick his knee to shut him up.

I kiss Milo's cheek when he joins our pack, then Colt's. But Colt's face is somehow haunted, as though he's lost in a bad memory.

I can't stop thinking about Colt. I don't know if it's because he's such a mystery or because we spend so much time together. Or if it's because, unlike when I think about Jacob these days, I get this sense of lightness in my body like I'm . . . anticipating something.

Why wasn't his dad there this morning? Why is his dad never even mentioned? Where does Colt live? I'm guessing not in a parking lot. Why won't he talk about his life? What are the tattoos a reminder of? Why are his moods so erratic? The questions grow from mere curiosity to a scratchiness inside my head that I can't ignore. They begin to consume me, and when I follow him home after practice the next day, I tell myself that it's because I want to help.

He doesn't go home, though. He parks the motorcycle at a couple of run-down tennis courts where he hits the ball against the wall until a girl—a woman—walks onto the court as if she owns it. Her long black ponytail matches a mostly black tennis outfit. Shoulders square and strong, waist narrow, she's a tad scary—Lara Croft-esque—and somehow familiar.

She gives Colt a whack on the butt with her racquet. He swings round and kisses her cheek. I'm shocked at the idea of Colt having a girlfriend, let alone one who's about ten years older than him. Why hadn't he mentioned her? My heart feels like it just got strung up.

I let the breath I'm holding dribble out. Why does this shake me so much? Am I here for more than friendship? I admit I feel . . . differently . . . toward Colt these days. But that's stupid. This is scary Colt, born aged eighty, wrapped in issues I'm not good enough to share with. And I love Jacob. It's not jealousy I'm feeling. It's disappointment. Colt doesn't rate me enough to let me into his life.

Whoever Lara Croft is, she's a top player and gives Colt a good game. I watch them, feeling as though I've been slapped across the face.

Despite the girlfriend discovery, I haven't uncovered any real answers, so when they're done, I keep following Colt.

If neither he nor Milo is going to tell me about this big secret, I'll just have to find out for myself. If I'm going to be Colt's friend, to be his partner at the Grand Slam, I deserve to know. Anyway, by helping him, I'm helping myself.

He parks his motorcycle outside an old, gray weatherboard house near the parking lot where I dropped him off. The picket fence might once have looked quaint, but now it hangs broken, the paint mostly peeled away. The lawn is uncut, crowded with weeds that extend across the two strips of concrete that serve as a driveway.

Colt bounds up the steps of the porch and reaches above the doorframe to grab a key. I park the Jeep farther down the road, doubling back on foot. The cars parked in the street are rusty and unloved and the air smells of gas and old trash.

I pause across from his house, wondering if I should knock. A trio of teenage girls, pushing strollers and smoking cigarettes, walks past me. A car alarm goes off, adding to the noise of traffic on the main road and the frequent trains that screech in and out of the nearby station. There's not a flower in sight.

We come from different worlds.

The screen door bangs. I duck behind a car as Colt sets off for a run. We've just finished a four-hour training session, including a 10K run, and he's going on another one? I watch the house while he's gone. There's no sign of his dad.

Forty minutes later, I'm about to leave when Colt sprints up the street and drops on all fours in front of his house, hauling air into his lungs. When he heads indoors I almost go home, but realize that apart from the fact that he's clearly not well-off, he's overtraining and risking burnout, and that he has a girlfriend, I haven't discovered any reasons for his erratic moods or for him having to take time off the circuit.

I wait a little longer, too embroiled and curious to give up easily.

Colt emerges wearing a retail uniform. He *does* have a job. That only proves he needs money. But surely there's more to this than Colt's shame about where he lives or his financial status. Because if that's all this secrecy is about, it means he thinks I'll judge him or look down my nose at him like that brat he once accused me of being.

I thought we'd gotten past that. I thought we were good friends.

Gunning down the road in my Jeep, stomach churning, my thoughts turn ugly with outrage. I don't want to train with someone who thinks I'm a tennis brat. It was one thing when he didn't know me, but now, after all these hours of training, us against Milo, the mirroring, the bond rope, the dinner at Milo's, taking him up the Mother Tree—I feel betrayed.

I decide to confront him tomorrow.

SEVENTEEN

MY GRASP TIGHTENS AROUND THE wire fence surrounding the two dingy courts. I'm glad it's between us. Colt serves ball after ball, then collects them using a pick-up tube. Several balls have rolled over to where I'm standing.

"You know you're overtraining?" I say as he comes near. "Milo would blow his top about burnout if he knew."

Colt's careful not to make any sudden movements, as though I'm aiming a gun at him, and slowly straightens. The gray tank top he's wearing reveals defined back muscles and powerful shoulders. He stuffs two balls into a pocket, then wipes the back of his neck and chest with the towel pinched in his waistband. When he lifts his eyes, they're so dark and stern I wilt under his stare.

Looking past me, he pokes his tongue into the side of a

cheek and exhales. "What are you doing here?" The question lacks any hint of friendship.

I shrivel inside. "I was in the area."

"Yeah, sure." His assessment of me is short, cutting to my bare feet. The first thing I do after training is to strip off sweaty shoes and socks. "You're spying on me." Spit flies from his lips. I curl my toes into the dirt. "Why?" He strides to the fence and dumps the word between us as if it's a grenade.

"Because you never tell me anything," I reply, rapidly. My focus ping-pongs around the court. "You're this big secret all wrapped up. I'm trying to be a good friend, and—"

"And what?" His words are bullets. I steel myself against them.

"And I want to know more about my tennis partner— to figure you out."

"What if I don't want you to know more? Everything you need to know you already know. You know my serve is shit-hot, my backhand is my secret weapon, my short shots let me down. That's the stuff you need to know." He drinks from a water bottle. A dark sweat mark gathers in the center of his shirt and all the way to his waist. He smells familiar—like hard work, like a good day's training, like a winner.

"Why didn't you want me to know where you live?"

Anger ripples off him and I'm no longer brave. He glares fiercely across the tennis courts. I'm about to walk away, thinking I've blown it, when he says, "It's not because I'm ashamed."

"It doesn't make a difference."

He approaches the fence again. "If it doesn't make a difference, why follow me?"

"I told you. I want to understand you. . . . You're such a closed book." His eyes hold mine, sending a shard of heat into my belly. It happens sometimes, but I figured it was because he's hot and I'm a teenage girl, that it was because I didn't know much about him, as if he were some mysterious prince. But now I understand something closer to the truth; he's no prince, no knight in shining armor. Now I'm thinking it's the heat of fear.

I turn on my heel and start walking.

The muffled tread of sneakers follows me, but I don't dare stop.

"This isn't exactly a safe area for a rich girl with her rich-girl car," Colt calls after me. As if to prove his point, a guy with several earrings in one ear approaches. He gives me the once over, lingering on my bare legs under my short tennis skirt.

I pick up the pace. "I'll survive." When I reach the car, I dig for the keys in my backpack. I sense Colt right behind me.

"Why do you need to understand me?" he asks, softer.

I shift to face him. He's close and I step back, butting into the car door. My heart raps against my chest like its volume is on high.

"I wish you'd be honest with me, Colt. Do you know what I think?" Nerves creep into my throat. "After everything, you still think I'm a spoiled, stuck-up brat who will look down on you if I find out you're not rich. You think I'll judge you." Indignation makes me bolder. "Thanks for thinking the worst of me." I stare at the park at the end of the street where the swings don't have seats. "Doesn't say much for our future as tennis partners, if you don't respect me and you won't trust me."

"I'm not very trusting . . . It has nothing to do with you. And we didn't always live in this shit pit." He flings his arms in a circle to indicate the area around us. "So I know that being rich doesn't make you a snob. I do have a more balanced view of the world. And I stopped thinking you were a spoiled brat a long time ago." He threads his gaze with mine. My heart squeezes.

It's also the most he's ever revealed. And I want more. "Where did you used to live?"

He shifts to lean his back against the Jeep, arms crossed. "Before my mom died, we lived on the Northern Beaches."

Coastal, middle class, and nothing like here.

A souped-up black car squeals past, the engine gunning.

"Then we moved to Florida because after she died, Mom's family offered Dad a job. That's where she came from."

"I'm sorry. About your mum." He doesn't respond. "When . . . did she die?"

He pushes his arms between his back and the hot chassis of the car. "It's been over eleven years."

"You lived in Florida all that time?"

"Yup." He hunts in the sky for something, tapping a foot.

I sense him closing up, Aladdin's Cave hiding its treasures. "That's where you learned to play tennis? Florida?"

"Yup." He straightens.

If he isn't ashamed of where he lives, why's he such a closed book? What's he hiding? "Then you moved back to Sydney? Why?"

"Didn't work out. I gotta go." He pushes away from the car and stands square-on, hands clasped behind his head.

I can't help myself. "Go where?"

He laughs, his shoulders shaking, a deep belly laugh. I take him in, enchanted for a moment by the sound; by the curl of his lips, by how open his face has become, by the way his eyes roar with energy. By the real Colt.

He catches me watching and reels in his smile. "Nosy, much? You're unbelievable."

I chuckle, eventually adding, "It makes no difference to me where you live. We're partners. So long as you keep up that serve and that backhand, yeah?"

As I speak, his eyes cup mine, then zone in on my mouth. My lips part to pull in oxygen, but it's somehow a sort of signal. Without warning his mouth is on mine, one hand clasping my jaw, the other wrapped around my neck, his shoulders surrounding me. His tongue fills my mouth. A firecracker goes off in my belly. I kiss him back. A hand moves to the base of my spine, compelling me closer. Our hip bones bump. There's a tripwire between us and we've set it off, but instead of blowing us apart, it's pushing us together.

An image of Jacob and Lara Croft causes me to pull away. Colt reels to the back of the Jeep. I clasp the door handle and mash my recently crushed lips together.

Colt smacks the roof of the car. "Not a good idea." He drops his chin to his chest. "On every level. I've gotta go. You should get out of here." Tromping to the court to fetch his abandoned tennis gear, he looks back at me, mournful, before pounding down the street. His shape shrinks until it disappears, and I keep clutching the door handle, my knuckles white.

EIGHTEEN

COLT LEAVES FOR A FUTURES tournament that night. I'm left to torture myself about the significance of the kiss until I join him and Milo in Wollongong in a week.

I distract myself by training harder than ever and playing brutal games of tennis with Kim Wright, half hoping to pick up on her "kill or be killed" attitude. Afterward, she hangs around the house with me, Jacob, and Aria. I've been trying to spend more time with Aria, but she says she's busy rehearsing, not a hint of apology in her voice. Jacob scrapes through his final exams, and with school over, his band—currently named Road Kill—uses his studio to rehearse while we're training. Then Jacob parks himself at our house for the rest of the day. Aria has stopped working at Mo's to concentrate on audition prep, and while she rehearses each piece the requisite twenty-five times, Jacob jokes around with Kim.

During breaks, Aria conveyer-belts food between the kitchen and Jacob, clearly loving the smile and cuddle she gets in thanks. And clearly failing to see the long looks he sends my way. Jealousy uncurls in my gut when he touches her, but he follows their hugs with an expression that tells me, *Wish it was you*. At first, I'm convinced Jacob will know I've been kissed by someone other than him, but it's not like Colt left a sign on my lips. Colt stirred me up, though, and I'm inside my head so much, Jacob's heated glances turn questioning.

"Jacob, you're so lazy," Aria complains. "I've rehearsed all my pieces and your flute is still in its case."

"You need to stop feeding him. He's like a pet monkey," teases Kim. "He'll choose food over work every time." Kim flips through a math assignment I've just finished. "Ugh. Glad I'm done with school."

"I've missed so much—even with tutoring," I explain.

"School's for suckers," says Kim, curt. "How many kids in your school will become world famous and earn a couple of million bucks a year?"

Driving to Wollongong, my stomach is concave with tension. Do I pretend that kiss didn't happen, even though the memory wakes me at night, my heart wriggling with confusion? I decide the kiss was thrilling because it was stolen. I can't like Colt like that. I love Jacob.

"Where's Colt?" I ask Milo when he meets me in the hotel lobby. I'm half relieved Colt's not there. I'm not sure how to have a conversation with someone who, when I last saw him, kissed me and walked away annoyed.

Milo guides me to check-in. "He's not staying here."

I pass a credit card to the receptionist. "But he's winning decent prize money."

"He's his own man. I can't tell him how to spend his money. Where he's staying is full of students and travelers, though. No way he's getting enough peace and quiet between matches."

"Will we see him later? We have to celebrate." This past week, Colt won the men's doubles and lost in the finals of the singles event.

"He's in full prep mode for tomorrow's tournament. You know how he gets." The receptionist passes me a key card. "Now call your dad. Then your phone is mine, *Dampfnudel.*"

For the next three days, I don't see Colt. Our schedules either clash or he misses Milo's training, plus we've entered both the doubles and singles events, making us time poor. Milo tells me Colt prefers to eat alone at night to get match ready, but with his eyes hidden behind those aviators, I don't believe him: the crinkled grin is missing.

Colt's closing me out again.

Because of that kiss.

I see him by accident. He's striding out of the players' lounge, texting as he walks. How is it Milo hasn't confiscated his phone, then? Colt seems thin and pale and tense. Probably from overtraining and lack of sleep.

Grabbing his shirt I say, "Hey. Howdy, stranger."

He doesn't seem surprised to see me. "Hey," he says, focusing over my head. And there's something wrong with the way he says it, like hearing a mishit on your racquet.

"You don't look like yourself. Are you sick?"

He scratches his nose. "I'm good. Match on soon. First round. Gotta go. See you later." He says the words, but I know he doesn't mean them—both the *good* bit and the *see you later* one. That was either a serious game face or he's torn up about our kiss.

I'm in a women's doubles match when Colt loses his first-round game. Milo's visibly upset.

"He looked pale when I saw him earlier. Is he sick, Milo? Please tell me because I'm worrying now."

"He's overdoing it. He's run out of money for food, and he's not getting enough sleep at the hostel." Milo taps at his forehead with a thumb knuckle. "I tried to persuade him to share my hotel room. I sent him takeout and he lost his temper. Stuff's going down at home that he won't even tell me about. But you must remain strong." Milo looks at me, taking stock. "Don't let Colt distract you. We need you to keep your ranking up—get you into that Aussie Open."

For the next few days, Colt's AWOL, but gets as far as the men's doubles final. I reach the singles final, pointing out to Aria when Milo lets me call her that it's a Futures tournament, which is less competitive than the pro WTA events. Still, it's my first-ever final on the professional circuit and my heart alternates between freezing with shock and pounding with excitement.

On the day of the final, I toss my gear on the seats next to the umpire and stoop to line up my drink bottles. Something purple catches my eye inside the tennis bag. It's a sweat towel. I search for Milo and there, next to him, is Colt. Milo said he was sick and sleeping, but he's here, a baseball cap hiding his face in shadows. A purple towel? It must be from Colt—I doubt he told Milo about Purple Time. I'm tempted to wave the towel, but instead I use it to wipe my neck even though I'm not sweaty.

Each time we switch sides, I use the towel. I conjure up Purple Time and stay relaxed and confident, and with the winning point, I abandon my racquet and run toward the gate where Milo and Colt wait. They swallow me in their arms and Colt, who appears not to have shaved today, rubs a stubbled chin on my forehead to make me squeal.

Then I'm surrounded by little girls requesting photos and autographs—and there's no feeling in the world better than winning, than knowing that others look up to me, that I'm someone's hero.

● ● ●

"That five-ball bounce before you serve is becoming a bad habit," says Milo. He's riding shotgun as I drive back to Sydney. Colt sprawls in the back, tired and economical with words, but he can't avoid me any longer.

"Superstition, not bad habit," I reply.

Milo turns the radio down. "Dangerous things, because when you don't or can't do them, mentally you can collapse."

"Tennis players live on superstition," says Colt, sounding gritty with exhaustion.

"Only the ones who need crutches," Milo returns.

Colt doesn't reply. He's having a text conversation with someone and his phone vibrates annoyingly often. *Lara Croft?*

I keep glancing in the rearview mirror, hoping to find Colt watching me. He never does. He rests his head back, eyes closed, but mostly he stares out the window, eyes dead. That kiss has ruined our friendship.

After I drop Milo home, Colt gets in beside me. Even in the dim evening light, I can tell he's shut the shop on chat. But I have a crack anyway. "Thanks for the towel."

Colt shifts his jaw from side to side.

"It was . . . thoughtful."

"It was nothing." He draws out a sigh. "It was purple. Made sense at the time."

A pulse of annoyance makes me push on. I'm in the mood for answers. "Why'd you stay in a hostel where it's impossible to rest? You're winning good prize money now."

"I wasn't avoiding you, if that's what you're thinking," he replies, surly.

"Now that you bring it up, I think you *were* avoiding me. After you kissed—"

"I don't do girlfriends. They mess— I made a mistake. I'm sorry." He rubs his palms up and down his thighs. "And where I stay and how I conduct myself at tournaments is my business. I got emancipated from my dad for good reasons, so I don't need *you* to parent me."

It's like he's slammed a door in my face. But at least I have another clue about his family. Is this what Milo meant when he said Colt had been through a lot?

Shrouded in fury, Colt flicks his head sideways. I want to pat down the ripples of irritation spiking off him, but I get the impression if I touched him, he'd open the door and jump out, thirty miles per hour or not.

But I'm angry now. "It *does* concern others—me and Milo. If it's affecting your game it affects our plan: the agent, the wild cards, sponsors, getting into the Open. It's not just about you. What is it about you guys and your egos? Share with Milo. Share with me, for Christ's sake. I think

I'll manage to keep my hands off you, *god* that you are. And you're overtraining. You shouldn't complete Milo's training and then do more afterward. Do I tell Milo or what?"

Colt doesn't reply. We simmer side by side, the silence between us thickening until it has its own form.

When I pull up at his house, he jumps out before I've fully stopped, snatching his bag. "Thanks for the lift and the lecture."

He enters a darkened house. It's impossible to imagine coming home from a tournament and finding there's not a soul to greet me. I ache for him.

is now more of a chalky white with light blue streaks, my knuckles pause in mid-air. I don't need to do this.

The curtains are drawn on the window to the side of the door, but there's a note, more of a letter, tacked to the inside of one of the glass panes. I squint and make out the words, *My Darling Madeline*, just as the front door lurches open. Colt fills the doorframe, dark hair tousled, wearing nothing but black boxer shorts. Behind him is the woman from the tennis courts, fully dressed—thank God.

Straightening, Colt glances over his shoulder at her—I was right, she's a woman, not a girl—then back at me. "This is getting out of control." But he doesn't look angry and I feel a wave of relief.

He gestures to the woman. "You'll recognize Natalie Barbie—a.k.a. Natalie Barbinsky. Natalie, this is Harper."

The Natalie Barbie! I knew she was familiar. She retired from professional tennis four years ago, ranked top twenty-five in the world. She's from England and at least thirty years old.

"Hi, Harper. Nice to meet you." Her English accent is tinged with a hint of American. Black hair cascades around her shoulders and despite the strong jaw and regal nose, there's a warmth in her caramel eyes that reminds me of Mum. "I'm on my way out. Don't mind me."

She's wearing a short, black sundress that swishes around her long legs as she steps onto the porch and offers her hand. I take it, thinking, *cradle snatcher*—she isn't exactly dressed for tennis—even though she's someone I'm in awe of.

is now more of a chalky white with light blue streaks, my knuckles pause in mid-air. I don't need to do this.

The curtains are drawn on the window to the side of the door, but there's a note, more of a letter, tacked to the inside of one of the glass panes. I squint and make out the words, *My Darling Madeline*, just as the front door lurches open. Colt fills the doorframe, dark hair tousled, wearing nothing but black boxer shorts. Behind him is the woman from the tennis courts, fully dressed—thank God.

Straightening, Colt glances over his shoulder at her—I was right, she's a woman, not a girl—then back at me. "This is getting out of control." But he doesn't look angry and I feel a wave of relief.

He gestures to the woman. "You'll recognize Natalie Barbie—a.k.a. Natalie Barbinsky. Natalie, this is Harper."

The Natalie Barbie! I knew she was familiar. She retired from professional tennis four years ago, ranked top twenty-five in the world. She's from England and at least thirty years old.

"Hi, Harper. Nice to meet you." Her English accent is tinged with a hint of American. Black hair cascades around her shoulders and despite the strong jaw and regal nose, there's a warmth in her caramel eyes that reminds me of Mum. "I'm on my way out. Don't mind me."

She's wearing a short, black sundress that swishes around her long legs as she steps onto the porch and offers her hand. I take it, thinking, *cradle snatcher*—she isn't exactly dressed for tennis—even though she's someone I'm in awe of.

NINETEEN

AFTER DROPPING OFF COLT, I arrive home as Milo calls to announce we have an agent. Dad cracks open a bottle of champagne and Mum cooks a celebratory dinner, but I can't stop imagining Colt, alone in that dark house, with no one to share the big news with. I itch to go to him. When Jacob slides his bare feet onto mine under the dinner table, it feels intrusive and I cross my ankles beneath my chair.

The next morning, I unravel myself from twisted bed-sheets. Aria's already practicing scales on the flute. I fib to her that I'm going training, and drive to Colt's house in time for breakfast. But half an hour after I've parked, I'm still stuck inside the Jeep building up the courage to climb the few steps onto his porch.

Hesitating at a front door that was once sky blue, but

"Congrats on your win yesterday," she adds.

"Thanks."

"Bye, Colt. Don't forget what we talked about." She tosses us each a jelly bean. I catch mine, studying it like it's some sort of secret message.

I sense Colt behind me and let my hair fall forward. I want to hide in my own shadow.

"Did you come to admire the outside of the house or are you coming in?" he asks.

Scuffing my sneaker on the deck, I face him. He steps aside. It's the last thing I want to do, but I can't leave now. I brush past into a sitting room containing a sofa, an armchair, a coffee table, and a TV on a cardboard box. The room smells musty and sour, similar to Jacob's music studio. Dented beer cans, dirty plates, and sticky glasses litter the coffee table and rug.

"I see you don't like tidying up after yourself," I say, defensive.

"Correction. My dad doesn't. I just haven't had a chance to clean up. My bedroom is the one tidy room in the house." He steps into baggy gray sweats and points with his chin to a door on the other side of the room.

Through the doorway, the image of his unmade bed, sheets coiled and rumpled, reminds me of what probably just took place in there. My cheeks tingle. The only other furniture in Colt's bedroom is a fan and a set of wire-basket drawers, and he's right, there's neither a dirty dish nor a single piece of clothing on the floor.

Sucking on the jelly bean, I almost step into a bowl of them. "What's with the jelly beans?"

Colt shrugs. "Long story."

"I thought you weren't into girlfriends."

"Natalie's my hitting partner."

I bite the inside of my cheek to kill the relieved smile that pounces to my lips. "A new girl every night then?"

He rubs his stubbled chin, grinning. He's way too smoldering-romantic-hero today. "Now you're fishing."

My palm shoots into the air. "Whatever. Changing the subject."

"I'd put on a shirt, but after two weeks away, they're all dirty and they stink. Breakfast?"

I look past ripped abs and a naked chest dark with curls, into the kitchen. Eggs, plums, bread, and juice spill from two shopping bags onto the cracked plastic counter.

"If it's okay with you—and your dad."

"He's not here. Juice?" Colt walks into the kitchen, chucks his jelly bean in the sink, and pours two glasses of orange juice. On the fridge is a note written in black pen: *If tennis is a mental game then you can win before you even start.*

"Nice quote," I say. "Venus Williams?"

"Something like that. Why are you here?"

I twist my hair, but stop myself from nibbling the ends, shoving my hands into my pockets instead.

He puts my juice on the kitchen counter and points to the one bar stool in the room. "Sit. I need to explain something to you." He leans against the far counter, arms crossed.

I comply, studying my glass to avoid scrutinizing his six-pack as it curves into his sweats.

"When I said I don't do girlfriends, I wasn't joking. I shouldn't have kissed you. I'm sorry. So if you're here because you've got some notion that you and me—"

I shove to my feet, cheeks redder than the Wilson sports logo. The bar stool thuds to the tiled floor. "That is *not* why I'm here. You kissed *me*, remember. I . . . I'm not interested in you in that way." Maybe I should tell him about Jacob . . .

I open my mouth to continue but only silence comes out.

Colt turns away, unpacks a shopping bag, then swivels back to me. "Why are you here then? On a Sunday morning. A no-training morning. At the crack of dawn?" He lifts an eyebrow.

I examine the wonky fence out the window, the green Dumpsters on the gray, flowerless street. There's another "Darling Madeline" letter tacked to the inside of the glass pane. "Because—"

Colt watches me over the juice glass and I forget what I'm about to say. He quits the staring match, picks up the eggs, and asks, "Scrambled or fried?"

"I'm worried about you. That's why I'm here. You once said I was an unexpected, but good friend. That's what friends do. When we see a friend isn't . . . coping, friends try to help."

"Scrambled, then. Saves me the extra dishes. You're very helpful."

"Are you laughing at me?"

He keeps smiling while he cracks eggs into a bowl, one-handed, and whisks them with a fork.

I pick up the bar stool. "He can play tennis *and* he can cook. Quite the talented seventeen-year-old going on eighty-eight."

He puts another pan on the stove. "Last year, in the States, I was into a girl." He grabs a tomato and slices it at a rate of one slice per second. "I hadn't realized how much I came to rely on her—being there when I got home or coming to matches. We broke up and it was as if her ghost haunted me night and day. My game fell apart. I fell apart. Love weakens people. I've got enough to deal with. Tennis isn't a hobby, it's my entire future. I won't let that happen again."

The whole time he's talking, he's chucking bacon into a sizzling pan and slicing mushrooms. He may sound like he's merely reciting a recipe, but he's finally opening up.

I moisten my lips. "Like I said, I'm here as a *friend*." But if that's true, why does the word "friend" in reference to Colt suddenly seem bittersweet?

With a crooked grin, he passes me a bread knife. "Put the toast on then, mate."

Put the toast on. Ridiculous words. Neutral, friendly words. But I'm beaming like I just won Wimbledon while my heart trips over itself. And when I'm next to him, buttering toast, it seems like he's standing too close.

"Natalie brought over breakfast. She's into mothering me," he says while we eat from our laps in the sitting room. "She's also a good friend."

"How'd you meet?"

"She used to train in Florida when she was a teenager. Her dad worked with my uncle, and my aunt helped her out with some personal stuff. I was in awe of her when I was a kid. She moved to Sydney when she retired, though. Now she visits my dad while I'm away."

"Your dad? Where is he?"

Sadness sprawls headlong over Colt. His Adam's apple bobs. "The night before the first Wollongong final, I had to admit him into rehab . . . Well, Natalie did it for me because I was away. He's an alcoholic. That's about as much as I want to say about it."

My gaze sticks itself to my plate. This explains the state Colt got himself into at Wollongong, the lack of money maybe, losing in the first round, the moods. It had nothing to do with that kiss. And it explains why Milo lets him keep his phone.

I change the subject. "Who's Madeline?"

"My mom. And I don't want to go there, either."

I gape at the note in the window, but keep eating. "Did you speak to Milo last night? About the agent?"

"No, what did he say?" Colt's shoulders pull back. "I was visiting the rehab clinic."

"We're in. They want us."

Eyes widening, Colt coughs and swallows his mouthful, slides his almost empty plate onto the sofa. The fork clatters to the floor as he bolts to his feet. "I can't believe it. Right when I've run out of money."

I giggle and lace my fingers together. "Apparently, two Aussie hopefuls racing up the rankings and playing doubles together is a PR dream—as Milo predicted. There's a press conference on Tuesday."

Colt paces around the sofa, hands clamped to the sides of his head, face going haywire with happiness. His excitement is contagious and I bounce on my toes. He bounds over and squeezes the air out of me as he lifts me clear off the floor.

"This means—everything," he says.

All I know is I want to make him smile like that all the time.

TWENTY

THE AUDITIONS FOR THE CON are tomorrow, and when I get home Aria and Jacob are practicing in our kitchen. Exhausted from the tournament, I languish on the sofa. With his long hair falling around his cheeks, the flute at his lips, Jacob resembles the Pied Piper.

We look up when there's a knock on the window. Jacob's dad points at Jacob and beckons him, then waves at us. I wave back, knowing he rarely comes inside. I think he's worried his Armani suit will get sticky or covered in dog hair.

"Gotta go, Gorgeouses. Parents remembered they gave birth to a son. They're taking me out to celebrate tomorrow's audition."

Aria snorts. "They're sure you'll get in then?"

"Nope," he says, packing away his flute. "They're out

tomorrow night with more important people than me." He hurricanes out of the kitchen, weaving through the dogs when they give chase.

Aria's gaze follows Jacob. Then she perches on the arm of the sofa and pulls at the scarf tied around her head. "Make pancakes with me?" Her shoulders slump and she exhales loudly. "I need cheering up and chocolate pancakes are the perfect cure."

Even though I'm not allowed to eat pancakes, this is the first time she's wanted to spend time alone with me in a while. "Your audition pieces are sounding perfect, don't worry. You'll do great tomorrow."

"It's not the audition." She nods at the door Jacob left through. "How is it we can have everything in common, spend all this time together, and yet . . . ? Why can't he love me back? I feel safe when I'm with him. It just feels right. Letting him go feels like letting go of everything I've ever known." Aria's pinched expression tightens, making my mind buzz. "What if I never get over him?"

"Pancakes it is." Leaping off the sofa, I lead the way into the kitchen and search for the right bowls. I stifle a yawn.

"Tired?" asks Aria. I give a noncommittal grunt and search for the eggs. "Maybe you shouldn't spend half the night talking to Jacob in your *bedroom*."

My heart stutters as if I dropped all the eggs. "What?" I fight to control how fast my head spins around.

Her eyes dart to the floor. "I heard you a while back. All

this time, I wouldn't let myself believe you and Jacob . . . I mean you would never . . ." She struggles to keep her face from crumpling. "I just want the truth."

"What are you talking about?"

"He was in your room after midnight . . ."

"But that was ages ago. Neither of us could sleep. He saw my light on. You know Jacob—never thinks, just does."

She crosses her arms over her chest. "What did you talk about?"

"The usual. Everything and nothing. I can't remember. Are you helping with this or what?" I thud a package of sugar on the counter.

"You remember our oath about boys—our blood on the pink guitar picks?"

"Of course. What are you suggesting? Jacob and I are finding our way, just like you are. We have to learn how to be the Raggers again. Stop seeing stuff that isn't there."

Aria flicks her scarf like a whip as she joins me in the kitchen and ties it around her neck. "Maybe you're right. I'm just being paranoid. But you two seem to be closer than ever and I'm back in your shadow, same as before I got together with Jacob."

"That's *so* not true." I open the pantry, ready to take a hundred years to find the flour.

Did she go out with Jacob to escape the shadow of the Harper Show? I realize she must've really resented me. My childhood ended abruptly . . . but thanks to me, so did

Aria's. I took Dad away, was gone so much it broke up the Raggers, and grabbed the spotlight at home. All while my dreams came true. For the first time, I see that I might have done the same thing she did had the situation been reversed. And now I have Jacob, too.

Aria seizes the measuring cups and dumps in too much sugar. She tips some back into the paper bag. We make pancakes, but she's quieter than usual, going through the motions. I jabber too much to fill the silences, certain I deserve nothing better than to strangle myself with Aria's scarf.

"Colt and I have been talking," says Milo, pulling at his baseball cap. It's six and raining. "He's admitted to overtraining and that's not good on every level—physical, emotional, mental. I'm telling you this, Harper, to ensure you don't get the same idea." Colt shakes the rain from his hair. "It's easy to get sucked in when you're determined to achieve your goals, but ultimately it's counterproductive."

With Kominsky, I'd trained hard, but now I see it was only a 90 percent effort, probably because I was afraid of not being good enough. If I didn't try hard, I couldn't fail. But now I want to give 150 percent. Every competitive cell in my body is screaming at me to win because I'm beginning to think I can actually do this . . . so I understand why Colt's overtraining.

"We're concentrating on that wandering ball toss of yours when Colt's hitting partner gets here, *Dampfnudel*. Then fitness training. One week until the Bangkok Futures. Let's go." Milo claps sharply.

Colt wipes at the strands of wet hair stuck to my face. My cheeks flare, his finger a match striking on skin, hot against the cool rain. I search for something to mirror for Colt as he blinks rain from his lashes, but I'm inexplicably embarrassed and take off for a warm-up jog instead.

Our fitness training is a tandem bike ride, but Milo converts the bike into an instrument of torture. We speed-race up and down a footpath in a nearby park until Milo finds a hill to scale. We work as a team. When one of us needs to pull back due to cramp or the fatal lack of air, we code-call *child*, and when we're ready to take on the main work, we shout *Milo*. Then *purple* when we stand in the pedals to pump up the hill.

When Milo calls time, we fall sideways off the bike, huffing next to each other on the grass. Milo's pleased face materializes above us. "Same thing tomorrow?"

Arms flung over his head, Colt says, "One day, we'll get you back for this, old man."

"One day, you'll kiss my feet with gratitude," replies Milo.

Colt sits up. "Only if they're made of bacon and eggs."

The heavens open and Milo waves and jogs to his Saab convertible.

Unable to stand yet, I tilt my face and open my mouth to drink the rain, which is both sweet and cool. From this angle, some of the drops look bigger and I bop around to trap them. When I glance back at Colt, he's watching me, his wide eyes sparkling.

"What?" I ask, wiping the rain from my face with a flat palm.

"You. I like that you enjoy the small things in life. And that you can be kind of silly."

I'm searching for a retort until I realize the look in his eyes is approval. My heart cartwheels like one of Milo's racquets.

I have an hour to eat and shower before Mr. Fraser arrives for my tutoring. The house should be deserted, but the French doors in the kitchen remain open and Aria is sitting out on the deck facing the pool.

She never simply sits.

She's always cooking or playing music or reading or walking. Besides, I realize with a prick of unease, she's not even supposed to be home.

"Aria? Why aren't you at your audition?" I step onto the deck. She stiffens. "Aria?" She's wearing pajamas. My stomach somersaults. "What's wrong?"

"I'd-be-playing-right-at-this-moment." Her words are soft staccato notes.

"Why aren't you?"

She sags and rocks forward, bundles herself into a ball on the chair, and sobs. I blanket her with my body, wanting to absorb all the sadness. She stiffens so it's like hugging someone who's wearing armor. I slowly loosen myself from her and slump into a chair, rub her arm. "You took a gap year. You've practiced and practiced. Did the nerves get to you?"

Her lips contort. "It's Jacob." She shudders and tightens the hold around her legs.

It's as if my heart is shriveling, panting. As if it got stuffed into a dark, tiny box too small to hold it. "Why? What's he done?"

"He's always there, being himself and making me love him more and more and it—hurts. Too. Much." The last two words are more of a wail.

The skin rips from my body.

She holds her breath. Hiccups. "How can I go with him to the Con every day for the next few years when the more time we spend together, the more I miss him? What if he finds a girlfriend?" Aria rocks herself, rubbing her shins. "I was stupid to think I could do it. I can't even sleep properly. What if I never fall in love again because my heart is broken?"

"But you've been fine." Guilt tears at me. "You're moving on."

Eyes pink and crammed with gloom, she says, "I didn't want to spoil everything. We had such a perfect childhood. I didn't want to lose that as well. But it's not working. I can't do it. It's breaking *me* instead."

Aria's worked toward this audition since she turned thirteen. She can't let a boy destroy her dreams. Love can't be this destructive. Yet heartbreak did the same thing to Colt last year. Except in Aria's case, it's me as well as Jacob who've hurt her, and now she's utterly lost. Why did I ever kiss him back? I slap a hand over the sob that's thickening in the back of my throat.

Aria grips her lips together, sits straighter. "I need to get away." Pulling her pajama sleeve over her fist, she uses it to wipe away her remaining tears. "I've decided to travel . . . Apply to a music school in Paris or Rome." She stares at the roof of Jacob's music studio just visible over the wall dividing our houses.

Life suddenly resembles those towers we used to build out of blocks—as soon as we perfected the tower, it would tilt and fall and explode into a hundred pieces. This time, there's more than a mess of bricks. This time, dreams are being lost, sisters split apart, friendships broken.

The side kitchen door slams open and Venus and Adagio bounce in, followed by their long-haired master. Jacob's face is fixed with worry. I'm taken aback by how handsome he is in a suit and tie. "Aria? Where'd you go?"

Aria rushes to her feet, silences me with a warning look, the tiniest shake of her head perceptible. "I decided I didn't want to go to the Con," she says. "I want to study overseas."

My stomach stretches and twists, knowing that each word must bite at her throat. I reach for her.

"Don't," she says. "I'm fine. I'm not unhappy about this decision. Honestly. I'm going to look up flights." She makes her face smile and sprints upstairs.

It's as if she's dropped a grenade and run away, leaving Jacob and me to deal with the fallout. Jacob sits, then stands. I fold myself in half on the chair. When I straighten, tears are tracking down Jacob's cheeks, and I desperately want to erase the memory of his empty stare into the garden.

"She didn't duck out of the audition because of me, did she?" he asks.

I pull up my knees. If he finds out she gave up her dreams because of him, he'll blame himself for the rest of his life. This isn't some childish argument to solve with a tickle and an ice cream. I have to minimize the damage. I have to catch the block tower before it hits the floor and explodes.

"She wants to travel." I hiccup into my knees. "It's not you."

"Really?" His voice cracks, making me look up. He bites his bottom lip and rubs a crooked finger along his eyebrow. "Crap. Everything's changing so fast." For once, he keeps his distance.

But space and a remorseful silence can't wash away my guilt. Aria must love Jacob more than her dreams, more than her future.

Jacob walks back into the kitchen and stares at Aria's violin on the table.

"Jeez, I'm sorry, Jacob. How did your audition go?"

"Good. I think it was good enough."

"I bet you blew them away," I say. He stuffs bunched fists into his trouser pockets and taps a rhythm with his shoe against a table leg. I want to hug him. Kiss him. Instead, I say, "I should go to Aria."

"Harps?" Jacob looks like a little boy lost. "Don't ever change, Harps."

But it's too late. I realize I'm no longer the person Jacob wants me to be. And that changing, moving away from the familiar and stepping into the new, is inevitable.

TWENTY-ONE

IF I DIDN'T EXIST, WOULD Jacob love Aria?

Losing myself in three-legged races, in repetitive serves and volleys, in tandem bike rides, in the monotonous sound of the ball on the racquet, helps me forget the riddle. But it doesn't erase the growing darkness inside me. It's like Aria's decision to abandon her audition, her dream, shut out all the light. Each day Aria avoids both me and Jacob, and each day any remaining chinks of light splinter, then vanish. The weight of darkness is crushing me because the only way to fix this is to turn back time.

I avoid Jacob. It's impossible to explain that we can *never* be together. I know he thinks there's still hope for us in the distant future when Aria finds someone else. If I'm honest, I thought that, too. But Aria gave up her dreams both now and forever *because of him*, and I can't deliver that parcel of guilt.

We could hide our love forever and it wouldn't be long enough.

Mum and Dad haven't changed toward Jacob, although I wonder what reason Aria gave them for her decision to study abroad. They're being supportive, but I see them watching her when she's not looking, trying to decode the riddle for themselves.

Everyone's more serious and subdued, as if someone turned down our volume. Except for Jacob.

The night before I leave for Bangkok for the final two Futures tournaments of this season, Jacob jokes around at dinner, even getting into a tickling contest with me. I know it's because he's desperate to get my attention, and to touch me. I know he thinks it's okay to act like this, because that's what we did when we were the Raggers. But we're not ten anymore. And he's my sister's ex. And she's still in love with him. His breath in my ear, I wriggle to escape, but he sits on my legs and pins down my arms. Instead of boyish victory in his eyes, the heat in his gaze makes my heart choke.

I slip into a crack of despair. How do I stop loving him just because he's the wrong person to fall for? Love isn't a pilot light that can be switched on and off. It's more of a fire you build and care for and stoke until it's no longer under your control.

When Dad announces bedtime, Jacob asks if he can steal a quick word with me. The darkness expands and sits like a truck on my chest. I guess he doesn't know he's the reason for Aria's choice, but while we're all changing, he's still acting like we're the Raggers. I glare at him and his eyes reflect the disappointment littered in my own.

Aria stacks plates so aggressively it's no surprise she chips one. While Dad scolds her harder than he normally would, I follow Jacob into the shadows cast by the woods, waiting for his questions with my heart hung on a hook.

Jacob nibbles on a cuticle. "What's happening with Aria? She okay?"

I wonder if he feels as wretched as I do about Aria leaving. I resist reaching for the comfort he could deliver in just one hug. "She's determined to persuade Mum and Dad she made the right decision."

"Is she definitely going to Europe?"

Freaking hell yes. "I guess."

He stops walking. "Are *we* okay?" Jacob's tone is pinched with worry. "Have you been avoiding me?"

Even now, I have no answers. We agreed to keep it friends until Aria got over him, found someone else, but now if I say we can *never* tell Aria we love each other, he'll know she's leaving because of him. And while I need him to back off, I still do love him; I won't hurt him with that truth.

"Sure, we're okay. But we need to keep our distance. . . . I think Aria's suspicious."

"Shit. Did she say something?"

I keep walking. He stays rooted to the spot, but reaches for my wrist. He threads his fingers with mine then frowns at our linked hands. I will my heart to stay as small and hard

183

as an uncrackable nut. But I've missed his tender touch. With Aria going, somehow I need him more. A Colt-shaped thought sneaks in. It makes me uneasy to think a hug from him would probably make me need Jacob less. So maybe I am a little hooked on Colt. But I shake the thought away—Colt's off limits, too. This is my punishment for betraying my sister—both Jacob and Colt are barred.

"Did she say something?" repeats Jacob.

Unlinking our hands, I shake my head and rub my upper arms. "Life will never be the same again," I whisper. I can't imagine Aria's bedroom without her. Something inside me unravels. My chin quivers.

Jacob draws me in, kisses my head. I want to pull away, but some part of me clutches for comfort. All it takes is for him to leave his lips on my forehead and a warm summer's breeze whisks through me, lifting the darkness. He feels familiar and safe and smells of popcorn and I lift my chin and can't stop myself kissing him back and kissing him back and the tears slipping down my cheeks are tears of wretchedness followed by tears of self-hatred because I am so weak.

I walk away from him in tatters, unsure I'll ever be able to let him go.

In the kitchen, Dad's seated at the table, hands frozen in a steeple. When he inspects me, anger and confusion war across his face.

"What the hell are you and Jacob doing, Harper?" Dad never yells, but his words are a shouted whisper. Lips drawn taut he adds, "I went to get something from the garage. I saw."

OhmyGodno.

It's one rip too many. I collapse into a chair, hug my shoulders, chin dipped onto my chest. Hunting for excuses and denials is pointless. My dad is not a stupid man. I could admit to everything—how Jacob and I have loved each other for years and never acted on it, how we tried to fight it but love came anyway. But I already know none of it matters.

"I don't know where to start," Dad mutters.

Scouring the ceiling, I blink wildly. "You don't need to say anything. I'm trying to stop."

"No, Harper. You *will* end it!" His flat palm wallops the table. My face warps. "It's bad enough that one of my daughters has given up her dreams for Jacob." I wonder if he guessed or if Aria explained. "Not you, too. Not after everything."

My chin juts forward. "I wouldn't let him affect my tennis."

"You can't be sure of that." Head in his hands, he massages his scalp. The dishwasher whirs and the fridge rattles briefly. "What do you think it'd do to this family if Aria found out? She's lost the future she worked for because of Jacob. It would tear two sisters apart. And your mum and I—" His voice stretches. "Do you think we could bear to see that?"

I chop at my thigh with the side of a hand.

185

"And Jacob. We love him like a son. But you and Aria come first. If he came between you . . ." Tension makes the words hiss. "Put a stop to this now." Dad's whole body is trembling.

I know he's right. I'm doing everything wrong, not only by my sister, but by everyone. I should be focusing on tennis, on becoming stronger, on winning. I've taken the sparkle out of Dad's eyes again. The only thing I can think of to make up for it is to win big in Bangkok. Maybe that will bring back Dad's sparkle and everything he just witnessed will be obliterated from his memory.

TWENTY-TWO

AT BREAKFAST THE NEXT MORNING, Jacob's not in the kitchen. His wet hair doesn't drip on the floor after a morning's surf, and his skin doesn't bring the smell of salt and coconut sunscreen. He's not stuffing himself with slices of buttery toast or talking Dad's ear off or filling the room with light as if the sun actually rises in our kitchen each morning.

The void makes my insides wrench.

The clatter of my chair against the wooden floor pierces the silence. Yet Dad doesn't look up from his iPad. "Dad? What did you say to Jacob?"

He stays locked on the screen. "I told him that if I ever caught him with you—doing anything like you did last night—he won't be welcome in this house." My chest judders. Tears threaten—not for me, but for Jacob. Dad lifts a heavy gaze, eyes tired behind his glasses. "It pained me to say that, Harper. Your actions have already hurt this family. As soon as you're back from Asia, set him straight before a war breaks out in this house."

"I will. And I'm going to play the best tennis ever. You've invested a lot in me and I am grateful. It's time I started to pay off."

I seek out the sparkle in his eyes. But it's gone.

Cities are always more magical at night; the colorful lights transform them into fairylands, ones I don't get to see much of because I'm usually tucked up in bed by early-o-clock. Bangkok is chaotic and noisy, like it's in constant party mode. The cab carrying the three of us jostles along the street while we, lethargic after the flight, silently watch snakes of people surging along crowded sidewalks. Eight lanes of traffic eventually creep into two and glass skyscrapers and ornate temples change into gray concrete buildings hunched beside each other, mimicking ancient gravestones.

My own world is changing, too. But it's too hard, too complicated, too painful. I want to go back—to when Jacob, Aria and I lived each day as the Ragamuffins, a nickname as powerful as the Three Musketeers, a label that told everyone we could not be separated; we were as one.

Colt sees my gloomy expression. I quickly pack it away.

We're crawling along a road uniformly lined with red canopies above every building's entrance. When we park next to a squat building so plain and absent of windows it could be a prison, for a second I'm confused. The hotels in Bangkok are always flashy, their standard of five star more like ten, and the exchange rate works in our favor. And then it hits me.

I round on Colt. "You're staying in a hostel again?"

Colt opens the door and climbs out. I scoot across the seat and follow him to the back of the cab where he's waiting for his luggage. "This is crazy. Why can't you share with us? Your stupid ego will lose you this tournament."

Up the street, people shout and whoop, throwing a bottle of something between them. Barreling nearer, they zigzag around us, hooting and colliding. Colt steps forward to protect me from getting knocked over. "Watch it," he yells, glaring after them until they disappear around a corner. He yanks two huge bags from the trunk. "Stayed in worse."

Seizing the strap on a bag, I shout, "Quit the pride crap and come with us."

"Cut it out, Harper." He tugs the bag from my grasp. "See you tomorrow."

I trail him inside the hostel where there's a tattered rug, a wooden desk, a rack of dusty postcards, and a corkboard littered with maps and flyers. On the right is a wood deck.

People lounge on mattresses or benches, swigging beer. Milo appears next to me as Colt speaks to the man at the desk.

"Milo, why can't you talk him into sharing with one of us?"

Milo scratches an eyebrow. "I've tried since before you came along."

'But this is insane. He needs peace when he's not playing." I peek over Milo's shoulder at the bare light bulbs hanging from the ceiling and take in the smell of damp. "Look what happened at Wollongong."

"I know, I know."

"Stupid ego. I understand the money problems, but we can share. I'm going to talk some sense—"

Milo traps my elbow. "It's more complicated than that."

"Complicated? No it's not. Unless there's something you're not telling me?"

Milo curses. "Don't tell Colt you know this . . ." Milo crosses and uncrosses his arms. "When I took Colt on, we agreed he wouldn't pay me until he could afford to. Now he won't spend what he sees as 'my' money on himself, and in his mind, sharing a room would further take advantage of me. Do you see?"

Colt approaches, jiggling a key. "All set," he says. "Room 14, if you decide to send room service."

"I want to see your room," I say.

Colt's grin grows. He tosses the key and captures it,

tilting his head at me. "She's a bit forward, isn't she, Milo?" I glare at them both.

Milo taps my arm. "Say goodnight, Harper." He walks outside as three guys amble in, passing a smoke between them.

I can't say much given what Milo just revealed. Instead, I hug Colt for longer than normal. The warm contact and Tiger Balm smell is comforting. "Not happy, Quinn."

Colt tugs my ponytail as I walk away.

Milo is sitting in the back of the cab, eyes hidden behind aviators. "You need to take this iron will onto the court with you."

"Did you take me on for free, too?"

"No. And it's not free, Harper. I don't see Colt as a gamble. He'll make it. I approached him. It was my idea. He will pay me back."

"Training us as the best ever mixed doubles partners wasn't why you took me on. It was to pay you enough to subsidize Colt's unpaid fees . . . to get your hotel paid for. Does my dad know?"

"He does. I was perfectly up-front with him about Colt's situation. Everyone benefited, and therefore you shouldn't have a problem with it."

I snatch his sunglasses off. "I have a problem with being treated like a child. Why did no one tell me?"

Milo takes back the sunglasses. "I have told you, and

you're acting like a toddler. Perhaps you've answered your own question."

I seethe in silence. Milo's just made me feel like Kominsky did—second-rate.

Our hotel, a huge glass structure lit with blue and pink lights, boasts a circular entrance, regal pillars, marble floors, and crystal chandeliers as big as cars. The churning in my stomach worsens.

Milo's room is at the other end of the corridor from mine. "'Night, Harper," he says. "Financials aside, I took you on because you have what it takes—and because you and Colt possess the X factor required for doubles partnerships. I'd been looking for that for months."

I say goodnight, my voice cold, but the bruised feeling swirling through my chest fades a little. I shove open the door to my hotel room. The king-sized bed is decorated with multicolored cushions. There's even a sitting area. I yank the curtains closed, shutting out the sparkle of the city below. When I turn and lean against them, the bathroom, with its walk-in shower, stone counters and spa, confronts me. *This is not right.* It's the sight of two white waffle dressing gowns hanging beside twin basins, orange blossoms peeping out of the pockets, that pushes me over the edge.

Minutes later, I'm in a cab traveling back to Colt's hostel. If it's good enough for him, it's good enough for me.

It's late when I get there and the desk is unmanned. I sneak down a diamond-carpeted corridor and struggle up a narrow staircase with my luggage. The door of Room 12 is open. It's crammed with four metal bunk beds. Next door is a bathroom containing rows of toilets and showers. I knock on the door with 14 inked on it. No answer. I rap harder.

"Harper, what the hell?" Colt emerges from the bathroom, a towel wrapped around his hips. The dark hair on his chest curls, damp, and there's a shaving cut on his jaw. *Holy hot guy in towel.*

I push my chin out, ignoring the rustling inside my belly. "If this place is so great, I want to stay here, too."

"This is bullshit." He rams the key into the lock, shoving me inside when the door flies open. The room's poky but clean, despite an old water stain across the ceiling. There's a neatly made double bed, bamboo blinds on the window, and a small wooden cupboard. Colt slams the door. "Does Milo know you're here?"

"Nope. You're not the only one who's stubborn, though. I'm not leaving." I ditch my bag and stand tall, but the room's tiny and he's a couple feet away, smelling of oranges and bristling with annoyance.

"I'm taking you back," he growls, yanking a white T-shirt over his head.

"You'll have to carry me downstairs, kicking and screaming."

He rubs his brow. "You can't stay here. For a start it's December. They're fully booked."

I glance uncertainly at the bed. "Good thing there's a double in here then." I pinch my bottom lip between two fingers. "Or you could share my room at the hotel. It's bigger—king-sized bed. More space for two."

Stony-faced, Colt waves me off. "No way."

Given that he won't tell me about the deal with Milo and how it means he won't share rooms with him, I go for a different angle. "Listen, I know Milo hates sharing and needs privacy. But I'm cool with it. It can be our secret. We can put a pile of pillows between us when we sleep."

He glares out the window at the view of a brick wall. "Not going to happen."

I haul my bag onto the bed, and start to unzip it. "Where do I put my stuff?" I drag out piles of clothes and dump them on the bed.

"Harper, come on. Stop." He seizes my wrist.

"I'm not staying there if you're staying here. That's final." I pull at more clothes until he snatches the bag, chucking it at the closed door with a thud. The door rattles.

He curses, shouting now. "What do you want from me?" My stomach dives.

I want him to put my world back together.

"Can you turn back time?" I yell. But of course he can't. So I need to do it myself. I decide to appeal to his sense of duty. "If you can't do that, I want you to come and share my room. You need to have a settled mind and rest. A good outcome for you is a good outcome for me. Your stupid ego is going to affect me, you see. And I can't have that. And if you're not at your best, it'll affect Milo—his future rests on your shoulders. Am I right?"

Colt releases my wrist, brushing a palm over his mouth and along his just-shaved jaw. He squeezes, leaving pale finger marks on his skin. "This is crazy. We can't share a room."

"Okay. You go to my hotel and I'll stay here. You said it's great."

"No way," he shouts, spinning and kicking the wardrobe.

The bedroom door jolts as someone bangs on it. Colt struggles to open the door against my bag. The man from the front desk peeks in at me, at the clothes flung around the floor, then at Colt. "One person paid for," he says. "Big noise. You go."

Colt holds up two palms. "Sorry, sorry. She's leaving. We'll quiet down." The man points a warning finger at Colt, who looks angry enough to bite it off. Colt shuts the door and pelts me with a glare.

"I'm not leaving without you," I say. "Accept my help. There are three options—"

"Okay, okay. Pack your crap," he says, stuffing his own things into a bag.

● ● ●

Colt scopes out the hotel room. He opens the curtains and ponders the lively scene below. "I can see why you were uncomfortable staying here, with me at the hostel."

"Good. Guess I'll use the bathroom. Feel free to unpack." After a quick shower, I change into an oversized sleep T-shirt that's as long as a tennis dress.

When I come out, Colt's perched on a chair, his back to me, watching Sky Sports. His bags, still unpacked, sit side by side against the wall. I pull back the blankets on the bed and build a wall of pillows and cushions down the middle. Colt heads for the bathroom and I yank the sheet over me. When he emerges, he clicks off the TV, then the lights. The other side of the bed shifts downward with a squeak.

The room is dimly lit by the clock radio and the light coming from under the door, so I can make out Colt when he peers over the pillow wall. "Try to keep your hands off me, okay?" He grins for the first time.

I work to slow my breathing and kick off the sheet, the room suddenly boiling. My nerves buzz. *I'm a friend helping out a friend. It's just somewhere to sleep.* Lying stiffly, I listen to Colt's steady breathing. He shifts onto his side. Then his other side. The smell of orangey shower gel mixed with Tiger Balm and muscle cream floats around us. Maybe I smell of the flowery soap I used. *I'm in bed with Colt!* Something more pleasant than nerves spirals through me similar to a streak of excitement only more intense. But then a dreamless, jet-lagged sleep grabs me.

I wake before Colt and sneak a peek over the pillow wall. He's on his back, in T-shirt and boxer shorts, an arm flopped across his eyes, denying the sun is up. Today we've scheduled a training session before Milo has to complete paperwork and other official tournament stuff. Though I'm still angry with Milo after his revelation, I acknowledge he's never treated me as second-rate. Maybe Kominsky did simply because I *acted* second-rate. I can sulk about Milo's deal with Colt, give 90 percent, or I can choose to be first-rate and act like an A-lister.

I get dressed in the bathroom and when I come out, Colt's changed into training gear.

"Breakfast?" he asks, throwing bags that are still bulging with his stuff into a corner. "I could eat a herd of buffalo." His smile is king-sized and my heart stutters.

"Not sure they serve buffalo at his hotel." I open the door and almost walk into Milo. Sunglasses in place, his mouth opens and shuts, brisk as a hiccup.

"Figured I'd join you for breakfast," says Colt smoothly, hands shoving into his pockets.

As we walk to the elevator, Milo puts an arm around our shoulders, pulling us into an awkward huddle. "I don't think that was appropriate, guys. Harper's a sixteen-year-old girl in my care, Colt. No room visits." He releases us and pushes the down button.

With my cheeks the color of guilt, we step into the elevator.

197

"And one last word on the matter. I didn't think I needed to say this but . . . we keep this partnership platonic. Yes?" I nod, scrutinizing the countdown to ground level. Milo cracks his knuckles. "I've been around long enough to know that relationships on the circuit can tear apart dreams."

"Enough said," says Colt. "It won't happen again."

Breakfast is served in a dining area the size of the Sydney Opera House, the glass walls overlooking muddled, rainbow-tinted streets. When Colt approaches the buffet for a second plateful, I follow, not for more food, but to lay down the law. I shoulder-bump him then pour myself a black coffee.

"We'll need to be more careful, but you're not moving back to the hostel. If you do, I'll turn up again." I swipe an apple and give him my *I'm not kidding* glare, but instead of the huffy reaction I'm expecting, his eyes sparkle with amusement.

TWENTY-THREE

WE'RE ENTERED INTO THE SINGLES events of two back-to-back Futures tournaments. Next week's is in Cambodia. I get to see Colt's first game with Milo and a few spectators. Futures comps rarely draw big crowds. Colt is winning and he pans over to us, smiling, having broken serve again.

"My pig whistles," says Milo, slapping a leg. "The boy's changing. I've never seen him so relaxed on court." Milo grants me that pleased look. "Colt tells me you've been a good friend to him. He needed that, Harper. Thank you."

I flush with the idea that Colt talked to Milo about me.

Colt wins the game in straight sets.

The atmosphere at Camp Milo is one of disbelief and excitement as we triumph over our opponents and even share celebratory dinners. My five-ball bounce and thinking of Purple Time help me succeed as much as choosing to win one point at a time, which is easier to believe possible than contemplating winning the whole tournament. I'm also fitter than I've ever been and have the mental edge on my opponents; based on my past form, they expect me to crumble, and when I don't, it freaks them out. Milo's pleased that Colt's not locking himself away, while Colt and I become practiced at sneaking him into the hotel—and out again early the next morning. At night, we lie on our bed, the pillow wall discarded, and dissect our games, strategies, and opponents, then roll over, back to back, and fall asleep. It works, and we plan for the same arrangement in Cambodia.

Five days later, Milo and I follow a victorious Colt into the media room for the post-match interview. Futures tournaments don't get a lot of attention, but we're obligated to attend media conferences and Colt has just reached the semifinals. We're both having an incredible tournament—my semifinal is tomorrow.

Milo and I wait at the back of the stark room behind rows of plastic chairs while Colt fidgets at the front. He hates these interviews, maybe because he's not someone who is comfortable talking about himself. A journalist asks what Colt can attribute his recent run of success to. Straining not to pace like a caged tiger, Colt keeps his answer short, prickly even, and rightly gives the credit to Milo. Another reporter asks what Milo changed in Colt's training. A third asks why Colt uses the surname Quinn when he was born Colt Jagger.

Colt's already tacked-on smile slips from his face.

Milo strides toward the group—I've never seen him move so fast. Colt suddenly darts for the door. The journalists knock over chairs to give chase.

"How is your father, Colt? Has he cleaned himself up?" calls the same journalist. But they stop short of pursuing Colt when he races down the corridor. They walk back into the room, furiously jabbing at their cell phone screens.

"Shit," says Milo, jogging down the corridor after Colt.

I follow and bang into Milo when he stops in the main entrance. "What's happened? What do they mean?"

Milo scours every direction, but Colt's gone. Milo stalks back into the media room, me in tow.

"Tell me, Milo. What the hell?"

The press crushes around us, talking over each other. Camera lights flash like mini midair explosives.

"Can we get an interview?" shouts someone.

"Tell us about Colt's father."

"Not going to happen, fellas," says Milo. "Colt and I will respond to questions about the game, but his personal life is his *personal* life." Milo swings Colt's abandoned bag onto a shoulder, forcing them to step back. He commandeers my elbow and barrels out the door. "I'll tell you in the cab."

I look around, frantic. "But we can't leave Colt."

"He's long gone." Milo marches into the street and hails a cab. Once inside, he punches a number on his phone and we peer at Colt's bag, hunched between us, when it rings. Milo curses.

"Tell me, Milo. I'm fed up with all these secrets. Has this got something to do with that tennis player, Jamie Jagger?"

"Jamie Jagger is Colt's father."

My hand flies to my chest, eyes popping. "He's Colt's dad? *The* Jamie Jagger? But there's no resemblance at all." Jagger has bright blond hair and blue eyes.

Milo presses his lips together. "Colt takes after Madeline— his mama."

I study the patchwork of steel and glass and color that forms the streets of Bangkok, and put together the facts. Colt told me his dad is in rehab and is an alcoholic. Jamie Jagger, nicknamed "Spitfire" because of a short fuse on court, is famous for blowing apart his own tennis career. World number 5, he was banned for taking performance-enhancing drugs, and then once the ban was lifted, he turned up on court at the Australian Open drunk. The media crucified him. His coach, his sponsors, his agent, all ditched him. That was his last ever appearance on a tennis court, maybe ten years ago.

"Are you getting it now?" says Milo. "Why Colt is the way he is? He has so much to prove. He's been Colt Quinn—his mother's name—since he started in the junior

202

circuit. Would you want to be known as Jamie Jagger's son? The son of a cheat?" Milo pinches the bridge of his nose. "Now they're going to dig out Jagger himself. This is not good."

I lean forward to search for Colt out the window, wishing I could see through buildings. "We need to find Colt."

"He's better left alone. He'll come back when he's ready."

But by dinnertime, there's still no sign of him. Milo's face is etched with worry. "You get to bed, Harper. Big game in the morning. Don't let this affect your state of mind. Colt is strong. He'll survive." He doesn't mention that Colt's semifinal is tomorrow afternoon.

I lie alone in the dark, unable to sleep. Colt inherited his talent and his temper from Jagger of all people. But Colt will never be free of his father's reputation. Every press interview, every match appearance, every drug test. It'll be hard to get sponsors or wild cards or keep his agent.

There's a beep and the door cranks open on its spring. A shaft of light from the hallway gushes into the room. Lying on my side, pretending to sleep, I squint at the outline of Colt, then the clock. 11:23. A rush of relief makes me grin. Light slinks away when the door closes, and there's the sound of static as Colt undresses. The squeak of bare feet on tile tells me when he's in the bathroom. He brushes his teeth in the dark. When the bed tilts with his weight, he exhales, a frail kind of sigh.

His back to me, he lies on the very edge of the mattress.

I shift closer, place a hand on his shoulder. He tenses. Then his cool palm covers mine, startling me. I want to ask if he's okay, but obviously he isn't. I quietly sniff for alcohol to see if he's drowned his sorrows in some bar, but he smells of chlorine. Had he gone for a swim?

"Tough day," I whisper.

He breathes in a hunk of air, compelling my hand to rise and fall on his arm. His hand presses harder on mine. I listen to our breathing, to the sounds of people in the hallway, talking, joking, slamming doors. He doesn't move, doesn't speak. I move closer. I have no clue how to comfort him or be the friend he needs now.

"You played a great game," I say. "You should be proud of yourself. I've never seen you play better. Your ground strokes, your serve placement, your returns, your footwork. Milo couldn't fault anything." He removes his hand and I shift mine to rest on his waist. "You've got everything it takes—"

He rolls over and holds both sides of my face, presses his mouth, close-lipped, onto mine. I don't object, thinking this is a moment of out-of-character emotion, an impulsive sort of *thank you* for saying what I said. But eyes shut, his lips stay against mine for a long ten seconds.

My wide eyes relax, then slip closed.

As if he's in a rush, he moves over me, muscles taut and unyielding, to kiss my nose, then across my brow, shoulders hunched around me. My breath quickens to match his. One hand slips to my shoulder and his lips travel along my jaw, teeth nip my ear, my neck. Sparks ricochet through me and a small sound, like a mewling kitten, shivers into the back of my throat. My mouth pops open, inhaling, needing his hard tongue.

But he pulls away and off the bed in one movement, striding toward the window.

"Fuck. Sorry. Shit." Arms rigid, fists balled, he whips back to me, his expression muddled. "That shouldn't have happened." He curses again.

I slip off the bed and step closer, wanting to say it's okay, I kind of liked it. But he snatches his sneakers and the keycard, and he's gone before the door cranks shut on its spring. My insides churning with not altogether unpleasant sensations, I fall back onto the bed, arms crossed over my face. *What the hell?*

For the next couple of hours, I relive those heavenly seconds—how his body felt super powerful, how he ignited a flash fire in me. The desire to kiss him properly had stung me in a way that has never happened before. Kissing Jacob is beautiful and safe and fills me with a familiar warm curling smokiness, and although he makes my pulse race, it was never like it was tonight. My heart has never verged on exploding, my skin has never prickled with anticipation so alarmingly, my mouth has never felt so starved of a kiss.

But why had Colt kissed me when he's made it clear he doesn't do girlfriends? He needed comfort and took it?

Maybe he craved my words of reassurance and got carried away—like before in the parking lot. And I guess a half-naked girl in bed is a temptation for any guy.

It's daylight when the door cranks and wakes me. I perch on my elbows. Colt stares across the crackling space between us, looking as if his soul just crawled out of a hurricane. I search for the words that will make it right again, but come up with nothing.

"That'll never happen again," he says, detached, clinical. He runs an agitated hand over mussed-up hair. The statement hurts more than it should.

"Where've you been? Have you been drinking?" I slap a palm over my mouth, remembering in that instant who his father is, and realizing that I've never seen Colt drink alcohol. Guess it's obvious why now.

His eyes whirl with hurt. He strides into the bathroom and slams the door.

I don't get to brush my teeth because over an hour later, when it's time to go, he's still under the shower. "Don't drown," I yell, trying and failing to slam the spring-door as I leave the room.

When my game begins, I'm still furious. But whenever we change sides, I use the purple towel and realize Colt had been dealing with his dad's rehab at Wollongong, yet he was thinking of me when he bought that towel. My anger cuts itself in half. But I have to blank out my changing feelings for Colt, and everything else that's bugging me,

206

especially what I have to say to Jacob when I next see him. I have to suppress the possibility that Aria knows about me and Jacob but can't quite nail us—or bring herself to face the truth. I know the pressure I'm feeling is a whisper compared to the pressure Colt must deal with, and that helps me remain strong.

My opponent gives me several puzzled looks and it dawns on me that she's expecting the old Harper. I focus on only the next shot, the next ball toss, the next smash, and let her self-destruct on her own. At one point, I go in for a smash and she actually winces and steps aside rather than attempt a return. It makes me feel powerful, like I'm hurling fireballs. Soon I'm trailing into the media room, Milo's congratulatory arm around me. About twenty reporters swarm us. Despite my win, I know they're not here for me.

"Mr. Stein. Where is Colt Jagger? Where is Jamie Jagger today?"

"Has Colt ever failed a drug test?"

Milo does a U-turn, leaving the room without a word. Someone shoves a microphone in my face. "Are you Colt's girlfriend? Where's Colt?"

Milo returns and tugs me with him. He marches into the administration office and rants at someone, complaining about the press hijacking my interview and demanding a dispensation for Colt after the game this afternoon to avoid a fine for missing interviews.

Will Colt even turn up for his game?

He does. And he's a machine, the racquet an extension of his arm. He never lifts his focus from the ball or the racquet or the court itself, as though nothing outside the edge of the arena exists. He loses some easy points, makes a few unforced errors, but his serve saves him and he plays himself into the final.

Colt exchanges a few words with the umpire and darts from the court.

Milo sighs. "And he's off."

"He was on fire today."

"Let's hope he doesn't implode."

We leave the arena and head for the players' lounge. Milo orders a beer and instructs me to go for a run around the complex to dispel any remaining lactic acid from my earlier game.

The complex is huge, with lakes, a gym, swimming pool—vastly different from many of the Futures tournaments, where the changing room can be a trailer in the middle of a field. I spot Colt's tennis shirt and dark hair from a distance, his hunched figure rock-shaped on the wooden bridge that curves over the resort pool. His back rests against the paneling of the bridge, knees bent, forearms propped. People walk by, swim beneath the bridge, and sunbathe in lounges around him. He's the image of the loneliest guy on earth.

He doesn't stir until I slide down next to him.

"Following me again?" His eyes remain fixed on the waterfall across the pool.

"Just a friend looking out for a friend." *And starting to want to be more than a friend.*

His head lolls against the bridge. "You haven't given up on me yet?"

"I'll never do that," I say, without pausing. He jerks his chin down. I hunt for the right words, but can't think of anything not related to tennis, dads, kissing, or the press.

"It's peaceful here," he adds. His mood seems pliable. Guess he has just made it into the final.

I reach over and untie his shoelaces, then pull off each tennis shoe.

"What are you doing?" he asks.

"Being your eyes and hands." When I strip off his sweaty socks, he chuckles and I want to absorb that smile.

He pegs my nose for me. "You got a death wish?"

"Quite possibly." I pull off my own tennis shoes and carry them all to the other side of the bridge, placing them under a palm tree.

"Milo's taught you well—the Distraction Technique. What are you up to?" he asks.

"Do something for me? Don't question, don't think, just do—live in the moment."

Gripping his wrist, I pull until he stands and follows me to the edge of the pool. We sit and dangle our feet in the water. His superior glance says, *See—I can live in the moment.*

Giggling, I shove him and he topples into the pool. When he surfaces, I'm relieved to see he's not mad. Instead, he tugs my legs until I fall in.

The water is clear and refreshing and I don't care if we're in our tennis gear and shouldn't be here. I surface near the waterfall. Colt swims through the cascade of water, mounts the rocks behind, and beckons me. It's intimate, as if I'm on one side of a shower and he's on the other.

I duck under and join him on the rocks. The noise is deafening and I barely hear him say, "You've officially hippied me up."

Colt's eyes rake over me. One corner of his mouth ticks up. I splash my reddening cheeks and then, in case he thinks I have any ideas about getting kissed again, I dive deep and swim where the world is muffled. I admit there's a part of me that wants to kiss Colt badly, but for a start, every time he kisses me, he regrets it and gets angry. Second, he doesn't do girlfriends. Third, Milo's warning. Fourth, Jacob. Poor Jacob, who'll be upset after Dad's scolding.

I think about the story Colt shared about his old girl-friend ruining his game, yet here we both are at a tennis tournament—

Then there's Dad's concern about my tennis, although he was referring to Jacob affecting my game. I consider how a relationship could've wrecked Colt's dreams and love did wreck Aria's. Even now, I shouldn't be thinking about this. I should be analyzing my next opponent and making game plans.

Boyfriends can't happen right now.

When I get out of the pool, I find a shirtless Colt back on the bridge, but this time when I approach, he pats the spot next to him. My belly wobbles.

"I needed that," he says, leaning forward to wring out his shirt. "I'll go back to the hostel tonight."

"No you won't," I snap. "Winning our finals is the priority. And don't flatter yourself. I'm not interested in you except as a friend and doubles partner. Go cuddle a pillow instead of lunging at me. If you're upset, stick to talking. I'll be there for you, but keep your lips to yourself."

Colt skims the horizon, a slow grin building. "Game, set, and match to Harper Hunter."

TWENTY-FOUR

BUT SOMETHING'S CHANGED.

That night, when Colt and I sleep side by side, I glow from the inside out as if I have something precious cupped in my chest.

In the early morning light, I devour him while he sleeps, his arm covering his closed eyes to keep the world out. I'm no longer confused. The friendship I'd nursed between us had changed to something hazy and exciting and just out of sight, but now it's changed again. It's loud and real and currently making my heart bounce around my rib cage like a tennis ball. But for so many reasons he's off limits, and I can't make the same mistake with him as I made with Jacob.

Milo has whipped me into the best shape of my life and taught me a lot about self-belief and mental toughness, and maybe that's why I don't feel as tired or anxious as I otherwise might when every set goes to a tiebreaker the next day. Maybe that's why the court seems smaller. Maybe that's why Hosek drops her racquet after one of my serves hurts her wrist, and maybe that's why I don't turn to putty; when Hosek loses a point I don't feel like I've taken something from her—she chose to give it to me. But my match play also improves because I have Colt openly supporting me, cheering for me, advising me, and somehow that motivates me more than anything ever has. His enthusiasm also makes me wonder if something's changed for him, too—like that kiss meant more than he's admitting.

After I beat Hosek in the final, Colt hugs me and spins me around and happiness busts out of me as though he unzipped a bag of it inside me. And when it's clear Colt's going to win his final, too, I anticipate the hug we'll share, my body thrumming with expectation. But how can I feel like this when I'm filled with all this love for Jacob? Is it simply that there's a hot guy sharing my bed and my hormones are out of control?

Hormones, and whatever's going on between us, don't appear to affect our games adversely, so we continue as secret roomies in Cambodia. We train and strategize together, win games, share breakfast, lunch, and dinner; Team Milo is inseparable.

One morning, I wake to find Colt lying on his side, studying me.

The earth pauses for a soft moment.

My heart floats inside my chest, a falling petal in the breeze. I return his gaze. And when he says, "Morning," rolling away to take a shower, I touch the sheet to absorb the warmth he leaves behind.

On the evening Milo announces the latest rankings—I've reached number 89 and Colt is 103 in the world—we lie on our bed and talk into the night, blitzed on excitement. Colt's face slips wide open. He's as relaxed as a lion stretched out in the sun and words spill out of him.

Hours later, we agree it's time for sleep. Colt switches the lamp off. A shaft of light dips into the room from under the door and I make out the outline of Colt lying on his back. He stares at the ceiling, hands behind his head. After a while, I roll over to face him. He looks toward me.

"Why did you come back to Sydney?" I expect him to tense or tell me to sleep, but he goes back to examining the ceiling, and licks his lips.

"We moved to Florida because my dad got a job. Then he lost the job."

"Didn't you say your mum's family offered him the job?" That conversation at the run-down tennis courts seems a billion years ago.

"I'm sure you're curious and I'm grateful you haven't pumped me for details." He pauses for such a long time I assume it's all the answer I'm going to get. But then he adds, "Mom's cancer pushed Dad over the edge—with the drugs and drinking and stuff." Colt stares right through me and into the past. "By the time she died, he was a mess. Loving my mom reduced him to this weak, broken man."

Colt untangles the sheet covering our legs and moves onto his side. "My aunt tried to help by offering him a job a few months after Mom died. They own a sports equipment manufacturing company. You already know what Dad did at the Open that year. He'd lost everything."

"You were six when she died?"

"She died a month before my sixth birthday." Colt says the words as if he's telling me today's date. "Dad was drinking heavily after the Open incident. For my birthday, I was given the gift of cleaning up his vomit." Colt's laugh is more of a snort. "If we hadn't moved to Florida a few months later, the state would've gotten involved. I got lucky. My aunt and uncle eventually saw my passion and found me a coach—they even paid for everything. And they put Dad in rehab. When he got out the second time—I'd just turned ten—things were going along fine, except Dad looked at me funny. He thought I'd betrayed him. He hates the tennis world. Said they'd turned on him and he wanted nothing to do with 'the vermin.'"

"Jeez. When I was ten, I was playing in the woods and running around in a bathing suit all day."

"I'll bet you were training."

I roll onto my stomach, cheek resting on my hands as I answer. "But I lived in a controlled bubble compared to you. I had all the support I needed."

Colt smiles, wistful. "I took Mom's name. That made everything worse with Dad. But I trusted my uncle's advice that I'd be held back if the world knew who my father was. Then last year my aunt and uncle helped me get emancipated so that I'd have all the legal rights of an adult. My dad hated that."

"But why did you leave Florida?"

"The last time Dad came out of rehab my uncle gave him an ultimatum: Dad better not fall off the wagon again or they'd stop supporting us."

"And he started drinking again?"

"The higher my ranking, the more Dad drank. And . . . he can't control his temper. That's why he earned the nickname 'Spitfire.' He fought with my uncle at the company board meeting and then went to their house and trashed the place. He blamed them for pushing me into tennis, even though it was me who wanted it."

"How could they punish you for your father's mistakes?"

He shakes his head. "They didn't follow through on the ultimatum. They said Dad had to go. They wanted me to move in with them, but when Dad announced his plan to return to Sydney, I couldn't let him go alone. It's my fault he can't stop drinking; my tennis rubs his face in the past and keeps him from moving on. And I knew he'd destroy himself if I didn't come back with him."

"Tough choice. You walked away from your dreams."

Colt's eyes lose focus, becoming glassy. Someone lets the door slam in the room next door, flushes a toilet.

"I tried to forget tennis, but it seems like the genes are ingrained in me and I was falling apart without it. I figured tennis might save us both. If I can become the best, I can support him, help him get better. Then Milo found me. A part of me knew it'd work out. It's as if I know my future is tennis and whatever path takes me there, I'll somehow make it. I'll be number one."

I jab Colt's shoulder. "Cocky, much?"

He chuckles and rolls onto his front. "I call it confident and positive thinking."

Our arms under our pillows, elbows touching, eyes burrowing, the moment suddenly seems intimate. Neither of us looks away and I wonder what it'd feel like to be his girl, but then quickly change the subject. "And your uncle and aunt haven't tried to contact you?"

"I haven't told them our address or called. There was a big argument before we left. I doubt they'd want to hear from me."

"Why wouldn't they? You made the . . . honorable choice."

"You think? Not the chump's choice?" He reaches out and strokes my cheek with the tips of his fingers, and in the same motion rolls onto his back away from me. In that one movement, I'm sure that whatever feelings I'm fighting, he's fighting the same ones.

Zipping off the bed, I escape into the bathroom. "The right choice if you're human and not some robot," I call, before shutting the door.

I slump onto the wooden laundry basket, alarm bells ringing in my head. It's one thing for me to find myself attracted to a scarily intense doubles partner who's unobtainable, but it's quite another for him to be attracted right back.

When Colt wins the final at the Cambodian Futures tournament, he breaks through the world top 100 barrier. Earlier in the day, I lost in my final, but it's still a reporter's Christmas Day. The story of two Australian players simultaneously shooting up the rankings in time for the Aussie Open next month makes the *Sydney Morning Herald*'s sports pages. The media shows replays of our recent games, rehashes interviews, and compares Colt's game to his father's. But mostly they ask where Jagger is today, repeating clips of his boozed-up appearance at the Australian Open nearly twelve years ago.

We arrive in Sydney in the bone-colored morning light. From the moment the plane hits the tarmac, Milo's phone beeps. While waiting for our luggage, Milo responds to texts and listens to messages. Colt and I survey the conveyer belt. Since Colt opened up about his dad and I got the sneaking suspicion he's into me, I've kept my distance and he's done the same—except he's been relaxed and cheerful rather than locked away and moody. I repeat the list of reasons why we can't hook up at least twice per hour.

"This is it. The moment before your lives change forever," says Milo, arms around us. "Your agent is working hard and you're in—the Australian Open mixed doubles event and wild cards into the singles qualifying tournament—plus two brands have offered 'his and hers' deals with all the tennis equipment you can wear and break."

And when we enter the arrivals hall, a spray of camera lights flash, making me squint. "Tennis royalty," says Milo. "Get used to it."

Milo's arranged a surprise—a stretch limousine to drive us home. I sit between him and Colt, sipping a glass of champagne mixed with orange juice. Colt sticks to OJ. I begin a boisterous round of "We Are the Champions," forcing them to sway from side to side. But when we arrive at Colt's house, he stiffens beside me, his face a cracked mirror.

He drops his glass into the footwell and shoots out of the car before it stops, jogging to where a woman in a sleek, black pantsuit waits on the porch. Milo and I watch as Colt dives his forehead into Natalie's shoulder. Her arms wrap around him, her face slack with sadness. I'm swamped by the need for his head to be on my shoulder, for it to be

219

my arms around him. I reach for the door handle but Milo stops me.

"Something's happened. We need to know," I snap. Natalie is talking fast, her hands holding either side of Colt's downturned face.

"Let him decide," replies Milo.

I tap my lips with my fingertips repeatedly until Milo lowers the window as they walk toward us.

"Natalie's driving me to the hospital," says Colt, bending to talk through the window. His gaze bounces around the car. "Dad's overdosed."

Milo rubs his temple, then shakes his head.

Colt slams a fist on the window frame. "And while he was in rehab. Someone has to take responsibility—"

"I'll meet you in the hospital soon, okay?" says Milo, and I can only nod in agreement.

Colt mashes his lips together, then straightens up. "I gotta go."

And he walks across the road, arm in arm with Natalie, away from us, away from me, away from my heart, which is weeping for him. And away from the space I've gotten used to him existing in, night and day during the last two weeks—the space right beside me.

TWENTY-FIVE

WHEN THE LIMOUSINE PULLS UP on our street I fake a smile, but it falls away when neither Jacob nor Aria appears in the welcome lineup.

Something's wrong.

Slightly numb, I'm cajoled through the usual hugs and kisses from Mum and Dad, who don't answer when I ask where the rest of the Welcoming Committee is. Then Milo and Dad go into the study to check through next year's tournament schedule—I suspect that's code for talking about Jagger—leaving me and Mum to prepare breakfast in the company of Beethoven's Sixth.

"Where are Aria and Jacob?" I ask again as Mum butters piles of toast.

Scratching her nose with a knuckle, she turns down the radio. "Aria's staying at a friend's house." My stomach hitches. *Oh.* Mum reduces the heat on the scrambled eggs then scrunches a sheet of foil until it's a tiny ball. "The thing is . . . Jacob didn't get into the Con."

I push down so hard on the knife I'm slicing watermelon with, that it gets stuck in the rind. Mum doesn't need to explain how devastated Jacob must be, or how it means Aria took a gap year and then gave up the audition for nothing.

Mum reaches over, yanks the knife from the rind and keeps slicing. "Sorry it's not much of a homecoming. I can't think where Jacob is today. By the way, Aria's booked her flight to Rome—straight after the Australian Open."

I suppress the urge to suck my hair. "I should go to Jacob."

Mum's usual bright smile slips into a frown that implies, *Don't start a war.* As I turn to go, she says, "I support your father on this subject."

Turning back slowly, I fold my arms. "Does Aria know?" Mum bites her lips, then shakes her head. I shut my eyes and exhale. "Neither of you get it, though. I love Jacob." But even as I say the words, I think of Colt.

"Love comes in so many forms." Mum discards the knife and leans against the counter. "I guess love resembles colors. Colors get broken into different shades, so if love is red, your feelings for Jacob are more of a pink."

I grind my jaw. "How can you possibly know that?"

"Because I know you. Everyone has a safe place. Yours is Jacob." Mum smooths her bob, tugging at the curl that

222

refuses to curve under. "When I was a young woman, I had lots of pink loves. I loved poets and artists before I learned who I was, and that my future needed more than sweet words and sketches—"

"You can't reduce what I feel for Jacob to a color and a need to be safe. But don't worry . . . I'll do the right thing, for Aria's sake." Even though some of what Mum's saying makes sense, I don't want to hear any more. I head out onto the deck.

What color is my feeling for Colt?

Whatever the answer, I can't avoid Jacob forever.

The wall between our homes may as well be a trench in World War One. How do I tell Jacob we're over, we can *never* be, when his world has blown apart? I should be picking up the pieces, helping to put him back together, but instead I'm stomping all over the debris.

Inside the studio, the curtains are drawn. I don't see the pyramid of beer cans until it's too late. When I kick them over, they make enough noise to wake the dead. I scrunch my nose against the smell of beer and bubble gum.

The shape of Jacob sits up on the red lips sofa. "Aria?"

"Harper," I say, yanking open the curtains. He groans, lies down, and puts an arm across his eyes, reminding me of how Colt sleeps. My heart cartwheels at the memory.

"You both look like angels," Jacob says, his tongue sounding weighted down.

"Are you tanked? At nine in the morning?"

"Hmmm. Come here," he says. I hover. He's wearing swim trunks and his stomach muscles flex as he lifts himself onto one elbow. He loops his fingers through mine and tugs me closer. I kneel on the floor beside him. "I'm not allowed to kiss you," he says. "Orders from your dad."

"I wouldn't want to kiss you. You're wasted." His eyes glisten as they bore into mine. I draw away. "Don't, Jacob."

"Don't what? Don't kiss you? Don't love you? Don't live here because it's killing Aria? Don't ever play music again?"

I bite the inside of my cheek at the sight of his war-torn face. I have no idea what to say because I can't say it'll be all right. Maybe it won't.

"Come on. Get showered." I drag him up. "Let's go for a walk in the woods."

Fifteen minutes later, Jacob pulls up with slicked-back hair, looking sheepish and smelling of coffee. He sticks his tongue out and jabs me in the ribs as we climb the wall.

Purple Time is always short, but this year it's shorter than ever. Already, the lilac haze has diminished and the sound of our tread is muffled by the spongy, purple carpet. The instant the woods swallow us, Jacob's hand rests on the curve of my spine, guiding me down a path I've walked a zillion times. Neither of us speaks. We settle under the Mother Tree, our arms pressed together. The river skips and coils around the rocks.

Jacob's feet tap a drumbeat only he can hear. He gnaws

on each cuticle in turn. "Heard about your tournaments and the Australian Open and stuff. You're flying now."

"Thanks. I can't believe it's happening." But we both know this isn't what we need to talk about. We slip back into an envelope of silence.

Circling my knees with my arms, I breathe in deeply. "I heard about the Con. I'm sorry." I rest the side of my head on my bent knees to watch him. "What will you do now?"

"Dunno." He stares into the branches above us. "Leave home to give Aria some space? She took the news worse than I did. I'm guessing that's because now she knows she gave up the audition for nothing." As he speaks, his gaze climbs straight into mine. "Am I right?"

"No. I don't think that's true. I think she feels bad for you. She threw her audition away as if it were nothing, and then you didn't get in when it means so much to you." The lie makes my ears turn red.

"You're sure?"

I nod a little too quickly. "And you don't need to leave. She's going to Europe in January."

He inspects the river, adjusting his jaw back and forth. "When your dad busted us—you and me—when he warned me off . . ." Jacob hangs his head. "Jeez, I'll never forget it. He's disappointed in me. But how am I supposed to stay away from you when—when I can't live without you?" He swings to me, face etched with hurt. There's a powerful need in his eyes, not just for me, but for comfort, for reassurance.

When you've known someone almost all your life, there's a deeper bond. It's not like a normal breakup. The bond jerks now, and I play a game of tug-of-war with it. Jacob scratches the scar on his hand, left from the knife he used to carve our names into the bark of the Mother Tree. I guess our memories are etched into our souls like carvings or scars and always will be, but they shouldn't stop us from growing up or moving on, any more than the carvings can stop the tree from blossoming.

"But Dad's right." I roll forward onto my haunches, facing away from Jacob, expecting cajoling words. When there are none, I glance over my shoulder.

Jacob sags against the trunk, staring into the canopy, so sad and so beautiful and so fragile; if the wind gusted now, it would blow pieces of him away like torn bits of paper.

TWENTY-SIX

TWO DAYS LATER, ON THE first morning back at training, Colt is a no-show.

"That boy's father is going to blow two tennis careers," mutters Milo.

Colt misses the next day's session, too, and isn't answering texts.

I drive to his home. He doesn't answer the door, even though I'm sure I hear someone inside. There's no chance of peeking through the porch windows because every inch of glass is covered in "Darling Madeline" letters. They mostly don't make sense or are illegible, though some parts could be described as love notes. Each one is signed, *Yours forever, JJ*.

The next morning, I meet Milo for practice and spy Colt slumped against the café wall. Relief swirls through me, but then I spot the split lip and swollen, bruised eye.

My arms melt down to my sides so that I drop the bag I'm carrying.

Colt's glance turns limp when he sees us. He hunches over his knees, dipping his chin. Tennis racquets and bags are littered around him, almost certainly thrown there.

When we reach him, Milo taps my arm. "Be right back."

There's a long silence. I think of Colt's rough neighborhood. "Did you get mugged?"

Colt snorts. "I wish."

Milo returns with ice. Colt winces when Milo pushes the pack onto his face. After a few minutes, Colt holds the ice himself and Milo settles down next to him. I kneel in front of them.

"Your dad's out of the hospital then," says Milo. His voice is cold and seething. I've never heard him sound so angry. Colt nods. Milo slaps his own leg. "Son of a—"

Colt's dad hit him.

"Said it's my fault he can't stay clean and wants to kill himself." Colt adjusts the ice. "Wants me to give up tennis . . . won't be reminded of the people who turned on him and will turn on me." Colt's words are hard and monotone. "Said how could I prefer to play tennis than stay and help him? And why do I want to mix with the people who did this to him?"

"He's not thinking straight. I'm assuming he'd been drinking?" asks Milo.

"What else? He saw the news about me breaking into the top hundred—and all the footage of him blitzed at the Open."

"Everyone has tried to help him. Your aunt and uncle, you, me, Natalie, the rehab centers. He won't accept help. You cannot throw away your life on someone like him, whether he's your father or not."

"He nearly died this time, Milo." Colt pulls the ice away and glares. "How can I not stop playing tennis? Except now I'm letting down you and Harper and her family. It's not just me. I don't know what to do."

"What you do is keep moving forward. If you don't, he'll bring you down with him."

Colt chucks the ice pack far into the grass. "I lost my mom! I can't lose him, too."

Milo kicks out at the wall, clearly needing to throw something, as well. "I'm going to talk to him. Is he home?"

"Take your boxing gloves." Colt glares into the clouds.

"Are you up to practicing with Harper?"

After a beat, one side of Colt's mouth lifts. "Yeah." He seems relieved. "I need to train. Might break a racquet or something, though."

Milo and I stand. "You're a winner, Colt. A winner never quits and a quitter never wins. Start with a run. You good with that, Harper?"

"Of course." I gather Colt's scattered racquets and Milo gives me a thumbs-up.

We set an easy pace as Milo screeches out of the parking lot. "Has this happened before?" I ask.

"Yeah."

"I hope you hit him back."

"He didn't understand what he was doing."

"If that's true, he didn't understand what he was *saying*, either."

Colt raises an eyebrow and sifts through every feature on my face, but then picks up the pace until we can't talk.

When we return to the courts after a quick 5K run, Colt executes a few thousand mile per hour serves, the equivalent of a punching bag. We practice our lobs, smashes, and drop shots, but Colt isn't really there; his eyes are a dark void and his body does what it knows how to do automatically.

It's only once we stop for water that he returns. "Thanks for putting up with me," he says. "Not the best session for you."

"Don't be stupid. It's fine." A loose strand of hair slips over my cheek, and he hooks it behind my ear, mirroring for me. Then he steps behind me, tugs out the elastic band, and rakes my hair into a ponytail. Unlike that first day of training, his actions are careful, more of a caress than the hurried slaps he used before. The skin on my neck tingles.

"Thanks," I say, spinning around.

"My turn for the bashed-up face," he says. He's too close. My heart gasps. I struggle to figure out the new language my body is speaking—I need an interpreter. I step back. Colt lifts his racquet and taps my cheek with the edge as a Saab screeches into the parking lot. He freezes beside me.

"That man won't change," says Milo, stomping toward us and smoking with anger. "Let's get you hydrated."

We huddle by the side of the café, away from prying eyes. Colt pours the Milo Potion. He drowns his stare inside the cup of orange liquid before drinking it. "What did Dad say?"

"What you said. But isn't this his chance to give the tennis world the finger? Why would he want you to give up on your dreams after what happened to his career? I was there back then. I watched him screw up and it was the saddest thing in the world. He just needed to accept help and—"

Colt throws the cup and punches the wall with a roar. He slides down the bricks, cradling his fist. His expression swerves from a chilling rage to haunted and empty, as if his body is being shattered, his essence sucked down a drain.

Milo squats, seizes Colt's forearms, and shakes. "He won't change, Colt. I threw everything I had at him. But you can't let him bring you down. I'll help you. Don't repeat history and refuse to be helped."

Right in front of me, Colt closes the door on the world. I stare at his slammed-shut face, the bloodied knuckles. His body slumps like the life is trickling out of him while Milo strives to shake the life back in. All at once, Colt isn't at all scary. His masks have gone and he's just a boy, afraid of losing his dad. Afraid of making the wrong choice.

And I think of Aria and how she gave up her dreams only to figure out she shouldn't have.

"You can't give up, Colt." I slump to my knees in front of him, take his uninjured hand, and pump it when it stays limp. "I know you love your dad, but he's not well or he wouldn't ask you to do this. And there's no guarantee he'll get better and stop drinking even if you *do* give up tennis. And then you'll lose everything for no reason."

"Harper's right," adds Milo.

Colt's jaw clenches. "But if I keep going . . . I'm as good as killing him."

"Are you the one making him guzzle a bottle of vodka?" asks Milo. "Only he can choose to beat this. You can't do it for him."

Colt stares into space. "He wasn't always this way. For my third birthday, he gave me a tennis racquet. He taught me . . ." Colt curls his arms over his head. His shoulders heave.

Milo gives him a minute, then examines the injured knuckles. "Let's get you to the hospital in case you've done some real damage. But you're staying with me for a while. You need some space to make the biggest decision of your life."

Shaking his head, Colt says, "I won't leave him alone, Milo."

My stomach lurches at the idea of life without Colt—training alone, attending tournaments without him, never seeing the smile that seems created just for me. My fingers splay and press against my chest. I rush to my feet, knocking over the Milo Potion.

I vaguely realize that this could mean we don't go to the Australian Open, but mostly I see that whatever choice Colt makes, he loses: his tennis career or his father.

TWENTY-SEVEN

JAMIE JAGGER IS KNOCKED DOWN by a car that night.

Milo calls to tell me early the next morning. "He was so drunk, he didn't see it coming. Colt's at the hospital now, and Natalie Barbie is with him. He blames himself, of course."

I hate that it's not me beside Colt. I feel like a child who's been told I'm not old enough to go out past eight o'clock, but Dad insists I stay away, keep training and focused. Dad needs to stop protecting me and let me grow up. I complain to Milo, but he won't interfere with parent-law.

When I hear Jagger's going to be okay, I text Colt: *Stay strong and take care of yourself.* He doesn't respond for two days, and then out of the blue a reply pops onto my screen. *He's agreed to go back to rehab. See you soon.* That's it. Nothing memorable, no smiley face, but it's the first text he's ever sent me and I can't bring myself to delete it. I like seeing his name in the list of messages.

At breakfast two days later, the atmosphere in the house is . . . unsettling. It's three days before Christmas, and Mum's making up the bed in the guest bedroom while Aria, who returned home from her friend's house twenty minutes ago, bakes gingerbread men for the Christmas tree, her white chef's hat wonky. "The First Noel" blasts from the radio. But at every lead-up to Christmas I can remember, Jacob would be beside Aria right now doing a great job of getting in the way and licking out bowls of raw cookie dough and horsing around loud enough to drown out the carols on the radio. Today, he sits across the room in an armchair, his head bowed as he strokes the dogs at his feet. Aria tells a stilted joke that I can't hear properly above the carol singing. Once Jacob and Aria had been so close they ate cereal out of the same bowl every morning, and now he's keeping his distance and fake-smiling at her jokes.

No one's saying Aria gave up the Con to preserve her breaking heart, or that now that Jacob has failed the audition, she did it for nothing, and no one's suggesting there's something going on between me and Jacob. Yet the ripples of truth are in the air like heat waves, threatening to burn us if we get too close. The truth is in each curt shrug, each fleeting glance, each awkward silence, each sigh. So this is how it feels to be alone in a crowded house.

Dad is talking on the phone in the study, his bacon and

eggs going cold on the kitchen table. He rushes in, scolds Jacob for not clearing up his spilled cereal, and yells that Colt is coming to stay . . . but he has to get back to the office and we'll talk later. I tear into where Mum is stacking towels on the bed in the guest room, humming "Silent Night" to herself. "What's this about Colt? Why doesn't anyone tell me anything around here?" My voice wobbles with excitement.

"Sorry, darling. Dad just organized it." She straightens, rubbing her back. "Colt's staying with Milo while his dad's in rehab, but Milo's visiting family in Germany for a week over Christmas and didn't want to leave Colt alone. Of course, we invited Colt to stay, and it means you two can keep training. Milo wants you to use our court—the press are camped out at the practice courts." She stuffs a pillow into a pillowcase. "They're excited about Australia's up-and-coming superstars . . . and with the Open next month—"

My phone rings in my pocket.

"*Dampfnudel*. Merry nearly-Christmas."

"Milo! You're sounding extra cheerful. Relieved to be escaping from me and Colt?"

"You've heard. I wanted to confirm you're okay with it—Colt staying. I realized we decided all this without you. Sorry . . . had to get the cow off the ice."

I giggle at the idea of Colt being a cow on ice. "Of course I'm okay with it." *This is going to be the best Christmas ever.*

"Can't have him alone on Christmas Day. Does this mean he's made a decision about tennis?"

"Not yet. Stay away from the press. Take care of him. He's a bit—been a tough time."

What Milo doesn't understand is that now that I've seen inside the real Colt, every part of me wants to make him feel safe and protect him from the big, bad world. Except my own feelings for him will have to be put aside because he needs help, not more complications.

● ● ●

When Colt arrives, he's folded himself away like an umbrella. He escapes the Welcoming Committee within twenty minutes, slipping into the guest bedroom next to Dad's study. He's barely said three sentences. Five hours later, the door is still closed.

But when he emerges, freshly showered and dressed in a short-sleeved, white cotton shirt and smart khaki shorts, he apologizes to Mum for falling asleep and asks if he can help with dinner.

With a look of pleased surprise, Mum passes him a knife and three tomatoes and he gets slicing. "Don't suppose you got a lot of sleep at the hospital," she says, then adds, "Were you a chef in a past life, Colt? See how thinly he slices tomatoes, Aria? He's earned cucumbumber duties."

Colt frowns. "Cucumbumber?"

"Harper could never say the word when she was little," Mum explains.

Colt chuckles, glancing at me. My chest warms.

The radio continues to blare Christmas carols, and the smell of mince pies fills the air each time Aria opens the oven. I'm better off out of the kitchen and grapple through a game of cards with Jacob, listening to Colt interacting with Aria and Mum. He's comfortable in the kitchen, even letting Aria pop cookie dough into his mouth.

After losing again, Jacob chucks the cards in the air, letting them scatter on the floor. He refuses to pick them up unless I help. Irritated, I give in to avoid a scene. On our hands and knees, he passes me his cards. "Your parents are keeping tabs on us," he whispers.

I shift onto my haunches to put some space between us. "You're imagining things. I told Dad we've talked and he doesn't need to worry. Be yourself, okay?"

Jacob reaches for more cards, flicks them at me. I duck before they hit my face. Piling the cards on the table, I survey the activity in the kitchen and notice Colt sizing us up.

Dinner is rowdy, with Jacob and Dad bantering and competing for the biggest laugh. Afterward, Jacob goes for a swim and Aria excuses herself to shower. Colt and I hang over the deck railing sipping on lemon water. Jacob moons us before jumping into the pool.

"Time he grew out of that," I say, mortified.

The garden is a fairy-light showdown. Mum is a sucker

for a traditional Christmas, and she arranges to swamp the tree line and pretty much the whole house and garden in lights. Even the tennis court is swathed—it belongs in Santa's garden.

When four members of Jacob's band arrive, Jacob grabs me roughly in a goodnight neck lock. "Jeez, Jacob. That hurt. *Getoffme.*" He calls me a crybaby and climbs the wall with his buddies.

"We training tomorrow?" Colt asks. "I've got some catching up to do."

My neck still smarting, I squash down the excitement so my voice doesn't sound too high. "You've made a decision about tennis?"

He lowers himself into a wicker chair. "After the car hit him, I realized Dad's drinking doesn't have much to do with me playing tennis or not being there for him. I hadn't thrown his ultimatum in his face or deserted him for the tour. He drinks because he's a sick man. And when he drinks, he makes stupid choices."

Relief trickles through me.

"Except I'm running out of time," continues Colt. "I have to make some big money so I can afford to keep him in rehab until he's completely better. I have to make that happen at the Aussie Open. It's the only way I can help him . . . before he kills himself."

"Aussie Open it is, then." We clink glasses, and I drop into a chair next to him.

"I kept thinking about what you said—about what would happen if I gave up on tennis and he didn't get better. That was the final thing that helped me decide." Colt play-punches my arm. "So, thanks."

His face is wide open, eyes filled with light and . . . something that makes my belly flutter.

"I'm sorry if that dumps a pile of pressure on you," he adds.

I hadn't thought it through, but he's right. If we don't win . . . no rehab. Suddenly, Jagger's life is in my hands, too.

TWENTY-EIGHT

IN THE MORNING, I TAKE Colt on my usual run to the beach. We reminisce about the paddleboarding session. "So much has happened since then," I say. His eyes wash over me, thumbing through memories. I swallow hard.

"That was way too short a run," he says, bouncing on his toes like a boxer. "Come on, slacker. That's not going to win us the Open."

We run six miles before racing home, competing for the lead. Colt wins, and we collapse on the front lawn in a heap of sweaty limbs. The thermometer is set to hit 98 degrees today. The sun flames hot in the sky, pulsing over us.

"Swim?" I remove my sneakers without untying the laces.

Colt follows me down the side of the house and I dive into the pool, fully clothed, expecting him to refuse. As I surface, there's an explosion in the water beside me.

"Last one to finish eighty lengths is a squished tomato,"
I yell, and push off the wall. He leaves me in his wake after
a lap and perches smugly on the edge of the pool when he
wins. I squint up at him.

He tickles me under the arm with his toes. "A squished
tomato? Where did you get that from?" I somehow don't
want to mention Jacob, and haul myself out of the pool.

Colt leans back on his hands and considers the pool.
"This is great," he says. "I can concentrate on getting fit—
it's a bubble the outside world isn't allowed into." Our eyes
link with a jolt.

I look away, nodding toward the court. "Good. You
could use a break. Now, let's go play tennis."

"Hello, Mrs. Milo. Can I eat breakfast first?" He stands,
offering me his hand. "Last one to the kitchen gets to wash
your socks." He lets my hand go and pushes me into the
pool. Under the water I laugh so hard I come up spluttering.

Later, Colt asks me to drive him to the store. He wants
to contribute supplies—before he empties Mum's pantry.

"Don't be stupid. Jacob's always over, and he's never
done that before. Mum wouldn't expect it."

"I don't care if she wouldn't expect it. I want to do it. And
does Jacob have his own bedroom at your house or what?"

"Told you. We're practically siblings. Mum and Dad
wouldn't want it any other way." But Colt's right—Jacob does
seem a bit entitled, taking what Mum and Dad do for him
for granted and never doing anything in return. When Colt

doesn't seem convinced, I add, "Jacob's parents are hardly ever home, and if they are, they're not exactly into kids. Not that Jacob's a kid, but we've gotten into a habit now."

After our shopping expedition, Colt rides his motorcycle to visit his dad and see the psychiatrist who's treating Jagger.

Somehow, when he leaves, the kitchen loses color.

I drift around making coffee, reading, clock watching, and end up on the sofa in the kitchen listening to Jacob and Aria play guitar. They quibble and criticize each other and where Aria once led their practice sessions, now they argue about which key to play in.

When Colt walks in, his eyes find mine. Shadows swirl around him. I feel a stab of panic.

He plunks himself next to me. "Hey," he says. The expression on his face nicks my heart so there's a permanent scar.

"Hey." I don't ask how it went; I can guess it wasn't easy. I go for distraction and tempt him with Aria's shortbread while Jacob and Aria compete to outdo each other on each instrument. When they're done, Jacob proclaims himself the winner.

"You can't say you beat Aria on the flute, Jacob," I tease. "She whooped your ass with her exam result."

"The examiner probably had the hots for her." Jacob snaps the latches on his flute case.

"Go die in a hole," shrieks Aria, chucking violin rosin at him. It would've hit him on the side of the head had Colt not shot out an arm.

"You nearly lost your last few brain cells, Jacob," I say.

Colt sniffs the rosin, then puts it on the table. "Are you three always ragging on one another like that?"

I phony grin at Jacob and Aria and they phony grin back, a thousand thoughts behind our eyes.

At dinner, Jacob suggests he get his guitar and teach Colt to play. I inspect Colt, hoping for him to loosen up more. But wearing his own sham grin, he shakes his head and keeps eating. Once dinner is over, Jacob pressures him again, and I join in.

"Come on, Colt. You're supposed to be upsizing your inner child," I say, even though I'm slightly uneasy that this may be Jacob's way of showing Colt up.

Scraping back his chair, Colt says through gritted teeth, "I said, no." He stalks out onto the deck. Jacob suppresses a snigger.

I march after Colt. "No need to flip out. We're only having some fun."

He spins around, features knotted. "My dad is trying to kill himself, the landlord wants to kick us out because my dad didn't pay the rent with the money I gave him, I can't afford to pay the bills—so, I'm sorry if I don't exactly feel like horsing around. It has nothing to do with lightening up. Sometimes, I think you need to upsize the *adult* in you." He swings back toward the garden.

Every word stings. He's right, of course.

"I'm sorry." I step closer to play-pinch a tensed bicep. "It was insensitive of me."

His shoulders sag forward. 'You couldn't have known." He exhales. "I'm a moody bastard."

"I know enough, and I shouldn't have said it," I say shakily.

Back inside, I tell Aria and Jacob to leave Colt alone and watch a movie or something, then kick myself when their faces go pale. I'm saying all the wrong things tonight. But when did watching a movie together become wrong?

An image of the three of us tangled in one another's limbs shutters through my mind; we were watching a Harry Potter movie after a morning of swimming at the beach and a picnic lunch in the woods where we re-enacted the attack on the giant basilisk. I can almost taste the salt from the popcorn, smell the aloe vera I'd rubbed on Jacob's burnt shoulders, feel the heat of our sun-warmed bodies squished together on the sofa, beach sand still flecking our legs. It was the day before I left on the junior circuit, and I now recognize that every time I came home after that, we tried to reproduce that moment in various ways. But it never worked. You can't plan perfect moments like those. Yet for everything my choice to play tennis has lost me, the tennis court is still where I want to be. It's still what I want to be doing. And that's why I have no plan B. The reasons for playing aren't tangible, they just are. And at some point, we need to acknowledge that we can't keep trying to recreate being the Raggers.

"We won't leave you with Mr. Cranky," says Jacob.

"He's not cranky," I snap. "Well, he is. But he's allowed to be. You're aware of the situation. Just grow up."

"You're no fun anymore," retorts Jacob.

I bite back my response—that I'd rather spend time with Colt than him—because I realize it might actually be true.

Aria clears her throat. "Do you want us to leave you and Colt *alone?*" She arches an eyebrow. Jacob scans from me to Aria and back again.

"He's my training and doubles partner. That's it."

"What? You don't see that gorgeous smile . . . when he chooses to reward us with it?"

"I *am* here," says Jacob. He mopes sulkily toward the fridge to grab a beer.

She's playing the Making-Jacob-Jealous game.

I retrieve Mum's juicer to make nonalcoholic drinks and we join Colt, but while the three of us try to lighten the mood on either side of heavy silences, Colt focuses on the tennis court, lost in his own hell.

In one of the silences, Aria watches me, but flicks her eyes to the sky when I catch her. It seems like she's always doing that these days, like somewhere on my face is an answer she's looking for. And tonight, when she talks, it's rarely to me, but part of the discussion as a whole.

For the first time ever, the Raggers run out of conversation and after another beer Jacob puts on some sixties music from Dad's record collection—he loves to play with the turntable. Colt returns to earth and is smiling again, although he refuses to join Jacob in a beer. He talks to Aria about her planned trip to Europe, giving the traveler's point of view on the various airports because they're all he gets to see on tour. She leans into him as he reveals which countries use holes in the ground for toilets, which airports are renowned for their prompt delivery of food poisoning, and which airline employs the most attractive flight attendants.

I like how he smiles and doesn't rush his words. Each frequent glance my way feels as though he's untying me and willing me nearer. An apology of sorts.

Something inside me chafes away, like a snake shedding its skin.

Aria goes to bed first, after presenting Colt with a double-sized ham and lettuce sandwich because she heard his stomach rumble. She even kisses him goodnight on the cheek. A tipsy Jacob dodges helping clean up, leaving Colt and me to stack dishes and wipe countertops.

"I've never realized how lazy Jacob is . . . He eats and leaves," I say.

Colt is quiet until we finish, then he carefully hangs a dish towel and says, "Want to go for a walk? I'm wide awake."

"Sure." I check the clock. Almost midnight. Guess he wants to talk—not something to pass up.

I grab the camping lantern from the deck and we cross the silvery lawn toward the woods, our low voices muffled in the soft night air. The path is narrow and we walk in single file until it opens up nearer the river. The trees have shed most of their petals and they're silky underfoot. In the muted light, the ground looks like it's covered in lilac snow.

Hanging the lantern on a small branch of the Mother Tree, I sit on a large rock protruding over the water. Colt joins me, still lost in thought, and we listen to the chatter of the river. I take a leaf out of Milo's book and wait for him to speak when he's ready. Shuffling forward, I dip my feet in the cool water.

"You were right, you know. I should loosen up," he says finally, staring at a whirlpool created by the rocks. "It's kind of a sore point. I don't want to get wound up, but I can't help it. I worry I take after my dad . . . and what if I become him?"

"Hopefully, the only thing you inherited from him is tennis talent."

Colt dips his feet into the water next to mine. To keep him talking I add, "You've had a lot to cope with. It's not a surprise you're a little . . . serious."

A smile quivers on his lips. "Serious? Is that what I am?"

I shrug. "There are worse things. I mean, you had to

grow up fast. You had a tough childhood, and you still need to take care of your dad and make these tough decisions. It's serious stuff."

"His psychiatrist . . . she said I need to stop doing everything for him when he's released from rehab. Says there's helping him and there's babying him. I need to let him stand on his own two feet—it'll give him a focus, a reason for getting up in the morning. But how am I supposed to do that when he's either fried or hungover?"

"What happens when you're away?"

"I try not to leave for more than two weeks at a time. Natalie checks on him. And I come back to a house that belongs in someone else's life. If I let him get on with things—who knows what'll happen?" As Colt speaks, I glimpse the boy in him, the one I saw at the practice courts, the one who doesn't want to lose his dad.

"See? Another tough choice. How do you concentrate when you're on tour? I don't think I could do it."

He looks bashful. "I get even more serious."

"Yeah. I noticed." I shove his shoulder. "You're better than you were, but your game face is seriously scary. What goes on in your head before a match?"

"The day before, I visualize my best serve with a wrist snap, my best lob, best footwork, best everything. Over and over. And I visualize winning. It keeps Dad out of my head. On the day of the match, I make myself angry. I go into myself, isolate myself. I think about my mom dying—the funeral. I conjure up things in the past that make me angry. Then I'm fired up for the match, ready to slaughter anyone who tries to stop me winning because if I can make it on the circuit, I can solve all the problems in our life."

Colt's game face. "No Purple Time for me," he adds. "Zero memories that cause the warm bath effect." Colt's eyes move from grim to shining. "Having you around helps, though."

A pulsing drumbeat strikes up in my chest. I don't dare ask why and instead pick at the fallen blossoms on the rock, throwing them one by one into the river.

Colt's chest heaves. "The psychiatrist says I've got to encourage him to get rid of Mom's stuff." He pulls his feet out of the river and props an elbow on each knee. "You should see his bedroom. It's floor to ceiling boxes full of Mom's things. There's only room for his bed."

"He's kept her stuff all this time?"

"Not just her possessions: the pit from the last peach she ate; the glass from the orange juice she drank that last morning; her toothbrush; fingernail clippings he found in the bathroom trash can—" He blinks away tears. "Messed up, right?"

Every part of me wants to hug him, but he's beyond comfort, and what I'm feeling for him is scarily new and powerful and shouldn't even exist.

"Want to climb the tree again?" I was going to ask about the "Darling Madeline" letters, but I think it's better

250

to change the subject. I pull both feet out of the river, flicking water at him on purpose.

He peers up at the branches above. "In the dark?"

I jump off the rock, hoping he'll follow. He does, and we race to the top by the light of the lantern below. When we poke our heads through the canopy, we whisper, "Whoa," in unison. It's a clear night and the stars are glitter-sprayed across an endless black canvas; the heavens have their own display of fairy lights.

We breathe in the sky, face to face with the stars.

"Maybe this is what it feels like to fly." Colt's words are full of wonder.

For a while, we stay in a comfortable silence, lost in our own thoughts.

When we get tired of perching in the canopy, we hang out on the lowest boughs, one of us on either side of the trunk. Our feet dangle above the carpet of petals and Colt traces the carving of my name in the trunk. We talk and talk about nothing important. I love Colt's chuckle, how it rumbles in the back of his throat and lights up his eyes. To make him laugh again, I tell him how I once huffed off the court, aged fifteen, refusing to shake the umpire's hand because he made bad calls.

"And as I swung my bag over my shoulder, my spare bra fell on the floor at the umpire's feet."

Colt folds over laughing and slips off the branch. "A Harper Hunter mood. That would be something to see."

He leans against the trunk and I kick at him with a bare foot.

"Coming from the King of Moodland?" I say.

"Guess I *am* the son of the Spitfire." Like turning down a dimmer switch, the glow of happiness in him fades.

"You're not your father," I say. Colt's shoulders flag. "You're stronger, more handsome, more talented, and you have way better friends."

I kick at him again, playful. He tries to grab my foot, but misses. Instead, he moves closer, and the backs of his fingers trace up my arm. My breath snags. His eyes are loaded with want.

The hot breeze stills, and the trees hold their sighs.

He maps my face as though I'm some fascinating creature he's never seen before. Then he watches his finger as it travels along my jaw to my chin and in an exquisitely slow, straight line, down my throat and chest to the neckline of my tank top. My lips part to grab air; my chest surges.

I fight to summon the trusty list of reasons to pull away, but it's like swinging a racquet in pudding. "I'm not sure that's what Milo meant about being my eyes and hands," I say, soft and gusty.

And what was it Dad said?

Colt shifts, facing me square-on, body touching my knees as I sway slightly on the branch. My thighs pinch together. *But Colt would never let me give up my dreams.*

His fingertips trace along the bone leading out to my

shoulder. He bends to kiss the hollow there. My stomach turns inside out. He murmurs, "Do you think the mirroring game is missing something?" Lips move against my skin, breath hot with each word. Goose bumps break out all over me—inside me it seems. His mouth traces up my neck, so, so slowly, and up to my ear, making my blood race with heat. He adds, "I've always thought it should include lips."

I wobble on the branch. He cups my hips, and I know he's going to kiss me. The notion makes everything inside twist and spark. To have this jammed-shut man-boy being so intimate, so gentle, wanting to kiss me . . . the other times felt like sudden emotionally charged reflex reactions to the situation, but this time, the way he's touching me . . .

But he doesn't kiss me.

His nose almost brushing mine, his breath is on my open mouth, on my tongue. I sip in air, hold onto his ribcage to steady myself; his body hums beneath my palms. He bends to kiss my shoulder, making my limbs go pulpy, then pushes aside the thin strap of the tank top to kiss beneath. The sensation rocks me. I grasp his waist. He presses against me, nibbles the hollow of my neck, and all I can think is that if he ever gets to my lips I'm going to faint.

When our eyes next meet, they ransack each other. I tilt my face, giving the all clear. He kisses the corners of my mouth, nudges my nose, his body heavy against my knees.

I open my legs, pull his hips to me. His breath hitches. Hands sweep up my back, lips brushing mine, nipping my bottom lip until I want to scream, *Kiss me.* When he does, his tongue slipping between my teeth, I wilt into him, in the clutches of the most powerful "warm bath effect."

He stops again, skims me with blazing eyes, checking in. I squeeze both legs around him. There's a grumble in his throat and he gives me his open mouth, more urgent now, pressing into me, limitless shoulders hunched, a fortress around me.

Time takes an extremely long changeover break. As the minutes crumble away, there's a wisp of possibility he won't abruptly stop and apologize and run away. He lifts me off the branch, my legs clamped around his waist, and leans against the trunk to settle us on the ground beneath the tree. He fists my hair, drawing my mouth to his.

He's kissing me, slow but urgent. He's not rushing. He's not going anywhere.

When he must be numb with my weight, I get up and reach for a hand. "Come on," I say, taking the lantern. We jump the rocks of the river downstream, the velvety night air wrapped around us.

The Purple Cave is initially a tunnel over the river where the canopy is low and thick with mixed foliage. The tunnel opens out on the left riverbank into a round, igloo-shaped space.

"When the jacarandas are in full bloom, the cave is completely purple," I say, stepping inside.

Years ago, the Raggers stocked the cave with a camping mattress, sleeping bag, pillow, and old cooler box containing pots for cooking on a fire. Before we reached double digits, we played house, two of us cuddled on the bed as husband and wife, while the other cooked. Then we swapped over. Aria always preferred to cook.

I sink to my knees on the single mattress, which is confettied with petals. Colt shadows me; his mouth on mine he tilts us sideways. I hold his face between each palm and he lowers me onto my back. The kiss deepens and the weight of him floods my senses. I swipe over the muscles of his back and shoulders. He groans and flops onto his side, scooping me up and gathering me against him as if I'm something precious that's about to disappear. He's big compared to me, his body tucking me in. I've never felt this safe.

The tangy green and soft honey smell of the woods is stronger in the cave. I listen to the wind in the treetops and our bumping heartbeats, and track the stars in the gaps of the canopy. Stroking the skin of his waist, I wander under his T-shirt to trace the chest muscles there. His eyes, filled with starlight, caress me. We communicate through our eyes and our kisses because there are no words that fit these perfect hours. When we're not mouth to mouth, he's breathing me in, cradling me, like I'm a memory he's trying to hold on to.

He doesn't push to go all the way, which I'm grateful for. Kissing and lying so close, our limbs twisted together all night, is enough, but it makes me wonder if he can tell I haven't done this before.

It's not until the dawn splits open the sky that I think of Jacob.

TWENTY-NINE

THAT MORNING, DAD HAS TO wake me. "Come on, lazybones. It's eight-thirty. Colt's waiting to train. It'll get extremely hot soon." At the mention of Colt, my belly levitates then plunges as though I'm on a trapeze. I pull the sheet over my head.

How is he up this early? "Ten minutes, Dad."

When I get downstairs, Colt's sitting in the kitchen with Dad. The sensations I experienced when he touched me last night take a repeat swim through my veins.

I mosey to the fridge, not daring to get too close.

"Morning," I say into the fridge, then confirm that Dad is busy on his iPad before crossing my eyes at Colt. He smiles self-consciously. I finish the carton of carrot juice in one long gulp, suddenly sure he's regretting last night.

Colt rinses his glass at the sink. "Beach run?"

We set off a few feet apart. I check in with him, but he's staring straight ahead. My stomach twists. Milo's words of warning come back to me, coupled with Colt's vow to swear off girlfriends.

"Wait up, dudes." I spy Jacob over my shoulder. "Okay to join you?"

"Sure," I say, my mood tumbling further. "I'm surprised you're not surfing, though."

"Been and conquered," Jacob says, out of breath.

Colt doesn't let up on our pace, and I guess he shouldn't—this is a training session. We stop talking when breathing becomes hard. Jacob is fast and fit, but as we launch up the hill, he falls back, and this time I don't pander to him and he gets left behind. He finds us at the summit, sprawled on the grass.

"I used to beat you up that hill, Harps," says Jacob, between gasps for air.

"I think you'll find we tied, and only because you held onto my shirt."

"Let's go," says Colt.

Jacob rolls onto his belly, groaning into the grass.

I struggle up. "I'll have you know I didn't sleep well last night. I might need a free pass."

Colt crosses his arms and cocks an eyebrow. "No free passes to the Aussie Open. You'll get your reward later." I can't tell if he's flirting, but his smile unbuttons me and my skin tightens with desire.

After lunch, Colt visits his dad, and I take a nap. Before I fall asleep, my mind cups the memory of last night in its palm. But it's ruined by imagining Jacob's reaction during our run if he knew that Colt had kissed me. I need to know what Colt's thinking. He hasn't made a move to even touch me today. He doesn't *do* girlfriends. This is going to be another "that will never happen again" moment. I'm shocked by how my heart feels as though it's been scooped out of my chest like ice cream. But how can I feel this way about Colt when Jacob's still sitting inside my heart, a place where he's reigned for so many years?

I startle awake in the pink afternoon light to the sound of Aria blow-drying her hair. She's left the bathroom door open, not caring if she wakes me. Jaw tightening, I get up, ready to slam the door shut. But before I can, I'm frozen to the spot at the sight of her.

"What do you think?" she says, watching my reflection and pointing at what doesn't need to be pointed out: she's cut her hair boy-short.

"Wow." I hold my expression neutral. "Pretty. When did you decide to cut it?"

"I don't know. Needed a change. Do you love it?" She double pats the nape of her neck. We'd always wanted our hair the same before.

I move into the bathroom and touch her hair, somehow sad. It's another sign we're growing apart, maybe needing each other less. Clearly, she's okay with that. But I feel as if life has ripped something away from me that I wasn't ready to give up yet. I want to hug her and never let her go, but something in her rigid posture tells me not to. Instead, I answer, "It's cool."

At dinner, Colt compliments Aria on her haircut. Mum and Dad have gone out with friends and Jacob joins us, unusually late given there's food available. When he spots Aria, he stops mid-stride and exaggerates a jaw-drop. He plonks into the chair next to me, smelling like he already swallowed a few beers.

"Which style do you prefer, Jacob?" asks Aria. "Mine or Harper's?" Jacob's lips move, but can't form words. He looks from me to Aria. As he's about to answer, Colt leans forward for a second helping of potatoes.

"It's a trap, dude," he says. "Stick with 'No comment.'"

Aria cuffs Colt on the shoulder and tosses what is now the sort of hair that can't be tossed.

It's Christmas Eve, and Aria's organized a pool party. Her friends start arriving along with members of Jacob's band. Aria confesses that while I slept away the afternoon, she asked Colt who we could invite for him and me and he'd suggested Kim and Natalie. Natalie arrives in a gunmetal-gray BMW. With her blunt-cut bangs, square chin, and feline eyes rimmed with dark makeup, she's the spitting image of Cleopatra.

As daylight seeps out of the sky, a starless, charcoal night lurches in. We take drinks and snacks to the poolside, and Jacob switches up the music before jumping from the deck railings into the pool. I taught him that years ago, but Dad threatened to dig up the pool and we haven't done it since.

Natalie attracts a crowd with a series of tennis tour stories, and whether she's telling them at the poolside table or in the pool, she's always next to Colt. After describing how the wind cost her three match points in a row at Wimbledon—"It literally gave my ball toss a life of its own"—she starts on an anecdote about Dominic Sanchez. I sit on the edge of the pool, watching her new groupies take in every word.

"I mean, Sanchez was about to compete in the final of the China Open and he's playing blackjack in the players' lounge," she says. "He lost his bet and afterward said that fired him up so much it helped him win the match. But Colt, don't try that—he's a total bullshitter."

Colt nods. "Zuri was lucky to make the final as it was."

Natalie wrings out her hair. "The headline read, 'Zuri lucks in while Sanchez lucks out,' which reminds me. I got stalked by a reporter when I went to the gym today. He wasn't interested in me, though. He was sniffing around about you." She rubs Colt's arm. "You'll have to be careful. He asked me if you get drunk or take drugs or steroids."

From the tilt of Colt's shoulders and the way his smile plummets, I want to shout at Natalie to shut up. I know she helps Colt, and I'm sure she's a great person, but I wish she'd go home. I'm trying to get Colt to relax and forget about the tennis world, like Milo asked. And it'd be nice if he paid a little attention to me.

Natalie follows Colt to a table, her fans in tow, while Kim mucks about with Jacob in the pool, getting tanked. I've recently overtaken her in the world rankings, but neither of us mentions it. She flings herself off the deck railings into the pool until Natalie yells, "If you don't stop that, I'll take my flip-flop to your bum. That goes for you, too, Jacob." Everyone cracks up.

But Natalie's expression turns dark when Kim ambles over and starts flirting with Colt, slurring and patting his arm. "Does only rubbish come out of your gob, Kim?" she scolds, but Kim has selective hearing.

My emotions are rolled up and dropped into a pinball machine when Jacob acts overly flirtatious with everyone, including me. I can't bear for Colt to see that. At the same time, watching Kim skirt around Colt makes me want to break her serving arm. I also can't decide if Natalie is just a friend to Colt, or a hopeful would-be girlfriend. Maybe last night was another one-off.

I take myself away from them and make small talk with

Jacob's band members until they're too drunk to make sense, at which point I seek out a lone sun lounger, nurse my juice, and monitor the dark clouds sailing across the moon.

My life is a chess game . . . and I don't know what the next move is. I should tell Jacob about Colt, but tell him what? That we kissed? We're together? But are we? I have no clue. What's the point of telling Jacob about a kiss that might never be repeated? He'd be hurt and angry. Especially as Jacob still thinks we're waiting to be together when Aria has moved on. I'm too much of a coward to have that talk with him. Or maybe I'm not ready to let him go forever.

I watch Jacob playing a game of chicken fighting. He's teamed up with Kim, and her legs are now wrapped around his neck. I realize that if they were to hook up later, it wouldn't worry me as much as it once might have. I feel as fickle as my ball toss.

Later, when most people have gone home, Jacob sprawls out behind me, straddling the sun lounger. He pours the last of a beer down his gullet. "Don't overdo the booze," I say, rubbing my always-stiff shoulders. "I don't want to be jumping in the pool to save you."

"I wouldn't say no to a little mouth-to-mouth." Leaning closer, he massages my shoulders. It's something he's done a million times before, but after everything we've said, after Dad's warning, why's he doing it now?

I shrug him off. "I'm good." But he peels away a streak of

sunburnt dead skin from my arm the way we used to as kids, flicks it, and moves closer behind me, kneading my muscles.

"When can we spend some time alone . . . to talk?" His lips brush my ear as he speaks.

Hopping up, I search the handful of partygoers in the pool, then the tables. Natalie is aiming jelly beans into Aria's throat and—crap. Colt's eyeing Jacob and me. Crap.

"Can I get you a drink, Jacob? Some water?" I ask, pulling a towel around myself.

"Good thinking." He waggles his eyebrows and slings an arm around my shoulders as we walk upstairs to the kitchen. I cringe, confused by the need to pull away. I *love* Jacob.

In the kitchen, he cracks open another beer.

"Shouldn't you switch to soda?" I prop open the fridge door and root around inside. I'm not even thirsty. Jacob moves behind me, breathing me in, his lips next to my ear, and massages my shoulders. I understand that he's doing this instead of kissing me, instead of cuddling me. And I'm sad for him. For us. But it still irritates me. We've gone over this, and it can't happen. "You're wasted," I say, more forcefully than I intend.

"Harper's right." Colt strides into the kitchen. "You've had enough to drink."

Jacob swivels toward Colt, and takes a swig from his bottle. "It's the fun police," he sneers. But Colt snatches Jacob's beer away and pours it down the sink.

Jacob squares up to him. "Who d'you think—?"

"Stop it." I slide between them. "Jacob, you *have* had enough, and Colt's had bad experiences with . . . Think about it, yeah? Back off." Jacob glares over my head and I wonder what Colt's expression must look like from behind me. When Jacob makes no move to back down, I push him backward and step him farther away from Colt. "Go swim it off. We're supposed to be having fun. It's Christmas Eve. I'll grab some mince pies, okay?" He peels his glare away from Colt and inspects me, his stance softening. Then he walks out, eyeballing Colt the whole way.

I whirl to face Colt. "Sorry. He's had too much to drink. He's having a rough time."

Colt grips the bar stool, ready to punch something. "He touches you too much. Does he—is there something going on between you two?"

This time, he's asked me straight out.

But what's the point of telling the truth now? The truth has changed anyway. Nothing can happen between me and Jacob anyhow. Isn't our brief relationship over and done with and therefore a secret better left alone? And how can I tell Colt when Aria doesn't even know?

Swinging around to open the pantry door, I step inside to find the mince pies. "I told you, we're like brother and sister. He's always tickling and fighting with me."

"And massaging you?"

"Yeah. I'm a sucker for it. My shoulders are always sore. Aren't yours?"

265

Balancing two Tupperware containers of mince pies, I bump the pantry door shut with my butt, then place the pies on a wire rack in the oven.

"Want ice cream with it?" When he doesn't answer, I look up. He's leaning straight-armed on the breakfast bar, head turned away. "Colt?"

"Double of everything for me," he says.

"Where do you put it all? Certainly not in that flat stomach I felt last night." The final words dribble from my lips, trailing off. I want to stuff them back in.

But Colt just laughs. "You felt pretty good, too." He brushes my arm with the back of his fingers, frisking my face with intimate eyes. My breath hobbles out of my chest and I command my eyes downward.

My cheeks flaring, I dip the ice cream scoop into a pitcher of hot water. I feel Colt's gaze on me and raise my chin. He slides a hand under my jaw, guiding me toward his lips, and kisses me, mouth warm and giving, and tasting like chlorine. My legs turn to pudding.

When he releases me, I'm holding the scoop in midair. He grins and takes it, dips it into the hot water, and pulls a ball of vanilla out of the tub. I grab some bowls.

"I didn't think you'd do that again," I say. "Every time you kiss me, you run away."

"Do me a favor and forget those first two kisses."

"You've been counting?"

He fails to flatten a smile. "I lost count last night." His neck flushes.

"But today you've acted as if nothing happened."

He keeps scooping ice cream, dumping one mound into every bowl. "I guess I'm still not sure if it's a good idea."

My stomach revolts into a ball of steel. I stab a spoon into each hunk of ice cream.

Colt wraps his fingers around the spoons in my hand. "But I do know you make the world a less scary place." His voice is low and smooth. "I can let my guard down."

I resist softening, tug free, and check the pies in the oven. When I turn back, Colt's leaning against the counter, arms crossed over his chest, a playful smile on his lips. "I'm sure your dad wouldn't approve, not right under his roof . . . And after what Milo said . . ."

But I'm hurt. "And because of what happened with that girl before. How it affected your game."

"Yeah. That especially." Colt's tone swings to icy. He straightens and loads the bowls onto a tray. "I'll take these down."

I wait for the pies to heat and for Colt to return, but the pies almost burn and he doesn't come back.

A skinny morning light sneaks around the curtains. I'm already awake. I hug a pillow and monitor the brightening dawn. Unable to face either Colt or Jacob last night, I'd gone to bed. But sleep had done nothing to improve my mood or resolve the secrets, the things left unsaid, the lines crossed. I haven't told Colt about Jacob and Aria's relationship, either, maybe because it's hard to talk about, but probably because if Colt knows that Jacob crossed the friendship line once with Aria, he may suspect the truth about what happened between Jacob and me. But should I even care what Colt thinks?

Wriggling into a damp bikini, I creep downstairs. It's Christmas morning, and the tree in the kitchen is surrounded by presents.

The sun still crouching behind the woods, I slide into the pool and my body opens up from sleep like a flower. The water is crisp against my skin after a humid night. Loving the sense of my own strength, I carve through the water, counting laps to still my mind. When my limbs grow heavy, I stop in the deep end and fold my arms on the ledge, my legs dangling. I rest my cheek on my arms and wriggle my toes.

Two hands capture my hips and Colt emerges from underwater. Arms as barriers on either side of me, his chest presses against my back, trapping me against the wall.

My insides whip up as if in a blender. "I didn't hear you get in."

He kisses me under my ear. "I've been watching you for ages." His lips brush my neck. I lean into him, rotate between his arms and soak up the brief warmth of his lips on mine. He looks toward the house, then pushes off the wall and freestyles to the other end of the pool. I wait for him to come back, to hold me again, but he tumble-turns and keeps going.

He does it again and again and I'm shocked by how much I need him to stop and kiss me.

THIRTY

MUM RULES CHRISTMAS—HER FLASHING EARRINGS
tell us so. A party hat propped on her bob, she presents a
turkey dinner fit for the Queen of England. As always, she's
invited Jacob's parents to join us so that Jacob can enjoy a
family Christmas lunch. Jacob sets himself up as barman
and makes piña coladas to snub his dad, who's brought
two bottles of Dom Perignon. "Let's see how long he takes
before he mentions the champagne," chuckles Jacob as he
downs his second cocktail.

The only time Colt and I spend alone is on a run before
lunch. We complete an hour's interval training, ending up on
the grass at the beach doing starfish impressions. Our arms
crisscross. Colt winds his fingers through mine and empties
a water bottle over his head to cool off. Just as I've caught my
breath, he rolls toward me and rests his forehead on mine.

My pulse pounds through me and into the earth.

Our noses almost touching, he pauses for an excruciating moment before brushing my lips open. But he breaks away again, pulling up enough to harness my gaze. Water from his wet hair drips onto my cheek. He wipes away the droplets, tenderly, as if they're tears. His eyes are smoky with desire, but they contain something even better—certainty. A promise of a future.

I slide my arm behind his neck until his mouth is on mine in the most exquisite, most perfect kiss in the world, because it contains a promise, too.

Aria must've put Colt on her Christmas list. She teases him, collars him to help in the kitchen, brings him orange juice and soda filled with cherries and cocktail umbrellas, and they chat easily and about stuff other than tennis. At first, it's comical, but then I realize Aria's probably a better match for Colt than I am. She's older, more earnest like him, and won't compete on the court.

While in the kitchen loading the dishwasher, I whisper, "Aria. Back off of Colt. He's my doubles partner, not your next boyfriend."

"I thought stealing *boyfriends* was off the table, not tennis partners." Her mouth in a hard line, she coughs, rubs her nose. "It's not Colt I want, anyway." She eyes Jacob, who's sitting next to his mother at the table. "I'll never be able to let him go." She takes a ragged breath.

I inspect Jacob. His expression is quick to jump into happy mode, but behind the clowning around, his mood yo-yos from wild to subdued. Aria must think her plan to make him jealous is working, but judging from the long looks he casts in my direction . . .

Something inside me shrinks and pinches. I silently promise to somehow make it up to Aria—to help her be happy again. And now that I'm feeling more sure of me and Colt, I have to come clean with Jacob. But I won't hurt him on Christmas Day.

After lunch, Jacob's parents leave. Everyone's relieved because they only talk about themselves, their cases, their triumphs, and argue elements of the law. Jacob's father is especially loud and forceful with his slurred opinions as he drains the last of the champagne; they drink like fish. His mother begins repeating how this is the only day of the year they take off work, as if it's something to be proud of, and that's the signal Dad needs to suggest a game in the pool. They'd rather be disbarred than play childish games.

Mum and Dad join the four of us for a rowdy volleyball contest, then after a leftovers supper, they go upstairs while we stay up playing cards. Although Colt positions himself next to me, his leg pressed against mine under the table, he's the first to go to bed.

"Sweet dreams," he whispers to me when he pushes back his chair. To everyone else he adds, "Not used to all these late nights."

I'm drifting into sleep when the bathroom door opens. I roll over, expecting to see Aria. But it's not her.

"Jacob? If Dad finds out . . ."

The shadowy figure looms nearer. "He won't. I need to see you, Harps."

"You've seen me all day." I suppress a ripple of annoyance.

"Without everyone else." He lifts the sheet and slides in beside me, wearing nothing but boxer shorts. "I'll go in a minute. Promise."

"Jeez, Jacob. What are you doing?" I sit up and lean against the wall, knees pulled up to my chin. "Last time you snuck in here in the middle of the night, Aria heard us. You've got to go."

He watches my retreat, his eyes pulsing with a hundred emotions. "I need to say this. I can't not."

I think of Colt, asleep downstairs, and wonder how this happened—sneaking around with not one, but two guys after hardly kissing a boy before. Is this growing up? I'm not sure I can survive it.

"Aria's going away in a month," Jacob says. "She'll be gone for a year or two. More. She'll move on. Jeez, she's already all over Colt."

Even the sound of Colt's name shoots a powerful tingle

through my veins and into my heart like a heat-seeking missile finding its target. "She's trying to get over you, that's all."

Jacob considers this, then adds, "Maybe. But she'll meet guys in Europe, and once that happens, we can be together. But in the meantime, she won't live here and it'll be easy to . . . Your dad won't catch us. I miss you. It's as if my life is over. We won't tell anyone until it's the right time."

Jacob is in my face, about to kiss me.

But this has to stop. I'm so gutless for not telling him the truth earlier. But what if he rants at me now, and storms around the room so someone hears us?

I take his face between my hands, search for the perfect words. "We can't do this. We can't lie. We can't risk tearing this family apart if anyone finds out. We've talked about this. We can only be friends, nothing more." I take a breath and then say the words I haven't had the courage to say until now. "Not ever."

He pulls away, balancing on his haunches. "What? Why not *ever*? Aria will move on." I put my palm over his mouth to hush him. He pushes it away. "Why not *ever*?"

"Because . . ." The words clump and stick together. I glance in the direction of the bathroom door.

"Because *why*, Harper?" His mouth distorts. "Don't you love me? Or is it Colt you love now? I've seen the way—"

"Because she gave up the Con for you."

Jacob's eyes widen and fill with something despairing, haunted even. His body hunches. "You said—"

"I'm sorry. I didn't want you to blame yourself. But do you see . . . how it means we can never tell anyone about us. She gave up everything for you."

"I hate myself for all this already," he mutters, balling the sheet. "And now it's even worse." Despair rolls off him in waves. "Remember when I said I would always protect you from dicks like that player's dad who riled you at your match?" I nod. Of course. It was the moment I fell in love with Jacob. "Now I'm the dick you need protecting from. You *and* Aria."

"No, you're not. None of this is your fault. It's no one's fault."

"It's messed up. It has to be someone's fault."

"Is it your fault we all live next door to one another and became the Raggers?" My pitch rises with certainty. "Is it your fault Aria fell in love with you? One thing I've learned recently is we make choices and then we have to live with the consequences. Aria chose to give up the Con. It wasn't your fault, and maybe it wasn't the right choice, but it was *her choice.*"

"What about my choice, then? I choose you."

"Guess we can't always have what we want." And with those words I wonder if that's Jacob's problem. He always gets what he wants. He asks for a music studio; it's built in three months. He wants a Jeep to match mine and Aria's, it arrives a day later. He wants a motorcycle; it's delivered to the door. He'd like six different guitars. No problem. His parents may think they're making up for the time they never spend with him, but instead they've created someone who can't cope with not getting what he wants. He might even want the things he *can't* have more.

We freeze with the sound of a thump and watch the bathroom door. The toilet flushes. A window slams shut.

When it's silent for a few minutes, Jacob exhales. "That was close."

"It's the middle of the night. Why would she *slam* the window?" We frown at the closed bathroom door. "You should go. Not through the window. Go downstairs. Leave through the laundry room. Aria might still be awake. She can't hear us talking. Just *go*."

His smile warps. "This can't be it. There has to be a way."

"I'm sorry, Jacob. But there isn't." My belly tangles and knots and I look away, knowing this is the moment his heart just got kicked across the room. By me.

THIRTY-ONE

CHRISTMAS ENDS ABRUPTLY.

When I come downstairs on Boxing Day morning, Colt's bag is packed and waiting by the front door. I bolt into the kitchen. He's alone at the table, downing a plate of pancakes topped with fruit. Jacob is worryingly absent. Mum's flipping pancakes to the sound of "The Phantom of the Opera" on the radio. She spots me and explains that Dad's caught the flu and Aria's asleep.

Mum pours batter into the frying pan. "I've never known Aria to miss chocolate chip pancakes."

"You're going today, Colt?" I ask. He nods through a mouthful, his stare fixed on the plate. I hide my dismay in the fridge, searching for juice. "But Milo's not back for two more days."

"Colt wants to get Milo's place cleaned and stocked up. He doesn't want to outstay his welcome here, either, even though I've *assured* him he's not. He's my favorite kitchen helper. Pancakes?"

Colt keeps chewing, meticulously loading his fork with sliced strawberries. My throat is thick with frustration. So we're back to "us" being a mistake. Or perhaps I was simply a diversion. With Christmas over, Colt's only focusing on the business of training and the final tournament before the Open. No girlfriend to distract him.

"Harper, I asked if you want pancakes?" Mum waves a spatula in the air, balancing a pancake. I shake my head, my appetite blown up with my heart. To buy time to find all the pieces of me and put myself back together, I make coffee. Mum keeps talking, but I don't hear a word.

The moment I sit at the table, Colt pushes back his chair and stands, plate not quite empty. *He always scrapes his plate clean.* "Thanks, Mrs. H. Please thank Mr. H for me. It was probably the best Christmas I can remember."

I'm vaguely aware of Mum hugging Colt, but when he refuses to meet my questioning gaze even though I'm standing right in front of him, I free-fall into a well of misery.

"Harper. Where are your manners? See Colt out, please." Mum lobs a dishcloth at me.

Colt walks out of the kitchen without glancing in my direction. I follow. He picks up his bag and opens the front door.

And I know I'm right. It's done. *We're done.*

I trail down the steps to where Colt's parked his motorcycle, willing him to get this over with, to get on the bike and ride away. Tomorrow we can start training and get back to normal. *If that's possible.* He doesn't get on the bike, though, and because my gaze is glued to the ground, I see his sneakers circle toward me.

"I meant what I said to your mom," he says, colorless. "I had a great Christmas. Hope you know how lucky you are."

I gather the courage to look up, to find a clue, then wish I hadn't; there's a hurricane swirling behind his eyes.

The edges of my mouth quiver. "Why are you going? Do you regret—?"

"I couldn't sleep," he barks, then reaches for a helmet and straddles the bike. He jams the helmet on. "I saw Jacob coming out of your bedroom."

A mountain falls on top of me.

It's as if a gust of wind fills my throat, because I can't get the words out before he fires up the engine.

And then he's gone.

Clouds collide above the house as I fall back against the brick wall, scraping my knuckles. Trembling, I push off the wall and run to Jacob's studio, bursting through the door. He's playing something maudlin on the piano, his back to me, and I have to yell to get his attention. "Did you talk to Colt last night—when you snuck out the house?" My body is rigid.

Jacob stands and comes toward me, reaching out to touch my arm. I flinch, and his eyes widen.

"No. What are you talking about?" His hand hangs in the space between us. "Did he bust us?"

I crush my face into my hands and slump onto the Lego sofa.

Jacob slides next to me. "Did he friggin' tell your parents?"

I shift my head from side to side.

"Then we're good." He rubs my hunched back.

What must Colt think of me? He'd finally let me behind his game face. He thought he could trust me, and now I've hurt him with my own secrets. And he'll be angry with himself for breaking his vow. If Colt dumps me as his tennis partner . . . What about Milo? Dad? I've messed it all up.

Jacob inspects my bleeding knuckles. "What happened, Harps?"

I swat at the tears, losing the battle not to cry. "Got a scare," I squeak. "Scraped them."

"Want a drink? For the shock?" I shake my head no. "Have you seen Aria?" he adds. But all of me is gaping open, and I can't speak. "I took the motorcycle for a spin to get McMuffins at about five this morning—couldn't sleep. Aria was walking up the road wearing pajamas. She'd obviously been crying."

I straighten. "Wearing pajamas?" I scrunch shut my eyes, as if to lock out what's about to come.

"When she saw me, she ran away." He gazes out the window and his face twists with sadness. "Guess she's still upset about the Con . . . and our breakup." He snatches a handball from between our feet, bouncing it over and over.

"I followed her, but she screamed for me to leave her alone and then ran down to the woods."

I rise off the sofa, legs like stringy elastic, hands fluttering, mind collapsing. My body tears with the truth.

"She knows," I choke out. A sob bulges in my chest.

Jacob drops the ball, whooshing to his feet. Hands on his head, he rotates on the spot. I dart to the door and he snatches my elbow. "I'll come, too."

A word balloons inside my throat until it explodes right through me. "No!" All the guilt and shame is rammed into that one word; it echoes across Jacob's bewildered, mashed-up face.

I fling open the door and run.

My bare feet batter the last of the jacaranda petals, now dark and shriveled, like tiny fallen angels. I charge down the path, trying to hold myself together. But there are too many torn parts. I seem to fly wide open. Bits of me hurtle through the air, never to be part of me again.

She's not at the Mother Tree. I spin in circles, and then race toward the Purple Cave.

Aria's sitting on the cooler box, her bare feet kicking at the mattress we'd once played with. When she sees me, her face falls open. She leaps to her feet, bends to retrieve her sandals, then throws them at me. They miss. I step closer. Her short hair makes her pink cheeks appear puffier, her bloodshot eyes bigger, her lack of oversized earrings starker.

"Go away! I never want to see you again." Her crimson

face is stamped with horror, as if I'm a monster about to attack. I brace against her anger, but can't stop sobbing.

"I'm sorry. Aria, please listen to me." I step closer. "We didn't—"

She slams a fist on either side of my shoulders and shoves me. "I heard *everything*." She stumbles backward. "You're in love. There's *nothing* you can say to make it better. You knew how I felt about him. I gave up the Con—" She throws the words at me, her usual smile pulled back into a snarl. "We swore a blood oath. You're my *sister*."

A squall stirs the dead leaves and petals into a whirling soup of debris around us. My hair billows. "Please listen to me." But the air is heavy with hate.

Aria opens the cooler box and throws a pot at me. Then another, and another. They hit my crossed forearms. She wants to claw my face off. "I suspected. I asked you straight up. I believed you because I didn't think you could do that to me . . ."

It's too late. There's nothing I can say. Although I stopped things before they got serious with Jacob, there's no undoing what we *have* done.

"I *hate you*," she screams, crouching and clasping her hands behind her neck. "Never come here again. You've taken *everything* from me. My memories. Jacob. The Con. My future. The woods are mine."

THIRTY-TWO

FOR THREE DAYS, THE BEGINNING and end of the world has been the edge of my bed. I stop training. I stop playing tennis. *I am no longer me.*

Every hope and dream I'd sewn into my heart unstitches itself.

I stamped out Dad's sparkle. Jacob is banned from the house. Aria never comes home. She stays at a friend's house before she goes to visit Mum's sister. After I've listened to Mum crying on the phone to Aria for the second time, I climb out of bed and tear at the tennis posters on the walls. Thunder rumbles closer. I want to crack every cloud in half, seize a thunderbolt, and stab it into my own chest. I slump to the floor, clutching my knees and rocking, surrounded by the ripped smiles of my heroes. With every flicker of lightning, they haunt me.

A week after the world implodes, my giant teddy Sharapova cuddled to me, I pull out of my first singles tournament of the year in Brisbane, refusing to hear the counterargument from Dad. He'd predicted this would happen, but to his credit he never says, "I told you so." I'm fined for a late withdrawal and Dad informs me the press have camped outside. They want to know what's happened to the girl they'd hung their hopes on.

One day bleeds into the next.

Before he leaves for the Brisbane tournament with Colt, Milo comes to visit. He settles next to me on the bed. His presence feels excessively big for my simple bedroom, like having the prime minister come to your home. He removes the aviators and I expect to see sympathy. I expect him to rub my back and tell me everything will work out.

"Your dad's explained," he says, his expression impenetrable and his voice too loud. "I'm sure it's painful, but why does throwing away everything you've worked for help? Will it solve anything?"

I don't deserve my dreams if Aria can't have hers.

"You did the wrong thing. You made a mistake. But are you going to pay for it for the rest of your life by giving up on yourself?"

It's all I deserve.

"Or are you going to grow up and tackle the consequences?" Tears pool under my closed eyelids. "I suppose you could lie there and give up. What will you do with your life instead?" He shoves over the stack of books next to the bed. "Lie here and read about other people's successes instead of having any of your own?" He stares at the mess on the floor. "We all approach crossroads in our lives and here's yours. Time to make a choice."

I glare at the ceiling.

"And Colt. I don't know what happened between you, but he refused to come here today." A rusty nail drives into my heart. "He's especially low about his dad and needs your friendship. It's going to affect his game."

Another person's dreams going down the toilet because of me.

I roll over to hide the tears from Milo.

The mattress lifts as he rises. "First Colt's father gives up on himself, then you do the same. Think for a moment instead of wallowing in self-pity. It's time to grow up. You made adult mistakes that had adult consequences. But you need to deal with them and go out into the world again to make better choices. If you don't, you're no better than Jamie Jagger. And I'm happy to tell the press that—and your sponsors, and your agent." Milo stomps out of the room and slams the door.

His sudden departure yanks a new series of sobs from me. I curl into myself, squishing my face in a pillow. When the door opens again, I wriggle closer to the wall, pulling the sheet over my head. "Please leave me alone, Dad," I hiccup.

"I want to tell you something I've never told a soul . . . not even Colt," Milo says, slow and precise. I grit my teeth against the next sob. When Milo says nothing more I sit up, pressing a hot cheek against the cool wall. The breath shudders in my chest.

He's over at the window, but the face staring out is no longer Milo's chilled, bemused one.

"Twelve years ago, I didn't try to stop Jagger going on that court, totally *betrunken*. He'd knocked me out of the Open and I was taking a day off, having a couple of drinks in a bar. He was, too. Only he had more than a couple. I even bought him one on my way out, despite him having a game to play that day. He was a cocky son of a bitch, always mouthing off. I thought he needed to learn a lesson. Later, I spied him staggering into the locker rooms. I could've tried to stop him, but instead I wished him good luck. I was young. I got it badly wrong."

I recoil at the sight of his trampled face.

"Big mistake, Harper. With big consequences. I played a big part in helping Jagger destroy himself. Christ, his wife had just died." Milo smacks the heel of his hand into his forehead. "I didn't know at the time, but it has eaten away at me every day of my life since. The guilt made me want to punish myself." His timbre becomes even softer, lower. "It's why my fiancée left me. I drove her away, because I thought that I didn't deserve to be happy. Could be why I never made it into the top ten as well. I believed I wasn't worthy." He swings to me, hooking his lips into a warped grin.

Fiancée? "Is that why you took on Colt for free?" I ask.

286

"No. Maybe. I followed Colt's progress." Milo moves closer. "Colt inherited all of Jamie's talent and drive, and then some. Except he's humbler than Jamie ever was. And less intense, if you can believe that. He's a safe gamble." Milo's eyes are glossy. "Don't do what I did." The corners of his lips arc downward. "Don't make yourself pay for your mistakes forever. A lifetime is a long time, *Dampfnudel*."

He opens his arms. I bowl into them, and he holds me, whispering, "This too shall pass," over and over, until I stop crying.

When he shuts the door behind him I starfish on the bed, staring at the bright squares of wall left by the posters. Milo, who has a handle on this world, also made mistakes. Who am I going to choose to be? A quitter like Jagger, a winner like Colt, or perhaps I'll live with regret my whole life like Milo.

I put on shorts and a T-shirt and lace up my sneakers. Then I run until my lungs split open, until the tear tracks dry, until the world stops being black and becomes a more normal shade of real.

I call Kim to ask her to train with me, but she reminds me she's at the Brisbane tournament with Colt, adding, "One less person with their claws out for my trophy."

After building the courage to call Natalie, she agrees to come over. If I can't fix Aria or Jacob or Mum and Dad, maybe I can be the friend Colt needs and help him reach his goals. He'll be lucky to get past the first round in the singles event at the Aussie Open. Mixed doubles is his ticket to higher prize money so he can help his dad get well. Jeez, he'd been staying in hostels and saving his money rather than eating so he could afford his dad's rehab. I'll concentrate on doubles and withdraw from the singles event. This is a short-term choice—for Colt.

Natalie is strong and no-nonsense, and makes me work hard. She asks me why I pulled out of Brisbane. I say I don't want to talk about it. But we become friends by the end of the week, and I let on that it's family stuff.

"You need to learn to compartmentalize," she says, sipping iced water in our kitchen. "Colt's good at it."

"What do you mean, compartmentalize?" I ask.

"Box up your life into separate compartments. Each box needs your attention, but they shouldn't overlap. There's your tournament box and your training box, your home life box, school box, whatever. And if you're at home, you nurture and pay attention to that box. Then when you're on the court, home doesn't exist. Only the box you're standing in exists. It's the way to stay mentally tough when other parts of your life get you down."

"Milo has me going to a happy place . . . when the pressure builds."

"Winning requires lots of strategies." She tosses a jelly bean and catches it on her tongue. "Just as you don't train one part of your body or do one sort of workout, you need lots of mental exercises to succeed. I wish I'd known that when I was younger. Instead, I became consumed with the idea that if I was a Rottweiler on the court, what sort of person did it make me?" She twists an invisible bracelet on her wrist. "The battle was within me, not on the court. I learned too late that who you are on court doesn't have to be who you are off the court."

The day before I leave for Melbourne and the Australian Open, I go for a walk in the woods. They're exposed and empty—the summer storms have decimated what blossoms remained, drumming them into the earth.

When I reach the Mother Tree, I climb onto the lowest branch and map the river toward the Purple Cave. Aria's final angry words slap at my heart.

She'd given up the Con for nothing in the end. And I realize I'm about to make a similar choice. Just as Jagger's decision to give up on himself and start drinking didn't bring back his wife, giving up on my singles career won't repair the rift in my family. I'll have to figure out another way to solve that problem, but what I do know is I'm no Jamie Jagger. And Colt said tennis brats are ungrateful types who squander their talent. I'm about to do just that. But I'm not a brat, either.

With a blast of adrenaline, I'm bursting with the need to prove it. I made some bad choices, but I'm not giving up on myself. That would be too easy.

This is my crossroads. I'm determined to prove Kominsky wrong.

My future is tennis, being the best I can be, written about in every sports section, living for the thrill of winning. I think of the children who collect autographs at the big events, how they look up to the players as if they're heroes who slay dragons, or gods who hurl fireballs. I want to be a hero to someone. That has always been the dream.

I decide I'm going to grab it with both hands.

I am Harper Hunter. I may be a daughter, a sister, a friend, and even a girlfriend, but none of that determines my future. Only I can do that. Tennis is the one part of my life that's down to me. Tennis is what makes me count in this world. And a Grand Slam is the biggest tennis event there is. Good thing Milo told me to think about it some more before he pulled me from the singles event.

It begins to drizzle, but I can't leave yet. Maybe it's because I feel closer to Colt here, or maybe it's because the ghosts of the Ragamuffins live in these trees and always will, and that makes me feel not quite so alone.

But as I take in the soggy ground, the gurgling river, the flowerless branches of the jacarandas, I realize it's over— the days we spent playing and laughing and loving each other in these woods are over, and I am alone. We all are. I need to grow up and stop gripping the past by the throat, and instead, reach for the stars.

A falling twig startles me.

"Up here." Jacob is high in the tree. He climbs down and straddles a branch. "Been wandering these woods for days now. Even slept here." He studies me with the eyes of a lonely child. "It's the only place I feel close to you guys."

I know he lost everything—his adopted family, his girl-friend, his second home, his chance at the Con. But even I can see that getting lost in the woods isn't going to lead him out of this mess. After Aria's skipped audition, he'd said, "Don't ever change," but what he meant was, don't ever leave; don't ever grow up. And suddenly I don't want to stay here with him, this aimless, ghostly version of Jacob left behind in the woods. Right now, he's as wrecked as these blossoms, never to bloom again, and if he doesn't choose to move on, he'll stay that way forever.

"Jacob. You have to move forward. We all do." I blink at the trees around us. "We can't be children in the woods forever. There's no future here." I jump down, reach for his hand and squeeze it. "Bye, Jacob," I whisper, tasting my tears on my lips.

As I'm winding my way back to the house, Jacob's voice ghosts through the trees. "But there's a future for us. I'll find a way."

THIRTY-THREE

OUR AGENT SECURES SPONSORED ROOMS for Colt and me at the official players' hotel, but I arrive in Melbourne alone. Colt and Milo fly in late, so I order room service and watch the sports news. Everyone's speculating about whether Colt has what it takes, if he'll pass the drug test, and if he has his father's temper. Mum and Dad plan to arrive next week—they're with Mum's sister in Canberra, visiting Aria before she leaves for Europe. Aria still refuses to talk to me.

The next morning, I wait by the water feature in the lobby, bouncing the heel of my tennis shoe on the gold-flecked floor tiles. I battle to pack some steel into my backbone. I'm sharing a car to the courts with Milo and Colt. I need to remain neutral—just Colt's doubles partner, his friend—because he won't want to hear any of my excuses. I'd lied to his face, I'd hurt him. That's the bottom line. And right now, he'll want to focus on his game, on winning so he can help his dad, not on why I'd lied. I'm just some stupid girl who could wreck his chances again. I have to put my own feelings aside and focus on my tennis, for his sake, for my sake . . . and for Jamie Jagger's.

When they step out of the elevator, I'm awash with nerves. Colt doesn't look up until he's two steps away. His gaze skids into mine, a detached, unsmiling mask in place.

I fold my feelings into the Colt box.

While Milo hugs me, Colt's attention flits around the reception area. Maybe he's in the midst of his match prep and has moved on from visualizing the win to making himself angry.

"Who've you got?" I say to Colt in the back of the people carrier, even though I've read the draw sheet. He'd stood aside to let me climb in first, and I figured he'd sit in the row behind me. He hadn't. And now my heart is trampolining around my rib cage. Milo, as usual, stays up front with the driver.

"I'm not in the mood to talk." Colt stares out the window.

He's a fortress without an access road. I wish I was anywhere but here.

Our arms bump when the car turns right. "Busy making yourself angry? Maybe I can help with that." I expect another retort, but something briefly alters in his eyes, like a crystal that sparks rainbows in the sunlight, only to become flat and dull when it swings back into the dark.

"You can put last week's tournament behind you, Colt," says Milo, twisting to peer at him. Colt lost in the second round at Brisbane, dropping his ranking back to 101. "It's done. Keep moving forward. Victories are the goal, defeats are the lesson." He braces himself as we take another mini-roundabout at high speed.

"If Brisbane was because of me, I'm sorry." If it's not the right time to explain everything, I can at least try to apologize.

Colt's mask slips right off. I can see how much I hurt him, squashed inside his face, before he forces the mask back in place. "I had a cold," he says, voice preset.

"That's from staying out all night at Christmas," I say. Milo swivels around, and Colt's glare says, *I can't believe you said that.* "Joking, Milo," I add. "He didn't put a toe out of line . . . unlike me."

"We all suffer family issues from time to time. You're here now," says Milo. "Colt respects that, don't you, Colt?" Colt broods out the window. "You're both on at eleven," adds Milo. "I'll tear myself in half."

When we're dropped off at Melbourne Park, Colt passes me my bag. "Good luck," he says and walks away, leaving me with Milo. I don't expect him to check back over his shoulder, but he does.

The true-blue Plexicushion of the Melbourne courts are akin

to the red carpet at the Oscars. Although I've played here as a junior, and again last year when I failed to qualify for the main event, I pinch myself. But then the two-inch negative version of myself that Milo sees on my shoulder shouts, "What if you repeat history?" I rub my shoulder as if to smother the voice.

I'm up against the American, Crazy Maisy—named for her off-court behavior and once ranked 48 in the world, but now 105 due to injury. I've fallen several places to 99. On paper, I should win. But no one knows I've lost my sister and my best friend, or that it's my fault my parents lost their children; that one plans to vanish in Europe, and Jacob is adrift in the woods. The spectators can't grasp how difficult it is to sever the bond between sisters and then play a game of tennis that could alter my future.

Although I win the coin toss and elect to serve first, my ball toss is all over the place and Crazy Maisy breaks my serve. Thinking about Purple Time makes things worse. Images of us in the Purple Woods charge into my head like savage ghouls—saying goodbye to Jacob, Aria snarling at me, Colt kissing me under the stars . . .

I can't do this. I ask for a bathroom break.

It's a timed break. I rush to the basin to splash water on my skin and glare in the mirror. Maybe I need to get mad. The problem is, the only person I'm mad at is myself.

Back on court, I play as if I'm twelve—unforced errors, heavy on my feet, lacking consistency. And then the biggest stroke of bad luck for Crazy Maisy saves me; she trips and lands hard. She hugs a knee and a linesman calls for ice, but she can't play on and retires from the match.

Colt's up in his qualifying game, but back to resembling a riled panther about to pounce. He doesn't even react to the cheering spectators when he stumbles and returns an impossibly long lob while on his knees. He pulverizes a higher-ranked player.

I smell trouble the moment Colt stalks across an interview room bristling with waiting questions. He plunks into a chair in front of the blue sponsors' board and the official invites the first question. Voices explode at Colt. He pulls the player's tag over his head and fiddles with it on the table.

"One at a time," says the official, pointing to a man in a baseball cap.

"How'd that game go for you, Colt?" asks baseball cap man.

Colt toys with a button on his shirt. "I executed my game plan. I won. That's it."

"Did you expect to win?" asks another.

"I won. What more do you want from me? That's what I came to do." I recognize the Colt I met six months ago in Cincinnati, the one who thinks he's alone, a targeted tower on a solitary island, vulnerable to attack from all directions. It makes him edgy, defensive, and closed off.

Another reporter calls, "We have information confirming Jamie Jagger is currently in rehab for drug and alcohol abuse. Have you ever failed a drug test?"

And the bomb detonates. Colt stands and addresses the

packed room. "If it weren't for the fact I'd get fined $20,000 for not attending this joke of an interview, I wouldn't—"

"Please take a seat, Mr. Quinn," says the press official.

"Or is it Mr. Jagger?" shouts someone.

Colt almost bites through his own jaw as he drops into a seat, then shoves at the chair next to him, sending it skating across the room. Milo pushes through the crowd and leans into the microphone on the desk. "Come now, ladies and gentlemen. Colt's won a tough match. Let's talk about that, and then let the lad go prepare for his next game."

When they're done with him, Colt charges out of the room without looking back.

The hotel's low-lit restaurant is packed with famous tennis players; I'd caught sight of the world's new number 1 ranked player, Dominic Sanchez, on the way in.

"It was as if I'd been set adrift in space to play tennis, and I couldn't find my footing or my serves or my ground strokes," I tell Milo, glimpsing another Hall of Fame player.

Before Milo answers, he beams over my shoulder. I check to see which legendary player he's spotted. But it's Colt, looking fit in a white, long-sleeved T-shirt and jeans. He slumps into the chair between us and rubs his face.

"One day down, seventeen to go. What are we eating?" He glances from Milo to me and back again.

"Steak?" Milo waves to get the waiter's attention.

"Double of everything," Colt says. He scopes the room, talent-spotting no doubt, then his gaze settles on me. He may as well have struck a match and set me alight. "Saw your game online. Not sure whether to lecture you or congratulate you."

I turn ketchup-red. "I'll take the lecture right now." I fiddle with a spoon, flattered he'd reviewed my game.

He swigs from a water glass. "What happened?"

"Is that honestly what you want to talk about? I mean . . . your interview . . ."

"I'm good. Talked to Natalie for about four hours. She set me straight. About a lot of things." Jealousy claws through me. "What happened?" he repeats. I rub sweaty palms on my jeans, thrown by his light mood.

"Harper says she felt like she was playing tennis in space," says Milo.

Colt smirks. "Looked like it, too."

"Seems Mr. Funny came to dinner," I say, playfully threatening to gouge Colt's arm with a fork. He snatches it away, placing it on the other side of the table. The waitress takes his order, batting her eyelashes, and I want to stab her with the confiscated fork.

Milo leaves to find the restroom.

Colt taps on his water glass, inspecting me. "What's really going on in that head of yours? You're going to bomb this tournament if you don't compartmentalize."

Suddenly I feel completely bruised. "Yes, I know," I say, defensive. "I talked to practically-perfect-in-every-way Natalie as well."

"Don't knock her—she puts me straight all the time, including where you're concerned." He'd been talking to her about me?

It occurs to me that Colt knows nothing about the casualties at home because he doesn't know about Aria and Jacob's past. I'm pretty sure Milo would've been discreet and given him the "family stuff" response to explain why I pulled out of Brisbane. Colt probably doesn't even believe that excuse. Therefore, Colt's referring to compartmentalizing what went on between us.

His knee bounces under the table. "What happened to thinking about Purple Time?"

"Gone." I make a "poof" gesture and spin a glass around and around. "Where's Mr. Grumpy from this morning?" The comment earns me a sexily raised eyebrow. I sit on my hands. "Not that you don't have a right to be grumpy with me."

His jaw clenches as he scrutinizes me. "I don't know a word to describe . . ." He suddenly hangs his head as if it hurts to look at me. "I'm grateful you're here for our doubles event. I'm in so much debt I can't afford any more rehab for my dad. I'm playing to save his life now. So I'm choosing to remember our friendship from here on out. You're a better friend than . . . anything else."

Milo approaches the table and pulls out a chair. Colt straightens. "You played great, Colt, but you've got to loosen up. Relax, or you're going to crack."

"Worked for me today." Colt tugs at the back of his collar.

"Up to a point, it will. But when the real pressure comes—"

"You may not have noticed, but the world's press is on my back in case I so much as take a drink of water that might contain drugs or alcohol. And if I don't win some big money, this whole dream will be over for me and Dad'll end up . . ." Colt breathes in deeply. The prickles he'd sprouted vanish. His voice low, he continues, "The interview. They goaded me to lose my temper . . ."

"Which you did, and gave them exactly what they wanted. People throw rocks at things that shine, Colt," says Milo.

The waitress dishes out plates of food, but my stomach churns at the idea that this could be Colt's last tournament. He inhales dinner, passing me the confiscated fork. "Avoid the hands and eyes, I need them tomorrow," he jokes.

"And please don't disappear after your game, Colt," says Milo. "Ten days to your first mixed doubles match. We need to get you on court together."

When we return to our rooms, having further dissected our games and opponents, Milo hugs me goodnight, and Colt chucks me a plum from the bag of food he'd bought earlier.

"Something purple," he says. He's trying to be a good friend.

I spend half the night attempting to conjure up Purple Time.

But it's gone.

THIRTY-FOUR

"YOU CAN DO THIS," MILO says, fiddling with the zipper on a bag. Colt's game is later today and it's just me and Milo walking through the gates of Melbourne Park. "You've come this far without Aria, and you'll keep going without Aria. You love her, and one day you'll patch things up, but right now you don't need her support or your parents' cheers to win this. You need to do this by yourself. *For yourself.*"

My Argentinean opponent, ranked 88, wins the toss and the first set. Purple Time has gone, and with it my self-confidence. I feel alone and exposed on that court and something—the loss of everything I once had—is sapping my energy. My knuckles seem to drag on the court as I haul over to the chair for a changeover break. The umpire stares, unsmiling, from his raised seat, making me feel small. I pour water over my head and use the purple towel.

Seeking out Milo, my heart bucks when I spot Colt beside him. He smiles—the one that could light up New York. I'm swamped with a warm thrill and overwhelmed with the conviction that while I blew it and we can't be *together* together, I want to be that friend, the one he turns to like Natalie. Does that smile mean he wants that, too?

When the umpire calls time, I snap up a racquet. "Come on," I yell. The crowd shouts their encouragement. Above the ripple of support comes one voice I can't mistake: "Choose to win." Colt.

He's still on my side. A sense of determination sparks through me. I won't be another Jamie Jagger in his life. My first serve kicks out an ace. "You got this." Colt, again.

I win each point just to hear him, even running for a drop shot so fast I can't stop in time and jump over the net. The spectators roar with delight, and I give them a quick curtsy, even though I lost the point. Colt's smile is a performance-enhancing drug. I don't lose another point, and I win the match.

Colt wins his game, too, and we're both in the final qualifying round. Sitting beside each other on an outside court, we wait for the mixed doubles hitting partners Milo has set up.

To break the ice, I untie my shoelaces, then his. "We need some mirroring practice."

He glances toward my lips. My pulse quickens as I realize we're both remembering our conversation at Christmas.

303

I push through the moment and plonk a shoe on his knee. He beckons for the other one.

"How about your net jump," he says, tying my laces. "I figure you'll make the highlight reel on TV tonight." He pats my shoes, and I get up to do his. When I stumble forward, he steadies me, his laughter blasting into my ear. He tied my shoes together.

"Milo would be proud," I say. "You're such a child."

When our hitting partners arrive, Colt puts on his game face, but can't help chuckling when they tease us for our calls, smelly Milo and purple child. I remember the bond rope, and we read each other's movement and energy, firing up when the other needs it, like on the tandem rides. We fist bump between points, smiling into each other's faces, somehow slipping back into our easy friendship.

As we leave the court, Colt gives me an approving back-slap. I smile so hard my insides stretch into a smile, too. He's no longer the intimidating stranger I once chucked green smoothie at. And he's become more than a friend.

He's my Purple Time.

THIRTY-FIVE

WE WIN OUR NEXT MATCHES and celebrate entering round one of the main event as wildly as two tennis players at the Australian Open can celebrate: with another training session. Afterward, Milo goes to meet someone for dinner, leaving us to return to the hotel without him. Hunting for something to say to Colt, I remember Milo's skeleton in the cupboard about Jagger. Yet *another* secret. I can't imagine how Colt would feel if he knew Milo could've stopped his dad going on court all those years ago. But it's not my secret to tell.

"What can you serve but not eat?" I ask Colt.

"There's nothing anyone could serve that I wouldn't eat," he answers.

"Maybe not a tennis ball?"

"Terrible joke."

I prod him. "Okay, let's hear your attempt then."

"Why should you never fall in love with a tennis player?"

Cheeks rushing with color, I bend to pick up my bag. "There are a thousand reasons."

"Because to them, 'love' means nothing."

I groan, and we walk toward the players' lounge in search of more cold water. We bat words between us until we find ourselves walking up to Kim at the bar.

"Congratulations. We're all in the main event," she says, raising a wineglass. Her boobs almost pop out of a skimpy minidress with spaghetti straps. "Wonder if we'll end up playing each other, Harper." Kim drains her wine and refills it from a half-full bottle. "Who would win, Colt?"

He pours water from a pitcher on the bar, then passes it to me. "My doubles partner, of course, but I'm sure it'd be a close game."

She sidles up to him. Too close. "I doubt that. I'd crush her like an empty Coke can." I hope she's joking and laugh into my glass.

Someone jostles Colt. He straightens and sweeps the room from over his shoulder. Dozens of curious eyes retreat. The players' lounge is infamous for its gossip spreading.

Colt downs the water, checks his phone, then me. "I gotta get out of here. You coming?"

"He keeping you on the straight and narrow?" asks Kim, already looking over my shoulder for someone else

to talk to. She's a cheetah on the prowl. "Don't you have tomorrow off?"

"Training tomorrow, and Colt's always up at the crack of dawn."

Kim kisses us both on the cheek, her breath thick with red wine.

Colt shoulder-bumps me when we get outside. "I'm always up at the crack of dawn? You should be careful how that sounds."

"Well you *were*, in Bangkok and Cambodia."

He jabs me playfully in the ribs. "Yes, but you're not supposed to know that." He's being lighthearted Colt—the Colt I wish would stay.

"And am I not meant to know how you sleep with your arm across your eyes?" I mimic him, raising my arm the way he does, and walk straight into someone. I gawp into the face of the men's number 1, Dominic Sanchez. He's a good-looking Spaniard, cocky, twenty-one years old, and he's gripping my shoulders.

"Ah, this is the jumping one. She nearly make love to the tennis net," says Sanchez. He looks over his shoulder at the six people in his entourage. They snigger as he gives me the once over. "And pretty."

"Sorry about that." I step back, forcing him to let go of me.

"I hope you keep your eyes open during matches, yes? I'd love for you to win so I can see more of those lovely

legs." He ogles me. I'm not sure if I'm more surprised by him or by Colt, who snatches my elbow and pulls me toward the exit.

Sanchez shouts, "Why don't you chill out and have a beer, Colt Jagger," And I'm suddenly pulling on Colt's arm as he rounds on Sanchez.

"Colt, no. Don't." But he's strong and drags me with him. "The media will say you take after your dad."

Colt stops and glares at Sanchez, who's holding up two palms as though he's a perfect angel. His entourage circles him. Arms rigid at his sides, fists bunched, Colt gradually turns away, still eyeballing Sanchez, then strides toward the transportation area. "He's an idiot who needs a brain transplant. Not worth it," I say as we wait for a car on the sidewalk. Colt's eyes crackle; they're a dark sky full of thunder and lightning.

"He's lucky I didn't punch in his face. How dare he say that stuff when I'm right there."

"That's guys for you. They're slimeballs. And it's not as if you and I are together."

Colt does a double take, then paces up and down like there's a tornado trapped in his head. Is he jealous?

"Someone left a bag of plums outside my room this morning. Know anything about that?" I ask.

"Probably some slimeball," he says, his expression grim. A car pulls up and he yanks open the door, waits for me to climb in, and says, "See you tomorrow."

He slams the door and stalks away.

● ● ●

Milo's a no-show for breakfast. When Colt and I spot each other across the restaurant, my heart stands to attention as a shadow passes over his features. He joins me and a waitress refills my coffee cup in an uncomfortable silence. *What's his problem?*

Colt orders the works and Kim slopes in, kisses us both on each cheek before dragging herself toward the juice bar for a Virgin Mary hangover cure.

"I think she's into you," I say.

"Too much of a party girl. And spoiled. She's going to throw it all away . . . just like my dad did."

"A tennis brat?" I ask. Colt thumbs his nose and silence spikes between us.

I fall back on a topic he'll always discuss, and ask about the Brisbane tournament. He slips into the trap.

"I needed to win," he says after he's told me every mistake he made. He taps a spoon on the edge of the table while I devour grape after grape.

"Maybe you should focus less on *needing* to win and more on the love of winning." I cut a grape and half of it jumps off my plate. Ignoring it, he leans on crossed arms on the table considering my words, and is about to say something when Milo appears next to us. We lurch apart.

Milo slaps a rolled-up newspaper on the table. "Okay. You guys screwed up yesterday. I've been doing damage control." He unrolls the newspaper, spreading it flat. There's a photo of Colt launching toward Sanchez with me pulling him back.

"But the press weren't there," objects Colt.

Milo waves his cell phone. "Nearly every person in the world has a camera in their pocket."

"Shit." Colt bangs the table with a balled fist. Our plates rattle.

"It's bad, but it's not terrible. At least you didn't hit the guy. Shame you chose the number one player in the world to pick a fight with, though."

"It wasn't Colt's fault. Sanchez goaded him," I say.

"Doesn't matter. Colt, you of all people cannot get caught on camera about to slam your fist into someone's face."

"I know, I know, Milo. Okay?" Colt says, popping his neck. "What now? Do I talk to the press?"

"Be prepared for their questions at the next media conference. They won't care about your match result. You'll need to stay in control. Don't do an impression of 'the Spitfire.'"

Training always cheers Colt up. We go for a run, then have some fun shooting hoops. I miss more often than not, but, in spite of everything, I crave the close physical contact with him.

"Let's hope your aim's better on court." Colt hauls me up after knocking me over. For a laugh, I pretend to be Kim and Milo playing basketball. To know I'm responsible for making Colt smile is better than holding the key to a treasure chest.

After another doubles workout, Milo rushes us into a cab. "Your parents arrive in one hour, Harper."

Colt needs a pit stop at a pharmacy, and while we wait, Milo turns to me. "You've had a good effect on him. He's more relaxed when you're around. You're a breath of fresh air—exactly the kind of friend he needs."

I peck Milo on the cheek. "I need a friend like him, too. And you."

We tell tennis jokes all the way back to the hotel until Colt announces, "Natalie Barbie's going to be in town." The cab rolls to a stop. "I won't make dinner tonight. Promise I'll have an early night, though."

A wrecking ball rams into my chest. Is this how Colt felt when he caught Jacob leaving my room?

Colt holds open the cab door for me, smiling. But it's Natalie who's putting the smile on his face, not me.

I dread to think what he bought at that pharmacy.

THIRTY-SIX

AT DINNER, I CHOOSE A seat facing the lobby and watch for Colt over Dad's shoulder. When I spot him, my heart warps. Colt's dressed in black jeans and a black cotton shirt, his hand at the base of Natalie's spine, guiding her outside. He never even turns our way.

And he's smiling.

Unable to stop imagining what Colt might be doing with Natalie, I don't sleep well. He's seventeen, girlfriend-less, parentless, and doesn't play his first-round match until the day after mine. He can do what he wants. But when I open my door the next morning, I'm surprised to find another bag of plums in the corridor. And my belly does a loop the loop when I stumble on Colt waiting downstairs with Mum, Dad, and Milo.

I'm playing Bisera Balakov, world number 41, in the

Hisense Arena. Every nerve is taut and twitching. Before I walk into the famous changing rooms, Colt says, "When I fractured your cheek and you made the choice to keep playing—that's when you proved you have the metal inside you to succeed. Believe it, okay?"

Colt hugs me, and I take the belief with me until I bump into Balakov in the rest rooms. How is it tennis opponents share changing rooms? That doesn't happen in any other sport, as far as I know. It's inhumane. Balakov resembles a bulldog. She's five years older than me and twice as wide. She eyes me like I'm a blister on her toe.

The arena is spaceship-like, with sloped rows of spectators reaching to the sky. Giant screens reflect me back at myself as I approach the chairs next to the umpire. My legs turn to jelly. I take deep breaths to calm the jumping beans inside my stomach. With thousands of eyes on me, I feel like the new student who sat down in the wrong classroom.

Milo and Colt watch me from the players' box. Next to them, Mum shrinks back into her seat, and Dad pats her knee. Colt's stare hooks into mine. He knows I'm feeling swept away by a surging river, about to go over the edge of the falls. I need a rock to hold onto. He blows me a kiss. I lift my racquet to catch it.

I win each point just so that I get to hear Colt's voice. I kiss the tip of my racquet between each game. And each time that Balakov eyes me like she wants to crush me, I return the look. This is a mind game, and this is my game face. If I start to wobble in my self-belief, I dig for that metal Colt mentioned. I compartmentalize Aria and stay inside my tournament box, and when Balakov falls on her butt after I've lobbed a ball high and long, I don't feel sorry for her. When she starts to argue line calls, I know I've got this. I send Miss Serbia home in two quick sets and don't even make it to the media room before a TV crew ambushes me. The interviewer asks if I'm Australia's new hope.

No more first-round graveyard for me.

Colt and I do a light training session after lunch and travel back to the hotel in the people carrier. In the gray afternoon light, the car ride is calming after the turmoil of the day.

"Good to see your parents last night?" Colt asks, sprawling next to me. My mouth dries and without tennis as a barricade, I'm aware how close he's sitting and can only nod in reply.

"I'm beat," he says, plugging the silence.

The two words reboot me. "Says the guy who didn't even play a match today. Late night?"

Colt beams. "Back by ten, Mom. Promise."

"But were you *alone*?" And there's my stubborn streak.

Colt whips off his smile and twists to read my face. "*Yes*. I was alone. It's not like that with Natalie and me."

Isn't that what I said about Jacob and me?

I should leave it alone. It's none of my beeswax, but an enormous part of me is confused. "Didn't look like it when you left for dinner last night. And you talk for hours on the phone. She's at your house at dawn on Sundays—"

"And she's a retired tennis professional who has helped me out and, I must add, helped you out, too." Colt bangs his head twice on the headrest. "She's a good person. A good friend."

"What did you buy at that pharmacy?"

He slaps his thigh. "Tiger Balm."

Even though I'm poking a tiger with a stick, I can't stop. Jealousy overtakes my brain. And he's definitely giving off mixed signals. "She's visiting you at the Australian Open. Seems *she* wants more than friendship."

"Maybe you need to learn more about friendship, then. You have your family here. I have no one, and Natalie offered to come give me some support." He rubs his palms up and down his thighs. "It's not like my dad's going to stop by."

My stomach writhes. *He's right.*

The car drops us at the hotel and we enter the lobby in silence. "I'm sorry. I didn't think." I hurry to keep up with him. "I guess I'm a bit jealous." The words stick like a pinecone in my throat.

After a couple of beats Colt stops. His mouth softens when he looks down at me. "You can never have enough supporters in that players' box, can you? And, by the way, Natalie's given you her stamp of approval—that's not a test many people pass. She thinks you're good for me. She's sorry she missed your game, by the way, but she had an appointment."

Angry with myself, I dip my chin.

Colt slings an arm around me, herding me toward the elevators. "Jealous, huh?" he says. "Friends aren't meant to be jealous of each other's friends."

"I kind of liked being a little more than friends. But then I'm a walking talking wrecking ball, and I messed it up." He removes his arm, and presses the button. "Am I allowed to ask why Natalie helps you with your dad if you're not . . . into each other? I mean . . . she's a saint."

Colt chuckles. "Saint Natalie. She'll love that." He slumps against the wall next to the elevator. "Maybe she can't let the tennis world go. Maybe she feels she owes my family for helping her out in Florida. Maybe it's because she understands where I am now; her mom died when she was young, too."

The elevator doors open, and Colt unhitches himself from the wall and follows me inside.

"About that friendship thing . . ." I say. Friends don't look at each other like Colt looks at me. They don't blow you kisses. He leans against the mirrored elevator walls, lips pressing together. "You know Jacob and I—"

He pushes off the wall, and for a moment I think he's

going to abandon me. The doors shut. Ramrod straight, hands balled in his pockets, he mutters, "I don't want to know. I don't want to talk about it." He glares at the ceiling grid.

"Then how will you ever know the truth?"

"I know enough, and it sucks." He remains in the center of the rising elevator, a rock that won't be moved.

"But you don't know *anything*," I shout, fists jammed on hips. "And if I wait for you to be ready, then the right moment to explain will never come. Did you know Jacob and Aria were together for two years? Jacob and I, we had to stay just friends because Aria is still in love with him and she gave up her chance to audition for the Conservatorium because of him. She gave up her dreams. Nothing really happened between us because we *couldn't* let it happen. A few kisses—"

"I don't want to hear this. And the details don't matter. I asked you if there was anything between the two of you, and you lied to me. More than once."

"But I *had* to lie." I throw my arms in the air. "We hadn't told *anyone*. And nothing was going on by the time you came for Christmas. I'd already decided it never could. So what was the point of mentioning it?"

"He came out of your room in the middle of the night, Harper." Colt's tone is unforgiving.

The elevator opens. I blow out a shaky breath. Neither of us moves. The doors begin to close and Colt jams the button and waits, staring at the carpet. "Your floor," he mutters.

I slowly pick up my bag. "That night you saw him leaving my bedroom . . . I didn't ask him to come. And we just talked. Nothing happened."

But Colt's a rock face I can't see into, go around, or climb. Stepping into the corridor, the doors close behind me and I wonder how life can go from crazy-amazing one minute to epically sucky the next.

THIRTY-SEVEN

COLT DOESN'T COME TO DINNER.

Both Natalie and Kim join us, and Milo excuses Colt by saying he's in full prep mode for his first-round match tomorrow. I hope our argument doesn't affect his game.

"He's putting on his game face," says Natalie, almost to herself.

"You mean his armor," corrects Kim.

As I'm about to hop into bed, I hear a knock at the door. Colt's smile is shamefaced yet cheeky, as if he's been caught with his hand in the cookie jar. I can't help but grin back, heart skittering around my chest.

"I need a good night's sleep, and I won't get it if I go to bed angry," he says, shutting the door behind us. I pick up the remote and point it at the TV, pressing over and over, but it won't switch off. He covers my shaking hand with his, takes the remote, and switches the set off at the screen.

"You were right." He grips the back of his neck. "I didn't know about Jacob and Aria. After you . . . explained . . . I sort of get why you couldn't let anything happen." He shifts from one foot to the other. "And when I caught Jacob, I did assume . . . the wrong thing. Bottom line is I trust you. I believe you."

I cross my arms, grabbing my shoulders.

"Besides"—his intense gaze shocks my heart—"I can't get you out of my head." He exhales loudly. "I've tried to . . . but you're . . . Then, when Sanchez . . . I guess I got jealous. And I'm glad you were jealous of Natalie." He hunts in my eyes, begging me to read his mind.

I don't dare breathe.

"I'm rambling. I'm not good at this pouring-your-heart-out stuff." He veers away, shaking out his hands as if he has pins and needles. "The point is, I can't think about you now because I'm at a Grand Slam, and that's where my head should be. Put up with me? I can be moody at tournaments but I need you to know . . . in my head we're good. And I hope we're good in your head, too."

I edge closer.

He steps back. "I've got to go." Grinning wildly, he crosses his forearms to warn me off. I punch his bicep and laugh, but inside I'm pleading him not to go out that door.

"You came and said all that, and now you're leaving?"

"I'm not mad anymore. Are you?"

Rubbing my arms, our eyes lock. "I wasn't mad in the first place. Just sorry . . ."

He crosses the space between us, and his mouth finds mine. My body's throbbing. I want more and press against him, but he ends the kiss. "And *that's* why I need to go . . . *right now.*"

The door shuts and every cell inside me is singing again.

Though I'm knocked out in the third round, it's farther than I ever hoped to go. It's a *Grand Slam*. Colt's a picture of determination, as though our conversation never happened. But his barriers have chinks of light—when he sits closer than necessary in the car or carries my bags or takes an elbow to steer me through a crowd.

We fist bump our way to victory in the first three rounds of the mixed doubles event and the media goes crazy with what's dubbed the *Australian Invasion*. They report our match play as entertaining—almost a dance. We move and think as one.

Colt advances to the fourth round. The night before his match, Natalie is leaving to check on Jagger. We gather for a goodbye drink, everyone except Kim, who lost in the first round. She had a public blowup with her dad, a man built like a tree with a clump of bushy red hair, after he fired her coach. Every night, they go sharking around the players' lounge for a new one.

"You *have* been more relaxed, Colt," says Natalie, the dim orange light in the bar making her appear deeply tanned. "I saw you wave at the crowd yesterday. I almost died of shock."

Mum nods from a bar stool. "The *Morning Show* presenter said you're less panther, more pussycat."

Colt grimaces. "Just what every guy wants to hear. She also said it seems like I'm not taking after my dad. *That* I did like."

Natalie kisses his cheek and wishes him good luck. "Focus on your game. I'll take care of your dad." To me she whispers, "I'm glad he has you." She presses a jelly bean into my palm. Colt overhears and looks down at me as if he lost something in my eyes. My skin evaporates, and I'm a mass of humming.

I pop the candy in my mouth. "What's with the jelly-beans, Natalie?"

"My mum used to give them to me to cheer me up. Before she died, she said each one contained all the wishes she wanted me to have. They're little capsules of possibility."

After I hug Natalie goodbye, I shift back to Colt. "How are you coping with the pressure if you're not making yourself angry anymore?"

He places a couple of jelly beans on the bar. "I still want to pulverize my opponent, but I remember what you said once: I do it because I love winning, love tennis, not because I *need* to or am angry. And thanks to you, I found my own Purple Time. I've never had a memory I could use before."

I check my parents, but they're chatting away with Milo. "Is it kissing me?" I tease.

Colt chuckles. Shaking his head, he focuses on his feet. "No. Because kissing you exercises the wrong muscles."

Eyes popping, I snort into my orange juice. He rewards me with his deep belly laugh. "It's the night we climbed the Mother Tree in the dark. Above the canopy—that vast sky. I felt small and grateful to live on this earth—to be born with this talent. It was kind of otherworldly. It felt like flying or like being in heaven. I felt closer to my mom."

"The warm bath effect?"

The heat imprint of his hand fades from the wood veneer bar, and he rolls a jelly bean into my glass. "Except I've renamed it the Harper Effect."

Colt makes it into the quarterfinals where he'll play Dominic Sanchez, a result the press prayed for. They pester Colt for a comment. He confirms he's just fine about playing Sanchez. His gaze trained on me he adds, "So long as he remembers his manners."

The match is a twilight game and while we wait in the

player's box in the famous Rod Laver Arena, I can practically feel the atoms in the air colliding with excitement. The announcer introduces Colt and he enters the arena to applause and a million camera flashes; it must be like standing in the middle of a star shower. He's composed, focused, strong. As is Sanchez, who saunters onto the court fist-pumping to the music coming from huge, orange cans. Sanchez settles next to the umpire, eyes closed, feet tapping, hands whirling as if he's dancing at a private party in his head and there aren't fifteen thousand people surrounding him.

Near the end of the first set, Sanchez is winning 5–4, but he's questioning line calls and then asks for a bathroom break. Colt strolls to his chair and rummages in a bag while he waits. I'd come across a navy blue towel with white stars during a shopping excursion with Mum, and secreted it into his bag. He finds it now and comically drops the towel on his upturned face. The spectators roar.

When play resumes, they win a set each, but Sanchez keeps the balls slamming at Colt, adapting his game to bring Colt to the net more often, a place Colt doesn't favor. Sanchez's serve reaches 150 mph. And even when Sanchez hits his winning shot, it's a result that'll earn Colt a fairytale amount of money and a lot of press coverage.

While Sanchez struts around signing autographs, Colt jumps the barrier and climbs through the crowd to the players' box, where Milo, Mum, Dad, and I have spent three hours cheering and half crying over returns he made that shouldn't be humanly possible. He tugs me against him, kissing me with all the passion of a guy who was holding back for a long time, but doesn't want to anymore.

The media embraces their new scoop in the next day's news, especially loving the astonished expression on Mum's and Dad's faces when Colt kissed me. Sanchez's comment about Colt stealing his airtime is often quoted: "The Australian Open is a tennis tournament, not a kissing contest."

Milo plays hardball and agrees with Sanchez—we still have a mixed doubles final to win. He wags a finger at us during our post-match analysis meeting. "He who chases two rabbits at once will catch none."

THIRTY-EIGHT

I'VE JUST STEPPED OUT OF the shower when Colt sends me a text: *Meet me in the bar.*

I'd left him downstairs with Kim when Dad insisted I go to bed. Our next mixed doubles match is the day after tomorrow. I hated the greedy way Kim was grazing over Colt when I swung around to give one last wave.

I sneak past Mum and Dad's room—Dad seems to think that by kissing Colt, I'll lose my ability to play tennis. He keeps muttering about how we've come this far and not to mess it up.

Colt's standing next to Kim, a square lightbox casting an oblong beam that cocoons them. She passes him a glass of champagne, which he puts down on the bar without sipping.

"Hey, guys," I say, hooking my fingers into the pockets of my jeans. Colt slings an arm around me and gives me a chaste kiss on the lips, but with a glance heated enough to set fire to Kim's cocktail.

"Get a room, you two," she says, lips knotted.

"See you later, Kim," Colt says. He leads me outside to where a Harley-Davidson is parked. He rattles keys in the air. "Always said I'd reward myself with one of these."

I gasp. "You bought it?"

He strokes the wide handlebars and the seat as though the bike is a pet. "Not yet. For now, hiring it for the rest of the tournament is enough." He passes me a helmet. I take it, reluctant.

"I've never ridden a motorcycle." I stare at the shiny hunk of red and silver metal. He takes the helmet and pushes it onto my head, and fiddles with the straps. "I don't know if I can."

"Have I found something Harper Hunter's afraid of?" He steps back. "You don't have to come. But I want you to. And I've never wanted anyone with me before. It's usually my escape. Makes me feel like I'm flying."

"You said you liked being above the Purple Woods canopy because it made you feel like you were flying. That's twice."

Colt scuffs his foot at the back wheel. "When I was a kid, I thought dead people could fly . . . like angels. I used to pedal like crazy on my bicycle, down the hill near our house, put my arms out and pretend to fly so I could feel closer to my mom."

I pass the second helmet to him and straddle the bike. His smile fills every edge of his face. I shelve Dad's warning. Time to make my own decisions, and Colt makes me feel safe. My cheek mashed into Colt's back, the bike revs and shoots forward. Through half-closed lashes the streetlights fuse into streaks of color. I shut my eyes. The hot wind whips us and it's easy to believe we're flying, just Colt and me, somewhere between two worlds.

Later, we stroll along the Riverwalk holding hands. Each time Colt's thumb sweeps over the back of my knuckles, I get the urge to kiss him. On impulse, I stand on tiptoe for a quick peck, but he bunches me into him. He kisses my mouth open and doesn't stop, right there in the middle of the sidewalk. When a couple of cars honk and someone whistles, he kisses me deeper, lifting me into the air as if to say, *Go away* to the world.

Eventually, he smiles into my mouth and sets me down. I cling to his elbows, staying caught in his gaze.

A cheer erupts, and several pedestrians encircle us. They're staring like we're rock stars, and thrust shopping lists and notepads forward for autographs. After we sign our names, Colt links his fingers through mine, and we run down the sidewalk and across a bridge. I'm laughing and he's whooping, and I hug myself inside because I've found the real Colt.

He stops in the middle of the bridge to appreciate the view. The moon shines a path across the water, a jetty made of light. "We're doing exactly what we want tonight," he says.

We cross the lawn of a park until we wander under a vast tree. Colt stops and cases the branches. The next moment, he's scaling it. I chase him and we climb until we can't go any higher. We take in the night sky, faces shining. The moon is so close I can see its craters, as though someone took a zoomed-in photo and hung it on a star just for us.

Colt watches me, unmasked.

"Come here," he says, his voice gravelly. Climbing across to where he's leaning against the trunk, I straddle the branch, facing him. I caress his face, this once-upon-a-time stranger, serious and unreachable. He leans his cheek into my palm, a lion tamed. I shuffle closer, needing to kiss him.

His eyes touch mine. My heart becomes a window and it flies wide open; love flares hot and strong.

My body trembles. The kiss lasts and lasts and makes the stars sizzle behind my closed eyelids. When I open them, the stars are trembling, too.

In the elevator at the hotel, Colt pushes the button for my floor. I press the floor number below mine. His brow puckers for a miniscule moment before he understands. He looks at me as though he's going to self-combust. "For a little while," he mumbles. He squeezes my hand when the elevator doors open, crushing my fingers as we approach his door. "I'm not sure this is a good idea." His eyes flare.

"Aren't we doing exactly what we want tonight?"

He swipes the key card too fast, over and over, until I double over in hysterics and he leans his forehead against the door, chuckling.

When the door eventually clamps shut behind us, I pull his mouth to mine. He groans and pushes me against the entry wall, kissing me back. My fingers drive under his shirt and he tucks me into his body.

I'm unbuttoning his shirt when he pulls back. "I'm not sure I have the willpower for this. I *am* only human," he says. I bend to kiss the triangle of chest I'd revealed.

"I don't need you to have any willpower." Colt's rib cage heaves and his mouth grabs mine. He walks backward into the room, drawing me with him. We topple onto the bed. My bones liquefy. He straddles me, pushes my hands into the pillows, then lowers himself to caress the exposed skin of my hips with his lips. I'm dizzy with wanting him, and the world blurs as he kisses my clothes off.

I stir once in the night, draped in Colt, and it's like prodding awake a hibernating bear. His hunger for me springs off him as he scoops me up. Our eager mouths crush against each other. My body blazes. He rolls us, settling between my legs. Arms snake underneath me, lifting my hips. He guides and I follow, and we no longer move as two separate blocks of ice, knocking and colliding, but instead like water in a wave pool, shifting and rising as one.

He lets my mouth go when I throw my head back to grab air, kisses my arched neck, my ears, my shoulders, enhancing the sensations ripping through me until I cry out. His gaze locks into mine, and we're flying together again.

THIRTY-NINE

THE EARLY DAWN LIGHT BRIGHTENS behind my eyelids—we'd forgotten to close the curtains. The clock radio, next to two empty condom packages, reads 5:44. I'm lying on my side with Colt behind, mirroring the curve of me.

It's Colt who's woken me, tracing fingers along my arm. I press into him. He lifts onto an elbow, thumbs my bottom lip, kisses me slowly. I soak him up for later.

"Better get you back to your room before your dad buys a shotgun," he whispers. I snuggle closer.

"Before I met you," he says, "Milo said I was a tightly packed parachute. All I needed was for the right person to come along and pull the rip cord and then I'd soar." He nibbles my ear. "I figure you might be that person."

"That's weirdly poetic," I whisper. "Is that your way of saying you like me?"

"No," he says, nose brushing my jaw. "It's my way of saying I'm in love with you." His smiling mouth finds mine before I can respond.

When we walk to my hotel room, I stay tangled in Colt.

"Now you've done it," he says, lips moving against my temple as he speaks. "Us Jaggers are like bald eagles—we mate for life."

"You're a Jagger now?"

He leans his forehead against mine, arms tugging me in. "I've always been more like my dad. With you at my side, maybe I won't totally follow in his footsteps."

I don't care if I've had three hours' sleep and have to train today. I don't care about Milo's warning. I don't care that when I switch on the TV, the news is broadcasting a photo of Colt and me kissing on the Riverwalk sidewalk with the headline, "Australian Invasion Stops Traffic." All I care about is that I'm in love with Colt Quinn . . . and he feels the same way about me.

At breakfast, Mum and Dad see the headlines and lecture me about sneaking out.

"But Colt and I have been together—secretly—since the first round," I argue. "The only thing that's distracting me is you wanting to put a stop to our relationship." They actually seem to take this in, because the subject gets dropped.

Safe in my bubble with Colt, we reach the mixed doubles final. The country is tennis crazy. Strangers in the street take photos of us on their phones, ensuring the Australian Invasion goes viral.

On the day of the final, we face each other across the bench seat in the famous changing rooms. The timber lockers create a hushed wall around us. "When you first step out there, it's overwhelming," says Colt. I remember how overwhelming the Hisense Arena was, but that was third round, not packed and a much smaller stadium than the Rod Laver Arena. I want to knot my fingers with Colt's for reassurance, but he's all match-psyched. "Stay prepared. The stadium is bigger than you realize when you're the one on court. Thousands of people have come to watch you. But keep settled. Remember Purple Time."

"I told you, I lost Purple Time."

The official beckons us and we make our way into the tunnel, lined with the giant-sized faces of past winners. "You didn't get it back?" asks Colt.

"Sort of. My Purple Time became you." Colt frowns. I bump shoulders with him, even though there's a TV camera trained on us. "It's okay. It was time to leave the woods."

I almost reach for Colt when we step out on court, though. The stadium is so huge it's like being swallowed by a whale; beyond the rising walls of faces is the open mouth of sky above.

In mixed doubles, the weak link is almost always the

woman, and Grigor and Katarina aim close to 80 percent of their returns at me. They work to tire me, then they'll target Colt. We use the same strategy. But I'm fitter than ever and used to returning Colt's massive serves, meaning even Grigor's doesn't faze me. What I'm not prepared for is Grigor's serve as it slams into my shoulder when I'm not even receiving.

Colt's beside me in an instant. I'm more shocked than anything, legs shaking. "I'm okay," I say, lifting the shoulder up and down. Grigor comes to the net to check on me; he'd risked losing a point. To hit me, his aim had to be way off on purpose.

"Watch it," says Colt, pointing his racquet at Grigor. Grigor dismisses him with a flick and saunters back to the baseline. Colt and I communicate using codes and remember the bond rope. We fist bump between points. Colt suggests new strategies behind a tennis ball held to his mouth. But half an hour later, when we've just won a tie breaker, Grigor's serve slams into my arms again when I'm not receiving. This time, the crowd boos and hisses, and this time Colt throws down his racquet and marches to the net, seemingly determined to rip Grigor's hand off so he never serves again. Grigor stays back, shrugging repeatedly to the umpire.

I play-punch Colt's arm. "Don't, Colt. I'm fine. Stay focused." Colt clenches and unclenches a fist, glowering at the ground. "We got this. Just fly with me."

The corner of Colt's mouth quirks up. He cuts to me, then Grigor, then the spectators. The crowd roars then chants, "Colt and Harper," until our names mesh together into one: ColtandHarper. I feel superhuman. Queen of the jungle.

Grigor and Katarina don't have a hope. They're not only fighting the crowd, but Colt and I flow together like we're each other's shadows.

It works out that I get to serve for the match. Colt passes me a ball, kissing it first. The spectators erupt until the umpire instructs them to take their seats.

At the baseline, before I perform my usual five-ball bounce, I check in with the players' box. Milo leans forward, elbows on juddering knees, fingertips covering his lips. Dad's arm surrounds Mum. I smile on the inside. After everything, they're here, supporting me and loving me. I'm the luckiest girl in the world.

Bounce, bounce, bounce, bounce, bounce.

I toss the ball dead straight, flick my wrist and launch the fireball across the net. Grigor returns it down the middle. Colt shouts, "Purple child." I take the shot, forcing Katarina back to reach the high ball. She lobs it, but creates an ideal opportunity for a drop shot from Colt.

And that's it. We've done it. We've won the Australian Open. Laughter bubbles out of me. Colt ditches his racquet. I rush at him and he lifts me, spins me, and the world whirls in a kaleidoscope of color.

FORTY

AT OUR CELEBRATION DINNER, EVERYONE'S upbeat. Dad even mentions Aria—she'd changed to an earlier flight and now she's in love with Rome, where she's landed a job as a cloakroom attendant at the Teatro dell'Opera. Colt wants to move his dad into a better neighborhood and admit him to the best rehab center until he's ready to cope. Milo is nicknamed Magic Milo by the media for creating us out of fairy dust, and Colt is no longer portrayed as moody and short fused like his father. Now he's the hero, protecting his partner—on court and in life.

When we get back to the hotel, close to eleven, Colt whispers, "Meet me in the bar." My legs turn to milkshake.

But it's not Colt who's waiting for me.

"There she is," Jacob shouts when he sees me, rising from the bar stool. He claps, slow and deliberate. A few people pretend not to notice. He lifts the wine bottle next to him and swallows a long swig.

"Jacob?" I tread closer, uneasiness splashing through every organ.

"I'm just about as great as always. Thanks for asking." This time, I hear the slur in his words. He glugs from the bottle again. "And thanks for the birthday card last week. My eighteenth was a blast."

Oh no. "I'm really sorry. I was so focused on . . . It's no excuse." I tug him out of the bar and across the lobby. When we get outside, he stumbles into a heap on the sidewalk. Red wine sprays onto my white jeans. Jacob hoots and rams the neck of the bottle to his eye, as if looking into a telescope.

"Gone," he says, rolling the bottle away. It gathers speed across the concrete and thumps into a streetlight, spinning off again. He gets up, an octopus arranging its tentacles, and steps forward as I step back.

"You're tanked. What's going on, Jacob?"

"What's going on is that I don't care. Why should I, Harps?" His bloodshot eyes narrow into slits.

It's early February, and I don't have a clue what he's decided to do now that he's not going to the Con. "I'd suggest going for a walk to talk, but maybe tomorrow," I say. "You need to sleep it off. Tomorrow, yeah? Where are you staying?"

"What's there to talk about?" he snarls at me, revealing wine-stained teeth. "Aria's three thousand miles away, you're busy letting every media outlet in the world photograph you sucking face with Colt, and I'm left behind with nothing."

That would hurt. I hadn't even thought about how it must feel for him to see Colt and me kissing, out of nowhere on some news broadcast. I'm so cruel. Thoughtless. Something inside me collapses, crinkles into itself, becomes very small.

"You forgot about me pretty fast, didn't you, Harper? Not even one text."

"That's not true, but I don't know how to . . . to be with you anymore. I don't know how to be your friend." It takes everything I have to stop myself reaching for him.

His anger-saturated face crumples with tears. "I thought you loved me."

"I do. I always will." But the words turn rabid on my tongue when I think of Colt. "We're the Raggers," I add. "All for friends and friends—"

Jacob seizes me, shakes me hard, breath sour in my nostrils, as though he'd slept inside that wine bottle. "The Ragamuffins are gone. Everything's gone. Except . . . I still love you." He doesn't stop shaking me and I go ragdoll limp. I scrunch my eyes to avoid seeing the pain sprawling across his face.

My mouth warps and tears rush my cheeks. "I'm so sorry, Jacob."

"Is that it? That's all you've got to say to me. You're sorry?" He slaps my face. His expression reels from angry to remorseful. "Shit, Harper—"

Suddenly furious, I wrench my arms from his grip just as there's a flurry of motion next to me, then a stinging flesh-on-flesh sound. Jacob jerks away and is lying flat on the sidewalk with Colt towering over him, a fist poised midair.

"No, no, no, Colt." I lunge forward. Colt straightens. I drag him back, canvassing for camera flashes. Jacob stumbles upright. Too drunk to gauge Colt's strength, he butts into Colt's stomach. Colt stays firm and shoves him back, but when Jacob pounces again, Colt punches hard and the crunching sound makes me wince.

"I mean it, Colt. Stop." I run into Colt from the side, pushing him away from Jacob, who's staying on the ground this time. "He's wasted. He doesn't know what he's doing."

"He hit you. What the hell's going on, Harper?"

"Don't get the wrong idea. Nothing's going on. He was in the bar when I went to meet you. . . . He's angry. He saw the stuff in the media . . . you and me . . ."

Colt's face moves from open to sealed tight. "He's in love with you. Do you love him?" My throat closes up. I can't breathe. Someone wrapped my head in cling wrap.

I consider Colt's straight, strong shape, holding himself like he owns the ground we stand on, yet inside he's not half as strong. And I size up Jacob, whose beautiful face is covered in blood and gasping for air; Jacob who I've known most of my life and will always love. Jacob who is also injured inside except this time, by me. I can't let him hear me tell Colt I don't love him. Seeing Colt and me together in the headlines is what drove him to this in the first place.

Silence sucks at my brain.

Colt's face slams shut. He stalks toward the Harley, jumping astride it in one movement.

Jacob sits. He reaches for me. "I didn't mean to hit you . . . I'm such an idiot." I should go to him.

Colt guns the motor. It's a split-second decision.

I run after Colt.

With every step, my feet seem to grow into flippers. I stumble over Jacob's discarded wine bottle, flying head-long, and crumple onto the sidewalk, hunching against the pain in both knees. Colt is suddenly there, lifting me to my feet.

"Stop running away from me." I grab his wrist. "It's complicated. And I can't explain it in one sentence."

Something between rage and disappointment glues itself to Colt's face. He snatches his wrist free. "Let me know when it's not so complicated. Whatever's between you and Jacob needs to be over." He twists away.

I seize his arm and he tenses, jaw jutting, fists curling. If I were a guy, he'd have decked me by now. "It is over. It never really started. But I can't tell you I don't love him. Just that maybe it's not that sort of love."

Colt snorts, scuffs the sidewalk, eyes rolling like a riled horse. "Brotherly love? Is that it?"

Words slur inside my mind, cling to my tongue. "Yes. Brotherly love. I guess." I'm sure it's more, but it's not as strong as what I feel for Colt.

"Except if it weren't for Aria?" Colt's voice is low, seething. "Tell me the truth. If she finds someone else, will you go to Jacob? If she weren't in the picture at all, would you and Jacob be together?"

The truth is a nail hammered into my heart. But he's only half right, because that was the truth before I fell for him. Doubt clutters my brain and asks if perhaps I love Colt because I can't have Jacob.

The fact is, I don't know, and Colt can see it scrawled all over my face. He yanks his arm away, waiting for an answer. I stand, shaking and reaching for the right thing to say, but it's as though he pushed me into a pool and I've forgotten how to swim. How do I explain that it was time to say goodbye not only to the Purple Woods but also to Jacob, except that I still love Jacob and no, it's probably not brotherly love . . . I just don't know what sort it is.

The sound of an engine revving startles me.

The Harley. The shape of Jacob.

Colt yells, "Jacob, stop." The bike catapults up the street.

My bones hollow out. Colt streaks past me. I run after them and when Colt stops, I keep going. But I'm not Superwoman. The bike accelerates away and I bend over, panting.

The dead chomp of metal hitting metal, of rubber

screeching on tar, makes my heart gag. Colt blasts past me. I take off after him, but then slow to a walk because I can't bear to see what made that noise.

● ● ●

Colt stays with me at the hospital until my parents arrive. I'm a blob in his arms and if he lets me go, I'll melt into a puddle on the floor. He can't look at me and I can't look at him, and as soon as Mum arrives, he passes me to her as if I'm a package.

He walks out the automatic doors of the hospital.

We wait for news of Jacob, and I watch the doors open and close, hoping Colt will walk back through them. Perhaps he's getting coffee.

But he doesn't come back. Not that night or the next day or the next night or the day after that.

Jacob is unconscious. The doctor's lips move, explaining. But his words get crowded out by the only two words that matter: *Don't die.*

Jacob's parents arrive in their expensive suits looking like they own the hospital. Everyone talks in whispers. I don't want to hear anyway. I already know this is my fault. My eyes ache with the bright lights, night and day, and the smell of bleach and medicine make me sick to my stomach. The efficient walk-trot of the nurses annoys me; their smiles offend me.

I watch Jacob through the window, shoving my hands into my shorts pockets. My fingertips brush something soft. It's a bruised jacaranda blossom, the one I caught that night with Colt when the Purple Woods rained petals in the breeze. Jacob's body is as lifeless as the blossom; tubes merge into him, bandages cover his head and half his body. I cradle the petal, afraid that if I let it go, I'll lose Jacob.

The doors open and close, and Colt doesn't come back.

I sit through the searing pain of my heart breaking.

But Aria comes back. The doors open and she rushes in with Dad behind her. She hugs me, her sobs echoing in my ears. My ribs cave in and crush my organs. Our tears mingle. We're inseparable. Squashed into the same stained, plastic chair. But neither of us utters a word . . . or sees more than the other's feet.

Maybe Jacob senses we're here, that if he just wakes up then the Raggers will be in the same room again. Because he opens his eyes.

FORTY-ONE

MUM AND DAD MAKE ME eat snacks from the minibar in the hotel room when all I want to do is sleep. Mum fiddles and puts things in cupboards. Dad rambles on about Rome and how Jacob is lucky to be alive, and when Aria insists on taking a shower, they agree. But they insist that they need to talk to me. I guess it's about riding motorcycles or Jacob and me behaving ourselves while Aria's here.

Dad draws me to perch with him on the bed. "We want to speak to you before you see the news."

The news? Colt. I pull away and stand. "Just say it."

"Jamie Jagger is dead. An overdose."

Sagging next to Dad, I pinch the skin on the front of my neck. "When? Where's Colt?"

"Milo tells us it happened the day of your mixed

doubles final. After Colt left you at the hospital, he took a call from Natalie and caught the next flight home."

I push my palms into my eye sockets to stop the tears. "Colt's all alone, Dad."

● ● ●

The next morning, Aria leaves for Rome. On the street outside the hotel, right where the Harley had been parked, she hugs Mum and bends to zip up her backpack. We've hardly spoken. Although we held each other in the hospital, I see now that was for Jacob; if we'd let go of each other, it may have meant letting go of Jacob. Maybe she blames me for the accident, too.

She seems bare without the long hair and quirky hats. A rush of sorrow swoops through me. When she straightens, I hug her. Though she stiffens, she doesn't pull away.

"I'm proud of how you've turned your life around," I say. "You were always your own person—never in my shadow."

She sags into the cab and hugs a bag, staring ahead.

The hollow in my chest expands.

I find Milo in his room, hoping he'll somehow fill the hollow before I turn into an empty space.

"I've promised the press a full statement if they leave you alone," he says. "You and I leave for Rio in a week. We must get home and back to training." He's glancing through our schedule. "You've had a rough time, *Dampfnudel*, but Jacob is okay now, isn't he?"

"I guess. He's being discharged next week." Home will be too still, too silent, without Aria and Jacob. Even the dogs will mope. "I'm worried Jacob drinks too much. Whenever he's upset, he gets tanked. And I'm worried about how Colt's going to cope."

Milo's features droop. "Many of us have crutches . . . We don't believe we're strong enough to cope without one. Jacob's crutch is alcohol. But he has to learn it the hard way—by himself." He licks his lips and seems to pull his face into place again. "And Colt will cope. He always does."

"I love him, Milo. But I love Jacob, too. What do I do?"

"Which one is your crutch?"

Jacob.

It's as if I've been trying to read a book written in Chinese and Milo has just handed me a translation. I want to hug him and absorb all his wisdom, but he's busy measuring out powders to make Milo Potion. I realize his words echo Mum's—Jacob is my safe place, my pink love. But I hadn't been ready to hear it back then. Colt taps into the core of me, waking the part of me that takes the world by its throat; he's found his way into the deepest, fiercest corner of my heart.

It's time to let go of my crutch.

● ● ●

On the morning after we return to Sydney, I drive to Colt's house. It's five a.m. I knock on the door, but no one answers. Milo hasn't heard from Colt in seven days. And he's ignoring all my texts. I check for the key above the doorframe. It's gone.

Committing to a stakeout, I wait in the Jeep, my phone keeping me company. I'll stay all day if I need to. But it's February, and by nine o'clock, the temperature in the car is oppressive. I get out to cool off, standing in a light breeze on the raised porch.

The porch window is still covered in "Darling Madeline" letters, as is the one next to it now. And the next. I traipse around the house, inspecting each window and trying to understand Jagger's state of mind. I can only decipher snippets, but it's like he wanted Madeline to read the letters from heaven. Every glass pane is a mosaic of love notes to his dead wife—including one window that's wide open.

The roller blind swings in the breeze. I push it to the left and slip into the house, then scrunch my nose against the reek of stale beer. I'm in Colt's bedroom. And there's a shape in Colt's bed. I say his name louder than I intend. He doesn't move.

Fear splinters through me.

I step closer. He's on his side—and breathing. And he hasn't shaved lately, given that he practically has a beard.

Blowing out air and pressing both palms to my forehead, I hunch on the bed next to him. He's an orphan now. I wonder if he has any family, other than his relatives in Florida. My feet knock over two empty beer bottles abandoned on the floor by the bed. His eyes drift open, unseeing, then slip closed.

He's been drinking.

I jog his shoulder. "Colt. Wake up."

This time, he lifts his head and registers me. He flops flat, covering closed eyes with an arm. Without a shirt, it's obvious he's lost weight.

I don't know whether to shout at him or kiss him. "You okay, Colt?"

"Get out of here, Harper," he mutters.

My smile falls away and my heart shrinks. I blink back tears and go into the kitchen to get some water.

The living room is pretty tidy except for two empty take-out pizza boxes, three drained bottles of red wine, and a quarter bottle of vodka. *His or his dad's?* A shape under a blanket moves on the sofa. I suppress a gasp.

A woman calls out, "Colt?"

Natalie. Despite Colt's assurances about her, jealousy smears itself through me. But the figure sits, hanging her red, spiky-haired head. I grip the sofa. "Kim?"

Even though Jagger's "Darling Madeline" notes block most of the sunlight, she squints at me as though the glare is blinding, then gives a brief wave. "Harper."

"What are you doing? Why are you here?" I round on her.

"Holy shit, keep your voice down." She pushes long fingers through short hair, squeezes her skull. "Colt needed cheering up."

I hover over her, taking in her bare shoulders. "And how, exactly, did you intend to do that?" When she droops farther into the sofa, eyes blank, my skin crawls. "You brought pizza and alcohol and yourself on a plate. You figured that would help, did you? His dad was an alcoholic, for Christ's sake. Colt's never touched a drop before."

She giggles. "He needed a li'l love and attention. No harm in that."

The ground buckles.

"Get out!" I yell, pulling her up. "Get out right now." But she's only wearing a boob-tube and panties and I ditch her wrists as if they've scalded me.

"Jesus, girls, keep it down, would you?" Scratching at his new beard, Colt traipses in the direction of the bathroom. "This is a decent neighborhood." The door slams. The shower cranks on, making the pipes groan.

Kim flops back onto the sofa, pulling the blanket over her. "Who made you the boss?"

Everything speeds up and I'm choking on too much air. I swoop around the house in a rage, collecting empty bottles and wrappers into a trash bag and scrubbing dishes. When Colt emerges from the bathroom, a shaving cut on his chin and a towel wrapped around his waist, I dive at him, fists slapping at his chest. "Is this your answer?

Getting boozed up and sleeping with girls? Throwing your life away like your dad did?" I intend every word to hurt.

He captures my wrists. His glare takes me apart, limb by limb, organ by organ. "I said you should go, Harper. I don't need your help." He pushes past me.

"Yeah, get going Harper," pipes up Kim from the sofa, snorting.

"You should get going, too, Kim," Colt calls from the bedroom, his voice firm and cold. "Thanks for the company."

I lean against the hallway wall, repeatedly knocking the back of my head against it. I can't just walk away. I have to stop him self-destructing.

A door to the left is ajar. Inside, the walls are lined to the ceiling with cardboard boxes that also block out the window. In the middle of the boxes is a single bed. It's the saddest thing I've ever seen. Jamie Jagger, tennis superstar, reduced to living in that miserable room, imprisoned by his own love letters and never able to leave behind the ghosts of his past. Never able to move forward.

I storm into Colt's room. He's perched on the edge of the bed, elbows on knees. He looks like a door that fell off its hinges.

"I hate that you're done with me, but I get it." I swallow the sob that's swelling in my throat. "But you're not done with tennis. I won't let you throw away what you have. If you do, you're no better than your father. I know you loved him and you miss him, but I also know you don't want to be him."

"I killed him, Harper." He snatches a pillow and chucks it at the wall. I'm glad there's nothing else in the room to throw. "I was playing tennis, and he was dying. I should've been here." Colt punches the mattress.

"You know that's not true. No one can protect someone twenty-four-seven. And Natalie was here . . . It's not like you abandoned him."

"I don't blame her."

"Then you can't blame yourself."

He slams himself back onto the bed, his hands covering his face. "He died in bed. Alone." Colt's shoulders judder.

I lie down and gather his rigid body to me. It's like hugging an armful of tennis racquets. His choppy breaths heave into my shoulder and my heart shatters for him.

It takes a long time, but after he calms down, I murmur, "It's horrible, I know. But he was already set on doing it. Second time, Colt. Second time. Whether you were there or not, he would've done it."

Colt rolls away, shutting his eyes. "So everyone keeps telling me." He takes a deep breath, taking back control.

"Maybe you should listen to them." I push myself up onto an elbow. "Maybe those people are right and they want to help you."

He exhales, eyes flicking open and toward me for a

split second before he sits forward. "Why couldn't he just be proud of me?"

"He was a sick man." I sit up, too, together but separate.

"He saw my matches on TV. The Australian Open—the very place where his career ended. That's what drove him to it. He asked me to stop playing tennis. If I had listened—"

"You'd have ended up bitter and angry like him. And it wouldn't have changed his decision." I pull at the frayed edges of my jean shorts.

Colt watches my fingers fidget in my lap, a smile quivering on his lips. "Not sure I can take your brutal honesty right now." His eyes grip mine.

"Don't make the same choice your dad did. Don't give up on yourself."

Silence holds the room.

"It's hard to admit he messed up big time. He was my hero—" Colt's voice splits. "And he's all I had—"

Colt fights to calm his jerky breathing. When he succeeds, he remains dead still, and I stay quiet to let him recover. Then he places his hand over my clasped hands in my lap. "It took guts for you to come here." When I don't respond, he squeezes my fingers to make me look up. "Still not giving up on me?"

"Nothing will ever make me do that." I try a small laugh, then remember Kim out in the living room. "I just wish you hadn't given up on me."

He sucks in a breath, exhales slowly, rubbing his face with flat palms.

There's a soft knock, and Kim's face appears around the door. "Colt. You okay?" She steps into the room, now wearing black shiny leggings with her top. My fingers ball up and Colt goes out of the room with Kim.

"Thanks for the company," says Colt. "I gotta head out soon. Have you got everything?"

"I had a great night. Thanks, handsome. Guess I'll see you . . . soon." I don't hear his reply above the clatter of the bolt on the front door and the squeak of hinges.

My heart thuds as I think about them being together last night.

I have to get out of here, but when I enter the living room my legs feel boneless. Colt has shut the door and motions for me to sit. I plunk into the sofa, completely sad-struck.

"Everything's messed up." My lips pucker and hot tears prickle in my eyes. "Did something happen with you and Kim? She made it seem like—"

"No, nothing happened." Colt's voice is steady and firm. His words echo in my head.

"What does it matter, anyway?" I lurch for the front door. Colt's fingers wrap around my arm. I pull away, but he's not letting go.

"I did not sleep with Kim," he says, more definitely. "I may be mad at you, but you're not leaving here believing some lie she sold you."

354

"You were probably too blitzed to remember."

"I remember everything. She made a drunken pass. I put her straight. I bored her with reruns of Wimbledon. She fell asleep on the sofa. I went to bed, fried but not paralytic."

"She was half-naked when I got here." I pull at my arm. This time he lets it go, a rumble of laughter filling the room.

"You're actually jealous," he says. "I thought you knew me better than that."

I blush to the tips of my ears, lift my gaze as far as his mouth. When I see he's still smiling, I check his whole face and it blows wide open. The parts of me that have whirled in midair since he left me at the hospital snap back into place.

"Thanks," he says. "For coming. And for what you said earlier. It might take me a while to believe it, but it helped. I need to keep hearing it."

"We should call Milo," I say. "He's worried. You need to get training again."

"I'm not going to Rio." Colt flops into an armchair, making the stuffing bubble through the holes in the fabric.

I step in front of him. "But you can't give up—"

"I don't know what I'm going to do yet." He picks at the stuffing. "There's the funeral. My family in Florida want me to move back. Landlord's kicking me out of this place. I need to get myself together, and that's not going to happen in two days."

I totter back into the sofa. "You won't find the answer in a bottle of beer," I say, thinking of Jacob.

Colt blows out a noisy breath. "Figured it's okay to have a drink on my eighteenth birthday. Some might say it's acceptable to have a drink in honor of a dead father, too."

"Your birthday? When?"

He shrugs. "Yesterday. I think. Not sure what day it is."

"Happy birthday."

"Not so happy. But I did learn that alcohol is overrated," says Colt. "Tastes like crap, and makes you feel like hell the next day. What's the point?" He doesn't look like he's expecting an answer. "Sorry I disappeared. I needed to be alone, you know? And the media invaded. I had to switch off my phone and lock myself in. I ate what was left in the cupboards, which wasn't much, so the only reason I opened the door to Kim was because of the smell of pizza."

But as he speaks, a swirl of gray invades my body. This is his crossroads. Where does that leave me? Every touch, kiss, and smile, every word we exchanged, is fading—always there in the past, but never able to lead to a future.

Colt gets up to fetch tall glasses of water, passing me one.

"You're going to be okay, aren't you?" I smile, but it's like my lips are made of wool and won't stay in place. "I mean, you're not going to follow in your dad's footsteps."

"Nope." He guzzles the water. "I've got a lot to work out, but I won't let alcohol make those decisions." He blows his cheeks out. "I'm guessing Jacob is okay? I called the hospital. They wouldn't tell me anything. But you wouldn't be here if he wasn't."

"He got lucky. And I'd be here no matter . . ." I stare at Colt, trying to work out what's going on between us. "I . . . we're good . . . you and me, aren't we? Friends again?" It's not the question I want to ask, but it's a start.

He flops into the armchair and considers the notes stuck to the window. "I quite liked being more than friends," he says, echoing my words in Melbourne. "But this Jacob thing . . ."

The expression on his face scrapes at my heart.

"I know," I say. "If I try to explain, do you promise you won't take off?"

"No point." He practically drops his empty glass on the table between us.

"You made the wrong assumptions before. And I got the Kim thing wrong. Even Natalie, once." Something tweaks in his jaw. "I needed to clear it up in my own mind before I could explain it to you," I plead. "If I mean anything to you, just listen. It's all I ask."

He taps his chin, then nods.

I rub my upper arms, and take a deep breath. "I do love Jacob. And no, probably not in a brotherly way." Colt shifts, pops his neck. "But I think I love him for the wrong reasons. Being together meant the future wouldn't separate us . . . everything would stay the same. I needed that, to feel safe. Or is it I needed him, therefore I loved him?" I swallow hard. "But we're not kids anymore. I am changing, and I'm making my own path. I love him. He meant so much for so long, how could I not? But I recognize now it's not a strong, forever love. It's not . . ." How do I explain the difference between pink love and the blazing, dazzling, heart-popping red love I feel for Colt?

Colt scrutinizes me, treating every word as a clue to a puzzle.

My toes curl up and I slump farther into the sofa. "When I was with you, it felt . . ."

My gaze plunges. *His dad just died.* This isn't the right time to tell him that I love him.

"All I know is that when everything imploded at Christmas, I missed Jacob and felt awful for him, but it's you I couldn't get out of my head." We watch each other with gazes that remember that awful day. "And I've thought about this a lot, but if Aria met someone in Europe, and she was okay with me being with Jacob, I wouldn't go to him. Going back to Jacob is moving backward, hiding in the past. It's staying with what's familiar and holding myself back, clinging to a crutch. Does that make sense? I'm ready to spread my wings . . . without him."

Colt's fingers drum softly on the armrest. "My dad. He married his high school sweetheart and got stuck in the past when she died. He loved her so much he could never move forward." Colt shuts his eyes. "I never wanted to love someone like that."

His face goes blank.

Silence slides like a barrier between us. I almost kick

the table over and grab him into a hug, but I don't dare breathe. Does he love *me* like that?

"He hit you, Harper." Colt shakes his head, jaw grinding, his gaze heavy on me.

"He's never done that before. It was the drinking . . . it turns him into someone else."

"Like my dad." I consider reaching for his hand, but something's off. He stands, cracks his knuckles. "I've got a lot of stuff to sort out. Thanks for coming over, though."

Tears prickle behind my eyelids and I rise. "Anytime." My voice cracks.

He heads for the door and holds it open, then follows me onto the deck and into the street. When he catches up with me, we stroll in the kind of silence you hope will never end because when it does, you won't want what it brings.

Colt stops next to the Jeep, hooking both thumbs through the belt loops on his shorts. "I don't know what to say to you right now. I'm a wreck. It's as if stuff is flying at my head and I have to duck all the time." He squeezes his eyes shut. "I won't take you down with me. You've got rankings to keep up."

My rib cage snaps in ten places and spears my heart.

Colt opens his eyes, and shoves his hands into his pockets. "I need to be with myself for a while."

The sidewalk tilts. *This is goodbye.*

I swallow the pebble in my throat, and because I can't

cope with seeing the truth in his eyes, I inspect my foot toeing the ground. "Is this your very indirect and subtle way of saying goodbye because you're already halfway to Florida?"

"I don't know. I just don't know."

Every happy memory we made just got vacuumed out of my head and replaced by a grief so big it needs its own funeral.

FORTY-TWO

MILO AND I LEAVE FOR Rio two days later. It's the same day Jacob is released from the hospital, and the same day Colt buries his father.

The atmosphere in the cab is thick with gloom. Despite the bruise-colored clouds, Milo is lost in thought behind his aviators. I resemble the tree house the Raggers once built in the Mother Tree, all pulled apart and broken, nothing left but a few bent nails as clues to the fact that life was once amazing.

In the hotel in Rio, I listen to the air conditioner, to the people in the hallway, to the muffled traffic twenty stories below. There's a sense that I've been climbing a mountain these last few months and I've finally reached the summit. I have nothing to think about but proving Kominsky wrong: Aria, Jacob, Colt—they're offstage, and I'm alone in the spotlight.

Everything has led to this point.

The morning of the first match, I know there won't be a bag of plums outside my door, but I look for it anyway. How can something that's not there hurt so much?

I'm fitter than ever and have upped my match play experience. I win the first match. During the postgame interview, they ask how Colt is. At the mention of his name my heart smashes through the windshield as though it were in a car crash.

"He's a son who's lost his dad," I say.

The second-round is tougher. After losing the first set, the pulverizing pressure closes in. If I don't find a way to dig deep and stay strong and determined, I'll get stuck in the first-round graveyard again. The concept garrotes me. I've had a taste of being a winner . . . and now I want more. I want a Grand Slam singles title. I want four Grand Slams. Ten! Maybe because I almost chose to throw tennis away after Christmas, only to win the Open mixed doubles, giving tennis up is no longer an option.

A powerful sense of purpose stirs within me.

Milo's words slide into my mind. *Do it for yourself.*

Not for Dad or Colt or Kominsky or even Milo. For myself.

I guess that's what I told Colt when I said he should concentrate on the love of winning, not needing to win for the sake of his dad. Playing tennis has to be for me because win or lose, Aria's, Jacob's, and Colt's lives continue along their chosen paths, and mine continues on mine.

The puddle of nerves in my stomach firms up, becoming steely. The umpire calls time.

Chin high, I visualize winning. I know I can do this. I want that moment. I want that win. I want the world to remember Harper Hunter. I want to achieve something big—to be number one. I won't waste this. I want to inspire others to chase their dreams. And I won't let my opponent take that away from me.

And I see on my opponent's face the moment she knows I'm going to win. The moment she chooses to lose.

I make it into the quarterfinals where I lose to Aletta Haas, ranked 5 in the world. It's seen as a great result. We head to a women's tournament in Brazil where I survive until the quarters again. Then it's America for a series of hard court events. Milo has scheduled the year in advance, and it's a long haul around America, only returning home after Charleston in six weeks. We'll then take a week's break in Sydney before going to Europe for the clay court season in the buildup to the French Open. I have no idea what he's scheduled for Colt, and I don't ask.

I don't text Colt because he said he needed to be by himself. Each day, I hope he'll text me something simple, like congratulations. But I remember how he watched me drive away that last day with goodbye in his eyes.

He does text Milo, though. We're on a court in Los Angeles trying to break my five-bounce superstition before the Indian Wells tournament when Milo stops feeding me balls to squint at his phone. "Colt's in Florida. With his aunt and uncle." My insides compress. "The coach he worked with before is helping him out."

It's like someone kicked me in the throat. "You got dumped, too." My voice squeaks.

"You two didn't manage to work it out then? Sorry, Harper. But all you can do is keep moving forward."

"And you? Will you keep moving forward or are you staying with me?"

He throws a ball at the net and advances on me. "Let's get this straight. I didn't take you on to facilitate the arrangement with Colt. That was a cherry on top. I took you on because you have what it takes—a little issue with your brain game, but not a big one. And I saw a mixed doubles partnership made in heaven. I was right, wasn't I?" He points at me. "You're destined for top ten in the women's tour, and I'm going to cheer from your players' box when you do it."

Sick with realization, I turn in a full circle. "Colt dumped you *because of me.*"

"Nope." Milo cracks his knuckles. "It was time for honesty. I told him the truth—how I didn't try to stop Jagger walking onto that court."

I suck in air. "Was Colt mad at you?"

Milo rubs his lips with a curled finger. "I don't think he was angry with me. He said there was probably nothing I could've said or done to stop Jagger anyway. But Colt needed . . . some distance."

Indian Wells is a tough slog. I lose in the third round after twisting my knee. We arrive in Miami early, and I celebrate my seventeenth birthday with Milo. He presents a cupcake with overly large 1 and 7 candles that tip it over.

There's nothing from Colt. I don't know why I thought there would be.

When I spot Kim at the Miami tournament, I decide to give her the cold shoulder.

"You can quit playing the blame game," she sneers, stopping me by thrusting an arm out. "I was only trying to help Colt."

"Help yourself, more like." I shove her arm and walk away. After that, she ignores me, too.

I hadn't realized how much I was hoping Colt would show up in Miami—he only lives a couple of hours away—until Milo gets another text: Colt has tendonitis in his wrist. "He's had to rest it. His ranking's slipped to 48, but he says he's training hard and is in the best shape of his life for when he hits Houston."

Houston is a men's-only tournament.

My heart flaps unhappily.

The Miami crowd is boisterous, and they cheer me all the way to my quarterfinal loss. I make the semifinals in Charleston, losing because of my lingering knee injury, but still pushing my ranking to 58. Colt blows through the men's tournament in Houston in the same week and wins his first professional ATP title after a four-hour, five-set game against Dominic Sanchez. Viewing the highlights on repeat, the clips show Colt making impossible returns while Sanchez self-destructs.

I watch Colt's athletic, powerful body, the one that had touched me gently and held me close.

At the post-match interview, Colt's face swarms with happiness—until they ask where I am. "You just beat the world number one. Are you going to celebrate with Harper?"

Colt shifts from one foot to the other. He snaps his neck. "She's going back to Australia. Taking a break before the European rounds."

How does he know?

The interview sets off the media. Why isn't Colt returning to Australia for his break? Why don't our schedules ever lineup? They keep speculating. It gives me the courage to call Colt—to say hello, to joke about the crazy media frenzy, to congratulate him.

But he's changed his number.

By the time we return to Sydney, I've given up hope of ever seeing him again.

"Who'd have thought a broken romance would be bigger news than the bombing in the Middle East," says Jacob, flicking off CNN. We loll on the sofa in the kitchen, one on either end, facing each other.

Earlier this week, I arrived home to find a more relaxed

Jacob. He'd cut his hair short because the hospital shaved it. He looks older. His face loaded with remorse, he'd led me into the dining room to apologize for slapping me.

"I hit rock bottom, Harps. It's no excuse, but when I saw you two kissing on national TV for all the world to see . . ." He'd dropped his chin to his chest and shook his head. I watched him steel himself to raise his gaze, and when he finally did, his eyes told me how much he wished he could take back that slap. "I felt betrayed. Angry. But what I did was unforgiveable."

"It was the alcohol that made your decisions that night," I said. "You have to stop drinking so much."

Not wishing to revisit those moments, I brushed off any further apologies. But after we rejoined everyone in the kitchen, Jacob's regret was far more meaningful when he declined the champagne Milo passed around.

Now we've slipped into an easy camaraderie that's simple and supportive. Perhaps he senses that I'm broken, too.

"Colt's doing well," adds Jacob.

Even after seven weeks, thinking about Colt hurts. I only let myself remember for short moments, like gasps for air.

I think of the text Natalie sent me after Colt's interview: Give him time, and change the subject. "Mum says you're reapplying to the Con?" My parents have taken Jacob under their wing, realizing he needs support, rather than outlawing him. Plus Aria isn't here anymore.

"Yeah, she encouraged me. But as I went through the

forms, I realized I don't want to go anymore." He lobs some popcorn at me. It hits my nose, and he busts out laughing.

"What do you mean you don't want to go to the Con?"

"I think I applied because Aria did. But it was her dream. Maybe I didn't want to disappoint her. It's always been the band for me. Why should I go to the Con when what I really want is to go on the road with my band? Now we're writing a lot of new stuff together."

So Jacob won't live next door anymore, waiting for me to come home. I should be wrecked, but I'm happy for him. "Wow. What do your parents think?"

"They're good. Weirdly, defending their son from a drunk driving charge has made them remember I exist. They're trying. We even do family movie nights."

"Jeez. What do you watch? French subtitled arty stuff?"

He purses his lips and sticks out his tongue, then adds, "They've helped me get my music lessons gig off the ground. I'm teaching in the studio. These kids are great. They're eager, and if they're not, I tell them to go play tennis, or something equally dull."

I kick out, playful. "I'm glad you're back on track and smiling again."

"Almost dying can do that to a person." He traces the foot-long scar on his calf. There's one on his scalp, too, but the hair has grown back over it. "Makes you a bit more grateful, you know? And I want to hang on to what I haven't managed to blow apart."

We gaze through a shaft of dust mote–filled sunshine at the woods. A silence that is snug and healing settles over the room.

"How's Aria?" he asks softly.

"Dad says she's happy. She was supposed to move on to Paris, but she loves Rome."

Quiet for a beat, he adds, "I'm glad she's happy."

"Harper, the TV . . . Colt's interview." Dad strides into the kitchen followed by Milo. He may as well have announced that Colt's at the front door. My heart shreds.

"It's official," says Milo, on the brink of exploding with excitement. "Colt's ranked number one in Australia."

Dad flicks through the channels. "And he's earned himself a nickname—'Bolt from the Blue'—because of his speedy run up the rankings and the power of his serve."

"And his true-blue Aussie roots," Milo adds.

And then Colt's on the screen, smartly dressed and standing on a street packed with honking cars. It's night-time where he is. He tells the reporter that becoming Australia's men's number 1 is the first of many goals, and he's going out to celebrate. I wonder who he'll celebrate with. My heart is an apple and Colt just took a big bite out of it.

As always, they bring the subject around to me. "What's happened to the Australian Invasion, Colt? Harper's in Australia and you're here. Not much of an invasion happening."

Colt beams cheekily. "We're working on a pincer move-ment." Even I can't help but blurt out a laugh, swiping at the tears.

"What a transformation." Milo nudges me from behind. "You did that, Harper."

In the top corner of the screen, there's an image of Colt kissing me at the Aussie Open. Jacob squints out the window.

"You sure did get Harper in a pincer movement at the Australian Open," jokes the reporter. "The score was love-all that day."

Colt grabs the back of his neck, chuckling. "Don't you know 'love' means nothing to a tennis player?" Even though I remember it was a joke we once shared, his words are spikes in my heart.

FORTY-THREE

LIFE BECOMES A BLUR OF tennis courts and interviews, the inside of cars, planes, trains, and hotels, the days set on repeat from Stuttgart to Portugal to Madrid. I lose myself in tennis, but a part of me still mourns Colt. Something precious has been lost forever, ruined and spilled, never to return.

Colt rises to number 21 in the world. He's focused, strong, and when the going gets tough, he doesn't let anger engulf his game, but seems to go somewhere serene. He sticks to men's tournaments, wins trophies, shakes hands with movie stars, waves at spectators, signs balls, and throws them into the crowd. And he uses the star sweat towel.

Milo receives a fat check. The note reads, *The first of many. Colt.*

During one of Colt's games, he's heading to the baseline and pulls up his shirt to wipe away sweat. I see the vision of his six pack—as does everyone else. In the hush before he serves, a woman calls out, "Colt, will you marry me?" Several thousand spectators react in a wall of sound that rumbles around the arena.

Colt straightens and smiles. "Speak to my coach. He has my schedule."

The media set the sound bite on repeat.

He's close yet far, familiar yet changed. The weeks roll by, pulling us further apart. I can't believe he once wanted me—loved me.

With the Rome Masters looming, I text Aria, hoping to repair some of the damage. Her response is, *I can't see you yet*. But I'm forced to pull out of Rome. The knee I twisted in Indian Wells hasn't healed properly. I'm devastated for more than one reason—Rome is a combined event and Colt will compete there. A week later, during a women's event in Strasbourg, I reinjure the knee. Strapped up, I study my competition and witness Kim's improved foot-work. She wins the tournament. A bigger shock is her new coach, Kominsky. The press photograph Kim's dad carrying her on his shoulders while Kominsky carries her trophy.

Milo pulls me out of the French Open, so I don't get to break into the 30s rankings. We head home to visit a physio genius and prepare for Eastbourne, the lead-up tourna-ment to Wimbledon, which starts in a matter of weeks. The French Open broadcasts in our kitchen twenty-four-seven. Kim has the best tournament of her life, charging into the quarterfinals, except that when she loses the match she smashes her racquet against a chair until it breaks.

Colt is a force of nature. With a 154 mph serve, he causes a major upset, serving thirty aces to beat Sanchez and reach the French Open final. Not sharing that with Colt—I'm no more than a stranger to him now—is the most bittersweet moment of my life.

Home feels different without Aria. Dad's barbecue smells replace her cookies and cakes, and the lack of blaring music makes it feel like the house is hibernating. Also, Jacob isn't a permanent piece of furniture in the kitchen. He's always busy with the band. I've never seen him so focused.

"Did I tell you the band's now called Purple Daze?" Jacob asks, the day before he goes on tour around Australia. We're lounging by the river, the rock cold from the autumn air. "Aria doesn't like it, but she'll have to deal. We've emailed each other . . . a little."

I feel no jealousy that she's communicating with him. Mine was the biggest betrayal. Maybe we'll all find a way back to one another, in time.

"It's a perfect name." My voice threads through the bare branches.

He shoves me, playful. "I still miss you, Harps." His grin shuffles into something more reflective. "But it's time to stand on my own two feet. Guess I've always relied on you guys too much. And I've always felt a bit worthless. I was never going to be a hotshot lawyer like my parents, or a world-class tennis player . . . and Aria always outplayed me. But this is my second chance." The dogs bound across the river toward us. "And I'm not going to waste it." Jacob hugs their wet bodies to stop them knocking me over.

The morning Jacob leaves with his band, he stands happily next to the tour van his parents have bought him. I can barely speak, barely breathe. It's as if Jacob planted a tree inside my rib cage that's grown overnight and there's no room for my organs. He hugs me last, eyes glistening. My head on his shoulder, I can't keep the sob in.

"I'm sorry, Harps. For taking you down with me. I was a shit who needed you and didn't think about the fallout."

As he climbs into the van, I wrap my arms around myself and, for a moment, I'm coming unfastened right there on the grass. I search for Mum and Dad among Jacob's friends, and they reach out for me, as they always have, ready to hold me together. But I shake my head. "It's okay," I say.

I run after the van, smacking the driver's door in one final touch before it picks up speed.

When we leave for our flights to London, Milo slides into the back of the cab alongside me. He does that these days. But he doesn't belong there; I can't help thinking he's sitting in the seat of a ghost. He rips open an envelope and whistles through his teeth at the check inside. "This is too much, Colt." He tucks it away in his wallet, next to a photo of a young woman with blonde hair. *The lost fiancée?*

"I hear Colt made it into the top ten," I say.

"Persistence is an art. Want to see the men's entry list for Wimbledon?" Milo unfolds a sheet of paper, points to Colt's name. "I like that he's honoring his father and putting the past behind him."

Colt Jagger.

So he's forgiven his dad.

But he can't forgive me.

The world warps.

It'll be the first time I've seen him in the flesh since we stood on his street almost four months ago. Feelings swirl inside me, and although I'm nowhere near the dining room, I can hear the grandfather clock. *Tick. Tick.*

FORTY-FOUR

ON THE GRASS COURTS OF Eastbourne, the injured knee feeling strong, my body and mind know what they're doing and I smash through games, visualizing victory. I take the pressure by the throat and pin it down. With each win, I grow more certain. I will have my dreams. I don't need to find a plan B.

But making it into the final of Eastbourne is the easy part. I'm facing Kim Wright who's having another great tournament, probably thanks to Kominsky. Bet he loves Kim—she never turns to putty.

The night before the match, I panic.

"Eat your steak," says Milo, shoveling peas onto a spoon.

I push a piece of steak around the plate. "Kim made it into the quarters at the French Open." I let my cutlery clatter onto the plate and almost knock over the water glass.

"That's it? You've decided she's the winner tomorrow?"

demands Milo. Sagging in the chair, I contemplate the inky damp night through the bay windows. He adds, "You weren't at the French Open to prove yourself and here's your chance."

"Did you hear what her dad said? That I'm all toy poodle to Kim's Rottweiler."

"He lets the media attention go to his head. They're fame chasers. Who says something like that?"

Superwoman does. With her kill-or-be-killed attitude.

She's just a girl like me, not Superwoman. She trains, she eats, she worries, she pees. Yes, we have history. Compartmentalize it. And Kominsky. *He's not Super Coach.* Wasn't he wrong about me? I'm no longer stuck in the first-round graveyard.

It's simply another match to win. One stroke at a time.

But not simply another opponent.

I screw up the napkin and squish it into my half-eaten dinner, wanting to do the same thing to Kim. She hadn't known about my argument with Colt when she went to his house. She tried to take him from me, screwed with his head knowing his dad's history with alcohol. And she timed her attack precisely. She moved in as soon as his dad had killed himself and Colt was at his lowest.

Leaning back, I observe Kim in the mirrored bar area. She's perched on a stool, muscled legs sliding out from under a short dress. Surrounded by three guys, she whirls a glass of red wine. *That's the real Kim. The one on court wears a killer game face.*

But I've never had one.

I drop into a Harper-sized wormhole; the table shrinks and everything and everyone whirls away into the distance. The pressure to beat Kim resembles a heavy rock tied to my chest, pulling me down, hurtling me farther away, faster and faster. I clutch the arms of the chair against the sensation of falling. Sounds muffle and blur so it's less my ears that hear her say my name, and more my heart.

My head whips round.

Aria's arms are stiff at her sides, a smile skidding across her face. I'm instantly out of the chair, wrapping myself around her, inhaling her rosin and oatmeal scent.

"I live in an *appartamento* in a building that's two thousand years old and there are Roman statues outside," says Aria. We fall into step on the wet sidewalk. She'd been drowning in guilt about refusing to meet in Rome and wanted to surprise me, she said.

Our knuckles bump. I expect her to pull away. Instead, she knots her fingers with mine, manically swinging our arms between us. "And I eat *biscotti* for breakfast, dinner's at nine, the pizza is to die for, and I drive a scooter."

"*Risky*. The streets resemble a *Mario Kart* course," I say, remembering a visit to Rome. "And still working at the Teatro dell'Opera, I hear." We dawdle along a cobbled street, a light drizzle reflecting hazily in the streetlights. "What else is new?"

She glances at me sideways. Her hair has grown and flicks up daintily at the ends. Spotted green feather earrings brush her collarbones. "I do have some news." I note the buoyancy in her eyes, and grin. "I met this guy at work. He won a scholarship to the *conservatorio* in Rome." She shakes me by the arms, needing me to share her excitement. "We're talking one of the oldest music institutions in the world." I chuckle and clutch her shoulders, too. "He's helped me with my music. I've got an audition!"

I hug her. The mist trickles down our cheeks, flattening our hair, but there's no place I'd rather be.

"That's not all," she says, continuing to walk. "This guy, André, we're kind of seeing each other . . ."

"You are? I'm"—speechless—"happy for you. What's he like?"

Her spaced-out gaze darts upward, face opening. "He's French, but speaks English. He's tall with dark, curly hair, and freakily intense about music. He'd practice all day if I didn't drag him outside."

"And you're happy?"

"Yes." She studies me. "I'm fantastically happy."

Our eyes have a conversation both of us can hear. She's let Jacob go and she's forgiven me. The sky splatters us with oversized drips of rain, forcing us to run for shelter. We huddle under the canopy of a shop and agree the rain smells grassy and coppery rather than the hot, wet-dust smell of Australia.

She pulls a lip gloss from her bag. "I heard about you and Colt. You okay?"

I slump against the shop window. "Gotta keep moving forward."

"True. I had to leave everything that was familiar behind just to *see* the next step. I realize now that sometimes playing it safe means you limit yourself." She mashes her glossed lips together. "I bumped into Colt in Rome. He said to say hello."

My heart flies into my throat. "Yeah?"

"I introduced him to André and Colt took us for drinks at his hotel. He's doing seriously fine. The place was dripping in crystals and a Coke cost $10. He was way more chill than before. Except I could tell he misses you. When I talked about you he got this look . . ."

I blink wildly. "What do you mean? What *look*?"

"Like someone turned a light on inside him. Or like his face came out of the shadows—even though it was broad daylight."

The rain drums at the cobbles.

Aria caresses my arm. "After Melbourne I thought you two were so in love."

The memory bites me. I straighten, bracing myself. "Love never lasts," I say. "Same as Purple Time. It's sudden and magical and beautiful, but it can't last." Streams of water run off the front of the canopy, splashing our ankles.

"Mum and Dad still love each other," says Aria. I scuff at the red mailbox next to us. "Do you think love is the color purple, Harps?" she asks. "I do. Love makes me feel all safe and happy and . . . purple inside."

My heart is aching too hard to answer.

Aria rounds on me. She pushes down her bottom lip and pokes my ribs. "Don't worry. I've proven it's possible to find love again."

"Wait. Oh my God. I'm *so* slow. You're in love!"

She covers her blushing cheeks with splayed fingers. She's glowing. We didn't realize back then, but when Aria gave up the Con, she let go of the familiar, spread her wings, and gave something better a chance to catch her.

And Aria's right. Childhood isn't the color purple. Love is.

Kominsky had instilled in me the habit of always packing a notebook to record training logs or reminders for myself. As I get ready for bed, setting out my kit for the final against Kim tomorrow, I grab the notebook. The purple blossom I caught and pocketed that night with Colt is now flattened between the pages. I had kept it safe after Jacob got the all clear from the hospital.

Walking over to the open window, I kiss it and toss it high. It falls with the rain onto the wet sidewalk.

It's time to spread my wings.

FORTY-FIVE

IN THE WOOD-PANELED CHANGING ROOM before the match, I perform my usual warm-up routine. Kim doesn't show until twenty minutes before we're due on court. Her eyes are heat-seeking missiles when she charges into the room. They flash and drill into me, narrowed, assessing, strategizing, and she's in full armor, no chink of human showing.

She slams a bag onto the bench, then herself. The room resonates with a low growl. "I'm going to put so much heat on you, you're going to melt like ice cream."

The hairs on my neck stand on end. "How *nice* of you," is all I can come up with. I pull my leg into a stretch.

"No room for *nice* on the court, darling. Don't you get that yet?" She chuckles like a serial killer. "It's about survival, and I'm taking you down."

I whip around, but my words glitch; despite her fighting talk, she's slumped on the bench, nursing her head in her hands.

"I wouldn't be so sure, Kim."

Palms slap into her lap and she lets out a strange, dark cackle. Her stare arrows into mine. "Did you see me at the French Open? A *singles* event? No doubles partner to prop me up with fist bumps, no one to protect me when the itty-bitty ball hit me. You're soft and sweet. Like I said, ice-cream. You may have won the war with Colt, but this is my win."

I walk to the farthest end of the claustrophobic changing room and run on the spot, bouncing up and down.

"Or did you win Colt? Reckon I've seen more of him lately. Colt and I, we're cut from the same cloth. After he stops needing all the sunshine and ice-cream pie shit you feed him, perhaps he'll make a different choice."

"You two? *The same?* You're an irresponsible lush, craving a spotlight. You don't give two hoots about the opportunities you've had handed to you on a platter—"

"Shut up, tutti-frutti." Kim waves me away. "And stop that pounding before I cut your feet off."

I keep up my routine. When the court official collects us, Kim's a wad of bubble gum stuck to the surface of the wood, and she peels herself off the bench. I wonder if she had a late night out on the town, and I imagine her slipping on the tiles and half grin.

The spectators erupt when we emerge on court. I seek out Milo and Aria in the players' box, but also spot Kim's rock of a father, a red bush of hair topping him off. He's chewing gum, ratlike eyes trained on me. He raises a thumb, as though hitching a ride, then switches it upside down. Kominsky is parked ramrod straight beside him, attention on Kim. I stare past them at the old-fashioned buildings visible beyond the rows of spectators, and watch a couple of red robins flutter into nearby trees. With the grass beneath my feet, I could be in a park . . . except for the few thousand eyes on me.

Having won the toss, I prepare myself opposite Kim. Her sluggishness gone, she glares into me from across the court, bouncing on her toes. My stomach ripples with nerves. I look beyond her game face. *She pees, too.* I've never wanted a win this badly, not because it's the final of Eastbourne, but because I want to grind her into the ground after what she did to Colt.

I take the first set 6–4, but she's not letting me win the next one without a battle—and neither is her dad. At the end of a changeover break, his words boom onto the court: "Take her out, Kim."

Kim sneers as we pass each other. I gauge her bloodshot eyes, and she reacts to the invasion of her personal space by knocking into me.

"Everyone wants you to win, Kim." I don't take the bait, but it's Kim's dad, for sure.

I grit my teeth. *I can do this. She's gone. I'm not losing today.*

I glance at Aria, her knees jiggling up and down. She's creating an amazing future for herself, and Jacob is touring with the band . . . While the Raggers have reconciled, the two of them are making their own dreams come true.

Now it's my turn. This is my dream, and Kim is not taking it away from me.

We go to tiebreakers over and over. Kim's power is amazing, her ability to stay settled during pressured moments allowing her to rob me of the second set.

"Your serve is da bomb, Kim." Mr. Wright again, careful not to say anything that could get him thrown out, but enough to rile me if I let him.

I don't.

During the final set, Kim's an advancing one-woman army. When I force her to run for drop shots, she sends in the speediest warrior. I get her running from side to side, but she finds reinforcements, and there are five of her on court. After I pull some power shots, she uncovers more power in her own arsenal. I pound her backhand, she attacks my backhand. Yet, despite her defense, I'm the one calling the shots. She's reacting to me. I'm in charge. That knowledge sends a surge of energy and determination into every muscle.

The next time we change over, Kim calls for a bathroom break. She stumbles over her feet as she walks away. *Step it up. She's tired. I've done that. I've tired out Superwoman.*

When we resume, I reach farther into myself, grunting with each stroke, powering the ball over the net. Always a silent, self-contained player, now I fist-pump the air each time I win a point. "Come on," I mumble, after losing a point. Then I yell, "You've got this."

I wipe the slate clean, as though every point is the first of the match, and I choose to win it.

The energy on the court rises. The spectators catch on, cheering and clapping. I absorb their energy, a battery recharging itself, and witness the energy dribble out of Kim. And then it happens. One point from my match point, 30-love, I lunge for a drop shot and strain the same knee I'd twisted before. I can walk, but it doesn't feel good. I should call for ice, strap the knee, protect it for Wimbledon, but Kim is a prowling wild animal and she'll target my weakness. I grit my teeth and head for the baseline. 30-15. Still two points away from winning. It has to hold. But my serve wallops the net, and a lightning bolt shoots through my knee. I push the signature of pain out of my face for the second serve, hitting the net again. *Double fault.*

Kim shrieks, "Yes! Ice cream." She pumps both arms.

I think of myself as a soldier with a bullet wound—it hurts, but I'm not dead yet. I can still fight in this battle. 30-all. My next serve is solid and I move to center, teeth gritted. I smash the ball at her feet and win the point. The crowd rumbles with anticipation.

"Match point, Hunter," announces the umpire.

One point and I can ice it. My knee on fire, I bounce the ball five times and serve. It hits the net and my knee gives way. I suppress a scream.

Kim points her racquet at me, as if it's a loaded gun.

One point. That's all I need. The throbbing tells me if I run on this knee, I'll damage it and have to drop out of Wimbledon. And if I don't win this point, we'll reach deuce. We could go to tiebreaker after tiebreaker again— and that's not an option. One chance. It has to be an ace. It has to be a steady, straight ball toss.

Choose to win.

I can and I will.

Kim hunkers down, a tiger ready to pounce. I perform the five bounces, but catch the ball, halting play. The crowd exhales. I put my weight on the uninjured leg, study the ball in my grasp.

This is it. The moment I win a professional tournament. The moment I prove I have what it takes.

I bounce the ball just three times, toss it dead straight, flick my wrist.

It's a fireball that not even Kim can stop.

It's an ace.

The knee iced and strapped, I practically float down the passageway for the post-match interview. Before I'd exited the court, fans thrust notebooks at me. A girl who had to be no more than nine caught my eye, and I reached for her notebook first. I'll never forget the expression on her face; she looked at me like I was a god—no, her hero.

I enter a packed media room and a tournament official gives me a bouquet of roses big enough to need their own cab. Every one of them is purple.

I look around for Colt, soaring even higher with a moment's hope. Could a movie-like ending happen for me? Instead, I find the familiar, perfectly round, shaved head of Kominsky parked at the back of the room. *He chose to attend my interview.* Our eyes snap together. Elastic lips sweep up at the corners as he bows his head to me. I smile and nod back.

"Please take a seat, Miss Hunter," prompts the official. I slide into a chair, laying the flowers on the table.

My voice comes out high and excited when they ask about the game. "I guess I had to dig deeper than ever before, and I liked what I found."

"You resemble the cat that got the canary, Harper," shouts the Channel Seven lady. "Who are the flowers from?"

Words swirl in my mouth, my heart suddenly stunned with love. "There's no note. But can you pass on a message?" The room ripples with nods and murmurs. "It's this: 'Child Milo, Milo child. Forever.'"

You me, me you. Forever.

When pressed, I explain it's a code for them to break.

But by the next day, I regret saying it . . . because Colt doesn't respond.

Hardening myself against the hurt that gnaws at me, I push him to the back of my mind. It really is over. The roses were his way of saying congratulations without having to call or text. The only purple I need to concentrate on now is the purple and green of Wimbledon.

Keep moving forward.

FORTY-SIX

I'VE ALWAYS HAD A SOFT spot for Wimbledon. I've played on the grass courts four times in the juniors, and once in the qualifying rounds of the professional circuit. Being the oldest tennis tournament in the world, they've clung to certain traditions, making it stand out from the other Grand Slams. There's a dress code for players—a mostly white kit—and there's strawberries and cream everywhere. And although last year I had to use the upstairs changing room, I did sneak into the champions' locker room, imprinting the details of the old-fashioned space in my memory. There's deodorant and hand cream next to each basin and an attendant passes out hand towels. The men even get shaving cream. This time, I'll be assigned to the champions' locker room. No more first-round graveyard changing rooms.

Milo, Aria, and I left Eastbourne yesterday afternoon to arrive in Wimbledon with two days to get settled. Dad's hired a physical therapist to join our team and my knee is feeling good. We've also rented a house rather than putting everyone up in hotels. Mum and Dad arrive soon after.

England is experiencing a heat wave and Milo doesn't want me to get dehydrated, so he sends me on crack-of-dawn runs. *The morning hour has gold in its mouth.* Milo's definitely right—I crave this calm hour when there's time to put myself together for the day ahead.

I run around the nearby lake, through the waddling ducks, the pale morning sunlight shimmering across the tranquil water. The paths around the lake are lined with bluebells and squirrels inhabit the oak trees, a contrast to the palm trees and kookaburras of home. As I run, I wave back at the rowers lined up in their boats and others who launch small sailboats, the water slapping at their bright hulls. Afterward, I walk to the end of a boat jetty to recover and to imprint the landscape into my memory. *I'm in the main draw of Wimbledon.* It's happening. My tennis dream is coming true.

Something knocks my sneaker and I look down. To the side of my foot is a tennis ball. Has Milo followed me to start another drill?

"Not a koala in sight," says a voice with a rumble of laughter beneath it. I spin around, and for a moment I forget how to blink.

After maybe a hundred years, I throw both arms around his neck. He lifts me and crushes me against him. He smells like Colt, and he feels like Colt, and he is Colt.

"What are you doing here?" I say midair. My belly shimmies.

He sets me down. "I'm playing in some tennis tournament. Forget what it's called. You?" I move to cuff him, and he captures my hand, grips it, and guides me back up the jetty. He's in running clothes and there's the shape of another tennis ball in his pocket. "Coffee?" His face floods with that smile.

"The park café isn't open yet. Believe me, I've checked." I search around like maybe an espresso bar might materialize. I'm not sure what else to do. He hasn't let go of my hand.

"Should we find another café?" he asks. It's as if he's forgotten we haven't spoken in four months.

I can't take him yo-yoing in and out of my life. I pull my hand away.

Colt grabs the back of his neck and dips his chin.

Before I can demand to know why he's here, a group of runners blur around us. We get jostled and Colt stands in front of me until the joggers thin out. Stepping off the concrete path out of their way, he pulls me with him. I continue to watch the stragglers. When I cut back to Colt, his gaze combs my face. My heart quivers. I can't ask the big question—not yet.

"Heard you bumped into Aria in Rome." I rub the

petals of a rose on the bush beside us. "I heard a lot of things, actually. You've climbed the rankings like a boy in a tree. You've even got a nickname. And you've married at least ten fans. Plus you've moved to Florida. . . ."

"That last part's not true," he says.

"And the married ten times part is?"

"In some countries, I believe they all count." Colt's grin fades.

He checks behind us and jerks a thumb in the direction of a thicket of trees. I walk beside him, feeling like my heart's being choked to death.

"I heard you're doing pretty well, too," he says, stringing a smile onto his lips. "Ranked 29? And Aria tells me the two of you are back on track."

My eyes bolt to him. "How would you know?"

"Aria and I've exchanged a few texts." He glances away.

I wrap my arms around myself. "Yup," I croak. "Aria and I are all good. She's fallen in love with a Frenchman." I can barely hear the words through the pounding in my ears.

"Yes, she has. I met him. They were Romeo and Juliet." We walk farther into the woods, the temperature cooler, the path narrowing, the green canopy thickening. "I missed you." His voice is low, coaxing. He stops. But I can't.

Arms covering my head, I blink up into the sky and keep walking. I want to be in his arms, but the hurt of the past few months . . .

"You me. Me you. Forever," he says from behind me. I

swivel to him. When he treads closer, I stay inside his gaze, chest rising and falling rapidly. "I'm here now," he whispers, near my ear. I make a series of small nods because I can't trust myself to speak, and when he braces my hips, kisses my neck below the ear, it's like my body is string and all the string just got twisted and muddled into a knotty ball in his palms.

"I don't understand. Are you back?" My voice is like sandpaper.

Dark eyes delve into mine. Longing leaps off him and straight into me.

But I'm shaking and pushing him away, needing space—and air. "I can't go through you leaving again." I turn away, frantically attempting to slot my thoughts into the right order.

He draws beside me. "Let's walk." The two words are doused with worry.

After several tongue-tied moments, we halt at the sight of an enormous willow tree. Its bright green branches sweep the ground as if it were a shifting, living hill. The boughs sway in the breeze and I walk forward, arms outstretched, parting the leafy vines and stepping inside the green cave. I hear Colt follow.

The tree is old and growing on a sideways slant, the thickest branch almost sweeping the ground. I outline a knot in the trunk that resembles an open wound, then press down on the smooth, flat surface of a branch once pruned away.

"I'm not planning on leaving . . . unless you want me to," Colt says.

It's all I've wanted to hear him say, but do I believe him? I'm just getting back on my feet and the thought of another goodbye . . .

"Maybe it's better that you do." I slowly propel myself around. He's too close. I back up against the low branch, lift myself onto it. His gaze tries to hijack mine, but I stare into the canopy above. The sunlight sparkles; stars in the leaves.

"Choosing not to be with you was the hardest choice I have ever made," he says, fiercely. "You'd become the skin that held me together."

"Why did you choose to leave me then?" My eyes claw at his.

"I had nothing left to give you because I felt so broken." Colt's voice fractures. "You were peaking, and there was no way I was going to bring you down with me. And when Milo admitted how he could've stopped Dad going on that court . . . It was too much. I didn't blame Milo, but the thought that one different choice could've changed everything . . . I had to put some distance between us. I realize now that my dad was always going to kamikaze his way out of tennis."

It's my turn to speak, but I can't; my throat is filled with a heart floating with hope.

"I had to be sure you were sure," he continues, hardly a step away. "I had to be sure that when it was okay for you to go to Jacob, you didn't. And I had to be sure I was strong enough to move forward without you before I could do it with you. Then, after a while, I thought you'd never forgive me for leaving. I thought you'd moved on—you were flying so high without me, and it was better to leave you alone. Until I got your code."

I slap a palm over my mouth to stop the sob of relief, eyes begging him to hold me. He bounds forward and wraps himself around me, burying his face in my neck. He lifts me off the branch, and when he sets me down our foreheads touch. "I never stopped loving you," he murmurs. "And I'm sorry if I hurt you."

My smile feels like it could never be erased. "I'm sure. Are you sure?"

"Yes," he whispers into my hair. "I wanted all of you, not just a piece of you. And you can have all of me now, because I know I'm not another Jamie Jagger."

Love beats in his eyes. He bends to kiss me.

And the world turns purple.

EPILOGUE

I SHOCK EVEN MYSELF WITH the risks I take on court at Wimbledon. The spectators can't stay in their seats. The chance-taking and bold gambles send me all the way to the quarterfinals where I bomb out, but not before earning the nickname "Lionheart."

When Colt beats Sanchez to win the Wimbledon singles title, I race down the stadium steps, jumping a block in one leap and vaulting over the barrier. Colt's laughing and covering his face with his hands, disbelief gushing off him.

In the post-match conference, Colt is asked if the Bolt from the Blue is going straight to number 1. Colt looks around the room until he locks onto me, standing to the side. "Do you mind if I do that tomorrow?"

ACKNOWLEDGMENTS

IF YOU'RE A WRITER, YOU'VE probably flicked to this page first to read the acknowledgments. I'm making a wish that you decide to read the novel. But if you're a reader, it's likely you've just finished reading my first ever published novel. And for that, I'm both humbled and excited. Thank you! I hope you loved reading it as much as I loved writing it for you.

It's been a lifelong dream to become a writer, but the thing I've learned about dreams is that it's pretty hard to make them come true all by yourself. The people who helped me are, in my imagination, my Dreamweavers; they each held a thread which, when weaved together, created a dream come true.

The first Dreamweaver I wish to thank is my agent in New York, Katelyn Detweiler, of Jill Grinberg Literary Management, for her unerring support of an overseas author who writes about characters who "twig" things rather than "understand" things. You keep me grounded and sane with insightful and savvy writing advice, too. Thank you to my US editor, Alison Weiss, who makes me believe that I can fly thanks to her positivity and enthusiasm. And thank you to her stunning colleagues who also have faith in me, including Kate Gartner who designed this amazing cover, Emma Dubin, Jennifer Chan, and Katrina Enright. Also thank you to the sales people and distributors and book sellers behind the scenes, always working on my behalf without expecting to see their names here. You definitely became the dream team.

I can't believe I'm blessed with two more dream teams in Australia. Thank you to my agent, Tara Wynne, of Curtis Brown for taking me under your wing. While we became the two T's, you will always be T1. Thank you also to Claire Craig of Pan Macmillan, for taking a chance on a new writer and making this whole process feel so magical. And thank you to the rest of the team at Pan Macmillan, especially Georgia Douglas, Brianne Collins, and Clare Keighery.

Other people who held important threads in making this all happen include my amazing friends in the Stiff Wigs Writing Group, acronym SWWiG, although we mostly swigged on tea. Thank you for your honesty, wisdom, and commitment Alison Quigley, Debbie Smith and Brenda Kelly.

The same goes for my critique partners and beta readers, Sandy Fussell, Kat Colmer, Ellie Royce, and Anna Carew-Miller. Also, thanks to the stars and back to early mentor, Laura Bloom and then Emily Martin who loved Harper enough to pick me from hundreds.

There are too many people to thank within the CYA Conference and the SCBWI, so I'll just say: you know who you are. Thank you for being a friend, a supporter, and a motivator. And for the organizers of these writing conferences: thank you for literally making so many people's castles in the sky become a reality. Ditto Brenda Drake of Pitch Wars USA.

A special mention should go to Varuna House, whose incredible work and residencies led me to meeting amazing friends and to finding a publisher. A friend I met there once suggested I buy myself a WRITER mug to drink tea from, to instill in my own mind that I am a writer. Every word of advice helped weave the dream.

By now, you can see how many Dreamweavers are required to make a dream come true. The list is long, but the following people provided some pretty important threads. Thank you to Eric and Ella, for all the times you wanted to disturb me in the writing room but didn't. Even though I'm shut away writing, I still hear your voices in my head and you'll find some of your phrases in this book. Know that you are in everything that I do. Child Milo, Milo Child. Forever. I hope you've learned that by believing in yourself, and never giving up, the seemingly impossible can become possible.

Also thank you to Mark for blindly following me into all this, and for never having any doubts. And finally, thank you to my mum and dad for making books and writing a part of my life from day dot. Thanks to you, I became addicted to the smell and touch of books, and to the stories inside. Thanks to you, I never ran out of colored pens so that I could rainbow write my early stories. Thanks to you, I can type at 80wpm so my fingers can keep up with my thoughts.

And to Andrew for all the Smurf stories. And Denise and Robin who put me up for a month so I could write, even though that book remains unfinished.

There's more; just to say I almost always write with music in the background, so thank you to Adele, Josh Groban, Backstreet Boys, Pavarotti, Pink, James Blunt, and Snow Patrol, for writing songs that help me find my muse. It takes a lot of diverse threads to weave a dream.

I hope to become a Dreamweaver for every one of you, as well as for all those I couldn't mention due to the need to stick to a word count.